THE UNCROWNED KING

AYLA MARIE

THE FOUR KINGDOMS MAP

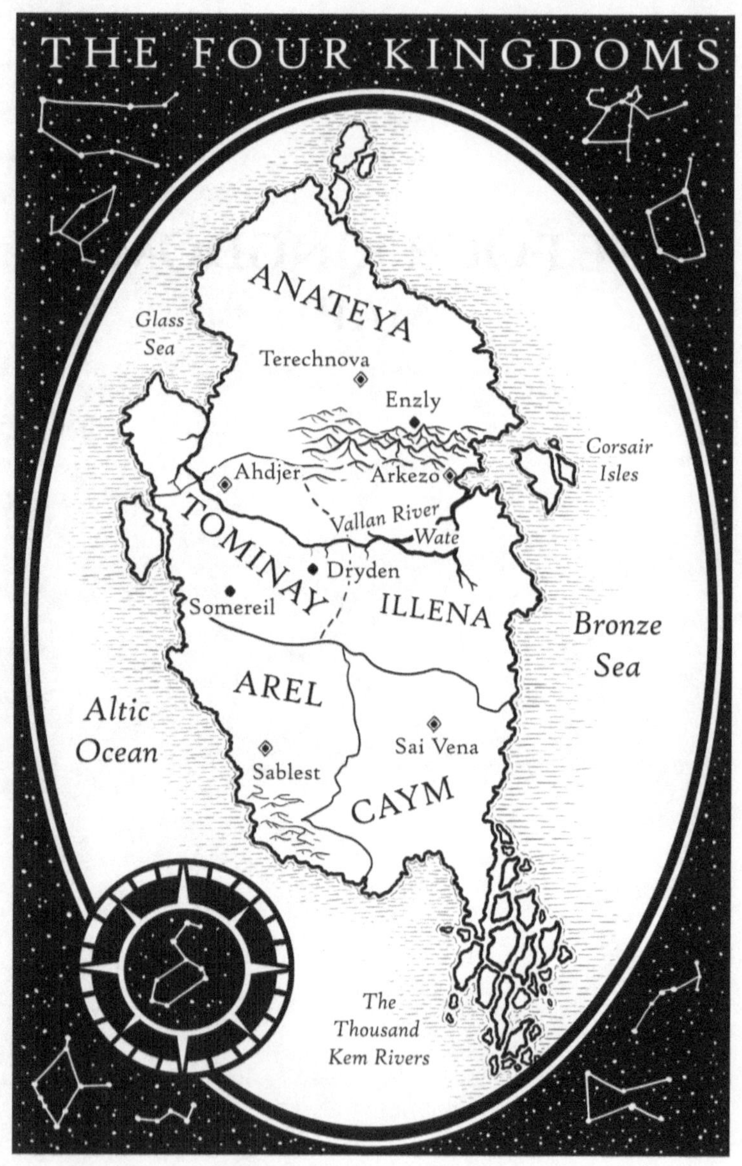

THE FOUR KINGDOMS
ANATEYA
Glass Sea
Terechnova
Enzly
Corsair Isles
Ahdjer
Arkezo
Vallan River
Wate
TOMINAY
Dryden
ILLENA
Somereil
Bronze Sea
AREL
Altic Ocean
Sablest
Sai Vena
CAYM
The Thousand Kem Rivers

THE UNCROWNED KING

By Ayla Marie

PART ONE
RIGHTFUL HEIR

CHAPTER

ONE

LEO

I'd thought that escaping Wate would mean no more captivity, no more cages or chains. I was wrong. When Byrne, Cael, the kids, and I met Emrys in the woods after making it across the river, he quietly led us into Illena's capital city and hid us in an old shed between two short buildings. As he warned us against leaving until he returned, I questioned whether I should have trusted him.

About an hour later, four soldiers—clad in black and sporting solid red masks that cover from their chins to just under their eyes—barge in, kicking down the shed door. The first thing I notice is the double-headed dog crest stitched over their hearts. I don't know what it is, but it feels... familiar. The second thing I notice is that every one of the soldiers carries enough weaponry to supply an armory and not one of them stops at the door.

Without thinking, I step in front of Saiph, Byrne, Cael, and the boys sitting on the ground and pull a dagger into each hand. The soldiers don't speak, leaping for me like a cat attacking a cornered mouse. The shed is small, but there's enough space to move strategically.

I pull the first masked guard toward me as he spins and swings his dagger in a deadly arc, narrowly missing my face. I duck under his arms and stab my dagger at his chest, but the armor around his torso doesn't budge. My eyes meet his as his head tilts curiously. I push him back and kick, hitting him right where my dagger had been. He stumbles and falls through the wall as if it were made of parchment.

The shed groans as another soldier sweeps through the door. Cael steps in front of me and grabs the man's arm. Cael pulls him to the side and throws his elbow at the guard's head, sending him sprawling into the opposite wall. Byrne holds Saiph tightly and pushes Antares behind her.

As another soldier steps inside, I raise my weapons, preparing myself for the next attack. She never gets the chance, suddenly jerked back by the collar.

Emrys bursts into the shed with his empty hands raised. His chest heaves as sweat drips down his face. He must have sprinted back. "Stop!"

Cael and I refuse to move. Though Emrys's expression softens as he looks at Byrne, his jaw remains tight with resolve. Emrys catches my gaze pleadingly before looking at Byrne and holding his palms up as if he were praying. Her lips are thin as she closes her eyes and takes a breath.

Byrne shifts Saiph on to her hip and puts her hand on Cael's shoulder. The tension lining his face disappears as he exhales. I look at Cael. For a moment, I don't think he's going to back down. I don't want him to. But this is the first step toward leaving behind Tominay and Wate, to leaving behind the mercenary Vela created. Cael nods slowly, and I sheath my blades.

Emrys watches me like a hawk as I raise my hands.

"Don't fight back," Emrys whispers. There's an apology written in his words. Then Emrys steps aside, allowing two guards carrying chains with thick iron cuffs forward.

Cael lurches back against the wall as fear flashes in his eyes.

"You won't chain us," I say as I stare down the partially masked guards.

Recognition flashes across their eyes before they exchange quick glances.

Emrys clears his throat and looks away. "The chains are only for you. The royals don't believe you're the crown prince as I've claimed, and though I tried to convince them, it is a crime to impersonate a member of the royal family."

My eyes narrow into slits as I stare at him.

"Lie on your stomach and let them cuff you," Emrys says. "When they realize that I've told no lies, they'll release you. It will only be until they're sure."

I shake my head slowly as my hands hang slack at my sides. I look behind me as Saiph buries her head in Byrne's shoulder. Antares slides over to stand behind Cael while Altair stays frozen in the corner, surveying the room with cold, sharp eyes.

Forcing myself to breathe, I slowly drop to my knees and raise my hands. A soldier side-steps Emrys and moves to stand at my back. She grabs my hand, but instead of cuffing it as I thought she would, she presses her knee into my back and pushes me to the ground. I grind my teeth and turn my face to the side as she clasps the cuffs on my wrists, then another set on my ankles. At least she allows me to keep my weapons, though they're useless when I'm bound in this position.

Nevertheless, my mind runs through every way I could gut them and run. I'm not helpless. I will never be helpless again. It takes everything in me not to kick her off my back, my muscles straining as my mind roars to break free. I can see Cael struggling to stay back as he glares at Emrys with clenched fists, but Cael doesn't make a move to help me. Cael knows, as I do, that this is our chance, and we can't afford to mess it up.

———

I'VE BEEN LYING on the ground for over an hour. Cael and Antares have joined me, their legs still too tired to keep them upright. Hunters took a physical toll we hadn't expected, and the exhaustion is pulling us down. The soldiers vacated the shed minutes after chaining me. Emrys explained that their presence put everyone ill at ease, and although he was right, I couldn't help the anger that flared inside me at his words. I won't forget about this little affair.

Emrys, Byrne, and Altair are the only three standing. Altair has yet to move from his corner, his chin held high as his eyes move over us. Something in me can't stand to look at him. The boy I raised is nowhere in his eyes, but foolishly, I still hope my brother is buried deep in the layers of his mind. Altair meets my gaze. His expression is cold, and it bites at my soul. I can't help feeling guilty for the person he has become. Had I not brought him to Wate, he might still be the witty kid who loved to climb trees and try to outsmart us. I shake away the thought as I avert my eyes. That isn't a grave I can afford to dig up right now.

Byrne and Emrys stand together against the wall, tucked into the corner. They're completely hidden from view of anyone outside. Byrne doesn't waste time filling Emrys in on everything that's happened. I grit my teeth as sympathy falls over his face. I don't want his pity—I want my brother back. I want a chance at Cassien. I want Elana here. I close my eyes when Byrne mutters her name. The memories of Elana's face and Cass's last moments replay in a loop in my head. I feel as if I'm going to vomit. Cass was so good, too good to have lived the life he did. He deserved better. After so much suffering, Cass should have had a proper burial beside his twin, but I couldn't even give him that.

"Leo."

I look up as Cael stares at the door. He pulls himself up and places a hand on Antares's shoulder to keep our younger brother behind him. I turn my head to follow Cael's gaze. An old, withered woman stands in the doorway. Her extensively embroidered red and silver gown is strikingly out of place beside the partially shattered walls of the shed. My jaw drops as I catch sight of the ruby tiara interwoven in her silver hair. I don't think I've ever seen so many jewels. One of those gems could feed a family for a lifetime. My gaze lowers to her face, and my heart stops beating altogether. The shape of her face is a reflection of my own, and her eyes... they're the mirror image of mine. The old woman's mouth drops open as she stares at me.

"Show me," she orders.

Though the words are not loud, they demand a presence in the room. Whoever she is, this woman is powerful. One of the soldiers steps through the door and frees my limbs from their cuffs.

"Stand."

I do as she demands, never breaking eye contact. The soldier who released me reaches to grab my wrist, but I step away and take hold of the soldier's arm, pinning it behind her back. I pull a dagger from the sheath at my thigh and hold it to her throat as Cael steps to my side.

"You won't touch us anymore," I seethe. My chest constricts as the soldier in my grasp swallows hard.

Laughter booms from outside the shed, startling me. A man—maybe a few years my elder—smirks as he watches us from behind the old, bejeweled woman. I hadn't seen him get so close. He too wears a crown, though significantly less extravagant. The ornamental suit he wears is stitched with the same red crest over his heart depicting the dog with two heads. His build is much like mine, but that is where our physical similarities end. His hair is jet black and immaculately styled, and his monolid eyes are a darker shade of silver than my own.

"Ares. That is enough," the woman spits.

Ares, as she called him, wipes the mischievous smile from his face and bows his head. "My apologies, Your Highness, I meant no disrespect."

He raises his eyes back to us. There's a glint of recognition behind them as his words click in my mind. *Your Highness.* I stare at the woman as my surroundings seem to become infinitely more real. Emrys said I was the son of a prince, but I hadn't truly processed what that meant. I thought maybe I had a far-away ancestor with royal ties and hoped it would be enough to plead for refuge. But this woman standing steps away is a *queen.*

"Let my soldier go," the old queen orders, her voice softer than it had been. Her head tilts to the side as she watches me with furrowed brows. Her eyes search my face as though they're looking for some kind of sign, an inkling of truth behind the stories she's been told.

I take a breath and force my arms away from the soldier. She quickly steps out of the shed and takes her place behind the old queen.

"Show me your wrist." The old queen's voice is barely above a whisper, her resolve clearly wavering.

Tension rises around us as I raise my arm, still flecked with dried blood from Wate. I show her the two bands that circle my wrist and encase the digits printed into my skin. 43201006. They're the numbers that connect me to my lineage. The first three digits are inherited from my mother, the last three would be identical to my father's, and the middle two tell of my birth order. I was the first and only child my parents were given the chance to have.

Before I have time to dwell on how I came to be, Ares steps forward and raises his arm next to mine. The air around us becomes electric as we stare at the digits. The band on Ares's arm is below the numbers etched into his skin, marking him as a pure blood-eye, but that isn't where the queen's eyes focus. Though the first five numbers on his wrist are far from mine, the last three digits are identical. 006.

Everyone remains still as my gaze slowly rises to meet the old queen's.

The tension bracketing her face melts away as the barest smile graces her lips. "You've come back."

LEO

"What?" The word slips from my lips before I can think better of it.

The old queen watches me with sad eyes, and it almost feels as though she's searching for someone else in my face.

She opens her mouth as if to repeat herself, but Emrys speaks first. "Perhaps we should allow our... His Highness... to clean himself up before you speak to him in private," he says, hinting at the gathering crowd.

My throat tightens as I catch a glimpse of the curious onlookers. They're... normal. Normal people. There are children pushing past their parents, trying to get a better view. Mothers grab their arms and scold them for being nosy, all the while observing the debacle out of the corner of their eyes. They look like the people who lived in the middle town of

Somereil, wearing worn clothes on the brink of needing patch-ing. A community that works hard but lives comfortably.

The old queen pulls me from my thoughts as she steps back. Ares retreats beside her.

"Of course. I'm sure you're all exhausted from your trav-els," the old queen says, eyeing the blood staining our skin.

The thought of it makes me want to step out of myself and burn the body left behind. It reminds me too much of Cass. Too much of his face as he fell...

"Call a carriage and have them brought to Ridge Palace. Arrange to have rooms prepared and clothing brought up. I will alert the queen and king and we will meet soon. We have much to discuss," she says before turning away. I can't help but watch her as her words replay in my mind and I realize with a start that she's not the true queen. We've been here less than half a day and my thoughts are already a tangled mess.

She walks toward a large, ornate carriage waiting on the cobblestone road. Two looming brown horses stand tethered to the front. I know next to nothing about horses, but I can tell these are no ordinary breed. They're unnaturally still and covered in lean, taut muscles. The people and soldiers bow as the old queen passes. Ares follows close on her heels, his back pin-straight and chin high. He extends a hand to help her into the carriage before climbing in himself. He looks back at us once and smiles before shutting the door.

Everything that happens next is a blur. I take Saiph from Byrne as Emrys leads us outside. The soldiers look unsure as to whether they should bow as we pass. After a moment of contemplation, they lower their heads. The loitering crowd stares at us with wide eyes, having no clue why these royal soldiers are saluting a rag-tag team of sleep-deprived kids.

A second carriage pushes through, forcing the crowd back as Emrys races toward the door. He throws it open and mutters something about meeting us at the palace. We cram inside and a soldier shuts us in. We don't speak or move as we ride. The carriage is so clean I'm afraid to dirty the velvet lining the seat and walls.

As it turns out, my stomach does not do well in bouncing carriages. I shut my eyes as nausea rises, and I rest my forehead against the shaking window panel. When the door opens, I race to get out, breathing in gulps of fresh air.

"Leo..."

At Cael's voice, I look up and my jaw falls open. A towering palace stands before me, gleaming in the sunlight. It must be at least ten times larger than the king's house in Somereil. The palace is built into the side of a wide, cascading hill. Walls of gray stone stretch up along with several floating bridges that connect one wing to the next. Most of the structure is framed with lush, green trees, but the three tallest spires rise above and pierce into the sky. Both clear and stained-glass windows paint the area between patches of climbing vines, allowing what must be an immense amount of natural light to seep inside. It's breathtaking.

Surrounding the paths leading to the palace are red flowers sprawled across the ground, growing up shrubbery, and falling from wispy trees. The garden leads to two intricately carved wooden doors, capturing my attention in a wild and curious way. In the middle of the space is a fountain with a stone statue of a two-headed dog standing like a guard looking over the garden.

A man dressed in a black suit with the same red crest stitched over his heart approaches us from a path to the left. We all stiffen, and Cael steps in front of Antares with Saiph in his arms as I pull Altair behind me. Byrne's hand twitches toward the blade she has tucked into the waistband of her pants as the other hand grips the bag carrying our meager belongings. The man stops abruptly as he notices our defensive stances. He swallows as sweat builds on his lip. I watch him fold at the waist and decide that I hate it when people bow to me. It feels... wrong.

"If you would please follow me this way, Your Highness. Their Majesties are awaiting your arrival."

I wince at his use of the title. *Your Highness.* I feel as if the words have been branded into my forehead and are slowly burrowing into my skull.

The man leading us through the grounds directs us inside, constantly throwing nervous looks over his shoulder. We step through the towering doors, and though my mind created an image of what the inside of the palace would be like, I couldn't have imagined this. The air is light in the sweeping hall as rays of sunlight give the walls a golden sheen.

We stare at our surroundings with wide eyes as we walk across a large mosaic floor. The tiles are various shades of gray and white, but they contrast each other in a way that creates a design of gradients and hard lines. I gasp as I realize that the night sky is drawn out beneath our feet, the stars we were named after shining amongst the brightest inlaid in the tiles. Across the walls are tapestries depicting wars won and lost, of heroes surmounting their fates and falling under the weight of their flaws. Everywhere I turn, a new detail appears. The amount of color alone overwhelms my thoughts as I imagine what life might have been like had the places we'd lived not been so gray.

At the end of the hall, bracketing two doors, is a pair of double-headed dogs painted in deep shades of red. Their ominous presence is jarring in this haven, yet I can't tear my eyes away, stuck in a stare-off with the snarling beasts.

The man leading us down the hall turns toward a wide stone staircase. Cael and I glance at each other as we follow, moving deeper into the building. I stay close to my brothers as we ascend the stairs and move into a narrower hall. The roof is completely transparent, the connected panels made of crystal-clear glass. The light flowing through illuminates a long line of royal portraits hanging on the wall. The first painting is of a woman donning a thick iron circlet that peaks between her brows. It sits perfectly placed on her intricately woven black hair as she sits, the picture of elegance. With her hooded eyes and round face, the portrait emits a strange feeling of serenity.

"Leo..."

I turn at Byrne's voice as she stares at a portrait a few steps away. Cael stands beside her, his gaze flitting from my face to that of the person captured on the canvas. As I step in line beside my brother, my lungs constrict. I feel the man who has been guiding us through the hall staring at me, but I don't turn. I can't look away. My mind is unable to form a thought beyond the portrait before me. The face mirrors mine.

"You really do look like him."

We turn to the voice behind us to see Ares leaning against the wall near the mouth of the hall. He walks toward us smoothly as a small smile pulls at his lips. I involuntarily stand taller. Ares's eyes dance at the reaction before he lifts his hands in a show of peace.

"Don't worry, I'm friendly," he promises. He stops a few steps away and shifts his gaze to the portrait behind us. "That, if you hadn't guessed it already, is your father, Dirix Matteus. The one to the right of him is my dear sire."

I glance back at the portrait of my father. He must have been around my age when the portrait was completed, and I don't think we could look more similar. My hair is a shade lighter and my eyes slightly darker, but I could *be* him. The portrait beside his is of a slightly older man. The familiarity is clear, but there's an edge to his features that my father didn't inherit. His cheeks are sharper and his mouth thin. That man seems as though he took on the responsibility dutifully instead of willingly and had no choice but to sit for the portrait. My father, on the other hand, looks as if he was built to hang on the wall. His shoulders are back, and his chin is high. He's completely at ease, as if he knew the power he wielded and was happy for it.

I turn back to Ares and note the differences between him and his father. He carries the same sharp edges but doesn't look unhappy in his duty. Ares strikes me as calculated, as if he has thought out every step before he moves each foot.

"How are we related exactly?" I ask Ares, holding his gaze.

He folds his hands behind his back. "Our fathers were brothers. Dirix was the eldest. This makes us cousins." He looks at the portrait of his father and his eyes narrow so slightly, I barely catch the change. "When Dirix disappeared—only a week before he was meant to take the throne, might I add—my father took his place. My father died of a sudden illness three years ago after reigning for most of my childhood, and he left Illena to my younger sister, our queen." Ares looks at me strangely, as if he's trying to see through me. For a moment, his warm demeanor drops away, leaving nothing to read on his face. "But I imagine you now hold more right to the throne than even I do."

"I'm sorry to interrupt, Your Highness, but Her Majesty is awaiting our arrival with many members of your Bloodline," the man who's been leading us says.

Ares slowly turns to face our guide as an easy smile melts back onto his face. "Of course. Lead the way."

The guide bows deeply before continuing down the hall. We follow him with Ares, and I catch sight of the last painting on the wall. It depicts a woman wearing the same unadorned crown as the rest of the royals, but she's different. This woman is regal and dark, sitting straight-backed without an inkling of warmth on her expression. She shares none of my features, nor those of Ares, but I can't help but feel recognition as I meet her eyes.

"That was the first Queen of Illena," Ares says from behind me.

Cael glances at me as a look of unease settles on his face. I stare at the painting as we pass and shake my head.

She's more than a queen. The thought catches me off guard and I only realize I've said it out loud when I notice Cael and Byrne staring.

"I'm not sure I follow," Ares says with furrowed brows.

I turn my head slowly to look at him.

"You don't recognize L—"

Cael gently knocks my side with his elbow and the fog on my mind immediately recedes. Ares watches me closely as I glance at the portrait again.

"I see a resemblance," I say instead.

Ares nods, straightening his posture as he tucks his hands behind his back. Cael keeps a close eye on me as we walk and stays a step behind until we reach a set of double doors. Two men in matching uniforms and masks covering the bottom halves of their faces stand guard with a slender staff at ready in their hands.

"Her Royal Majesty is expecting us," our guide tells them.

Moving as one, the guards pull open the door to a dimly lit rectangular room. The walls are solid stone, and the only way out seems to be the door through which we're ushered by our guide. Tables have been set in a wide semicircle before us, most filled with frantically chattering people who quiet at the sight of us. In the middle of them all stands a dais on which is a smaller table with a man and a woman fitted with heavy regalia. Jewel-encrusted gold crowns sit like halos on their heads. *These are the royals,* I think as my stomach turns. *The Queen and King of Illena.*

The people around observe us carefully, noting every detail of our beings. It's obvious they don't take kindly to newcomers. I take Saiph from Cael as he shifts his attention to keeping Antares at his side. Byrne moves so she's shoulder to shoulder with Cael as her gaze flits to the corner of the room where Emrys stands. His jaw tics as he watches her. I can see the fear in Emrys's eyes, and it does nothing to ease the tension strung tight through the room.

Ares steps out from behind us and makes for the podium. He sits in an empty seat directly to the left of the queen and leans back and casually crosses one ankle over the other, not caring that those around him are on high alert. On the other side of the dais stands the old queen. The sorrow on her face cuts deeply as she stares at me. I realize with a start that though her eyes are set on me, she isn't truly seeing me. She's looking at my father, the son she lost, resurrected before her with a different name and soul.

"Sit," the queen says. Her voice is soft, yet it cuts through the room like steel. In unison, those standing take their seats without averting their gaze from my family. "I've heard you have quite a story to tell us."

I glance at Cael, not knowing whether I should speak or stay silent. He only nods as he continues to watch the queen, spinning the ring our father gave him around his finger.

I think for a moment, wondering where I should start. The silence weighs heavily on my shoulders as the glares from around the room burn my skin.

"My name is Leo Heal. These are my siblings," I say, deciding that I will only give as much information as they ask. We may be here to seek refuge, but I won't go spewing my life to strangers.

The queen lifts her brow as the king leans back and crosses his arms.

"Is that all?" the queen asks softly, glancing at my wrist.

I breathe deeply and keep going. "We grew up in Tominay but were run out of our home."

Gasps ring through the room as eyes narrow on me. The queen nods, urging me to continue.

I steady my thoughts and block out the rest of the room. "We traveled through Tominay's forests until we reached Wate, where we stayed for a few months."

"The gold-eyes provided you lodging?" the queen asks.

I swallow the emotion clogging my throat. "You could say that."

The king sits forward and tilts his head. "Have you ever been in the presence of a royal?"

I shake my head. "Not in the way you mean."

The entire room seems to hold their breath. The queen only smiles.

"It's all right," the queen says as she lays a gentle hand on the king's arm. It seems to disarm him almost immediately. "I'm sure with time you will learn the customs of the court. They look at you in such a way because you do not address us properly."

Meaning I didn't call them Their Heavenly Majesties. I pull my shoulders back and narrow my eyes in frustration.

"I'll work on it," I say.

Angry murmurs rise through the space as the queen leans back. Cael kicks my leg, silently telling me to cool off. My heart is beating louder than a drum.

"Do you know why we've brought you before us today? Why members of every Bloodline are present?" the queen continues unruffled.

"I'm the son of a prince. Dirix Matteus was my father," I answer.

The entire room seems to exhale. The old Queen beside the dais closes her eyes and clasps her hands on the front of her dress.

"Grandmother, you've seen the proof?" the queen asks lightly as she turns to the old Queen for confirmation.

She dips her chin and opens her glistening eyes. The queen shifts her full attention back to me. "Raise your arm."

My brows furrow as I comply and raise my wrist to make the numbers etched into my skin visible. Many around the room strain to see, but the queen only turns to the king beside her, who takes one glance at my wrist and nods. For a moment, I wonder what they've agreed upon. I'm nowhere close enough for them to see the digits, but the queen passes over the matter as if it's been settled.

"Do you know where Dirix is now?" the queen asks, moving on as my thoughts spiral.

Some of these people might have known him. Some might even be his friends. His companions. I steel my emotions and fist my hands to stop them from shaking.

"Dead."

The old Queen winces at the harsh word, but I see no point in trying to soften the blow.

"My mother was gold-eyed. Her people killed her for having me, then murdered Dirix when he came to save her. My siblings' parents stowed away with me before the gold-eyes could get their hands on me. That's how I came to grow up in Tominay."

The old Queen turns away as tears fog her eyes. She must have been hoping he was still out there. I glance around and note the pale faces of some of the guests. *They must have all thought there was a chance he would come back.* They're foolish to have held on to hope for so many years. Hope never manages to do anything but infect an already gaping wound and prevent it from healing.

"The gold-eyes did this?" the king demands.

I nod stoically.

"Do you know who committed the crime? Specifically?" the queen asks as tension brackets her mouth.

I glance at Byrne as she closes her eyes. I would love nothing more than to throw Cassien to the wolves for what he did to my parents. And to me. And to his daughters and to Cass. But if I say his name, what happens to Byrne if these people go after her father? What happens to Elana? I swallow my unease and shake my head.

"I don't know. He was killed in Wate, but I can't tell you who finished his life."

Byrne lets out a heavy breath.

I glance to the side and see Emrys do the same. He gestures gratefully before I straighten my gaze back to the queen. "Is something going to be done about his death?"

The king narrows his eyes. "We will discuss the matter and decide whether the situation is worthy of further investigation."

Shock hits me like a whip. I don't want to hurt Elana and Byrne, but how could the queen and king possibly sit by and do nothing? How could they not send someone to find out what Wate is doing to its people?

"You're going to ignore this?" I demand loudly.

The room goes deathly still.

"Whether or not it is true, we have no proof of this crime. We cannot persecute an entire city for a murder we do not know for certain happened," the king states. His fingers clutching the arms of his throne are the only sign that he feels the tension in the room. "For you to be here standing before us, we know that Dirix broke rules of his own by entering their lands. The gold-eyes also have their own ruling systems. We do not know what transpired on their territories and refrain from interfering with their justice system as much as possible."

I'm about to retort when Cael grabs my arm.

"I understand this is a lot to take in. I think we have all the information we need for the moment. We will continue this conversation at a later date," the queen declares, shutting down the discussion before it's even begun.

I grind my teeth to keep from spewing my thoughts.

"Rooms are being prepared for each of you. You will stay here, as is customary for our Bloodline. Everything you need will be provided," she says.

"One room will be fine for us," I add, not wanting to be separated in this place.

The queen acknowledges my request with a wave. "We will make sure the rooms are adjoining. One of our men will take you there now." She quickly looks around the space before standing with the king. "You are dismissed."

CHAPTER
THREE

ELANA

I miss my sister. I've never been so far from Byrne. I have no way to know if she's all right or even alive. No matter how many times I tell myself that Leo and Cael will keep her safe, I can't help but picture her locked in a cell or cornered in an unfamiliar street. I saw the sincerity in Leo's eyes when he promised to take care of her, but still, I question my faith. I hate that I told her I would join her, knowing I would never get off this island. I hate myself for having believed I could escape. But, had I chosen to go with them, someone else would have died. So I stayed.

I try to disguise my limp as I walk down the street—keeping my chin high and back straight—but it's impossible. This is the first day I've been able to get up.

After bringing Cass to the Council building when Byrne and his brothers escaped, I went back to the house, unsure of where else to go. I wanted to stay with him. No child should be left alone, regardless of whether Lady Death is in the room. But when Cassien sent someone to inform me that I was to return home, I did. There was no point in hiding or trying to put it off. Byrne was already far away and I could handle a beating. He'd helped me prove that more than once.

When I walked through the door, I was prepared for the drunken fists and cold anger. But what greeted me was something I had never seen before. Cassien's eyes were void of the haze I'd come to fear, and his hand sat empty on his lap. He wasn't drunk. There was nothing to blur his conscience. My mind shut off as I met his gaze. I hadn't thought he could hurt me more than any other time, but knowing he was sober and choosing to do this opened a wound inside me that made me want to scream. He wanted to hurt me, to break me so thoroughly that the cracks in my soul would finally give way and make me shatter.

I can't remember exactly what happened. He stood slowly and stepped my way as I shook. I know he grabbed my face hard enough to bruise and forced me to meet his eyes while my body refused to move. I know he ran a blade along my face, cutting deep into my cheek. I remember him putting my left hand on the table and smashing my fingers one by one, screaming words I didn't understand through the fog of panic in my mind. After the fourth finger, I know my eyes shut and my mind blocked him out. There's a blank in my memory that I can't fill—or perhaps it's more that I choose to keep it empty.

I woke up in a pool of blood a day later. The house was eerily quiet and so were my thoughts. There's always a moment when I wake up after the storm that seems so serene. I can almost pretend that nothing has happened. But then my mind turned on and started to scream. I could feel the injuries: the crooked fingers, bruised legs, broken ribs, cut cheek and brow, the burn on my hip.

While I clawed my way to my room, my thoughts raced. I

imagined Cassien coming around the corner and pressing his boot to my neck. I was terrified. I pushed my door shut and pulled myself up to my feet. I threw my weight into the side of the wooden wardrobe until it tumbled in front of my door, locking me in. I sat down facing my mirror and took in my reflection. There was blood crusted in my hair, and the entire left side of my face was so bruised and swollen I was unrecognizable. I pulled out the medical kit I kept hidden under the vanity and laid out the supplies. But no matter how many supplies I gathered, they would never be enough to fix what Cassien had done. No bandage or salve can relieve the ache that wraps around my bones or erase the image of his face from my mind. Even when my wounds begin to heal, the scars will always be there to haunt me.

First, I set my fingers. I bit down on a piece of cloth and cracked each one back into place, feeling the bone shift. There were tears in my eyes even though I felt no pain. I threw up after setting the second finger straight. Placing wooden stabilizers under each digit, I wrapped them tightly to stop the bones from moving, but no matter how hard I tried to keep them stable, I couldn't get it right.

Once my head stopped spinning and I finished with my hand, I wiped the blood from my face and disinfected it with an old bottle of alcohol I'd stolen from Cassien. I'd taken a beating for that too, but he never actually found the bottle. I took a few swigs before throwing in some sloppy stitches to seal the slice down my cheek and the one over my brow. Both lacerations would scar deeply, but I couldn't bring myself to care. I scanned the rest of my body, counting off the broken ribs and bruised bones.

Finally, I lifted the seam of my shirt where it met my pants on my right hip. I don't know what I expected, but it was anything but this. My lungs heaved as my heart raced. Branded into my skin was a triangle with three lines starting from each corner and running through the middle of the shape to pierce the opposite sides. A silent sob racked my body as I stared at the mark burned into my angry, raw skin. I couldn't do anything but stare.

He'd branded me with the Tripoint. The man who had been my father had wanted to hurt me so completely that he'd denied me peace in death. He'd made it impossible for me to escape him.

I couldn't look at myself in the mirror, the glass reflecting too much for my mind to process. I moved to stand, but my knees buckled, sending me crashing to the floor. I scrambled frantically to my bed as tears gathered in my gilded eyes. The blanket seemed to be made of lead as I climbed onto the mattress and pulled the comforter over my broken body. Gasping for air, I lifted the cover over my face, needing to disappear as the door rattled. I heard Cassien screaming and pounding on the wood until the hinges shook. Even though I knew he couldn't reach me, I would never be safe. Cassien had branded the monster into my skin. I wouldn't ever escape him.

I HAVEN'T SEEN Cassien since the day he beat me. I've shown up to most of my normal duties and worked painfully through each passing day, but my mind has retreated to a hollow place. I ignore the smirks and disgusted sneers thrown my way by the people who used to fear me. Whether a child or an elder, no one shows me an inkling of sympathy. Even pity is hard to find amongst the faces I've grown up with. These people laugh at those who can't find a way to protect themselves, even when they fight back with every breath. That way of thinking seems so foreign to me now. How could I have once considered myself one of them? How could I have respected them? Idolized them? With every step forward, I realize my own ignorance, and it never ceases to make my thoughts burn.

I hobble toward the Council building, clenching my teeth through the pain as I force my eyes to stay silver. I couldn't bring myself to care about covering up the wounds, nor can I let myself give in to the numbness. It would be so easy to shift my eyes and relieve my pain, but Cassien's voice rings in my head each time I dare to consider it. *How weak must you be if you cannot endure pain? You will die a coward if you allow yourself to hide from the world.* I force myself to blink away the words, concentrating instead on my labored breathing as I continue on my path.

I ignore the dais in the courtyard as I pass an opening between two of the Council buildings. There isn't a doubt in my mind that had Cassien thought it wouldn't affect his own image, he would have strung me on the post and had me skinned. There would have been no saving me, but here I am, walking and breathing. These are the thoughts that set tangles to the strings of reason that should be straightforward. I should be able to kill Cassien. I should have run years ago. But I never fail to stay, no matter how broken he leaves me.

I shake away the thought as I walk toward the laundry room door I've been using to get inside the Council building. Cassien always uses the main doors to make sure he's seen. So far, my indirect route has saved me from running into him.

I reach to open the door with my good hand, but it swings open before I can grasp the handle. My mouth goes dry. Cassien's piercing cold eyes lock on me as I stand frozen in place. I tell myself to move, to go around him, but even my eyes are too afraid to look away. He scans me from head to toe, noting every injury, apparent and hidden. He knew what he was doing that day and he remembers every second of it.

I catch his expression soften as he stares at me, and for a fraction of a moment, my father returns. Lines dig into his face as he watches me. He swallows and clenches his jaw before pushing past me without a word. I flinch as he moves, feeling my entire body shake.

I trip as I stumble inside and the handle crushes into the brand on my hip. I double over in pain as the door swings shut. I force myself to breathe as I press myself against the wall. Finally, the pain recedes enough to stand straight. I raise the edge of my shirt and take in the bloodied bandage around my side. *I'll have to change that at some point.*

I've been tracing the same path for the last few days. I turn four corners before walking down a long, red-tinted hall. I check for lingering workers before shuffling over to the room I'm looking for. The door is light as I push it open and step inside. There is a window near the roof allowing a small amount of light to filter into the dull space. It's outfitted with only a chair, bed, and crooked side table. There are no fancy furnishings or comforts here. It was the only place I would think of bringing him.

I pull the chair beside the bed and place my hand on the knitted blanket I stole from Byrne's bed. A small form shifts underneath to face me. Soft silver eyes I've come to know well meet mine, and I can't help but smile.

"Hi, Cass."

CHAPTER
FOUR

My head spins as we follow a guide to the rooms that have been prepared for us. I can't believe what just happened. Cael appears to be deep in thought as he stares ahead, spinning his onyx ring around his finger. My father truly was a prince, and it makes no difference. The royals are his blood and don't care he was murdered. I shake my head as the woman guiding us through the winding halls stops before a door guarded by two burly sentinels. Each wears the same livery and half-faced mask as the rest of their counterparts. Their eyes don't waver from our forms as the woman opens the door.

I was expecting a small, sodden room outfitted with a few beds if we were lucky, but this... I never imagined any person could have so much luxury and space. We stand in a sitting room larger than our entire home in Tominay. There are couches set tastefully across the large area and a table in the corner sitting under a wide window that spans the entire wall.

Various doors to what must be bedrooms pocket the walls. To the left are rows of shelved books, stacked from floor to ceiling in three wooden bookcases. I turn to the guide as she watches us silently.

"All this is for us?" I ask. There must be a catch.

She tilts her head as her brows furrow. "Yes, Your Highness. We can procure you a larger room should you not find this one adequate."

My mouth drops open as my wide eyes meet Cael's.

"No, no! Thank you. This is more than perfect. We've never had so much space to ourselves," Cael admits with a kind smile.

The sentinels' stares bounce between us. The guide glances my way, as if waiting for me to speak. When I stay quiet, she nods and steps forward.

"The three doors on the left lead you to the bedrooms, as well as the door closest to us on the right. The second on the right is a nursery of sorts." The guide smiles softy as she waves at Saiph, who has laid her head on my shoulder. She must be exhausted from today's events. "The door beside that is the bathing room, and the last one is the royal suite. If you ring the bell on the wall behind you, a servant will come to see to your needs. Guards will be posted outside of your room at all times and will accompany you wherever you go."

I look at Cael as his eyes narrow.

"Will that be necessary?" I ask, eyeing the guards standing outside the room.

Their brows shoot up at my question. The taller of the two guards, a man with piercing green eyes and brown skin, bows his head curtly before responding.

"We are here to serve and protect you, Your Highness. It is required that all members of the Matteus Bloodline have personal guards with them at all times," he explains. His voice is edged with curiosity.

"I can protect myself and my family just fine. I didn't earn these scars by letting others walk over me," I tell them.

The other guard, a woman with chestnut hair tied in a tight knot at her nape, stares me down. "Pardon my bluntness, Your Highness, but you may not have received such scars had you had a personal guard."

My blood goes cold as I glare at her. "I never had a personal guard, yet every person who dared scar me never saw those wounds heal. Do you know why?"

She shakes her head slowly as she flinches away.

"Because I put them in the ground." I take a breath to allow my words to settle through the room. "We are more than capable of protecting ourselves, and *such scars* should be held as proof."

She swallows audibly as she bows her head. "Of course, Your Highness. I meant no disrespect. We are bound by duty to stand guard. That is all."

I nod slowly and reel in my resentment. Getting angry will do us no good. Cael exhales beside me, seeing that I've stood down. He stops spinning his ring and places a hand over Antares's shoulder. I shake my head and sigh, wondering how my life has come to this moment.

"Please, call me Leo," I tell them, rubbing the spot beside my temple that's starting to ache. "I feel inhuman when people call me *Your Highness*."

The guards exchange a quick glance before bowing deeper.

"Of course, Your Highness," they chorus.

I smile tightly. I'm going to have a hard time acclimating to that.

The guide moves to the door and bows at the waist. She reminds us that should we need anything, we can ring the bell or ask the guards. She offers to send in a nanny to take care of Saiph, but Cael and I quickly decline. I want nothing more than to be alone with my family to process the events of the day. None of us dare to move when she finally steps out and shuts the door behind her.

After a few moments, we turn to face the wide room. Looking at the space, I find myself completely and totally unsure of what to make of it. This is better than my best dream, but I can't help but feel as though I'm walking into a nightmare.

We don't speak much for the rest of the evening. I don't think I have it in me to reminisce or make conversation simply to fill the time. We search through the rooms and decide that Cael, Saiph, the boys, and I will take the room the guide called the royal suite. The bed is big enough to fit us all and still have space to spare. Byrne takes the room directly across from ours, and though it's much smaller, I like it better. This space makes me feel unsafe. There are too many corners to hide lurking dangers and it sets me on edge.

The large windows on the adjacent wall look out onto the city. It's... spectacular. That's the only way to describe it. The entire city is built on a slope that angles down to a wide bay. The water is a deeper blue than the sky and absorbs the color of the sun as it sets over the horizon. The Bronze Sea just beyond the bay glimmers brightly through a small opening between two tall cliffs protecting Arkezo from wind and storms. They stretch into the air like claws erupting from the ground and are split right down the middle as if the Lady herself had cleaved the stone apart. It's more than a wonder to behold.

The city bleeding away from the bay is just as mesmerizing. To the north are rows of large houses and markets and a port docking boats with sails like wings waiting to set flight. The bustle of people milling around is strange to watch from so far above. Regular people going about their days, clueless to the blood-eyed mercenary observing them from Ridge Palace. It's an eerie feeling, yet all I can think is how good it would be to be free as they are. To live simple lives and have simple problems. All I've ever wanted was to worry about the ordinary, about my brothers attending school and showing up to work on time. I'll never know that life now. I'm starting to believe I was never meant to.

I shake away the thought as Cael comes to stand beside me. I follow his gaze to the sprawling estates on the west side of the city. From what I can see, the properties are lined with high fences protecting the manicured gardens circling houses far bigger than those belonging to the rich in Somereil.

The few people directly below us seem to be in a rush, hurrying to their next destination as if their lives depend on it. In front of the Ridge Palace gates are rows of shops, hostels, and pubs. The buildings are painted with vivid colors and adorned with banners and hanging signs. Cael disappears from my side without a word, leaving me alone by the window.

I continue to survey the city and move my gaze southward. It's as if the life radiating from the city gradually gets choked off with every block. The buildings lose their color and the streets become visibly bleak and dirty. The roofs are full of holes, and the walls are falling apart. Abandoned buildings are scattered across the south, and the ones that remain standing lean on each other for support. Stretching into the bay are long, rickety docks connecting a series of weathered buildings built right on top of the water itself.

As the sun sets, the city lights up. To the west, the windows of the estates project light as if the day's been captured within their walls. Those to the north are dimly lit with flickering lights, while to the south, the streets are completely dark.

Cael returns to his spot by my side with a shriveled piece of paper. I recognize it instantly—Mum's letter. My eyes meet his as he smiles softly.

"We really made it this time," he says, handing me the letter.

I open it slowly and read the scrawled words as her voice rings in my mind. *...Follow the Vallan River to the Bronze Sea; you'll find people before you get to the ocean, but do not stop until you reach the bay...* The bay. I remember reading the words as though it was yesterday, but seeing them written out again is something entirely different. I look up and stare at the darkening body of water. A sad smile pulls at my face as I carefully fold the page back up.

"Yeah. If only Cass could have seen it." I look down and focus on my palms. "If only they all could have seen it."

The hole in my chest cracks deeper when I glimpse the sorrow on Cael's face. He nods slowly and raises his eyes to the city below.

"We did the best we could. They would be happy that we got here, and we have to be content in knowing that."

I let the truth of his words settle. My heart squeezes as I think of everything we've sacrificed to be here, but unease still sits heavy on my mind. We've been in this situation before. We've been hopeful. That hope usually turns out to be a red herring distracting us from the nooses being tied around our necks. By the Lady, I hope this time is different.

Cael suddenly goes still, his back straightening as his gaze flies to the corner of the window furthest to the right. Behind us, Byrne, Saiph, Antares, and Altair are completely silent. A soft crack shakes through the air, and without a second thought, I pull two daggers from the sheaths I have yet to take off. Byrne holds Saiph against her hip and pulls out a dagger of her own as she ushers Antares behind her. Knowing that she would protect them brings me a slight sense of comfort. I toss Cael the longer of the two blades I hold as we each move to either side of the window. We crouch as a louder crack sounds right outside the pane of glass.

There's a slight scratching noise, then a faint pop as the window swings open on a set of thin silver hinges. For a moment, I'm impressed at the ingenuity of it, but my mind goes clear as a set of hands grasp the ledge. Cael moves his hand, signaling our next move. I nod and pull on the instinct sitting impatiently just beyond my fingertips.

The intruder grunts as he tries to pull himself through the opening. Cael and I each grab a hand and pull the intruder into the room. I push him onto his knees and place my dagger at his throat as Cael closes the window. The intruder's hands go up as he feels the steel against his throat.

Cael catches my arm before I can press the blade any closer, immobilizing the weapon in my grip. I glare at him, wondering why he would stop me. Byrne gasps as she sees who I'm holding beneath the dagger. I look down and slowly let all the oxygen out of my lungs before releasing my hold on Emrys. His hands are shaking as I step back to stand with Cael.

Byrne puts Saiph down and runs to help Emrys up. He stands on weak legs as he runs his palm over his face. He starts to smile at her, but the expression doesn't have time to fully set before Byrne shoves him back. Her brows are pulled together and her mouth a thin line as she stares at him.

"What were you thinking?" she rages, her arms waving madly. "He could have killed you!"

Emrys's eyes go wide as his gaze flies from me to Cael to

Byrne. "I didn't know you'd be waiting at the window with a dagger! I needed to see you!"

"And you thought the best way to do that was by climbing through a window!?" Byrne yells incredulously.

We wince as she reels in her anger. I pity Emrys for having to be on the receiving end of the glare she's pinning to him. If it's anything compared to Elana's, it will crush him.

"Yes! I would never have been allowed to see you, and had I asked, they would have found it suspicious!" he yells, clearly desperate.

Byrne exhales as she lets the truth of his words sink in. Cael and I exchange a wide-eyed look as I take back the blade he passes me and sheath them at my hip and thigh.

"I'm sorry, you're right. But don't *ever* do that again," Byrne amends.

Emrys's shoulders relax as he steps forward and folds her into his arms. "Next time, I'll knock." With a soft laugh, he releases her. As if remembering we're here, Emrys turns to us and plasters a weary smile onto his face. "Your Hi—"

"Please don't. Just call me Leo," I stop him, cutting off the title that might make my brain explode.

His brows shoot up as he looks at me quizzically. "Well, that's definitely a first." Emrys's smile grows more genuine. "I don't think I've ever heard a Matteus refuse their title."

I cross my arms as I hold his gaze. "Thankfully, I'm not a Matteus."

His head tilts as if he's seeing me differently than before.

"No hard feelings about the whole dagger thing, right?" I offer with a tight smile.

He breathes out a laugh and nods. "You didn't slice my neck open. In my books, it never even happened."

Emrys filled us in on a few things that had happened since we'd come to this room. The public had found out I was here, and the reactions were... mixed. Overall, my presence was making the people uneasy. Some had even gathered outside the gates, demanding to see me. It made people nervous to learn that someone with more right to their country than their own queen had simply appeared out of thin air. I can understand their concern, and I'm sure it will reassure them when they find out I have no plans to take any throne.

More surprisingly, Emrys explained that a part of the root of the discomfort with my presence is that I am, and I quote, a *half-breed*. I'll have to add that to my list of unwanted titles, right next to *Your Highness*.

Exhaustion pulls on us as we relax on the couches that seem too pristine to be used as they're intended. I move to pick up Saiph to bring her to bed and catch sight of my stained hands.

"Is there a way we can get water brought up to scrub this off?" I ask Emrys as I lift Saiph off the couch.

He nods toward our room as he leans into Byrne, who sits curled into his side. "Just use the shower in one of the bathing rooms."

Cael and I exchange a questioning glance before looking back at him.

A crease appears between his brows. "You do know what a shower is, right?"

Cael and I shake our heads. Even Byrne manages to give a tired no.

"Wow. All right. Well, I guess I'll show you." Emrys stands and walks into the main bathing room.

There's a square stall made of glass beside a bath. He steps through an opening and turns a knob on the wall. Within seconds, water streams from a square piece of metal connected to the ceiling. We all watch in wonder as steam floats through the air and fogs the glass.

"How does that work?" Cael asks.

Emrys's gaze bounces between us, seeming concerned as he turns the handle once more, cutting off the flow of water. "There are pumps that bring the water from the bay to basins under the palace. From there, the water either gets heated and sent up through pipes or is pumped directly here."

I try to imagine it, but my mind can't grasp the concept. "How do the pumps work?"

"Electricity, I guess. I'm not sure. All I know is that they move the water so it can get to where it needs to go." Emrys's eyes are wide as he watches the confusion play across our faces. He looks at Byrne as if to back him up, but she shakes her head.

"We never had any of this in Wate," Byrne tells him.

Emrys looks at Cael and me, urging us to explain further.

"We got our water from a stream and heated it in a pot over our cooking fire."

Emrys's jaw drops, and I find myself wanting to defend our primitive ways. We did just fine with what we had.

"You never had power? Lights or anything anywhere in Tominay?" Emrys asks.

Cael and I shake our heads. He takes a few steps toward a switch in the middle of the wall and flips it. Instantly, the room that had been dim a moment before is illuminated as if we were outside in the middle of a cloudless day. We stare at the bulb hanging from the ceiling, throwing a bright yellow light across the room. Antares holds up his hand and stares as the rays of light play through his fingers.

"How is that possible?" I ask softly, as if it might disappear if I speak too loudly.

"We make power with turbines built into wind tunnels in

the twin peaks on the other side of the bay. The wind that comes off the Bronze Sea funnels into the wind tunnels and makes the blades on the turbines spin. That spinning motion powers the generators that in turn create electricity. It's transported here through cables that run underground. The light bulb contains tiny wires that heat up when the power goes through them. That's what creates the light," he explains, now staring at the bright bulb as if realizing how amazing it truly is.

"In a way, it's like flameless fire? Only it gets fed electricity instead of oxygen and creates less heat?" Cael says, absent-mindedly spinning his ring as he stares at the bulb.

After a moment of consideration, Emrys nods. "I've never thought of it like that, but I guess it is. The Death Dancers invented it. They carved the wind tunnels in the peaks and drew out the plans for the water and power systems. They were centuries ahead of the world. They still are. I never really considered that we're the only ones who have this level of technology. I assumed every country had access to something similar."

I laugh under my breath as a surreal feeling washes over me.

"We are the technology, Emrys. Same as the water and light. They created us for their own purposes." I walk out of the bathing room as the amazement that had taken hold of my thoughts a moment before becomes tainted beyond repair.

CHAPTER
FIVE

Cael keeps a close eye on me as we tuck Antares and Saiph into bed. I offered Altair his own room if he wanted it, but he chose to stay with us. I find myself standing taller as he follows us into the bedroom. The pain of losing Cass has left a mark on Altair. He knows what happened is partially his fault and I can see the regret flash across his face every time the subject comes up, but he still seems unsure of himself and of us. When he looks at me, I can barely see the boy I raised. But as time passes, I know I can't continue to hold what happened against him. He's my brother. He could commit the worst crime and I would still take him under my arm.

Altair chooses to sleep on the couch across the bedroom, with a thick woven blanket from the massive wardrobe to keep himself warm. The wardrobe was also packed full of simple, yet durable clothes. By the time we had gone through it all, every one of us was wearing a fresh outfit, making do with the larger sizes that hung off the boys' frames.

Though they're exhausted, Antares and Saiph refuse to fall asleep. Cael sits beside Antares, who plasters himself to Cael's leg. With his head resting against the headboard, Cael runs a hand down Antares's back and speaks softly, trying to coax him to sleep. I move around the bed and take Saiph in my arms as she fusses in the blankets. Her bottom lip quakes as she sniffles, overwhelmed by the day. I bounce slowly until she lays her head against my shoulder and her breathing evens out.

Being in this room is strange. The comfort feels unnatural in comparison to our usual sleeping arrangements of hard ground or dilapidated cots. I look at Cael as his eyes droop shut.

"Is she asleep?" I whisper, turning so he can see Saiph's face resting on my shoulder.

He nods with a tight smile. "Antares is too. Is Altair?"

I tiptoe to the couch where Altair lies facing away from us. I listen to him breathe evenly. He stays still as I approach, undisturbed by the creaking of the aged wood planks.

I turn back and nod to Cael. "He's out."

Cael watches me for a moment as sleep pulls at his features.

"You do know that you being who you are isn't all terrible, right? It's not always the curse you make it to be," Cael whispers, referring to what I said in the bathing room.

I shake my head as I sigh. "At times, that's hard to believe."

He smiles tightly and lets the subject drop, understanding I don't want to speak about it further. I've lost too much to think of who I am as a gift.

"Are you going to be all right with her?" Cael asks softly.

I nod as I sway, not wanting to disrupt our sister. "I slept yesterday. I'm good for another night."

Cael sighs and leans back against the headboard. There's a dagger on the side table beside him—a testament to his unease. Cael has always tried to reduce how much the boys are exposed to weapons, but I think the past few months have changed his perspective. The thought makes me want to disappear.

"Get some rest, I'll be all right," I tell him.

His eyes shut instantly. "Don't do anything stupid until I wake up."

The corner of my lips kicks up as I walk out of the room. "I wouldn't dream of it."

I've been pacing for hours. I don't know when I started humming, but a tune my mother used to sing floats lightly from my lungs. Maybe it's a way to keep myself calm while my every nerve ending sparks. I need to run, or spar, or do anything to get this restlessness out of my bones. I glance at the moon shining through the window and sigh. It's well past midnight, so I settle for wearing a path into the floor.

Just when I think my legs are going to give out from under me, I hear someone murmur in the hall. I recognize the voices of the guards, but I'm surprised as the queen's voice chimes into whatever conversation has ignited. My brows furrow as I move closer to hear them speak.

"Have they been out?" the queen asks, the words barely decipherable through the door.

"No, Your Majesty. We've barely heard a sound from them," one of the guards responds.

"Are you sure they're still inside?" she asks calmly.

Silence weighs heavily in the air. I lean forward and place my hand on the knob. Cael's voice rings in my head telling me to consider my actions, but I can't help myself. I open the door, and the eyes of four guards and the queen of Illena instantly find my face.

"I can assure you that if we did not want to be here, we wouldn't have been found in the first place," I tell them, keeping my expression blank.

The guards' eyes flare wide as they glance at the queen.

"I wondered if you'd still be up. Do you have a moment to speak?" the queen asks. Her eyes flit to Saiph still swaddled in my arms as I bounce gently.

"If you can whisper. I'd rather she stays asleep."

The queen nods and moves away from her concerned guards. "That won't be an issue."

I step aside and allow her to come in. All four of the guards stay a step away and take up posts around the sitting room. My brows shoot up as one moves to stand by the bedroom.

"My siblings are sleeping in there. Byrne is in the room across from it. I'd rather they get as much rest as they can before the nightmares wake them," I warn the guard with a low voice.

It's not a lie, but I know Cael woke the minute the door opened, and I would rather avoid dealing with their surprise should they find Emrys in the room with Byrne. The queen watches me closely, then waves off the guard. He moves closer and takes a place along the wall. The queen takes a seat on the couch across from me.

"Having trouble sleeping?" the queen asks.

"We're used to sleeping on the ground. The finery is foreign," I explain.

She nods, but I don't think she grasps what I mean. "Did you try to get some rest at least? We have a big day ahead of us tomorrow."

I breathe out a laugh without meaning to. I clear my throat at her confusion. "I don't sleep."

Five pairs of eyes narrow on me. I shake my head and explain the terrors, how I live eight different deaths every time I lie down to rest. I expect them to react with the same fear Elana did, but they seem... shocked. Their mouths hang open as if they can't believe what I'm saying.

"You get them every night?" the queen breathes.

I nod stoically as I try to read her paling face. For a moment, the strength drops from her appearance, and I can't help but see a scared and curious girl.

"I haven't had a night without them in years," I tell her. "Are they normal? For people with blood-eyes?" That damned hope blooms in my chest once again. The question bounces in my mind as she chews on her words.

"Well, to some... yes. They are."

I feel as though I'm going to crumble to the floor and smash to pieces. I never thought I would hear those words.

She takes a deep breath as I try to stop the world from spinning. "In the Matteus Bloodline, those who take the throne have been known to get these terrors. We believe it is a sign from our ancestors that the person would make a good ruler."

I don't know how to react to that. All that suffering, and they take it as a sign from a bunch of bones buried in the ground that the person should oversee the strongest nation on the continent? I guess it's the same as thinking Lady Death put the terrors into my mind, but for some reason, this is harder for me to believe.

The queen smiles softly and sighs. "In truth, we believe they come from the DNA the Death Dancers molded with ours to create us. During that mixture, shards of the past conscious-ness were maintained and passed down within our genetics. In most, it lays dormant in their minds, but our Bloodline is said to share the most DNA with those they created us from, so we are prone to reliving pieces of their lives."

I force myself to breathe.

She doesn't stop as I shake with panic. "Some also believe that the terrors are simply an extra punishment and that the DNA that gives us our abilities comes from a being that walked on these grounds as the world was being formed. They say there are pieces of its consciousness in our own, and that link allows us to relive the last memories of others whose genetic code was combined with our ancestors." She shakes her head as she looks past me, deep in thought. "It's all more complicated than I have ever been capable of understanding."

We sit in silence for a long while as I try to process this information. Everything I've lived is... normal. Something difficult to explain, but explainable.

"But..." she starts.

And that word, that single word, manages to make the world come to a screeching halt as my face falls. That flame of hope burns out like so many times before, and for a moment, I wonder if there's enough left in me to ever light another fire.

"Those who get these terrors get them once or twice in a lifetime. The only person I know who was said to have more was your father, and still, he was only known to get them on rare occasions."

I nod slowly as the information registers in my mind. I block out the flood of emotion pressing painfully against my thoughts. "Have you ever had one?"

Her face hardens as she meets my gaze. "I have not."

"Has anyone who still lives had one?" I press desperately, and something flashes in her eyes.

"Ares had one about four years ago. Three days before our father died. Some say our grandmother also had one when she was very young, but she's always denied it," the queen explains softly.

"By your rules, shouldn't Ares have taken the throne then?"

The guards go very still. The queen's eyes narrow as she tenses.

"It is not a rule defined in stone, only a fact that every ruler before me has had them. Dirix's disappearance unleashed chaos onto our ruling system. My father was not ready to take the throne, but he did. Years later, when he passed, I assumed Ares would be named king as he's the eldest. But with my father's death came the announcement of my inheritance. I was not prepared to be queen, but I did not stray. Your father broke every rule in our books, so I would hope that you are not questioning my legitimacy." There's sorrow hidden under her harsh tone, and it manages to break down the defenses I've put up.

"I'm sorry. About your father," I tell her softly.

Pain shakes behind her eyes. It's a pain I feel every day. An endless pit. No matter how far you fall, you can always get sucked deeper.

She takes a deep breath and nods. "Thank you. It was sudden. Sometimes I'm still surprised he is not with us. My father was a good king."

"I'm sure he was," I say.

The queen watches me for a long moment, as if she were trying to see into my thoughts. "You've lost people. Who?"

I force myself to breathe as I push away the flashes of my family's faces. My entire body tenses as a wave of nausea crashes through me. Saiph shifts in my arms, and for a moment, I don't remember where I am. All I can see is the pain in their eyes, begging for help while I ran away. I always run away.

"Let me take her, Leo." Cael is standing beside me with his

hands outstretched. He breaths out slowly as I come back to the present.

Careful not to wake her, I hand Saiph to my brother and sit down facing the queen. The guards' eyes shift from where Cael stands behind me to the pommel of the dagger now sticking out from under my shirt. Their hands move to the hilts of their weapons, a threat neither Cael nor I miss.

"We lost our father to Tominese fighters, our sister to Tominese law, our mother to childbirth, my younger brother to sickness, and his twin in our escape from Wate." My words are abrupt. I can't muster the strength to pretend I can think and speak of them easily. Let her see that whatever she struggles with, I've felt it too.

The tension in the room becomes so thick I could cut it with a blade.

"I've lost friends and killed my fair share as well. I've lived in more vile places than you could imagine and seen horrors told only in legends." I meet her gaze and hold it, forcing her to understand my words. "I don't want anything but a place where we can live peacefully. I don't care what I have to do, I just want to keep my family safe and raise my siblings where they don't have to fear for their lives or worry about going hungry." I force myself to take a breath as Cael sits beside me. "They're kids. All I want is to give them the childhood I was never allowed."

The queen smiles tightly. "That is the main reason I came here tonight. I wanted to ask about your plans with regard to your birthright." She seems nervous, but her chin stays high. The queen leans forward and braces her hands together. "If you choose to take the throne, it will be yours. If you desire it, I will act as an adviser until you are adjusted to your daily tasks, as well as the country as a whole."

Her words are genuine, but there is fear buried in her offer. What I can't decipher is if it's a fear for her people if I choose to take the throne, or if it's a fear of losing power.

Cael and I exchange a surprised look. I never imagined my blood would allow me to take control of a throne with just a few words. The queen has taken her entire kingdom and laid it at my feet. Thousands of lives handed over as if they were tokens. The insurmountable responsibility of it all makes me want to run toward the mountains as fast as my legs will carry me.

"I don't want it. The throne, the country, or the crown. Any of it," I say with clear finality.

The queen leans back and sighs. "All right. But you must understand that even though you refuse to take the throne, you must take your place as part of the court. Your blood demands it, as will the Bloodlines."

I look at her strangely.

"Aren't those the same thing, my blood and bloodline?" I ask.

She laughs to herself as she straightens her gown. "The Bloodlines are the thirteen blood-eyed families that hold power over Illena. They are nobility, of sorts. The Matteuses lead Illena as the kings and queens and are known for our abilities to survive. You've probably found that it's difficult to get severely injured or be killed. We also rarely get sick and can go for long periods without food, water, or sleep. All this belongs solely to our Bloodline."

I exchange a wide-eyed look with Cael. That explains... a lot. I always wondered why the boys never showed the same signs of being near immortal.

"We figured that out a long time ago," Cael says as he turns to look at the queen.

She nods as a small smile graces her lips. "The other Blood-lines help rule over different sectors of the country and make up the royal court. As an example, the Alinsky Bloodline, from which my husband hails, can see great distances and have command over many manufacturing cities across Illena."

Cael and I stare at her, dumbfounded. This is a lot more information than I have the will to understand.

"We will host a dinner in a few days' time where you will be presented to my court," the queen continues, changing the subject. She looks at Saiph and her brows knit together. "Though for this event, I'm afraid you will not be able to bring your younger siblings along."

Cael and I tense.

The queen shifts her gaze to my brother. "Both you and your eldest sister may also attend." It takes me a moment to realize she means Byrne. I don't have time to argue against leaving my siblings before she continues. "Tomorrow, we will tour the city. Appropriate clothing will be brought up along with breakfast in the morning."

Cael and I watch as the queen stands and moves toward the door. Her entourage follows closely, but she stops before stepping over the threshold.

"Pardon my curiosity, but I must ask. What did you do in Tominay to survive all these years? I assume it was nothing so simple or you would not have left," she questions.

I blink at the confidence of her words. Smirking, I slowly let the monster beneath my skin seep into my expression. "At first I fought in the arenas, but I was so proficient in bloodletting that I was hired soon after as a mercenary. I earned my keep by taking lives."

The guards plaster their hands to their weapons. I lean back as an ease coats my skin. I'll regret allowing myself to fall into this state later, but for now, I can't help but bask in the power. The queen's lips thin as she swallows.

"The Bloodlines will be pleased with that answer," she whispers as a guard hastily grabs hold of the knob and slams the door shut behind them.

CHAPTER

SIX

CAEL

After last night, Leo and I were both unsure of the day to come. I'd woken up beside Antares the minute the door had opened. I had no idea why the queen had showed up, but the conversation proved to be insightful. It explained a lot, including how, by the Goddess, Leo was still alive after so many years of constant injuries.

I tried to get back to sleep once the entourage had finally taken their leave, but it was no use. My mind was racing. Leo and I spent the rest of the dark hours sifting through every word the queen had muttered. It was... overwhelming. When the sun rose, Byrne and Emrys came to sit with us. We filled them in before a worry stricken Emrys gathered his things to climb back out the window.

Before leaving, Emrys explained that the vines that climb the lengths of the walls are grown on trellises so that they won't destroy the stone of the palace. Conveniently, the trellises beside our window were broken years ago, and instead of tearing them down, they installed new trellises on top. There's now a gap just wide enough to climb through, all the while being hidden by the new growth. As Emrys dropped out of view, it seemed almost too perfect of a cover.

An hour later, Antares wakes up screaming. It's something he's done so many times since we left Wate. Leo and I are by his side in seconds, but it's hard to be any sort of comfort to a grieving child. There's nothing we can do to change what happened, and we're useless in erasing the memories that feed his nightmares. I have a hard enough time dealing with my own nightmares, so all we can do is sit with Antares until his hands stop shaking and his breathing evens out.

Once Altair and Saiph wake, we funnel into the main seating area. No sooner have I sat down than a knock rings out from behind the door. Leo opens it and a flood of servants with two-headed dogs stitched over their hearts come bursting in. They leave trays of food on the table and lay a dozen long bags over the couches. They float around us as if we're ghosts and are gone before we can even thank them.

"Well, that was—"

"Strange," I finish for Leo.

Our words hang heavily in the silent room. The smell of breakfast wafts over to us, and in an instant, our eyes are on the tables. I don't think I've ever seen so much food. There are eggs, several types of meat, bread twisted in braids and covered in sugar, and giant bowls of fruits I can't name.

Anyone watching would think us feral as we set to ravaging the platters. In minutes, the impressive spread is gone. There's with barely a crumb left.

"I think I'm going to explode," Leo groans from his chair.

I grunt in agreement as I look at Antares, who's lying face-down on the floor. Saiph waddles over to him and bends to tap his head. When he doesn't react, she flops onto his back, giggling madly. I can't help but smile as Antares winces.

"She's getting heavy," he wheezes as he flips over and wraps Saiph in his arms.

To my surprise, I catch a smile bloom on Leo's face. He blinks and the look is gone. I sigh as I spin my ring. *He'll get there.*

"All right. Why don't we see what's in those bags?" I offer, though I'd much rather roll over and take a nap.

Byrne runs a hand over her face. "I think I'll just stay here and wait until they bring in the next meal."

I huff a laugh as I stand and pick Saiph up by her feet. The wound in my shoulder stings at the movement, but it's healed enough to ignore.

I got lucky with that arrow. It didn't strike too deep, and it missed anything vital. It still hurts like all hells though. Even my back still stings from time to time, though the scabs are almost gone and the scars are healing as nicely as can be expected.

Saiph squeals and tries to wrestle from my grip as she hangs upside down. It takes her less than a second to give up and decide that hanging limp is her best course of action. Byrne laughs softly as I flip my sister around and place her back on her feet.

Leo stands and grabs Antares under the arms. "Up, Antares."

Like Saiph, Antares decides on the limp strategy, forcing Leo to drag him over to the couches.

Leo lifts him and catches his gaze. "One…"

Antares's eyes go wide as Leo swings him. "No, wait, I'll walk!"

Mischief is written all over Leo's face as he swings our younger brother again. "Two."

"No, PLEASE!"

Leo laughs softly as he pulls back. "Three!"

He lets go, launching Antares into the pile of cushions on the couch. Antares's scream is so high-pitched two guards come bursting through the door, weapons in hand. The ease that had started to settle over us quickly evaporates. We go still as the guards' eyes rove over the room and pin to Leo. My hand moves to the dagger tucked into my waistband as Byrne stands behind me.

"We were just playing," Leo says coldly. The guards don't let up, their eyes flitting to Antares and back to him. "I wasn't hurting h—"

"Silence," a woman says, her hands clutching her blade.

Leo closes his eyes and visibly forces himself to breathe.

"He didn't do anything," Antares pleads. His hands are shaking as he stands and moves behind Leo.

The guards look at each other for a long moment.

"We would never hurt each other. I hope you both understand that. No matter who I am to you, I would never hurt my family," Leo says with a deathly calm.

The guards take a second before nodding. Leo's shoulders get infinitely more tense.

Finally, they retreat with a murmured, "Our apologies, Your Highness. It won't happen again."

When the door clicks shut, Leo lets out a shaky breath and meets my eyes. He turns to Antares as he clutches the back of Leo's leg.

"Are you all right?" Leo asks softly.

Antares smiles tightly, looking rattled. He turns to me and asks, "They don't trust us?"

I shake my head. "Not yet."

Something breaks behind Leo's eyes.

"They will when they get to know us. This is as new to them as it is to us. Give it some time," I tell them.

My brothers nod, but Leo's face is blank as he gently lays a hand on Antares's shoulder. I can tell the words do nothing to comfort him. It doesn't help the surge of worry eating through my thoughts either.

WE'VE BEEN DIGGING through the bags the servants left and quickly discovered an entire wardrobe contained within. We pull out more clothes than we've had combined over our lifetimes, all made from fabric finer than any I've ever owned. They feel durable yet look so delicate I don't want to touch them. Soon the empty bags are strewn across the floor and the outfits are laid haphazardly across the furniture so that we can get a good look at what we've been given.

"They only gave me gowns," Byrne says as she riffles through the last of her bags.

I turn to look at the pile she's made, and sure enough, there isn't a pair of pants to be seen. Leo and I glance at each other with raised brows.

Byrne stares at the dresses as her hands hang slack by her side. She raises her eyes to look at us. "I've never worn one. It was rare to see anyone wear a dress in Wate, but when we had the opportunity, Cassien never permitted it. He said they were impractical. That they would create a weakness we could not afford."

Sympathy floods my chest as she touches the fabrics longingly. None of us speak as we watch her pick up a simple, dark purple gown.

She smiles sadly and laughs to herself. "I guess they aren't the best for brawling."

"I'm sure you'd beat us both no matter what you wore," I tell her jokingly.

She sighs and carefully places the dress back down. "Not me, but Elana could." She nods absentmindedly. "She could will the world to fall at her feet and it would crumble to please her."

Byrne's lip trembles as she takes in a long breath. I knew she missed her sister, but I don't think I understood how deeply she's hurting. I doubt they've been apart for more than a day their entire lives. Their relationship is so different than the one I share with Leo. Elana is the only family Byrne has had for years. Elana took care of her, sheltered and protected her. Now she's on her own, and I can't imagine the pain of knowing that the person who shielded her for so long is no longer here to divert the chaos.

"She could do much more than that," Leo whispers, admiration shining in his eyes.

I smirk as I catch the emotion on his face. I don't think I've ever seen that look on Leo before, and by the Goddess, I hope it lingers.

Leo snaps out of his daze as Byrne turns around. "You can search through what we have and see what fits you," he tells her.

I nod, gesturing at my pile with a mock bow. "What's ours is yours."

She laughs before moving to pick through our clothes, holding out a few items as she tries to size them up. In the end, she doesn't take much, only a few things from Altair's pile— since they're the closest to her size—and two shirts from the items Leo and I were given.

Half an hour later, we're dressed and ready for the day. Saiph watches Byrne with wide eyes as she braids her own hair with nimble movements. Altair is perusing the bookshelves, though he doesn't take any books. He seems to find enough interest in simply considering the titles etched into the spines. Antares, on the other hand, is building some sort of track to roll his ball down. He's been trying for ages to bounce it off a line of tomes and land it in a bowl.

"I think Saiph likes having another girl around," Leo says, breaking my attention away from Antares as the ball rebounds off a book and hits him in the chest.

Chuckling, I follow Leo's gaze to where our sister is now demanding Byrne braid her hair. I can't help but grin as I watch them.

"Yeah. It's good for her to have someone to look up to. She's going to be something when she's older," I say as an image of a grown Saiph appears in my head. She reminds me so much of Pleiades. A memory of my sister swinging upside-down from a tree without a single care in the world floods in, sending a hurricane of emotions through my mind.

After tying off her own hair, Byrne happily obliges Saiph. She weaves Saiph's short hair together effortlessly. Leo and I are transfixed by the movements of her hands when steps from behind the door catch my attention. My head swivels toward the hall as we hear a knock. Leo steels his expression, stands, and makes his way toward the door.

I'm quick on his heels as the door swings open. Ares, Emrys, and four guards stand waiting for us.

"Are you ready to see the city?"

THE QUEEN and king meet us at the entrance of the palace with their own slew of guards. They introduce us to their most trusted adviser, an old man named Ceto DeLang. His wrinkled, dark brown skin and coiled silver hair shine in the sun. His smile is kind in the way only a weathered family member's can be. He takes his time to learn each of our names, and Leo and I nod gratefully as he listens to Saiph speak about her plaited hair. He seems trustworthy, yet I see hesitation in Leo's eyes. I can't blame him. Ceto appears to be most genuine man we've met in a long while, but we've been tricked before.

The queen and king lead us down the streets as people flock outside, coming out of hostels, bakeries, shops, and pubs in hopes of a glimpse of the royal pair. They wave and call the royals' names as we walk straight down the main road to the bay. When the people catch sight of us, the entire atmosphere changes. The calls quiet to hushed whispers and the eager glances turn to wary stares. I spin my ring as I take it all in, holding Saiph closer when she stirs in my arms. Chills run down my back as Leo pulls Altair and Antares to his side.

The adviser, Ceto, steps away from the queen to walk alongside us. "Don't be nervous. They're only uncertain of what to make of you. Of what story they should believe. Give them an image they can be sure of."

Nodding, Leo takes a deep breath and morphs into the picture of calm confidence. His back straightens as his chin lifts, an easy smile gracing his face. Ceto walks proudly beside us.

"Thank you," I tell Ceto, soothing my nerves as Byrne transforms her expression into one of ease.

Ceto winks with a childish grin as his eyes wander forward once more. The crowd around us feeds off our change and relaxes. Their excited smiles return as they wave. Children lean out of windows as they try to get a good look at the royal blood walking the streets. The feeling is surreal.

"The streets are... beautiful," Leo says as he scans the buildings around us. "Everything feels alive."

Ceto nods as he folds his hands behind his back. I couldn't

agree more. Somereil was a suffering city and Wate was always eerie, but this place is like a living being, full of sound and action.

"It is definitely one of the most vibrant cities in Illena. Though Keria holds a special place in my heart." At our confused looks, Ceto continues with a light laugh. "It is a city to the west from which I hail, though I have always spent equal time in Arkezo as I do at home. Being a DeLang, I have duties to the court that often call me here."

The crease between Leo's brows only grows deeper as he watches the man. "You're a Bloodline then?"

Ceto nods. "That I am. The DeLangs can sense weather changes. Days ahead, might I add." He smirks as he turns to look forward once more. "Here we are. The Lady's Bay."

We follow his gaze, and the breath is sucked from my lungs. A wide bay lies before us surrounded by black sand darker than ash. Directly across are the twin peaks we saw from the window last night. The crack between them leading to the Bronze Sea shines in the sunlight.

"As legend goes, the sand turned black when Lady Death forged the Ash Sword on this very beach," Ceto says.

Leo turns toward the man with neck-breaking speed and blinks as if trying to straighten his thoughts. "I thought the Ash Sword itself was only legend."

I know the story well. It was one of Mum's favorites. She used to tell us how Lady Death forged the sword with the ashes of the fallen. It was supposed to have brought together the survivors of the Death Dancers' reign, ultimately creating the band that defeated them.

"My boy, it is much more than that. It was your Bloodline's sword for generations. Supposedly, Lady Death bestowed it upon the Matteus Bloodline to lead Illena to prosperity when the war was won."

We stare open-mouthed at the old man.

"Where is it now?" Leo asks eagerly.

I look at my brother skeptically. For a moment, Leo seems different. Shadows play across his face and his eyes darken. I shake away the thought and focus on Ceto.

"It is in Anateya now. It was a peace offering many generations ago, gifted by a former king as a show of good faith. Anateya is the only country we continue to have a relationship with and whose people are openly aware of our existence."

Leo's brows furrow as he falls deep in thought. "I never knew that."

"It would have been impossible for you to know. You grew up amongst the Tominese, and Anateya is the only country who recognizes Illena as its own nation. The rest choose to ignore our existence. But as long as they abide by the treaties, we have no need for them and find it easier to keep to ourselves," Ceto explains stoically. There's no missing the pride in his voice.

We turn a corner, and the crowd grows tenfold. But this time, they don't pay us much heed. As I scan their faces, my attention catches on their eyes. Well, more specifically, the color of their irises. They're all different—silvers, blues, greens, browns, and blacks accentuating every person's appearance.

"Welcome to New Corsair," Ceto says lightly as he nods to a passing group of people dressed in sun-bleached clothes. "The getics we trade with keep to these streets. Some own businesses and hostels, but most are here only for short periods of time while their ships are docked."

Pressure on my chest seems to lift as I watch these people go about their days, interacting with blood-eyes comfortably as I have with Leo for so many years. They're like me. I never realized how good it would feel to see this. To know that I'm not the only one who dares live amongst them.

"I thought you said Anateya was the only state to have ties with Illena?" Leo asks as we continue down the street.

Antares watches everything with wide eyes. He steps closer to Leo as a man with a gruesomely scarred eye walks past on a wooden leg.

"The Corsair Isles aren't considered a country—by law anyway. They are simply a middle ground for merchants and marauders from across the globe. It is a place where they can be safe under the laws of the sea instead of the laws of land. Where they can gather with their own people," Ceto tells us.

Leo and I nod as we watch the crowds milling around us. Almost every group wears foreign clothing, all of which displays an array of color wider than the sky as the sun sets. Languages from around the world merge into a symphony of droning melodies. It's a beautiful type of chaos. A being made of spare parts that somehow manages to breathe.

After turning another corner, we come face to face with an extensive building that stretches for blocks. The first level is made of solid stone, and there are stairs leading to the open second and third floors set at equal distances in the wall. There are large painted signs on display, along with a multitude of flags and tapestries that sway in the wind. The strong smell of sugar and spices wafts through the air as we walk along the street.

"This is the Killarian market. Most of the goods brought in by the getics, as well as the products people make or harvest in Illena, can be found here. The second and third floors are full of anything you can ever imagine," Ceto says with fond eyes.

Leo's forehead creases as he scans the bleak stone wall. "What about the first floor?"

Ceto's eyes narrow as he turns his gaze to my brother. "Everything you don't want to see. Killarian is a wonderful place, but only if you know who to deal with." His tone is suddenly eerily cold. The change feels like a punch to the gut.

Leo nods, but I can see the curiosity bloom in his eyes. He catches my glare and puts his hands up in mock defense.

"Don't even think about it," I mutter as he laughs maniacally under his breath.

Ceto points out the different districts as we pass through the twisted streets. Some are business and residential areas, while others are designated labor quarters and factories. We walk along the manors to the west. I can't help but think they're even more impressive in person, though the people scurrying about look anything but taken by the view.

Ceto explains that these are the primary domiciles of the Bloodlines. Each house has been in the various family's possession since the founding of Illena. Though they have appointed rooms within the palace for their personal use, the houses are more comfortable and therefore their chosen residences when they find themselves in the city. Ceto tells us we will never find a Bloodline without their kin nearby. As he speaks, I notice those who are walking through the yards keep their eyes down as they hurry to their next destination. I can't miss the dread and stress pulling at their faces, and I know Leo notes it as well.

"We will dine with the Bloodlines in two days," the queen announces as we pass the last of the houses and turn south. "Servants will be sent up to take measurements for your garments. They will also discuss a nanny to watch over your siblings in your absence."

My eyes lock with Leo's as my stomach knots.

"We aren't leaving them alone," Leo states, his voice ringing with finality.

The queen observes him for a moment before her gaze

leaps to the hand he holds on Antares's arm. After a moment of deliberation, she nods. "That can be arranged."

I let out a tight breath as I exchange a grateful look with Leo. Had she not agreed, I don't know what we would have done. I couldn't leave Leo or Saiph and the boys alone and I doubt this dinner is optional.

We continue through a particularly thick crowd when I feel a tug on my pocket. I turn and catch a hand seconds before it's pulled away. Leo draws a dagger from the sheath on his thigh as a tall boy around our age turns his wide, surprised silver eyes on us. I don't miss the fear flash across his expression as he tenses and tries desperately to escape. Ares is instantly by our side, grabbing the pickpocket's arm from my grip. The guards pull their weapons as the boy closes his eyes, his brows furrowed under a braided leather halo wrapped around his forehead.

"Seems like we've got a thieving slumblood on our hands," Ares seethes, his voice so cold it stings.

The boy stays completely still even as his hands tremble. Ares shakes him so violently that his captive stumbles back a step and turns his face to the side.

"There are so many things I could do with you," Ares sneers. There's disgust written on his face as his eyes light with anger.

"We only ran into each other. I grabbed his hand to keep him from falling. He did nothing wrong," I tell Ares.

The pickpocket looks at me strangely, seemingly trying to understand if this is some kind of joke. I know what it's like to have to thieve your way through life. The fear on his face is evident, a feeling I've shared a hundred times before. It's all-consuming, taking over when you know there's no way out and no second chance to barter for. As I meet his eyes, I recognize the hardened acceptance of a person who's never had the option to live simply.

Leo steps up beside me when Ares doesn't make a move to let the boy go. "It was an accident, Ares."

After a moment, Ares nods and peels his hand away from the boy's shirt. "I'm sure you'll be more careful next time, yes?"

The stranger nods before bowing deeply. "My apologies, Your Highness." He turns away, but not so fast that I don't catch the surprised gratitude in his eyes.

Leo and I exchange a long look.

"Did he go for your pockets?" Leo whispers. I nod once, and the corner of his lips kicks up. "He's lucky we hate rules."

The urge to smirk pulls at my face, but I bury it as Ares glances at us. *That thief truly had the Lady on his side.*

As we continue southward, Ares drifts closer to us. No one speaks as the buildings grow taller and block the midday sun from the grimy streets. The crowds gradually thin until very few people are left wandering the winding roads. Broken wooden shutters are slammed shut as we descend into the squalid neighborhood.

I glance at Leo and see his muscles relax in contrast with the growing tensions of our party. It makes sense. This place is almost identical to the low town of Somereil. That was Leo's territory, the place he knew the best and where he felt at home.

Dirt-stained kids watch us from behind crumbling alley walls as rag-clothed people linger in the street. A group of dirtied workers come out of a home as we turn the corner and start to head back the way we came. They watch us as though we're prey, and I have a feeling they aren't the only ones keeping an eye on us.

"This place is different," I whisper to Leo.

He nods absentmindedly as he scans our surroundings.

"There are canals farther along," he says softly as he glances over his shoulder.

I nod, having noticed them before we turned back. Leo switches his attention to Ares.

"Why didn't we go all the way down?" Leo asks quietly, as if speaking too loudly might disturb the peace of the area.

"The Riv is not a place you go to be safe, so we stay on the outskirts. That way we are seen but not in a dangerous position," he replies without averting his eyes from the queen ahead of him. "The people deep in the Riv aren't fond of the queen."

I hear the guards behind us bristle.

"The people seemed to love the queen earlier," Leo remarks as memories of the waving citizens flash in my mind.

Ares nods shallowly as his eyes dart from the royal pair ahead of us to the guards on their flanks. "By most, yes, Kalani is loved. But those in the Riv believe they are the bones on which the system was built, and their blood is the fuel that allows it to operate. They do not feel they deserve to live in these conditions and claim their suffering is a wound that cannot heal in this world. It is truly a simple fix; however, the people would rather complain about their filth than clean up their lives. If they would simply contribute to society in a way that was productive, perhaps they would not be confined to such slums."

I hold Saiph tighter as I look over my shoulder. The gilded filter through which I'd seen the city shatters, and Leo's face becomes strategically void of emotion.

"In the end, we may have only run in a circle," Leo says under his breath as Ares steps away.

By the Goddess, I hope he's wrong.

CHAPTER
SEVEN

I don't think I realized how small Cass was until I carried him to the Council building as he bled out. He seemed so fragile. The memory of his eyes fluttering shut as his lungs heaved is more fuel for my nightmares. I barely remember calling for a doctor. When they refused to treat him, I eventually pulled rank and forced the medic to help. It turned out the sword had been set to pierce his lung but instead hit a rib, sending the blade ricocheting through the flesh on his side rather than dealing a deadly blow. Though the wound would be incredibly painful, it wasn't life-threatening as long as we could get the blood loss under control. The Lady had truly bestowed a miracle by saving him and I didn't know what to do with the emotions that overtook me.

For a while, Cass slept as he tried desperately to recover from the injury the doctor had dutifully sewn shut and cauterized. It would leave two thick scars, but at least he was alive. When Cass finally woke, he asked for his brothers. I didn't know what to tell him, so I said nothing. He stared right past me, understanding the words floating in my mind.

"They left me," he said, his voice a ragged, broken wheeze.

I saw the tears well in his eyes as his lip quivered. I shook my head as my soul severed in two. "No. No, they didn't leave you. They've gone to set up a place for you to live, then they'll be back. Until it's ready, I'm going to watch over you, all right?"

He nodded as a tear rolled down his pale face. I didn't leave his side for the rest of the day, holding his hand as he fell asleep. From that moment, I knew I couldn't abandon him. I'd protect this boy with my life, even if that meant keeping his survival to myself.

IT'S BEEN JUST over a week since Cass was well enough to speak after his injury and he hasn't said another word. I've come every day to keep him company, bringing him books and making sure his bandages stay clean. I've become accustomed to my new routine. Waking up in the cabin after a fitful sleep and walking into the city as pain shoots through my body. Going to the mess hall in the Academy to pick up food, ignoring the sneers and calls of those who once feared me, then visiting Cass. I feel a new sense of pride, watching him silently regain his strength. I finish the day by making my rounds of Wate just to make appearances around the city before crawling back through the woods to the cabin.

I haven't been back to the house and decided I never will. I won't be hurt there again. I won't be beaten only to wake up staring at his chair or the cabinet of pristine crystal glasses. If Cassien wants to take out his anger, he can do it in the streets in front of his people.

I sit next to Cass's cot as his eyelids droop. For a little over an hour, I've been reading a book my mother used to read to us when Byrne and I were children. Cass seems to be enjoying it as much as I enjoy reliving the memory of my mother's sure voice. She used to carry the words off the pages and set them afloat in my mind. I slowly close the heavy tome and set it on the table beside Cass's cot. His eyes track my every movement, knowing I'm about to leave. I stand and pull the blanket up to his chin.

"I'll be back tomorrow, all right?"

Cass nods once as a flicker of fear dances across his face. I place my hand palm up on the bed, and after a moment, he folds his own over it.

"Just try to sleep and the time will pass. Before you know it, I'll be back by your side," I reassure him. "I promise I'll be here tomorrow."

The corner of Cass's lips turns up into the only semblance of a smile I've been able to get out of him as he drags his hand back under the cover.

I head to the door and gently pull it open. Turning back for a moment, I watch the brand-new candle burn in the corner as light dances across the room.

"I'll leave it lit for you?" I ask, as I do every day.

Cass's smile grows—though only slightly—as he nods. My heart squeezes as I step out. The feeling's become a daily occurrence.

I hobble out of the Council building, bypassing anyone I can. I sigh when I step outside as the sun sets, warming my cold skin. For a moment, the world goes silent and the pain fades to a dull whisper in the back of my mind. There are only rays of heat and me. I stand with my eyes closed, breathing easily. The warmth builds under my skin until it burns. I feel myself frown as the pain returns. It crawls under my skin as the golden light becomes molten against my face.

I open my eyes to a group of commanders who had been in my class at the Academy standing only a handful of feet away. Their expressions remain blank as they watch me. They don't try to cover their stares as their eyes note every injury scrawled across my body. Not one of them shows the smallest sign of sympathy. It makes sense, seeing as we were raised not to.

A person who cannot protect themselves must wear their wounds as a brand of shame. I've heard those words a million times and muttered them myself on more than one occasion. I was so wrong. Wounds are not signs of weakness but of strength. They show what you have endured in order to survive. Not so long ago, I would have beaten anyone who dared to think otherwise. I guess I've become what I always imagined the enemy to be. Now I'm completely alone, waiting for the people whose fear I fostered to skin me alive.

I turn away and walk with my chin held high, even as I limp. I feel their gazes follow me, but I pay them no heed. I don't turn as a few members of the group break away and approach me. I close my eyes as I force myself to walk. Time slows as they get near, the pounding of their boots rattling the earth. I breathe out heavily as the air moves around me.

I quickly pivot and dodge the blow Emila sends flying at my head. Her eyes shine with a pure, molten rage. We stand still, watching each other with less than three steps between us. Emila's lips slowly curl into a smile as she bares her teeth.

"Traitor!" Emila launches herself toward me and sweeps her leg at my feet.

I barely avoid the strike, slowed by my injuries. The only way I'm going to get out of this alive is to be smart. I jump into the offensive, throwing everything I have into the movements. I land a nasty elbow to her jaw as she throws a body shot at my broken ribs, injuring them even further. She laughs when my body crunches in on itself.

"No one's going to save you, Elana," Emila sings. "We are never merciful." She's trying to get into my head. It's working.

Seething, I jump at her. She evades the punch I throw and wraps herself around my middle, taking us both to the ground. As we fall, I spin and pin her down. My vision is blurry as my lungs heave. My fist pounds against her again and again as blood splatters on my skin. Emila lifts her leg to flip out of my hold, but I push my knee into her stomach to keep her down. A burst of air fades from her lungs and she struggles to get it back.

Something feral breaks out of me as I beat her. I don't know when she passes out, but I don't stop, every ounce of emotion overflowing from my body pushing me further. As her head falls to the side, bouncing off the gravel, I manage to freeze my fist midair an inch from her face. I lean down beside her ear.

"I am my own savior," I whisper. I slowly stand, feeling the new bruising across my body throb. Staring at Emila's blood-covered face, I do exactly what Wate has taught me. I feel no sympathy. I feel nothing.

I raise my eyes to watch the stoic group of people who had once feared me just enough to respect me. They hold no respect for me now.

"Anyone else?" I call, stepping away from Emila as her chest quivers with a shaky breath. They don't move, as if I had frozen them in time. A grin grows across my bloodied face. "Cowards."

They bristle but never dare to step forward.

"You're all a bunch of cowards." I turn away, limping heavier than I had before but unable to bring myself to care.

Let them see me like this. Let them see that I will not fall, no matter what they throw at me. They chose to cross the wrong woman, but they won't make the same mistake again.

CHAPTER

EIGHT

I'd rather do anything than attend this dinner. Ceto came over yesterday to give us a lesson about the usual court proceedings, the order of the feast, and the most important part of the evening—the introduction of Bloodlines. There are thirteen in total, each having their own respective abilities and powers within Illena. Ceto spent hours explaining everything from the leaders of the families to their responsibilities, and it only fed my nerves.

After our lesson, tailors were ushered in to take our measurements, promising to have even more new outfits prepared ahead of the dinner. They keep their promise, delivering the garments right on time. I slip on a shirt before a comfortable black suit jacket with red detailing around my shoulders. A two-headed dog sits stitched over my heart, as well as imprinted into the black metal buttons running from my neck to the bottom of the jacket. I do each one up slowly, scared I'll ruin the finery. Cael walks out of the bedroom wearing a dark blue suit with silver embroidery cut similarly to mine.

"At least they know how to make good clothes," Cael says as he straightens the neck of his jacket.

I nod, still slightly dazed by what I'm wearing. Saiph slides off the couch from beside Antares and waddles over in the little silver dress they made for her. She stumbles over the puffed tutu as she walks in shoes that took three of us to get on her feet. They're the perfect size, but it seems our little sister has an aversion to new footwear.

"Do you think they would get mad if we put her back in her old boots?" I ask Cael.

The tulle of Saiph's skirt pools around her as she goes boneless on the floor. Cael laughs under his breath as I pick her up. Saiph refuses to straighten, becoming dead weight as she flops around.

"She has to learn to accept change at some point," Cael remarks.

I look at him with raised brows as I pull off her shoes. "The only thing she knows is change. What she *should* learn is how to deal with continuity."

She immediately perks up, wiggling to be set down so she can run around bare-footed. Altair comes out of the washing room wearing the same outfit as Antares: a black shirt and pants detailed in bright gold. The two-headed dog can't be found on any of their clothes. Altair steps our way and I find myself holding my breath, wondering what he'll do. For a moment, all he does is watch us. It's as if he's taking his time to straighten out his thoughts. He hands us Saiph's boots with a flat expression. I take them gratefully and muster up a half-smile in response.

"Thank you," I tell him.

Without acknowledging me, Altair sits on one of the

couches and pulls out a book he had been devouring. I glance at Cael, and I see the hope flare in his eyes, mirroring the warmth in my chest. Whatever that was, it was good. A step forward. It seems like the time away from Wate is allowing Altair to see a bit more clearly.

"Do we have to go to this thing?" Antares grumbles as he sits cross armed on the couch.

Cael sighs as he walks to Antares's side.

"You want a home, don't you?" I ask.

Antares nods, though his eyes are bleak.

"Then we have to attend. All of this is happening to solidify our place here. You won't have to do anything, just be good and eat as much as you can possibly fit into your stomach," Cael says, winking as he straightens Antares's collar.

Our younger brother smirks as the cloud hanging over him disappears. Nothing makes a Heal happier than the idea of a good meal.

Byrne walks out of her room, and our eyes fall on her in awe. She had been hesitant to wear a dress, but what the seamstresses put together is... beautiful. Even though she didn't say it, we all knew it was because of Elana. Wearing the dress meant accepting a new life while Elana is stuck in the past, stuck in Wate. Byrne is living in finery and going to a royal diner, knowing her sister is trapped in a life she can't tear herself from. Though I'm happy Byrne's wearing the gown, I understand why she feels guilty. I wonder if Elana would even wear a dress if given the choice. Byrne smiles at us, her eyes shining as brightly as the simply cut silver dress draped across her frame.

"Emrys is going to faint when he sees you," Cael says, smiling gently.

Byrne blushes and looks away.

"Honestly, we might have to make sure he doesn't hit his head," I tell Cael as I paste a serious look on my face.

Byrne's smile brightens even more, battling the shimmer of the pins holding back her midnight-hued hair. She laughs as she waves us off. "He won't faint."

I shake my head dramatically. "My lady, he might simply pass away."

For the first time in what seems like forever, my mind feels at ease. I wonder for a moment if this is how normal people live. If this feeling, this uncomplicated and unrestrained joy is something not so rare.

A knock at the door jars me from my thoughts and the comfort that had settled around us instantly melts away. I pull Saiph's old, stained boots onto her feet before we drag ourselves to the door.

"Is everyone ready?" I ask.

Only when I get four sure nods do I pull on the knob and step out of the safety of our room. I don't know what will come next. All I can do us pray it doesn't end in disaster.

I THOUGHT we'd be taken directly to the dining room, but we're ushered into a small, dimly lit sitting room. The guards shut the door behind us. We're the only ones here. For a while, we stay close to one another as we wait for what comes next. Nothing happens. No one comes to retrieve us or inform us of what is happening at the dinner.

As the minutes pass, we slowly relax. Antares takes to jumping from couch to upholstered couch as Saiph runs in dizzying circles, trying to catch him. Cael tries desperately to replace the disturbed pillows as Antares plows through the space.

"This is turning out to be some dinner—"

I don't get the chance to finish as the door swings open. Antares loses his footing and goes flying into the air. I move to break his fall, catching him awkwardly around his middle before his head can hit the floor. Cael straightens the last pillow and scoops Saiph into his arms.

The queen, king, Ceto, and their guards look aghast as their mouths hang open. I flip Antares around and place him back on his feet, then pull on his shirt to straighten the collar before he shuffles behind Cael and me. After a moment, the queen folds her hands on the front of her extravagant red gown, the layered skirt hissing against the ground at her movement.

"I hope I will not regret the decision to allow your siblings to attend tonight," she says with a raised brow.

Cael shakes his head as his lips form a tight smile. "You have no need to worry, Your Majesty."

None of the group seems convinced. After a tense moment, the queen sighs. Ceto directs me to stand beside the queen and king, then places Byrne and my siblings behind us.

"I pray to the Goddess you all remember the etiquette lesson I taught you," Ceto whispers pointedly, keeping his eyes forward.

He was such an easy-going man when we first met him, taking in stride everything life threw at him. That is not the overstrung man beside me. Ceto's brows are set in a frown and his hands are solidly stuck behind his back. There isn't a crack in his image, and it makes me shiver. I look at Cael worriedly as they open a large set of double doors. A flood of chatter and faint music overtakes my senses.

I wince as the light from the brightly lit dining hall hits my eyes. After a moment, my vision clears and all I can do is gape at the crowd of silver-eyed nobles dressed in their finest. At least, I hope it's their finest. I can't imagine more elaborate and elegant outfits than the ones before me. I suddenly feel under-dressed.

The entirety of the room bows deeply as their eyes stay fixed to our group. Ceto and the guards around us bow as well. Byrne hesitates as she begins to bow, watching Cael and I closely. She swallows before straightening, pushing against the years of training etched into her bones.

"Rise," the queen says. Her voice carries over the room with a power I've never seen.

The court straightens as a unit, not bothering to hide their curious stares.

The queen and king walk the few steps down to the main floor and stand behind their seats at the head of the table. We don't follow, staying with Ceto as he instructed yesterday. Ceto told us that there will be half an hour before the dinner starts to mingle with the guests after the queen and king introduce the evening.

The royals take their seats, and the queen raises her hand. "We are glad to see you could all attend such a special occa-sion." She turns her eyes on me, and I feel the entirety of the crowd's attention move with hers. "Tonight, we celebrate the return of a lost line. The son of the Crowned Prince Dirix Matteus, Leo Matteus, has joined us to once again make our Bloodline complete."

I shift uncomfortably as the name rings in my ears. I've lived my entire life as a Heal. Suffered and survived through impossible odds with that name. I'm no Matteus. Cael nudges my foot lightly, reminding me to stay composed as Ceto warned. *These people can smell fear. They can see every sign of uncertainty, hear every muttered word. Do not give them anything to exploit,* Ceto had said with such conviction that neither Cael, Byrne, nor I had dared ask him to elaborate.

"Let us welcome him and his companions with open arms

and show him the light Illena lives to shine." The queen smiles easily, but it only puts me further on edge.

I slide in front of Antares and Altair, trying to protect them from the piercing gazes of the people surrounding us.

The room explodes with applause until the queen waves to end the ruckus. The people return to their previous conversations, but I know the topics have changed. We stay on the stairs in front of the doors for a long while as we take it all in. Suddenly Cael goes still by my side. When I catch his blank expression, worry flows through me. I follow his gaze and immediately see why.

At the opposite end of the room, two guards stand post at the door. It's not their appearance that is off-putting, but rather the living, breathing two-headed dogs standing vigilantly by their sides. They bare their teeth each time someone gets too close, and I swear I see their eyes lock onto me. I look away as a shiver creeps down my spine.

"Those are what we call double-dogs," Ceto explains softly, his body tense. "They are a creation of the Death Dancers, just as we are. They are the symbol of the Matteus Bloodline and so, in a way, are considered sacred. The only weapon deadlier than one of those beasts are our own hands. The good thing is they are incredibly hard to breed, so there are very few in existence."

I watch Ceto carefully, noticing the sliver of fear in his eyes. *Don't mess with the two-headed demon dogs. Noted.*

Ceto starts down the stairs without a word, carving a path for us to follow. We stay close on his heels with Byrne staying a step behind. I turn as she finds Emrys in the crowd. The uncertainty that had plagued her expression melts away as she holds his gaze. Emrys doesn't seem to care where he is, staring at her with eyes brighter than the sun. I call to her softly and she snaps out of her trance. Byrne swallows quietly before rejoining our group, her attention now trained dutifully ahead.

Ares is the first person to approach us. He welcomes us with a warm smile, but I can only greet him stiffly. Ceto glares at me, and taking the hint, I try to relax and pull on that mercenary's mask I've spent years perfecting.

Though most decide to keep their distance, two men and a woman approach us. They bow deeply, wearing clearly forced smiles.

"Your Highness, I present Adya and Cyrus of the Kalu line, and Einar of the Melian line," Ceto says. He watches the trio closely as they straighten.

I nod in acknowledgment, unsure of how this will go. If my memory serves me, the Kalus can adjust their core body temperature to suit any climate, while the Melians are able to hold their breath and swim as though they were born in the waves. Neither Bloodline was amongst those Ceto warned us to avoid.

"So, you're Kenzo's son," the tallest of the two men, Cyrus, says. He watches me with careful eyes, though he doesn't seem threatening.

"Pardon?" I say, not sure who he's referring to.

The trio smile at each other, the memory of a secret clearly passing among them.

"My apologies, Your Highness. We knew Dirix when we were children. Kenzo was a nickname given to him during our time in training," Cyrus explains.

"You really do resemble him. It's like looking in the past," Adya adds, watching me with sorrowful eyes.

Both men nod.

"So I've heard," I tell her lightly, trying to shake away the tension whipping at my bones. I clear my throat and raise my chin. "Why Kenzo?"

My need to know more about my father suddenly grows insufferable. These people knew him and may have even been his close friends. A wide smile appears on their faces.

"Ke—Dirix hated the attention he received from our tutors growing up. One year, a new combat instructor had been hired from a small town in the south, and he'd not yet seen Dirix. Since we all wore the same uniforms to train, there was no clear sign that he had royal blood in his veins—other than his skill in combat. The instructor, not familiar with the Bloodlines, thought Kenzo Cadmus was Dirix because he was the strongest among us. Kenzo drank up the attention and Dirix enjoyed the reprieve. For a full year, to keep the instructor thinking Dirix was truly Kenzo, we had to call him so. After that, the name stuck." Cyrus laughs to himself, as if reliving the memory. "The instructor only found out when he finally realized that your father was by far the best fighter in our ranks and healed ten times faster than any normal person should."

"We were punished for weeks afterward. I don't think I've ever trained so hard in my life," Einar adds, his voice rough. His eyes meet mine and I have to fight the urge to look away. "Is Dirix still around? Surely if you're here, he's told you of us."

My back goes pin straight. *They don't know he's dead.* I blink, wondering how that could be possible. They catch my hesitation and instantly tense.

"I've never met him. My—their mother and father took me from Wate days after I was born," I say as I nod back toward my siblings.

Their gazes shift to my arm, as though they could see the two bands on my wrist hidden under the thick sleeve.

"Your mother truly was gold-eyed?" Adya says as surprise flashes across her features. "Perhaps I shouldn't have disregarded the rumors so soon." I grind my teeth as she speaks to her counterparts as if I were not standing mere steps away.

"My eyes bleed red like my father's," I tell her.

"Then what of your mother? Is she alive?" she presses, focusing back on me.

I look to Ceto, but his attention is willfully averted. I clench my jaw and look directly at Adya. "She was murdered for having me."

Ceto's eyes cut to me, a clear warning in his gaze. I don't care where I am—what they did to Dahlia wasn't right. I won't stand by and allow them to see past it.

"And Dirix?" Cyrus asks warily.

The groups around us have gone silent, clearly listening.

"I was told when he begged for aid in retrieving me from Wate, he was ignored. This forced him to come looking for me himself. The gold-eyes knew he would come and were prepared for it. They strung him up and made him bleed for all to watch," I say softly, though I know the entirety of the room hears the words.

Ceto winces as the trio's anger becomes apparent. A few gasps ring out in the quiet space as the memory of the records room floods into my mind. I force it back and stand taller. I won't let them push me down. Dirix screamed for me. I won't let his last breaths fall silently to time.

"Those are big accusations from a boy so new to our court," Adya says carefully.

I don't have time to reply before doors on either side of the wide room burst open, bringing with them the sweeping aromas of our dinner. Ceto sighs heavily as the trio moves toward their respective seats at their tables.

"I would choose my next words very carefully if I were you," Ceto warns under his breath before he heads to his seat at the table adjacent to the queen and king.

I meet Cael's eyes as resolve fills my chest. I expect him to caution me, but instead I see a look of pride as his lips quirk into a smile. Confidence works through my body as the tension straining my muscles bleeds away.

We head toward the open seats as Ceto instructed. Ares smiles from where he stands behind his chair as we wait for the queen to allow us to sit. I take my place behind the one next to Ares and pull Antares to stand beside me. Altair takes the next seat, followed by Byrne and Cael. The rest of the crowd mulls around, finding their seats with ease.

The last people to approach the table are three men and a girl, all dressed in deep purple. The girl is around our age with olive-tinted skin and curly shoulder-length hair. Half of it is braided up and tied neatly at the back of her head. Her black-lined eyes make her silver irises stand out starkly. The three men share her features. Though they are clearly related, the men give the girl a large berth, as if scared to get too close. Ceto's warning echoes in my head as the girl's eyes lock with mine. *Whatever you do, stay away from the Damaris line. They are more dangerous than you can possibly imagine. If you must be around them, do everything in your power not to touch them, especially the youngest, Kaja.* He'd sounded so distant, as if even speaking of her was to condemn himself.

Though I don't see a weapon on her, this girl feels dangerous as she takes her seat. I think of the first time I saw Elana and the power that radiated from her being. This girl is different. Where Elana felt strong because she embodied a ruthless leader, Kaja pulls her power from those around her. Everyone in the room recoils as she comes near as if her gaze could kill.

Well, almost everyone. Cael is unmoving as Kaja approaches. He speaks to Saiph to keep her calm and doesn't bother raising his eyes. He tenses so slightly when Kaja stands beside him that only someone who's known him for years would see the change in his posture. Kaja watches him carefully as if expecting Cael to step away like all the rest. My brother holds his ground and lifts his gaze to hers. Kaja's eyes widen as he nods in greeting before politely turning back to Saiph. I don't know if he realizes it, but a smirk pulls at his lips. I shake my head as a laugh bubbles up in my chest and turn to watch the queen.

"Be seated," she commands with a wave.

We pull out our chairs and take our seats. The room fills with conversation as food is placed before us. Blank-faced servants walk between the two tables and fill our plates with a variety of meats and vegetables. Cael and I glance at each other with wonder as we watch the food pile onto our dishes. Antares stares at the meal as though it might disappear before his eyes. The Bloodlines are unfazed by the quality and sheer amount of food before them. They barely note their plates as they speak in hushed tones and throw piercing glares at different families across the room.

Even as the Bloodlines eat, I can only stare at the delicacies before us. I feel the hunger rip at my stomach, but my hands refuse to move as the weight of the evening becomes unbearable. Three silver forks sit to the right of my plate, and I don't have a clue which one to use. I've never felt so small.

"You do know this food was prepared for us to eat," Ares whispers beside me.

Snapping out of my trance, I sit straight in my seat, glancing at Antares as he watches me. "Of course."

I pick up the middle fork and dig into a piece of meat. When the taste hits my mouth, every bit of doubt that had been floating across my mind disappears. I laugh under my breath as I take another bite, wondering how we got here. My siblings inhale their dinner without hesitation. Byrne is the only one of us who has any restraint.

"It's as if they've never seen food before," a man sitting

beside Emrys across the table says loudly enough for the entire room to hear.

The space falls quiet. The disgust weighing on the words pulls my eyes up to him as my fork hovers halfway to my mouth. I glance to the side to see Antares's face smeared with sauce. Our plates are the only ones almost empty.

"You'll have to excuse my family. We aren't used to court etiquette yet," Cael says diplomatically as I lower my fork.

I pick up a silk napkin that feels too expensive to be using as a rag and hand it to Antares, motioning for him to wipe his face.

"Or etiquette of any sort," the man sneers. He must be Emrys's relative. They're wearing the same shade of turquoise.

Emrys winces, an apology clearly written in his eyes as he looks at Byrne. She doesn't dare meet his gaze.

"We lived very differently in Tominay. I would hope you could give us the courtesy of time to adjust," I tell him, my voice cold as ice. The man scoffs and the monster in my depths roils. "I suggest you watch how you speak to my family."

All eyes shoot toward me as the man's round face grows red with anger. The rest of the room remains silent with calculated restraint, but this man doesn't seem to care. I remember Ceto telling us the Lord of the Ceruleen line had a temper.

"Is that a threat?" he says, his voice packed with heated emotion.

My face goes blank as I sit back.

"Take it as you will," Cael says, his expression mirroring mine.

The lord's eyes fly between us. "You let a getic speak for you?"

Emrys leans back, trying to disappear as Cael and I grow livid.

"I let my *brother* speak for me," I tell the man pointedly.

A few people around the room shake their heads in response as if it were such an impossibility. Others who do not react watch us closely, as though they're trying to see past the conversation at hand into our ulterior motives.

"And I wonder how a crown prince of the strongest country on the continent gains a family like yours?" a woman farther along the table says, taking the weight off the Ceruleen Lord.

"We survived together," is all I say.

The woman wears a tightly fitted green gown that contrasts harshly against her white hair. *She's the Lady of the Keres line,* I remember Ceto saying, *the Bloodline with superior intelligence and intellect. You won't be able to outsmart or lie to these ones.*

"And how is it you survived in a country where you would be hunted for the very blood in your veins?" the Lady of Keres asks as her eyes bore into me. "I don't expect it was by following their laws..."

"I worked in exchange for our safety," I tell her, a non-answer.

Her eyes narrow as she watches me. "Doing what exactly?"

"I'm quite sure you do not mean to pry, Lady Keres," Ares says, staring the woman down.

I glance his way, knowing Ares is trying to take the pressure away from me. A moment of silence passes, but the piercing gazes of those around us demand answers. I give Ares an appreciative nod for the effort but decide to continue. Hiding who I was isn't worth the risk of them finding out later. Plus, as Ceto said, the Keres line would see through any lie. I won't chance it.

"I was employed by one of Tominay's arena bosses," I tell her easily.

Her brows rise as she nods, clearly piecing the information

together. "You're a killer," Lady Keres says, her tone light as her head tilts to the side.

I don't break her stare even as murmurs float around the room. I nod as my stomach twists with nerves.

"I was... once. I fought in the arenas to earn enough money to feed my family, then was forced into working as a mercenary," I explain.

"Forced?" a man from down the table asks.

"The boss who held my employment knew what we were, what we are. He knew the laws we were breaking by living on Tominese soil. He found joy in using my siblings as incentive to get me to do his bidding."

No one speaks as they watch me, clearly trying to decipher the truth in my words.

"You speak of him in the past tense," another woman interjects, trying to wring the story out of me.

"I am not accustomed to speaking of dead people in the present," I state.

The woman nods in acknowledgement. Half her face is covered in long scars, as though someone tore one side off and sewed it back together in a rush. I recognize her as the daughter of the Alinksy Lord. Ceto told us about her horrible scars, but I never imagined anything like this. I shake the thought away as curiosity buzzes through the room. The people here know we're dangerous and they aren't afraid.

I crack my neck as I survey the table, having forgotten about the food before me. Looking the Bloodlines over as they whisper amongst themselves, I realize they will not be as civil as I had hoped.

CHAPTER

NINE

CAEL

The dinner was tense from the moment we walked in, and the air only grew thicker after Leo told them of his past employment. We kept to ourselves following that ordeal, and the Bloodlines seemed to be sated. Throughout the rest of the night, the queen watched us curiously, while the king looked ready to order us out of the Illena. Ceto had made it very clear the king would be difficult to impress. He was known for being guarded, and right now Leo is a risk.

After the meal, the people stayed late into the night to drink and speak amongst themselves as was customary, but we wanted nothing more than to escape. Saiph was tired of being held, and Antares wouldn't stop fidgeting with his clothes, tearing two buttons off his cuffs. Finally, exhausted and fed up, Leo found Ceto and asked permission for us to leave. Seemingly regretful, Ceto declined, so we settled for hiding in an alcove just out of sight of most of the guests.

Finally hidden from prying stares, we deflate as the image we've been upholding melts away. Leo leans against the wall and closes his eyes for a long moment. I let him be as I watch Antares and Saiph test how many times they can spin in a circle before falling. I count absentmindedly as they move, happy that they're tiring each other out. Byrne stands by the other wall beside Altair, deep in thought.

Hearing steps near us, I turn to face the room. I breathe out slowly as Emrys walks our way. He and Byrne had been stealing glances at each other the entire night, yet luckily, no one had noticed. He checks over his shoulder and slides into the alcove.

"This could go incredibly wrong if you're caught here with us. It's safer if they don't know about you both," I tell Emrys with raised brows. "I wouldn't imagine the Bloodlines would take kindly to learning about your escapades in Wate."

He waves me off as he moves to Byrne's side. She sinks into him, and his arms move around her protectively.

"I couldn't care less at the moment," he says. "My father wants me to speak with you, Leo. He believes that because I took a part in finding you, you'll tell me something he could use as blackmail should he ever need a favor."

My brother's eyes are tired, his will drained from the events of the evening. "Being a murderer wasn't enough?"

Leo rubs a hand over his face. I can see the shadows dancing in his mind as the memories taunt him. Emrys laughs mirthlessly.

"The Bloodlines love anyone who can carry a knife, and they crave a good show from anyone who holds power," Emrys says. "Their entire system is built on who has the ability to bestow the most fear and gain the most respect. You might have just accomplished both."

I huff an incredulous laugh as I think of the irony of our

situation. We had to hide for years because of Leo's employment and who my siblings are. Now the very thing that would have damned us is what might save us.

We stand in silence for a while, listening to the idle chatter of the Bloodlines from the main room.

"Are you all right?" I ask Leo in a whisper.

A muscle in his jaw feathers as he stares at the wall. "I'm just trying to figure it all out."

I nod, knowing full well he's going through every minute of the last few hours in his head. "We will, it just—"

My head swivels toward the main room as I hear someone coming. Leo straightens beside me and steps away from the wall to cover Saiph and the boys. Kaja appears, her sharp eyes roving over us. Though Emrys steps away from Byrne, I know she's seen them. Her attention moves to me, and I don't know what to do with myself. I return her stare, noting every feature of her face: her strong jaw, straight nose, high cheekbones... Her indigo dress is made of a layered, sheer material that seems to float, making her all the more surreal. I can't read a single emotion on her face as she scans me. We stand there for a long moment with our stares stuck in place. For some reason, I don't mind it.

"I hope you found the dining to your liking," Kaja says, pulling me out of the daze I'd fallen into.

I swallow as I regain my bearings. Leo passes me a questioning look, which I ignore as I wonder how long I was caught in her stare. I nod, the motion overly stiff. "It was the best we've ever had."

Confusion passes over her face as her brows furrow and her hands fold together.

"In Tominay, it was rare for us to eat anything more than what we could forage or steal. Even in Wate, Cael and I were only given scraps," Leo explains with a cold voice. There's a warning in those words: she should keep her distance.

She lifts her chin, holding her ground. "I understand you did not have much in your past life." It's a statement more than a question.

Leo shakes his head. "We had each other."

Kaja doesn't say anything as she bows her head in what seems to be... respect.

"And that is still more than so many," she says, her voice strong and sure as she moves to step back. "Welcome to Arkezo, Your Highness." Her eyes linger on me for a moment before she makes her way to walk back to her entourage.

"Kaja," Emrys says before she's out of earshot.

She looks back over her shoulder. Her expression warns him to be careful about his next words.

"You've seen nothing," Emrys says, his voice promising violence.

A smile pulls at Kaja's lips as her head tilts. Emrys shrivels into his skin at her undivided attention, fear seeping into his resolve.

"Your business is only yours, Emrys." Kaja watches Byrne for a moment, who stands slightly hidden behind Emrys. "Though I would advise you to be more cautious in the future. I shouldn't need to warn you about the consequences of deceiving the Bloodlines."

Without another glance, Kaja reenters the crowd in the main room. I watch her walk back to her Bloodline as every person she passes moves to carve a path. She doesn't speak a word to anyone, nor does she cower under their stares. She walks with confidence, letting the people bask in their own fear.

Emrys lets out a long breath as he closes his eyes.

"Do you think she's going to do something?" Byrne asks worriedly.

I think the question is meant for Emrys, but I answer instead. "No. If she wanted spectacle, she would have made a show."

LEO

It's well past dark now. Antares, Altair, and Saiph all found sleep hours ago. Though it's taken them some time, they've grown accustomed to the new environment. Since the dinner three days ago, we've fallen into a sort of routine. The servants bring in our daily meals without ever varying the times. Between lunch and dinner, we're brought out to see the city to acclimatize to our surroundings and learn the blood-eyed lifestyle, as Ares likes to put it. Besides Ceto, he's spent the most time aiding us in adjusting to our new setting. In the mornings, the pair comes in to teach us some of Illena's history or to show us around the palace, a building that has turned out to be more elaborate than I could have imagined. We have yet to see the whole thing, even after spending hours walking through its halls and discovering its hidden chambers.

In the evening, we silently watch the flames dancing in the fireplace as the moonlight shines through the windows. Emrys sits on one of the couches, holding Byrne close to his side as he does every night. Emrys has been punctual to the point where we now wait by the window to help him through, knowing the exact moment he'll appear.

Cael sits beside me, absentmindedly spinning his onyx ring as he stares at the hearth. He's been lost in his thoughts a lot recently and has refused to tell me what's going on in his head. Whatever it is, it doesn't seem to be dragging him down, so I've let him stew in peace. The only problem is my mind now has the insatiable need to wonder about every detail of our lives as well. This worriless lifestyle is what I've always prayed for, yet now it all seems incredibly... dull. I need something to keep me busy or I might go insane.

I stand as I crack each knuckle in my hands and head toward the bookshelf. I need something, anything, to keep my thoughts from wandering. I feel Cael's eyes follow me as I fidget, trying to read the spines of the tomes.

"Restless much?" Cael points out.

I turn as he raises a brow in question and the corner of his lips kicks up. I smile flatly.

"It's that obvious?" I say sarcastically, knowing full well I haven't been able to sit still in hours.

Cael sighs as he crosses his arms like an exasperated parent, nodding toward the shelf. "I don't think reading will do you any good."

I throw my hands in the air and flop ungracefully onto the sofa. "Well then tell me what I should—"

Cael stops me with a rather annoying shushing sound. I'm about to retort when he turns toward the window, his brows drawn together. Emrys and Byrne stay deathly still as they watch us. Ever so slowly, Cael rises and picks up a dagger from the table. I pull my own from the scabbard against my thigh and stand. A faint whisper of wind slips through the open window closest to the trellis. My stomach knots as Cael and I step toward it simultaneously. The window was closed after Emrys came in. Cael and I both checked it. Someone's out there.

Emrys and Byrne stand, watching us carefully as we crouch beneath the window. Cael nods and I rise to look outside. A pair of wide silver eyes meet mine so suddenly, I almost stumble back. I knock open the window and throw my hand out to grab the spy. I get a hold of his shirt, but he spins and wrestles out of my grip. The sound of a struggle against the trellis followed by a loud thud rings dully through the air. I lean out and catch a glimpse of a dark figure hobbling away. I make to jump out the opening, but a sure hand pulls me back.

I look at Cael with wide eyes as my heart races. "I'm not letting him get away."

His jaw tightens as he moves briskly into the bedroom, returning with a pair of black hooded jackets. "I won't either."

I look at Byrne and Emrys as I slip on the coat Cael throws to me. Seeing the question in my eyes, Byrne nods stoically.

"Go. We'll watch over the kids until you get back," she promises.

"You think he sent someone," Cael says under his breath as he pauses in front of the window.

My thoughts reel. *Cassien.* If he sent someone to us... by the Lady, we're far from safe. And Elana... I need to convince her to leave Wate. I don't know how I'm going to do it, but I'll find a way to get her out. And if she doesn't run, then I'll take the safety to her, though that strategy requires a bit more of my mercenary expertise than I would like.

"Who sent someone?" Emrys asks obliviously.

Byrne shivers and he tucks her tighter to his side. Sharp worry dawns on his face.

"We'll find whoever it is," I assure Byrne.

She manages a nod before I move to the window and pull up my hood. I've seen Emrys swing out of it enough times to know how to do it. I drop out feet first and find my footing on the trellis beneath the new foliage. Cael follows, closing the window behind him. A storm of dread builds in my mind as I climb away from Saiph and the boys. I have to believe they'll be fine, but I can't stop myself from thinking the worst.

Cael stops a few feet above me as his foot breaks through a rung.

"Are you all right?" I whisper.

"Yeah... whoever was up here cut themselves going back down," Cael says absentmindedly.

I lift my hand to find a small splatter of blood on the wood. A bleeding runner is always better to track.

Cael and I race down and get out of the open area by slipping behind a manicured shrub. I scan the ground for signs of anyone who would have rushed past but come up with nothing.

"Look," Cael whispers, motioning for me to come over to him.

A streak of blood is splattered amongst the dew on the grass. A smile pulls at my lips as I look at my brother. *Whoever this is won't get far.*

A faint trail of blood and footsteps appears as we push forward, leading us to the north end of the grounds. We follow the signs to a small, dilapidated shed. It's a perfect place to hide until the gates open tomorrow. Whoever this is must have been planning to watch us for a while if he's been staked out here.

Cael and I each have a weapon ready as I place my hand on the door. Taking a deep breath, I swing it open and burst in. The shed is empty except for a few wilted potted plants and an old gardening trunk that's seen better days. I groan as I run my hand down my face. Cael takes in the shed with furrowed brows. This doesn't make sense. The intruder clearly came in here and now he's gone. There's no way out. Nowhere to hide. Yet he's not here.

Cael steps into the confined space and his breathing grows heavier. He scans the walls, dragging his fingers along the boards.

"We better just head back," I say with a sigh as frustration grinds at my mind.

Cael steps across the shed and crouches, staring at the floor beneath a pile of cracked pots. He turns to me as the beginning of a grin pulls at his face.

"I never took you for a quitter," my brother says with a raised brow.

He knocks on the floorboards, and I hear it. The dull thud of hollow space is music to my ears. I shake my head, impressed once again at how Cael manages to see everything past its disguise.

"You have a gift, you know that?" I tell him incredulously.

His smug grin grows wider. "Of course I do. It shouldn't have taken you this long to realize."

I roll my eyes as I move to his side. As one, we pull up the boards to reveal a deep tunnel dug into the ground.

"Well, that explains a lot," I mutter.

Cael huffs his agreement as he stares into the darkness. Setting my jaw, I pull open the lid of the gardening trunk.

"What are you looking for?" Cael asks as I search through the old tools left to fester inside the trunk.

My lip kicks up into a smile as I turn toward him with a half-burnt candle and a water-marked box of matches. They're thickly coated in dirt and dust, but they'll do perfectly. Cael's expression eases as he nods in thanks.

"How'd you know they would be in there?" he asks as we move toward the tunnel.

"Vela used to have a gardener at his largest estate. The man did all the work at night so that the garden was pristine for the day. Apparently, he burned through candles faster than Vela bothered to buy more."

Cael nods as a shadow crosses his face.

We sit beside the tunnel and set to lighting the wick. After a few tries, a spark finally catches. Cael and I lock eyes before we stare at the tunnel. The dim candle won't do much, but it's better than complete darkness.

"Shall we flip for who goes first?" I say jokingly, knowing we have nothing to flip.

Cael rolls his eyes as he shoves my shoulder. "You're a fool if you think I'm going in there first."

I shake my head with a grin as I move over the entrance, salute my brother, and drop down.

Moments later, we're stalking down the dank underground corridor, listening to the shifting earth under our feet. The large wooden supports built into the walls must be at least century old, maybe even from pre-wartime. Most of the beams are moldy and rotting away, while a few have had chunks eaten out of them by some type of animal. I touch the walls, and to my surprise, they're solid. The earth is packed so tightly it almost feels like carved stone.

"Look at the beams," Cael says, stopping us both in our tracks.

I follow his gaze as he holds the candle close and brushes dirt off the wood. Sweeping engravings have been carved into the grain. It looks like script, but it's like nothing I've ever seen. The lettering is mesmerizing. Each character flows into the other like a work of art.

"I've never seen anything like it," Cael says.

Though it might be a meaningless pattern, the longer I stare at it, the more it *feels* like a language. It's almost... familiar. There's an itch at the back of my mind as I trace the lines with my eyes, like a memory triggered by the letters is staying just out of my reach.

"It's the Death Dancers' writing," I surprise myself by saying. "The language they spoke. This was how they wrote it."

Cael watches me curiously as I stare at the letters as though I could read them.

"How do you know that?" he asks.

I tear my eyes away from the markings and my mind stumbles for an explanation. I blink once... twice. "Because that's what it is. Does it not look like a language to you?"

Cael slowly shakes his head as he glances between the engravings and me. "It's definitely some type of writing, but I've never seen a written language similar to this."

"It's from the Death Dancers. I know it is."

Cael nods with a drawn expression. I can tell he doesn't understand, but something is drawing me to these symbols and it's terrifying. I force myself to take a breath and keep walking. I can figure out what tricks my mind is playing later.

The howling of the wind grows stronger as we approach the end of the tunnel. Several foot slots have been carved into the surface of the wall, allowing us to climb out. There's fresh blood smeared on the holds, and I can't help but feel relieved we're still on the right trail.

Cael climbs out first. He snuffs out the candle before pulling himself up through the opening that'd been covered by an empty crate. I pull myself out after him, accepting the hand he extends to help me up. My brother relaxes instantly as the cloud of tension from the tunnel fades away. As I take in our surroundings, I realize we're standing in an alley between two buildings along the main street in front of the royal grounds.

Cael picks up a piece of blood-stained cloth lying on the ground beside the opening.

"We can't be too far behind," Cael says as he moves toward the road.

I pull my hood lower over my face as we walk along the quiet street. "He wouldn't have stayed on the main thoroughfares."

Cael nods and we head toward a side road leading south. I palm a dagger, holding the blade tight to my wrist as we move through the city. I try not to take notice of the sounds in the darkness or the animals skittering just out of my view. I breathe easier as we head deep into the Riv. This is where I thrive. We push well past the limits the royals set for us and I instantly understand why they kept turning us around.

Half of the people on the street seem to be too drunk to pay two hooded men running through the darkness any heed, while the other half seem to be too busy attempting their own illicit missions to care. We fit in seamlessly as we follow the faint trail of fresh blood. Cael stops and stares at a dark figure walking down the road.

"That's him," I say, recognizing the thick black clothing and build of the man.

Cael nods, and we set to following him from a distance. He turns down the winding streets, avoiding the unnatural puddles littering the street. After a few minutes, a canal appears, slicing the road in two. The sound of softly lapping water mingling with the stale wind and the smell hanging in the air reminds of the nights in Somereil. Looking around, it seems like a bridge pocketed with holes and charred planks is the only way across the dark water. By the Lady, I've missed this.

When our target gets halfway across, he stops and turns so quickly Cael and I barely manage to conceal ourselves from his view. His silver eyes gleam as he searches the darkness. They're the same pair that looked at me from outside the window.

"That's the guy who tried to pick my pockets," Cael whispers.

Whoever this man is, he's pushing his luck. He got off once when he tried to steal from us, but he won't get away again. Seemingly satisfied that no one is following him, our target continues on his path, moving more swiftly. Cael nods and we resume our pursuit.

After crossing two more bridges, we enter a part of the city more eerie than even Dryden. The atmosphere feels dangerous, as if the wind is whispering to run. The man moves off the street toward a crooked, deteriorating building. The paneling is falling off and the chips of paint left on the walls are curling away from the surface. Most of the windows are boarded up, and the front steps are littered with holes. It's in such terrible condition, I can't imagine it ever being new.

As I scan the rest of the street, every building is in similar, if not worse, shape. Two buildings down the road have obviously succumbed to a fire, left charred with collapsed roofs. Though there are signs of life pocketing this ruin, there's a lingering sense of fear floating in the air. I jolt as someone screams in the distance. The sound is cut off in an all-too-familiar manner. Cael and I exchange a serious glance as we approach the building our target entered.

"What's the plan?" Cael asks as a group of black-clad people hurry silently down the street beside us.

"We'll scale the wall to the top floor and slip in the window," I say, nodding toward the broken pane on the third floor that has yet to be covered.

Cael glances at me as a grin pulls at his lips.

"Don't look at me like that. I've never let it stop me."

"You were the most feared mercenary in Tominay, and now

you're the Crown Prince of Illena, a country more powerful than any other, yet heights continue to be your worst enemy. How incredibly human," my brother says sarcastically. He winks at me before he moves toward the building.

I mutter a retort Cael chooses not to hear as I follow him.

Standing in the narrow alleyway, Cael waves for me to go first. I scowl at him and set to scaling the crumbling structure. He's close on my tail, and I have to fight the urge to kick him as he watches me clutch the wall and snickers. Careful not to cut myself on the shards of glass still attached to the frame, I slip through the third-floor opening. Cael follows, his feet hitting the floor without a sound.

We stand together motionlessly, listening. Not a sound floats through the dusty air. As my eyes adjust, I take in the room. There's nothing more than an old chest half covered by a sheet in the corner and a wooden door directly before us. I bend down and swipe my finger along the floor, tracing a line through the thick layer of dust. I meet Cael's gaze. *No one's here?* My brother shrugs as a seriousness sets into his eyes.

We slowly walk across the dark room and stand by the door. No light filters through the cracks, nor does a sound reach our ears. The silence is off-putting. I open the door and the hinges scream.

A blinding light sparks to life as a giant figure runs straight into me, sending me sprawling backward. Faster than I can see, my attacker takes two blades in hand. My eyes bleed red as I twist out of the way and catch him by the arm. I spin and kick at his chest, throwing him off long enough that I can stand back on my feet.

Another attacker floods into the room, heading straight for Cael. My eyes meet my brother's as resolve solidifies on his face. I crack my neck and hold up my fists. The man charges once more and lands a blow to my brow before I can turn away.

I spin on my toes, catch the back of his knee with my foot, and pull him down. Still standing, I shift and take on the broad man with flaming red hair who had been assailing my brother. I grab the wide man's shoulder and yank him around to knock him in the jaw as Cael wrestles the other man onto his stomach. Cael manages to hold the man's arms tight behind his back, incapacitating his attacker.

The man I hit stumbles back a step as his red-flushed eyes gleam. I land two blows to his stomach before knocking him onto his knees and placing a dagger flush against his throat. He swallows as I turn to look at Cael, but my brother isn't looking at me. He's turned toward the illuminated doorway where two smug-faced women lean against the wall.

"Well, isn't this a wonderful surprise," one of them says. "Welcome to the Riv, Your Highness."

ELEVEN

CAEL

Leo and I stare at the women, unsure of what to do next. I dig my knee further into the man held captive beneath me as he tries to roll away. The taller of the two women—a lady with cool brown skin and a shaved head tattooed with a symmetrical bird whose wings reach out just shy of her eyes—leans against the door with crossed arms. A second large flower tattoo peeks up over the collar of her high-necked shirt. The fine lines of the artwork are stark against the cold disdain radiating from her.

The woman beside her could not be more her opposite, radiating a buzzing energy as she smiles widely. She's shorter and thicker than her counterpart, and her face is oddly like that of the man I hold under me. Her pin-straight, ebony hair hangs slightly disheveled over her shoulders, and there are ink stains on her hands. She scrunches her nose as she looks at us, pushing her thin-framed glasses up her nose.

"I'm never letting either of you forget this moment," the wild girl sings as she bounces on her toes.

The man Leo holds rolls his eyes, clearly unaffected by the blade begging to slice into his throat. "They caught us off guard, Emmani. You and Deca would be in the same position had you pushed through the door first."

Emmani laughs before crouching to look the man I hold to the floor in the eyes. Leo pushes the dagger closer to his captive's neck as she moves, gaining a sharp-eyed glare from the other woman, Deca. I can practically feel Leo itching to run, but the confusion on his face keeps him rooted in place. It's the same feeling that keeps me still.

"How you doing under there, Soren?" Emmani says with a crooked smile, full of childish joy.

Soren grumbles under his breath as he presses his forehead to the floorboards. Deca shakes her head as she pulls Emmani back up to her feet. The movement reveals various weapons hidden beneath Deca's clothing, including a deadly ax hanging on her hip. She smirks as if she knows exactly what the move-ment revealed.

"We would appreciate it if you let them go. We have no desire to hurt you," Deca states matter-of-factly.

"We swear it on the Lady and the Gods," Emmani adds, touching the braided leather circlet around her brow. It's iden-tical to the one Soren wears.

I lock eyes with my brother, and a silent conversation passes between us. After a moment, we step away, moving closer to the window. The man Leo had been holding sighs as he leans forward and presses his palm to his neck.

"Aw, you get scared Kiro?" Emmani coos.

Flames light in his eyes as he straightens and drops his hands to his side. Kiro plasters on a smug smile as he turns to face her. "I had him right where I wanted him."

Leo's eyes roll as he stares Kiro down, clearly imagining burying his fist in his face once again. Kiro sees it and stands with a challenge clear in his posture. I push myself in front of Leo to pull the group's attention away from my brother.

"Why were you watching us?" I ask Soren. I know the dangerous look Leo wears without having to glance behind me.

"Because I ordered him to." The voice that sounds from the hall is like a frozen wind scraping against the earth.

Leo and I brace for an attack, setting ourselves into defensive stances without a moment's thought. The group clears the way as a woman who challenges my height and is built thickly with muscle walks through the doorway. Her jet-black hair is braided tightly to her head, allowing a perfect view of the large red birthmark spanning the length of the right side of her face. A gruesome scar follows the edge between the mark and her raw sienna skin, as if someone had traced the outline with a knife.

"You are not supposed to be here," she says, her words low and even.

"We go where we please," Leo challenges. He says it not because of his bloodright, but because of who he's made himself.

The woman's eyes thin. "You won't survive long in Illena believing such notions."

"Lady Death and I have an agreement," Leo says evenly.

The tall woman nods slowly as she crosses her arms. "So it would seem."

For a moment, no one speaks. The silence grates on my ears, allowing the tension to thicken through the room. Soren seems to blend into the wall as Kiro's eyes dance between us.

"Do you know who we are, Your Highness?" she asks, her voice revealing nothing as her head tilts.

Leo and I stay deathly still as a cruel smirk appears on Deca's face.

"We are the ones the Bloodlines hunt. We wreak havoc on your cities to sever your grip on our people," the woman says.

Leo only smiles, leaning back on the wall. "We got that sense when Soren over there tried to pick my brother's pockets. It makes no difference to us if you're the Lady reincarnate—we don't take kindly to people who put their noses in our business."

I jump as a loud cackle fills the room. Kiro is bent over, heaving for breath as he laughs hardily. Leo and I exchange a confused look as Kiro finally straightens and wipes the tears from his eyes.

"They caught you?" Kiro says pointedly to Soren.

He doesn't answer as he lifts his head in defense.

"Are you finally losing your touch?" Kiro pushes with a wink.

Soren flips him off with a bland expression.

"Enough, Kiro," the woman in the doorway warns.

Kiro shuts up, the mirth dropping from his face as he stiffens. The tall woman's eyes find ours once again and I can't help but shiver.

"I make it my business to know what happens in this city, for my survival and that of others," she says icily. "Since you are quite new, I'll give you a rare chance. We do not allot more than one, so do not expect any more kindness." Taking our silence as agreement, she continues. "No matter who says your blood rules Illena, they are mistaken. We are Hela's Bond, and this city is ours. The Bloodlines think they can do as they wish, but you will be sorely disappointed when you come face to face with the repercussions for your wrongdoings. Now leave before I decide to renege my generosity."

I nod slowly.

"I don't care about who you are or what you do. I only want to live in peace with my family. You have no need to worry about us, and I would hope we will have no need to watch out for you. Now just to be clear, I will only tell you once to stay out of our way," Leo counters.

The room goes cold as the group stares us down, my brother's threat hanging in the air.

"And next time, if you're truly feeling curious about our escapades, just ask. It will be much more efficient for you." Leo signals to me, steps back, and slips out of the window.

As Leo drops, Kiro launches at me. I backpedal and kick him in the chest before moving toward the opening to follow my brother. I salute Kiro as he stands, and I drop from their view. By the time Kiro's head is out the window, Leo and I are out of sight, hidden deep in the shadows of the night.

CHAPTER

TWELVE

Today marks two weeks since Byrne left. I've somehow prevailed in avoiding Cassien, and since word of what I did to Emila spread like wildfire, I haven't had to deal with the rest of Wate's hateful population either. I've thanked the Lady time and time again for that.

Cass is healing incredibly well, considering the situation. He has yet to speak to me, but his spirits seem higher. I'll catch him smiling when we play a game or when I tell him stories of my childhood. He seems to enjoy hearing about the memories that keep me from sinking too far. I think he imagines himself in some of them, living with parents as mine had been so long ago. As his had most likely been as well.

A few days ago, it hit me how young he was when his parents died. I wonder if he even remembers them: the sound of their voices or the expressions on their faces. Those are the things I cling to the most, and the memories that are the easiest to forget.

It's pitch black as I hobble through the streets, making my way toward the Vallan. The pain is slightly more tolerable than it has been, but every step still sends a flash of discomfort through my muscles. I drag my feet through the woods until I have to stop and lean against a tree to catch my breath. *Almost there. Just a few more steps.*

I sigh in relief when I finally get to the shore. Bending down carefully, I run my hands through the shallows. It's warm today. I slowly build up the strength to stand back up and head toward the boat hidden in the brush. Getting myself across will be more than a challenge. I stare at the far-off shore, wondering if Leo and Byrne will be there waiting for me. I don't know what I'll do if they aren't. I don't know if I'll have the strength to come back.

As I watch, a shape moves away from the trees. A hand moves up and waves, signaling his presence. A smile pulls at my lips in time with a string in my chest. All of a sudden, the Vallan doesn't seem so wide. I shift my eyes and pull the narrow rowboat onto the water.

Even with the current on my side, my body screams with every pull of my arms. I'm dreading the moment I'll have to battle it to return home. That word rings strangely in my head as I row. *Home.* Wate isn't my home. It may have been once, but I haven't felt that way in years. After what seems like hours, Leo's shape comes sharply into view. He rolls up the legs of his pants and throws off his boots before wading out to meet me. As he approaches, my arms go slack.

"How strange to meet you here," Leo says with a smirk.

A wide smile lines my cheeks as I chuckle softly. "I could say the same of you, Your Highness."

Leo's face scrunches into a look of disgust. "I'm begging you, do not call me *Your Highness.* I need someone to treat me like a normal human being."

As he grabs onto the side of the boat, his eyes meet mine, and for a moment, his smile falters. His gaze lingers too long on the tell-tale signs of my injuries. Leo frowns but refrains from saying anything, thank the Lady. I don't think I could handle him mentioning Cassien right now. Seeing him melts the wall inside me. All I want to do is break down and cry as every bit of courage I've built up over the past few weeks disappears. He opens his mouth to speak, but I cut him off.

"I think your begging skills need some work," I tell him as the boat hits the shore.

He smirks, though his eyes aren't half as bright. "I'll work on it."

Leo extends his hand and I take it gratefully, shifting my eyes back to silver with a wince. A frown creases his face as he helps me out of the boat. I scowl at how soft he is.

"Where's Byrne?" I ask as we walk into the woods.

We find a clear spot to sit down. Leo stays stuck to my side as if he thinks I might crumble right here. I hate it. He stares at my splinted hand, and I hear his breathing go shallow. He looks up and smiles apologetically.

"She's trying to guilt you into coming back with me," Leo says, turning his deep silver eyes toward me. "Do you think it will work?"

There's hope in Leo's expression, brightening his face. I have to look away as I shake my head, knowing full well I can't leave with Cass alone in Wate. But for now, there's no way I can tell Leo he's alive. If I did, he would run into Wate blindly, doing exactly as Cassien expects him to do. When they accept Leo and Cael aren't coming back for Cass, they'll loosen their security, giving me a chance to get him out. I just need to bide my time.

"I can't yet," I answer.

Leo doesn't push it. He only nods defeatedly as he picks at

a loose thread in his pants. They're finer than any I've ever seen. My mind blanks for a moment as I take him in. The pristine outfit and the way he's filled out. He looks healthier, brighter. I must look like a monster painted in black and blue.

"He hurt you, Elana."

I shift, startled by the words. Leo is staring at me, his eyes like shards of ice. I don't know what to do but watch him silently. It's answer enough for him.

"How bad did he hurt you?" he whispers.

I swallow as tears gather. I hadn't realized how badly I was hurt, not only physically. I look away. I can't let him see me like this. This isn't me. I close my eyes as his fingers sweep under my chin, guiding my face back to his. He runs his thumb along the gash on my cheek as I force myself to breathe. My every sense narrowing in onto that small bit of contact. When I open my eyes, he's searching my face.

"Let me help you. Let me take you to Arkezo. You don't have to be strong, Elana. Nobody expects anything from you. You've done more than enough," he pleads.

I hear the desperation in his voice, begging me to see him. I shake my head as a tear rolls down my cheek. All I want to do is go with him. To see my sister and be rid of Wate. All I want to do is leave.

"I can't," I tell him.

He looks at me as though he can see my thoughts, all the things forcing me to stay. Slowly, he wipes away my tears.

"Then at least let me help you with the wounds," he says softly.

After a moment, I nod. It takes everything in me extend my hand, but I do it. He unwraps the bandage, careful not to jar me in any way. My hand is a mess, my fingers swollen and bruised. Leo winces as he turns to the bag he brought with him and pulls out some medical supplies.

"Byrne told me to bring it," he says at my questioning look.

I should have known she would assume Cassien would hurt me. She was right to. I turn the other way as Leo fixes the splint and sets to wrapping each finger.

"Your fingers don't seem to be too bad. You'll probably get decent range of motion back," he remarks as he secures each one with care. I want to vanish. I'm shaking by the end, but he manages to get the splint set straight again. He takes out the old, crooked stitches and rebandages the cuts on my face that are rimmed with red. When he's done, he digs in his bag and pulls out a small metal flask.

"It'll help with the pain," he says, a forced smile pulling at his face.

I open it cautiously and gag at the smell.

"I am not drinking that," I tell him, confident the odor is strong enough to mask my pain.

He grins as he crosses his arms. "It's Cael's special recipe."

I roll my eyes as I stare at the concoction, wanting to do nothing less than drink whatever vile substances are mixed inside.

"Don't think about it, just swallow," he says, watching me as if he knows exactly what'll happen next.

I breath out heavily as I hold it up. "I can't believe I'm doing this."

I toss back the drink and am hit with immediate regret. I plaster my hand over my mouth to keep from spitting it up. I finally swallow, but not without gagging as I toss the bottle at him in revenge.

"That was the worst thing I've ever tasted," I wheeze.

Leo laughs hysterically as tears build in his eyes. I scowl as he cackles, glaring at him as my mouth burns.

"I'm sorry. I'm sorry," he manages through laughing spurts as he wipes away the tears. He digs into his bag and pulls out another, wider bottle. I eye it skeptically as he hands it to me. "It's water, I swear."

After careful inspection, I gulp down the liquid, thanking Lady Death for the reprieve.

"Better?" he asks as I hand back the bottle.

I nod and lean back so that our shoulders are touching. "Much."

Though the taste was atrocious, the pain darting through my body is subsiding to a dull ache. We sit together in silence, simply content with being where we are. My head slides onto Leo's shoulder as my eyes shut. He freezes as I lean into him. I laugh inside at the panic on his face, but I can't bring myself to care about keeping my distance. Especially when he's so warm.

"I beat up Emila," I mumble. Leo shifts, allowing me to curl into him.

"That's my girl," he says, pride woven though his voice.

I feel his hand wrap around my back and slowly land on my side. I wince when his fingers graze the brand. We stay frozen for a moment, stuck in time.

"What did he do?" he asks gently, as if he could tell his fingers had touched an injury unlike the rest.

I don't know what to say, so I say nothing. I squeeze my eyes shut, scared to think about the mark burned into my skin. Leo moves his hand so it rests below the wound and pulls me closer to his chest. Any strength I had left leaves my bones as I melt into him. We sit like that for a long time, listening to each other breathe and finding solace in knowing nothing can reach us here.

"He branded me," I whisper as I stare at his arm.

Leo tenses but says nothing, holding me tighter. It's a strange feeling, being so near someone and not feeling like I need to escape. The way we're sitting allows me all the control. I could move away in a second if I wanted to. He makes sure I don't feel trapped in his arms, and I can't do anything but be grateful. I don't remember the last time I was held.

"With the tripoint," I finish. I hadn't said it out loud until now.

Leo rests his chin on the top of my head as his hand moves in small, soothing circles across my arm. Tears well in my eyes.

"You don't deserve that," he says tenderly.

I hadn't realized I was shaking until now.

"You never deserved that."

I can only nod.

"Lady Death won't refuse you, no matter what's written on your skin."

I look up and meet his warm eyes. The corner of his lips pulls up as his gaze travels my face.

"And if she does?" I ask.

Leo laughs under his breath and his smile makes my lungs squeeze. I've never seen him smile like this. It softens his expression, almost making him look younger. It's peaceful, the look of someone who hasn't suffered or known pain.

"Then you can spend the afterlife with Cael and me. You do have the patience of a Goddess, right?"

I laugh softly, sniffling as I lay my head back on his chest. "I think I can find a way to tolerate your presence."

His heart races as he leans back against the tree. "I'll take it."

CHAPTER

THIRTEEN

LEO

"The court is definitely something," Ares says with a grin as Cael and I walk beside him along the street. A pack of guards walk behind us, and it sets Cael and me ill at ease. "The Bloodlines are chaos wrapped in skins of monsters who hold the power of a country in their hands. We put on false smiles in front of the people we've known since we were kids, then stab them in the back the first minute they avert their eyes."

I exhale heavily as I rub the back of my neck. Ares has been reviewing the ins and outs of Illenian court for an hour now and it isn't becoming any less daunting. Though Ceto had gone through most of the formalities before, Ares has taken the time to explain some of the unspoken social guidelines he's learned from personal experience.

The Bloodlines control the economy, deciding the rules on production and distribution within their own sectors and ruling over the cities that provide their goods and services. The only people able to overrule them are the queen and king as the ultimate decision-makers in the country.

"And all the Bloodlines are the same?" Cael asks, eyeing Ares closely as if he's trying to dig up some type of truth hidden beneath Ares's honest face. "They care only for their own blood?"

Ares laughs darkly as we head into the Riv. "As far as the people are aware, yes. But what is never said and often not understood is that a Bloodline does not care for their own because they are family. They are only motivated by the power their blood can give them. They will turn against anyone, no matter who they are, to gain strength. We are taught to be wary of everyone, even your own Bloodline."

Cael and I exchange a strained glance. Being willing to betray someone you love simply to rise up in society is a concept neither of us will ever understand and it complicates our situation tenfold. Cael stops and turns toward the Riv, squinting.

"What is it?" I ask Cael as Ares turns back toward us, his brows knitting together.

My brother doesn't have to respond as an ear-piercing shriek rings through the air. Looking ahead into the Riv, flames lick the sky and smoke billows into the air. Without a second thought, Cael and I start toward the burning building, but a hand catches my sleeve before I can step into the street. I glare at the fingers clutching my sleeve as my body goes still.

"Let go," I tell Ares quietly, my voice cold as ice.

Ever so slowly, Ares peels his hand away and lets it rest at his side. The intensity of the screams increases.

"You can't go that way," he says sternly. There's uncertainty in his voice as his gaze flies between Cael and me.

"They need help," Cael says decisively, standing tall by my side as he buzzes with adrenaline.

"We can't put our lives in danger for them," Ares says as he waves his hand vigorously through the air. I shake my head as I back up. "Wrong answer."

Cael and I turn in unison and sprint toward the fire. I hear the boots pounding behind us as the guards follow in pursuit.

As we approach, people drag themselves away from the scene, covered in soot and coughing incessantly. We stop and stare at the flames as a feeling of helplessness creeps into my bones. I scan the crowd, at a loss for what to do. Two men pull a panicked woman away from the building as she screams and claws at their arms, begging to let her go back.

"Someone's still in there," Cael says as his face pales.

We push past bystanders entranced by the blaze. Some step aside, even more shocked as they realize who I am.

"Please! Please I have to go back, they're still in there! I can't leave them," the woman cries as tears flow down her face.

Cael steps beside her to grab her attention. "Who's inside?"

The lady turns her feral eyes on us as she shakes wildly. "My sons and husband. Please, you have to help them! They were sleeping in their room when my husband went to get them."

I look at Cael and see the resolve in his eyes. I nod, already knowing the thoughts that spin like a whirlwind in his mind.

"Are they on the first floor?" I press.

She nods as a sob escapes her throat, understanding what we're about to do before we turn away. Using a bucket of water, Cael and I drench our shirts and head toward the door. I pull the fabric over my nose and nod to Cael as he mirrors my actions.

Ares screams from somewhere in the crowd as I ram my shoulder into the door, busting it open with ease. Cael and I drop to the floor as thick smoke covers the ceiling. My eyes burn as I bleed them red. Heat singes my skin as Cael stays close to my side. I shudder as a scream rips through the air. A child's scream.

I stop when I see Cass stare at me through the flames, his eyes wide as a spot of blood grows on his shirt. *He's not here,* I tell myself. *Snap out of it.*

I shake myself as blood roars in my ears. The roof above us cracks as beams start to come crashing down in an explosion of embers. A deep scream sounds from farther down the hall.

"We need to move," Cael yells as he grasps my sleeve and pulls me forward.

I follow and call out into the space, hoping desperately that the person trapped inside will reply. After a moment, a voice calls back from one of the rooms. I stand to touch the handle and recoil from the scorching heat. When another high-pitched scream sounds from behind it, I stand and throw my shoulder into the wood. It doesn't budge.

"It's blocked," Cael says frantically as he helps me push.

Together, we throw ourselves into the door once, twice, three times. On the fourth, the top half of the door finally gives way, allowing us to break through. A large, heavy beam is jammed against the bottom of the door. My eyes water as I climb through the hole and look around the room.

A young, soot-covered boy cradles a baby in his arms, huddled in the corner. I move toward them, but his small eyes don't shift. They stay fixed on the fallen beam. Glancing over, I realize he's not looking at the beam, but at the man pinned beneath it. I sprint to the kids as Cael moves toward the unconscious man. The kids shake, and the infant wails weakly. I reach for them, but the boy shrinks away.

"It's all right. I'm going to help," I murmur as I extend my hands.

He doesn't fight when I pull him toward me. His skin is boiling with the heat. I block the memories flooding through my mind as I take him and the infant into my arms.

"We need to lift it off," I tell Cael as I step toward him.

The beam is crushing the man's leg, blood staining the floor around him. Cael bends down and places his hand against the man's neck before nodding.

"He's alive."

The entire house shifts as a cracking sound rings through the air. The boy screams as I meet Cael's eyes.

"Help me," Cael coughs out, wincing from the heat.

I place the kids down beside me and tell them not to move before bending down and wedging myself under the beam alongside my brother. The embers burn numbly through my skin as I grit my teeth.

"I'm going to lose it!" I yell as my lungs seize.

"Just a little more," Cael heaves.

I take a smoke-filled breath and give one last push. The timber shifts just enough to allow Cael to move the man's leg out of the way. I drop the beam and fall to the floor.

"We need to get out now!" I pant as Cael nods.

He pulls the boys beneath him as the smoke creeps closer to our heads. He clutches them against his chest so he can crawl with both kids while I take hold of the man and drag him through the hall. I cough so hard I wonder how much oxygen is left in this house. Cael moves slowly beside me, his skin stained with ash and drenched in sweat. He flinches with every movement as sparks float around us like fireflies in the night. Finally, I see the light peeking through the front door and push Cael to go first. My brother scrapes his way outside as I stand and throw the man over my shoulders.

As we breach the door, the guards run to our sides and pull us from the home. Seconds later, it's gone. I don't look back as a wave of searing heat bites at my skin. The sound of the walls giving in and splintering into rubble overwhelms my senses as I push myself farther away.

As soon as we reach a clearing, the mother sprints over. She pulls the boys into her arms as she weeps, falling to her knees. The boy and the infant clutch her shirt as they cry. She scans her children from head to toe as two medics approach. One takes care of the father as the other moves toward the children, now huddled in the safety of their mother's arms.

Cael and I collapse to the ground and lie beside each other, panting and coughing as the world moves around us. As the adrenaline subsides, a laugh bubbles past my lips. The sound is jarring against the chaos of the moment. But no matter how hard I try, I can't stop it, and within minutes, Cael is cackling along with me.

"Why did we do that?" he asks with a raspy voice.

"I don't know," I tell him as I wipe the tears from my face.

We lie silently, staring at the sky.

"We did the right thing though," I say quietly. I turn my head to look at the family. All three of them would have died if we hadn't gone in. The woman would have been left alone.

"Yeah, we did," Cael says.

Someone moves to stand above me, and I squint to make out his features against the light shining around him like a halo. As my eyes adjust, I realize it's Ares, or a very angry version of the cousin I met only days ago. Cael and I slowly sit up. I can't help but catch sight of the group of people ogling us. Even the guards are staring, hands slack by their sides and eyes wide.

"I don't think I've ever seen anything more foolish than

what the pair of you just did," Ares seethes, his back pin straight.

I glance at Cael and shrug. "It would have been foolish not to help."

Ares bristles, his chest rising and falling with deep, measured breaths. "What you don't understand," he scolds quietly, "is that you are important. Your blood is connected to the very soul of Illena. You *cannot* be so thoughtless with your life, because every drop that spills from your veins has consequences. Your life is not equal to any of theirs, because when you bleed, Illena bleeds. If they die, another will take their place. If you die, a part of Illena will fade with you."

"What's the point of staying safe when the people I am tied to are dead?" I slowly pull myself to my feet, then offer my hand to Cael. When we're both standing, I stare Ares down and allow him to see the emotion of every word on my face. "There is no Illena without its people, Ares. I have not been here long, but that is something I know. A country is made by its people, not the other way around."

Cael and I walk over to the family. The father is awake and has been tended to, holding his sons tightly with his bandaged hands. When Cael asks if they're all right, the woman breaks into heaving sobs. She moves to bow awkwardly from where she sits, but I stop her. She looks confused but smiles through her tears as she thanks us repeatedly for saving her family. We offer to help move her husband to where he might be more comfortable, but with a nervous glance at the guards behind us, she declines the offer.

When Cael and I finally pull away, we walk back toward the guards. Every pair of eyes that has gathered stares us down. Each person murmurs as we pass, speaking hushed words of kings and Bloodlines.

Cael stops suddenly as we break through the group of

people and turns to look behind him. I follow his eyes and find the woman with the red mark on her face staring at us from the crowd. She meets my gaze and nods in approval, an expression of gratitude clear on her face. I open my mouth to point her out to Cael, but before I can blink, she's gone.

CHAPTER

FOURTEEN

"By the Lady, how does this thing get heavier every time I pull it out?" I grumble as the wind whips at my hair.

This rowboat will be the death of me. Never mind that I still haven't healed from my various... encounters, I have to pull a boat out of the damned woods and row it across the Vallan every three days.

The first time Leo came to meet me in the woods, we decided we would visit twice a week. Or rather, he decided. I simply didn't object. When I see him, I feel as if I can breathe. As if I've been drowning and for a moment, my mind numbs enough to forget about the missing air. I've come to enjoy his company and the feeling of waking up with his arms loosely draped over me. It's the only time I'm able to sleep soundly.

After several minutes of pulling and digging at the rocky ground, the boat finally comes loose. I sigh in relief as I push it into the water and jump in. The current pulls the boat downstream toward Arkezo. The stars are out tonight, shining bright like pin pricks in the blanket of night.

When I approach the shore, Leo's already waiting with his hands folded across his chest. A smile lights up his face, and I'm taken by it, forgetting about the pain wreaking havoc on my mind and body. He wades out and helps me pull in the boat. I take his hand gratefully when he offers it, keeping me steady on my still-weak legs.

"I have a surprise for you," he whispers as his smile softens.

I narrow my eyes at him, trying to decipher whether he's toying with me. He bites his lips as he fidgets.

"You can't tell me you've got me something only to stay silent. I hardly think that's fair," I tell him. "Don't tell me, you're the surprise," I deadpan.

"I think I'm quite a nice surprise," he quips with a wink.

I roll my eyes as I step away from him. "Honestly, your ego is..."

I can't breathe as Leo steps up beside me and softly places his hand on my back. He leans in close to my ear. "Though my presence is very much a gift, I figured you would probably appreciate this more."

Tears spring to my eyes as Byrne's gaze locks with mine. I haven't seen her in weeks, but it feels like so much longer. She looks... incredible. There are smile lines etched into her face, deeper than I've ever seen. *She looks happy.*

In the time it takes me to step forward, she's crushing me in a hug. I squeeze her right back as I sob. I hadn't realized how much I've missed her.

"I'm sorry I didn't come sooner," she cries, shaking as I hold her.

I sniffle and pull away to hold her face, forcing her to meet my eyes. "It's all right. You're here now." I wipe a tear that falls down her cheek.

"I missed you," she says with a smile.

I laugh lightly. "I know."

I look over her shoulder to see Leo grinning. His eyes lock with mine. I don't think I've ever been happier than this.

"... and I can't even begin to explain how amazing the food is," Byrne gushes from across a small fire.

I laugh as I lean back against a tree, my mind at ease as my sister—healthy and glowing—sits before me, telling me every detail of her time in Arkezo. She hasn't been able to wipe the grin from her face.

"I'll never argue with that," Leo says as he slowly turns over my hand.

I wince and he stills, his gaze flying to mine. At my nod, he continues to look over the fractures with a calm confidence. He told me he wanted to check my hand to make sure it was healing properly, and I managed to fend him off for an hour before he finally wore me down enough to allow him to take off the splint.

Despite all his nagging, Byrne is the real reason I let him have a look. She was so concerned and demanded to know what happened. When getting the story from me proved impossible, she insisted on seeing the injuries herself. She was fuming, at both Cassien and me. I suppose I felt letting Leo take a look was my compromise.

Byrne continues to speak, but her words get lost as Leo's fingers run over my palm, tracing the fading bruises as if he could see how they'd bloomed.

"... and Leo jumped out of the castle window."

My head snaps up as Leo shifts uncomfortably beside me. Realizing I wasn't listening, Byrne stares between us with interest and crosses her arms. Leo gently releases my wrist and clears his throat.

"Yeah, apparently, we attracted the attention of a crime band from the Riv. One of them climbed up to spy on us, so Cael and I jumped out after him.," he says, running a hand through his hair.

My eyes narrow. "I thought you were afraid of heights?"

His gaze snaps to mine. "I never said that."

I scoff as I lean my head back. "It's not hard to figure out if you know what you're looking for."

His brows shoot up as a sly half-grin pulls at his lip. He picks up the splint sitting beside him and sets my hand again. "So you admit you've been watching me?"

I hold his heated gaze as my cheeks flush. Byrne coughs awkwardly, breaking the trance like a splash of cold water over my senses.

"Fire's getting low," she says, nodding toward the flames.

I look at my sister and frown, knowing Leo fed it a few minutes ago. Leo finishes wrapping the splint around my hand and moves to lean into me but freezes when he catches Byrne glaring at him. He finally gets the hint and stands.

"I'll get some more wood," he says before heading toward the river. I stare after him as the darkness of the woods swallows him up.

"I don't think I've ever seen you enamored before."

My head snaps toward my sister. "What?"

She smirks. "You're smiling, Elana."

My hand flies to my face, and lo and behold, the corner of my lips is lifted.

She turns her head to look at the woods where Leo disappeared. "He looks at you in a way that most people are never seen, you know."

"What do you mean?"

She locks her gaze with mine. "He looks at you in a way that says he'd burn the world to keep you happy."

I don't know what to say. She must be wrong, because there's no way anyone, never mind Leo, would feel that for me. It's not possible.

"You look at him the same way, Elana," Byrne whispers. There's a sadness on her face, something raw in her expression that wounds me deeply.

"I found more wood," Leo announces as he appears out of the brush.

Byrne straightens and wipes away the deep emotion that had painted her face a minute before. "Thank you."

She watches him settle back at my side after placing a few logs into the flames. As Leo sits, I notice water drip from the front of his hair as if he'd dunked his head in the river. My brows furrow as I look at Byrne. She's watching me with a smirk.

"How are things with Landris going?" I ask her.

Her eyes narrow as she crosses her arms. "You mean Emrys?"

"Right, yes. How has Emrys been?"

Even though she tries to act as if my asking doesn't affect her, she can't help the blush staining her cheeks. "He's good."

"You see him a lot?"

Her face goes entirely pink. "When he's around," she says with a false calm.

Payback, I think. Her eyes narrow as if she can see the thought float through my mind. I take a breath and lean against the tree at my back.

"He treats you well?" I ask seriously.

She catches my tone and softens, smiling lightly as she nods.

"Good. I should hope so, after everything."

She laughs softly, and I catch Leo smiling at me. I'm glad Byrne is doing well. I've given everything for her to live a life where she can find peace and maybe even love. As I look at Leo, I can't help but be a little jealous of the freedom she has. Of the choices she can make. I blink the thought away and tear my eyes from Leo's. Strangely, pulling away first doesn't feel as terrible as it once did.

FIFTEEN

LEO

Byrne and I walk through the tunnel that runs under the palace grounds back from seeing Elana. Since we discovered it, I've been using it to get off and onto the grounds. It's much easier than climbing over gates and taking the chance of being seen. We have yet to run into anyone else using the tunnel, but I keep a blade in my palm just in case. This place has a way of putting me on edge.

"Elana has been through a lot," Byrne says. "More than you know."

I glance back at her, though I can barely make out her face in the darkness. "As have I."

She doesn't say anything as she follows a step behind me. I know what she's thinking before she says it. "Just don't hurt her. She's always been there for me and there aren't many things that I can do for her, but I can save her from this. If you don't feel anything real for her, you need to back away."

I stumble as my mind spins a million miles an hour.

"I don't know what you mean." I say softly, almost in a whisper.

"I can see it, Leo. Whether you realize it or not, I can see your feelings. You wear them on your sleeve when you're around her. So just promise me you won't hurt her."

I stay silent as my heart beats out of my chest. The lump in my throat grows larger with every step I take, stealing the air from my lungs. Finally, when we get to the hatch under the gardening shed, I turn to look at Byrne in the light. I don't know how to respond, so I speak the first words that come to my mind.

"Even if I wanted to, I don't think I could ever hurt Elana. I couldn't live with myself if I were the cause of her pain," I say, and in this moment, I'm hit by how deeply I believe it.

WHEN I PULL myself through the window, I'm completely exhausted. Physically, I don't need to sleep for another day, but mentally, I need to shut down and process everything that's happened. The terrors seem to be an entirely new type of nightmare here, making it almost impossible for Cael to keep me tied up. Even when I wake, I can't shake the images that play through my head for hours at night. I step into the sitting room as Cael sleeps on one of the couches with a frown etched into his face. Antares is curled up against him with a blanket wrapped tightly around his shoulders. He must have had a nightmare. As Byrne heads into her room, I quietly open our bedroom door to find Altair and Saiph sound asleep on the bed. When I close the door and turn back to the main room, Cael is awake and watching me. I head over and sit across from him.

"How was she?" he asks.

I smile as I lean back against the chair. "Better. It was good for them to see each other."

Cael's face stays neutral as I tell him about Elana. He barely reacts at all, and a pit of worry digs into my gut.

"Did something happen?" I ask him.

He is quiet as he chooses his words and slowly spins his ring around his finger. "Earlier today, I heard a noise and thought someone was outside the window. When I went to look, I found that letter wedged between the panes." He nods toward a small red envelope on top of a pile of books between us.

Dread tightens my throat as I stare at the paper. Taking a breath, I pick it up and read it with a nervous glance.

It seems Illena's lost prince isn't what we thought him to be.
Come tomorrow night.
And by the Lady, use the front door this time.

I hand it to Cael as my brows furrow. "You think it's Hela's Bond?"

He nods absentmindedly. "Who else could assume we know where to meet them?"

"Do you think we should go?" I wonder aloud, asking myself the same question.

Cael's jaw feathers as he thinks. "Do we have a choice?"

"We always have a choice."

Cael dips his chin. "If they wanted to kill us, they would have attacked us here. Why call us to them? We could just as easily report them."

"Agreed. From the sounds of it, they want to talk. Although I couldn't tell you what about, it doesn't seem malicious."

Cael nods, his thoughts visibly straightening. "Then it's decided. We meet Hela's Bond tomorrow."

We stand across the street, watching the door of the building Cael and I scaled not so long ago. We've been here for some time, still unsure if we should trust Hela's Bond and their vague letter. I lift the envelope out of my pocket and scan the script, rereading the simple phrasing for the thousandth time.

"If we're going to do this, we should just go. Hesitating will do us no good," Cael says without a lick of confidence.

I glance his way with raised brows as my stomach knots. Byrne is with Saiph and the boys back at Ridge Palace. For some reason, leaving them felt too familiar, like in Somereil when that damned red cloth was tied to the tree. It makes me want to turn back and run.

I scan the quiet street one last time, take a deep breath, and roll out my shoulders. "All right. Let's go."

In seconds, we're on the stoop and staring at the door. We each hold a dagger ready for whoever might answer our knock.

I rap my knuckles near silently against the door. Movement sounds from inside, some shuffling and muffled speech. It seems like a lifetime before the door cracks open to reveal two dark silver eyes. Soren, the pickpocket, nods once before stepping away and gesturing for us to enter. The small room is dark when we walk in, sparsely lit by only a few candles.

I count five people in all. Emmani is to the right of Soren, sitting on an exposed ceiling beam at the back of the room as her feet dangle in the air. Opposite Emmani, the tattooed woman, Deca, stands stoically beside an eager-eyed Kiro. I can feel the violence emanating from his bones, ready to jump the minute we step out of line. Directly in front of us is the woman with the red birthmark. She watches us with a predator's eyes as I swing the door shut.

"Should we be surprised you showed up or do you simply

have no regard for your survival?" she asks evenly, crossing her arms.

I glance at Cael as his shoulders ease. She meant for that sentence to be an offering of peace, a white flag to bring peaceful conversation. We won't deny the opportunity.

"Either is possible," Cael responds, waving our own flag in return.

Her expression remains blank as her gaze roves over us. "We invited you here to thank you."

My brows shoot up in surprise. That was not what I was expecting.

"I'm not sure why we would need such a gesture," I say as I glance at Cael.

Emmani's eyes bulge as she sways on the rafter, as if she were trying to keep herself from saying something she might regret. "You saved our people. The man and children you dragged from the fire. They were not meant to survive. The fire was a punishment for showing up late to their employment in Sai house."

The words hang heavily as I try to absorb their meaning. One of the Bloodlines—those who hold power of the county and its people—planned to burn that family alive out of spite. If Emmani's story can be believed, that is.

I nod slowly, not knowing what else to say.

The woman with the birthmark says, "I showed up to try to pull them out, but when I saw the flames, I knew there was nothing that could be done. Fires devour the Riv on a regular basis. People don't get out of blazes like that. I had prepared myself to comfort the woman who had lost every-thing, but instead I found the two of you laughing hysteri-cally on the ground, covered in soot as the family held each other."

The group watches us with wide eyes, as if this is the first time they've heard this story. Something seems to click in them as they stare.

"I know what loss is, and what it's like to feel helpless as the people you love are ripped away. We weren't going to let them die without trying to save them," I state.

"That's the thing—walking away is exactly what's expected of people, never mind a royal. Yet the two of you decided to go against human nature itself and run into those flames." She nods once, as if saying the words reaffirms the ideas in her head. "So, I will offer you this as Hela's Bond now owes you a debt: should you need anything in the future, Your Highness, we will be there."

Once again, her words manage to stun me.

"Anything?" I ask as my brows lift. There must be a catch. No one makes such an offer without their own motives, especially not a group like this.

"Within reason, of course." Her face remains stoic.

"Why would you offer this to us? This debt is not yours to repay, nor is it something we will accept reparation for. We've done enough wrong in our lives that saving three lives cannot begin to tip the scale. And even at that, you don't seem like the type of people to simply hand out kindnesses," Cael says carefully, revealing a piece of our lives before all of this... before royal blood, gold eyes, and Illena.

The woman with the birthmark is the only one who appears unaffected by Cael's words, as if the group has taken offense to us knowing they exist outside the law. By the Lady, there is no way that Hela's Bond is innocent, existing unblemished by this world.

"You're right. We aren't used to making such arrangements. But this is a special case," she says.

"Because of my blood," I state.

She nods once. Cael's brows furrow as he watches her.

"You do know neither of us holds any power? Leo won't take the crown," my brother says, expressing the exact thoughts that had been flying through my head.

She smirks as if we're ignorant to some obvious truth. "Your blood deems you powerful whether you wear a crown of air or iron. And even if you didn't have power, you have the ability to become powerful, a gift most of us are never granted. You can't blame me for wanting to align myself with someone who has such a choice, can you?"

There it is—the motive. She wants an ally in court. Someone who wouldn't decline an offer of partnership. I'm not against the idea.

"And you want nothing in return?" I ask carefully, trying to find the hidden lines within her pretty speech.

"For now," is all she says.

My gaze is locked on my brother's as uncertainty plays on his face. After a moment, he straightens, as if to say *what do we have to lose?* I look back at the woman and, in a show of good faith, sheathe the blade I've been holding in my palm. In the same moment, each member of Hela's Bond does the same, making a show of laying down the weapons they've been concealing. *At least they have good senses.*

"If we're going to trust you, shouldn't we know your name?" Cael asks.

I'd been wondering the same thing.

"Red," she says plainly. When we don't push with more questions, she nods as the tension that had been bracketing her mouth fades away. "As you are probably aware, this is Kiro." Red points at the largest man of those standing behind her.

He's the flame-haired man I took down during our last visit. When I meet his eager eyes, he smirks, a clear challenge written on his face. It's a look I've seen a million times before in the arenas. Unfazed, I return the glare, daring him to try his hand at me.

"Beside him is Soren," Red continues, gesturing to a man with a tall, lithe figure. His eyes are cold and calculating as he assesses our conversation. "And hanging from the roof is Emmani—"

"I'm Soren's sister. It's very nice to make your acquaintances," Emmani blurts, her voice bubbly as she sways her feet through the air and waves.

"You as well," Cael says.

"And finally, we have Deca," Red says, motioning to the tattooed woman standing closest to Emmani.

If Soren is ice, this woman is death herself. Deca seems as though she could turn us into broken heaps of flesh and walk away with the same flat expression on her face. The mask of a murderer. Deca dips her chin in acknowledgment.

Cael's head swivels toward a doorway at the back of the room as his hand inches toward the blade he concealed in his belt. "Someone else is here."

I tense, preparing myself for an attack. Red raises her hand to call us off as a boy around Altair's age walks into the room, rubbing his eye. He stops moving abruptly when he sees us and looks at Red as his brows knit together. She turns toward him and moves her hands fluidly. The boy tracks the movements with ease, nodding along as he glances our way. My hands are slack at my sides as I watch, entranced by what seems to be a conversation. The boy faces us and meets my eyes.

"It's nice to meet you. My name is Gray." His deep voice catches me off guard, pronouncing the syllables in a way that melts the words together before they scrape out of his throat.

"You too," I reply.

He smiles shyly, reminding me even more of Altair. Or at least, how Altair used to be.

"I'm Leo, and this is my brother, Cael."

Gray turns toward Red as her hands move once more. He smiles and explains when he sees the confusion crossing my face. "I'm deaf. We use signs to communicate, but I can speak and read lips to a certain degree."

That makes sense. Red was translating. There's pride in her eyes as she watches him.

"That's amazing," Cael says, his head tilted slightly.

My gut sinks as I see the happiness in Gray's face. This language would have been good for Cass. It would have changed his entire life. I tear myself away from the thought and turn back to Red. The raw emotion drops off her face as quickly as it appeared.

"If you tell anyone about us, whether it be Kiro or Gray, I will pull the innards from your guts and string them on the Ridge Palace gates," she threatens.

I smile, recognizing the protectiveness. "I swear on the Lady, I won't tell a soul."

CHAPTER

SIXTEEN

ELENA

The air smells like smoke. Something's burning. Something big. Cassien must have set something ablaze. Nothing ever burns in Wate unless he means it to. That's how Cassien knew Leo had burned down the lab, and it's why my gut knots. There hadn't been a fire in years before Leo, yet here I am again with the cloying smell of smoke filling my nose.

I walk slowly through the side streets with my eyes trained ahead and back straight. I know people stare, but I was trained to ignore them. *It makes them see us as Gods,* Cassien used to say. *These people should bow to us. Never show that you notice their presence. They must know that they are below us, as the meek are much easier to control.* I used to find it easy to separate myself from them, but holding the weight of their attention on my shoulders has become a chore. All I can do is tell myself to keep moving forward. Besides, tomorrow I go over the Vallan. Tomorrow, I can rest.

As I make my way closer to forest line, clouds of billowing black float into the sky. At first, I think it's Daeta's market, but the closer I get, the more I'm sure I'm wrong. My heart beats like a drum in my ears as I move faster. *He couldn't have found it. He never knew it was there.*

Through my panic, I catch a glimpse of a black figure right before I'm yanked into the alley between two houses. A scream sticks in my throat as I'm thrown to the ground. My head bounces off the wall as a sharp pain sears through my skull. Footsteps slowly crush the earth as he nears. I hear his clothes ruffle as he crouches before me. My ears ring when my eyes finally decide to focus. The pounding headache fades as the world takes on a gilded sheen. Cassien stares at me with a cold grin. I swallow my dread as I stare into his eyes. They're the mirror image of mine. He watches me for a moment before lifting his hand. I don't mean to flinch, but I do. There's nothing I can do to stop it as my breathing goes shallow.

"You've been avoiding me, Ella." All at once my mind and body revolt against the nickname. My thoughts sputter as it rings in my ears. *Ella.*

A shiver runs down my spine as he runs the back of his knuckles down my cheek. Though the touch is soft, it makes my soul scream, scratching at my mind like a caged animal surrounded by flames. It knows what's coming but can't escape. I try to shake my head, but only manage a quivering exhale. Tears gather in my eyes as his hand snaps away and grabs my jaw.

"I didn't raise you like this," he spits, his lip curling in disgust. "Whimpering like a child. Pull yourself together." He throws my face to the side as he stands. "Get up."

I stay frozen. A disappointed sigh escapes him as he leans down to grasp my neck and pull me up. I sway on my feet as he steps back, never taking his eyes off me.

"What do you want?" I ask as my hands tremble.

He laughs lightly and pulls two blades from his belt. "Let's play."

I freeze. He says it as if it were a simple thing. Maybe it should be, but when he played with us it was never just that. His playing was a beating until I learned how to block. His playing was nothing but training with a different name. It was a test to see how much blood I could lose before passing out. Training was breaking bones and forcing me to get back up, again and again and again.

I never disobeyed him because I was afraid of what he would do. I still am, but everyone he can hurt is far away now, and he won't touch Cass. He's too smart to risk injuring the bait before the right time. What do I have to lose?

"No," I wheeze.

His smirk grows wider as the hunger flames brighter in his eyes. "Pick your weapon, Ella."

"No."

He stares at the blades and shrugs lightly before sheathing the smaller of the two. "Fine. But know I gave you your chance."

I don't have time to blink before he swings, hitting me square in the jaw. I don't know when I hit the ground, but one minute I'm standing, and the next I'm being pummeled by a boot.

"Come on, Ella. Fight me!" he screams, his foot pounding into me over and over. "Fight back!"

I can't. After what could be minutes or hours, he finally steps away, breathing heavily. Beating up your daughter is exhausting. He growls as he grabs my arm, dragging me to stand again. I can't get my feet under me as he pulls me out into the street. My mind screams to beg for mercy, to plead for leniency, but my mouth does not open. I won't give him that power. It's the only thing I have left.

"They're watching you, Ella. Do you see them? They all see you for what you are now. You can't hide anymore."

I manage to lift my head just enough to catch sight of Emila standing with a group of commanders. Her grin shifts something in me, and for a moment, my mind breaks through the wall Cassien so torturously built.

I yank Cassien's arm and twist, sweeping my feet under his and throwing my weight into his body. He taught me that move years ago. I roll to my feet as he catches himself on his hands. Blood drips from my hairline as I stand over him. I swing my foot and connect with his jaw, throwing him to his side. Gasps ring out from around the street as he lies on the ground, holding his face. My lungs squeeze shut as he turns and his eyes meet mine. He's going to kill me. With slow, controlled movements, he stands and takes two blades into his hands.

I expect my body to freeze as he steps toward me, but instead I raise my fists and shift my weight onto my toes. There is nothing left of me to destroy. He's already burned it all away. For a moment, I think about my life and mustering a will strong enough to want to live, but no one powerful cares for their own life, for they are only vessels of conquest.

When Cassien swings, I deflect and spin out of the way. I make my attack, but he anticipates it. As I move through a sequence of quick, jarring movements to try to land a blow to his head, he stabs. I feel the blade slice into my gut before I can step away. He's on me again in seconds, shoving me to the ground. With my face in the dirt, he holds my head down with his hand, pressing all his weight onto my skull. He sets his knee on my back and grabs my hair, exposing my neck enough to place his bloodied dagger against it. I try to twist away, but he leans in further, trapping me as I struggle to get oxygen into my lungs.

"Kill me," I pant, trying to lean against the blade. "I'm a burden to you and your image. You never wanted me as your successor, so finish it."

He stays silent above me as his breathing grows ragged. I close my eyes, waiting for the swipe of the blade. It would be mercy. This is my final stand against the man who has caused me so much pain. The reprieve will never come. Cassien snarls in frustration as he takes a handful of my hair and pulls me up with him. My eyes water as he drags me along, keeping the blade pressed to my throat as if he were just moments from beheading me.

When we reach the forest line, he throws me to the ground. "You are not my daughter. You have nowhere to go, no one to run to."

I look at him, spitting out the blood pooling in my mouth. I almost smile as I see the damage I've inflicted.

"I would love nothing more than to rid this world of you," he hisses. A smirk grows on his lips as he backs up. My stomach sinks as he stares behind me. "But death is not a suitable punishment."

Slowly, I turn to face the woods. A sharp exhale bursts from my lungs as I see the orange flames dancing in the distance. The cabin. He found the cabin.

"You will never win this fight, Ella. I will always be two steps ahead of you."

I can't pull my eyes away from the fire. Even as I hear his footsteps recede, I don't look away. I force myself to stand and drag my feet through the woods. Tears fall as I pray again and again that this is some kind of cruel joke. *He can't have found it. He never knew. I was safe here. We were safe here.*

Byrne and I built this cabin together so long ago, assembling it board by board. Now flames shoot through the roof and from the trees around it. I fall to my knees as I watch it all crumble to ash. *He knew. We were never safe here. He knew exactly where I was the whole time.*

———

I HAVE to force every breath into my body as I keep a hand on my side, staunching the steady flow of blood from the knife wound. I've lost too much. I push the boat into the river as I pant, needing to get away. *He knew where I was.* I pull myself in and row as my muscles burn. *He was always there.* No matter which way I face, I can see the flames burning away the last shred of my sanity. When I get to shore, I barely manage to step out of the boat before I collapse. Sobs rack my body as I curl up on the beach.

I was never safe. I've never been able to outrun him. He's always waiting. He's always here.

CHAPTER

SEVENTEEN

LEO

Byrne hasn't seen Emrys in three days, and the only time he can sneak away is late tonight, so Byrne said she'd meet up with Elana and me at the Vallan in a few hours. It's unusually cold, the temperatures dropping the farther I venture into the woods. I have a blanket in my pack along with the usual medical supplies, but maybe I should have brought something warmer. I never know what state Elana will be in when I get there, but I've come to expect the worst.

It's strange to walk with my own thoughts. The last few visits, Byrne had accompanied me, helping to keep the silence away. Now all I can think of are bruises and cuts. Bleary eyes and blood and broken bones. I know that's what I'll see when I get to the beach, but I'm never able to prepare myself completely. It's impossible to shield the emotions that burst to the surface when I first meet Elana's eyes.

I breach the forest line and step onto the beach, scanning

the dark water for the rowboat. Nothing cuts through the ripple. No boat. No Elana. A chill runs through my bones.

"Elana?" I call, barely more than a whisper.

I swallow as I continue down to beach, moving faster. The only thing I see ahead is a pile of driftwood. My eyes come into focus. No, that's not driftwood. I sprint toward the overturned rowboat as my heart pounds in my ears.

"Elana?" I call as I round the craft, but no one's here.

I run a hand through my hair as I look through the darkness of the woods. She has to be somewhere. Why won't she come out? *Maybe she can't.* I lean against the boat, trying to clear my mind. *Think.* I hang my head and take a breath. *She's all right. Maybe this isn't her boat. Maybe she's still on the island.* Then I see it. The drop of red on the canvas of black stones. I crouch and run my finger over the spot as I hold my breath.

"Elana!" I stand and head toward the woods, finding drop after drop of blood. There's a rustling farther ahead. "Elana!"

I burst through the brush and there she is, her back facing me. Elana doesn't move as I step closer.

"Elana?" I fall to my knees beside her, my hands shaking as I turn her over.

Her chest is barely moving as her eyes crack open. There's blood everywhere. The ground is stained with it. She's stained with it. My heart stops beating all together.

"It took you... long enough," she wheezes as her eyes flutter.

I rip open my bag, scattering the medical supplies. "Where are you hurt?"

"I'm fine. Don't... don't worry." She raises her hand to push me away, but I catch her wrist.

"Where are you hurt?" I repeat.

She watches me for a moment, every breath shaky and shallow. She raises her other hand from her side, and it comes away slick with blood to reveal a deep wound in her stomach. My jaw clenches as I gather bandages and press them into the wound. She tenses as she clenches her teeth.

"Anywhere else?" I press.

She shakes her head as a wheezing laugh passes through her lips. "Only bruises and broken bones."

I scan her quickly, deciding my best course of action. There is no choice to be made. I won't send her back. I unfold the blanket and carefully pull it around her shoulders. She watches with glazed eyes as I pull out a bottle of water and hold it for her to drink.

"I can do it," she wheezes.

I meet her gaze, shaking my head at her stubbornness. I let her try to take the bottle, but she's too weak and her hand barely grips it. I place my hand on hers and help her bring it to her lips. After swallowing a few sips, she coughs and pushes the rest away.

I pack up the bag and sling it over my shoulder before taking in a slow breath. "I'm bringing you to Arkezo."

She shakes her head slowly as her eyes widen. "No. I can't."

"Yes, you can."

"Then I won't—"

"I'm not taking no for an answer. I can't keep coming and seeing you hurt only to send you back like it's nothing. I'm not letting him do this to you anymore," I tell her as my teeth grind.

"You can't control me," she seethes. "I do as I please."

"Can you not see what's happening? Every time I see you, you're hurt worse than the time before. Each run-in, you're one step closer to Lady Death's door."

"I don't need you to explain my life to me."

"Maybe you do. Whatever you say, whatever you do, I'm not letting you go back. Call me selfish, call me anything you like, but I'm not letting you go back. I will carry you to Arkezo kicking and screaming if I have to." My mind is on fire as I see the determination burning in her eyes.

"You will not touch me," she says, staring through me as she leans away. She winces at the movement, and every spark of anger that had taken over my mind drains away.

"Then tell me why?" I ask desperately. "Why can't you leave?"

She stays silent, watching me as if I were a monster.

"Please, Elana," I beg. "I'll do anything to get you out of there. I don't care what it is, but you have to tell me the reason so I can help. You have to let me in."

She stares at me for a long moment. Tears fog her eyes as she pulls the blanket tightly around herself.

"Please, Elana. Trust me. Trust me with this and I'll help you."

"Cass."

My blood freezes as my spine straightens.

"What did you say?" I whisper, pulling away from her.

"He's alive, Leo."

I shallowly exhale as I turn to look at the island. Something cracks in my chest. We left him. Alive. For months in that hell. Alone. And she knew. *She knew and never told us.* I shake my head slowly. She must be lying. That can't be true...

"I saw him die," I say, my voice breaking.

"He was wounded, badly, but he healed. They've been keeping him in the Council building, and I've been taking care of him. I've been with him every day."

"He's alive..."

"I protected him, Leo. No one's put a hand on him," she explains, pleading with me to understand.

I turn back to look at her, and her eyes are different from

the ones that take up so much space in my head. How could I let this happen?

"You lied? All this time, you've been lying," I accuse, my voice high and sharp.

Her mouth moves as if she were trying to explain but couldn't find the words. I take a deep breath as my entire world falls off its axis. When I return my eyes to hers, I don't recognize the Elana I've grown to care about.

"You're coming to Arkezo with me," I tell her without room for argument.

"Leo—"

"You're not allowed to speak. You can't have that. Do you know how long Cass didn't speak before we got to Wate? Years, Elana. He was silent for years. Now he thinks we abandoned him. You let him think *I* left him. So you don't get to say a word anymore. Not when you let us grieve him. Not when I grieved him and I told you about the pain."

"Leo—"

"Don't."

Her lips thin into a line as her eyes water. She doesn't let a single tear drops. She swallows before looking away. "I can't walk."

A hysterical laugh bubbles up from my lungs as I look back toward Wate. "You really don't know me at all if you think I'm going to let you walk."

Carefully, I slip my arms under her back and knees and lift her. Her face is pale, and it takes no more than twenty minutes before she's asleep in my arms while all I can do is fall deeper into my own thoughts.

RIGHT BEFORE I reach the outskirts of Arkezo, I hear light footsteps approaching. I duck behind a tree and tuck Elana tightly against my chest. My back is cramping from holding her for so long, but I can't chance resting. When Byrne's face appears through the brush, I exhale a long breath. She sees me and her brows knit together. She runs over, her eyes wide as she sees her sister in my arms.

"What happened?" she demands, her hand moving to touch Elana's face. She meets my gaze as tears well in her eyes. "Is she alive?"

"Barely," I tell her softly. "We need to bring her somewhere safe."

Byrne's hands cover her mouth as a wounded sound escapes her lungs. The cry tears open a hole in my chest. "Where are we going to take her? There's no way we can bring her into the Ridge Palace."

I shake my head as I grind my teeth, knowing what I have to do. "I'm going to call in a favor."

I BANG on the door as hard as I can as I stand on the steps of Hela's Bond's house. A slot slides open, revealing a pair of dark silver eyes.

"Who... what are you doing here?" I recognize Kiro's voice through the hatch. There's surprise in his tone, understandably.

"I need to call in that debt," I say.

I hear the smirk in his voice as he says, "In trouble so soon, Your Highness?"

"If you consider a girl I carried for miles bleeding out on your doorstep trouble, then yes," I seethe as my arms shake.

He stays silent as he holds my gaze.

"By The Lady, Kiro, let me in or I swear I'll break through the door."

He must catch the edge to my voice because the door swings open instantly. He swears as he takes in the sight of Elana and quickly shuts the door behind me. Soren and Emmani rush over to the table in the middle of the room.

"Set her down here," Emmani says as she clears the clutter from the space.

Deca appears from the hall a moment later.

"What happened?" Soren asks as I carefully place Elana on the table.

Deca grabs a medical kit and spreads out its contents as she scans Elana's injuries.

"It's a long story," I spit.

Elana stays unconscious as Emmani and Deca work to try to patch her up.

"We need to know if we're going to help," Emmani says frantically as she hands me new bandages to staunch the bleeding on Elana's side.

Elana gasps awake as her eyes shoot open. They shift gold in an instant and her tense muscles calm. "Where..."

"Relax. They're going to help," I tell her.

For the moment, I have to push any thoughts of Cass aside or else I might run back and burn Wate to the ground. Now is not the time. Elana's eyes are fixed on me as Emmani tries to keep her calm. Deca pulls out a needle and a vial of clear liquid. She fills the syringe as Elana flinches, and my arms wrap around her instinctively.

"What is that?" I demand as my gaze flies between the syringe and Elana.

"It will just put her to sleep," Soren explains as he deposits a handful of supplies on one of the chairs.

Deca nods stoically as she steps toward us.

Emmani must catch the fear on our faces because her expression softens. "It won't hurt you. You need the rest, and we need to be able to sew you up without you moving."

Elana looks up at me with wide eyes. Scared. She's so scared. Without thinking, I gently sweep the hair from her forehead and hold her tighter.

"You'll be all right," I whisper.

She searches my face as her throat works.

"Trust me," I say.

Tears gather in her eyes as she nods. Emmani moves forward without hesitation and injects the substance into Elana's arm. Within seconds, Elana's eyes flutter shut. I swallow the emotion that had risen in my throat and peel myself away.

A knock sounds from the door and Kiro moves to see who it is. I know that knock. It's the one we taught the boys when we were in Somereil.

"It's Cael and Byrne," I tell Kiro without looking.

He glances my way with furrowed brows as his mouth opens to speak.

"My brother and her sister," I explain before he can say anything.

He nods and slides open the latch to confirm. Kiro opens the door to let them in, and Cael rushes to Elana's side without a word to anyone in the room.

He moves me away from her as he takes a look at the damage to her stomach. "How long?"

"I don't know, a few hours maybe," I answer shakily.

Cael's expression evens out as he pokes at the wound. "Why does your voice sound like that?"

Kiro and Emmani share a questioning glance as Byrne stands beside me, her hands having fallen slack by her side.

"Like what?" I say evenly.

"Like your soul's been ripped out." Cael glances my way and his hands freeze. "What happened?"

Everyone looks at me and I forget how to breathe. "Cass is alive."

I hear Cael's breath hitch as he stares at me. Devastation takes over his face as his lips part.

"All right. One of you needs to start talking or else we're throwing this girl back into the street. What in all the hells is happening?" Kiro demands, his voice too loud in my ears.

I glare at him as my spine straightens. "This is Elana. She's from Wate, and the High Lord beat her half to death. We usually meet up every few days, and tonight I found her on the shore like this. Cass is our youngest brother. He was killed with a blade through the stomach the day we fled Wate. As it turns out, he's alive and she knew about it. Is that information adequate for you, or do you need the minute-by-minute recount of the past three months?"

They gape at me—whether from shock from what I've just said or my reaction, I can't tell. I'm gasping for air under their attention. Cael shakes his head as if to clear his mind and sets his focus back on Elana.

"We make sure she's all right, then we worry about Cass," he tells me, slightly breathless. "We'll get him back."

There's only confidence in Cael's voice, as though he believes we could walk into Wate and Cassien will be waiting to hand him over. But it's never that easy, not when it comes to my family. I can only hope this doesn't end with one of us bleeding, and sometimes even that seems to be too much to ask.

CHAPTER

EIGHTEEN

LEO

It doesn't take them long to patch up Elana. They get her bandaged with clean linens and apply salves to help with the smaller cuts and bruising before setting the breaks straight. Cael takes longer to sew up the wound in her stomach, but it was relatively clean, so he thinks it should heal well. Thankfully, the dagger didn't puncture deep enough to damage anything major. She'll pull through.

Red walks through the door, her skin and clothes covered with blood. None of us ask, instead filling her in on everything that's happened. Taking it in, she nods once before glancing at Elana and disappearing down the hall to check on Gray. He's slept through the whole ordeal. I guess any type of noise wouldn't bother him, so he remained unaffected by the chaos we created when I came through the door.

Emmani brings in a fresh blanket and drapes it over Elana as Byrne sits by her sister. She smiles sadly at Emmani and thanks the group for their help.

"So, what are we going to do about Cass?" Cael says tensely as he wipes the smears of blood from his hands.

"We have to go get him."

"It will be a trap," Byrne says, not looking our way. "You know that's why she didn't tell you. Father will be using him as bait to lure you back, the same way he used your mother to lure your father."

"Wait, hold on. Your father did this?" Emmani asks Byrne, aghast as she pushes her round glasses up her nose.

"That's what you're focused on?" Kiro asks incredulously. "Did you not hear that Dirix was murdered in a gold city?"

Deca not-so-discreetly kicks his ankle, making Kiro yelp. He shuts up as he catches sight of my expression.

"We would have figured out a way to get him out, Byrne," I tell her coldly.

She leans away from me as the blood leaches from her face. I read her reaction and realize with a jolt that the monster that crawls beneath my skin has surfaced. I close my eyes and do my best to piece myself back together as I run my hands through my hair. After a moment, I take a deep breath and manage to reel in my emotions.

"Elana said he's in the Council building," I tell Byrne.

She nods slowly as her brows knit together. "He'll be kept where you were. In the North Halls. They keep a list of the prisoners in the laundry room at the end of the hall. If you can get in there, you can find out where he's being held. But they'll have people guarding the doors and the whole place will be crawling with soldiers."

"When I'm done, they'll have to restock the platoon," I mutter to myself.

Byrne's voice goes soft. "Some of those people are good, Leo. They don't know any other way of life."

A laugh bubbles from my lungs as I watch her, remembering how I had muttered the same words not so long ago. "My brother is good... and they ran a sword through his gut and locked him in a cell. Those children in the puppet barracks are good... and they're beaten and starved. You and your sister are good, and your own father takes pleasure in ripping you to shreds. Just because people are good does not mean they are protected from bad things."

"That's enough, Leo," Cael scolds, his voice tight.

I immediately quiet, feeling his words burn through me.

"You're upset. I understand that. But you don't get to talk about us like we're a tragedy," Byrne seethes, her soft voice strong.

I nod, unable to meet her eyes.

"If the timing is the same as before, they'll do a guard change at midnight. There's always a grunt who falls asleep during the night shift. Find them and slip past. I'll draw a map to get you to the laundry room, then it's up to you to figure out what room he's in. There's a window at the end of the North Halls that has a broken latch. You can escape from there."

I meet her eyes and hope she sees the apology in mine. "Thank you." I turn to the four Hela's Bond members gaping at us. "Thank you all. For everything."

They nod as I hear Red walk back into the room.

"She'll be safe here until she heals," Red says. "The debt is repaid."

I nod, unable to say or do anything more. I'm going to get my brother back, and no one will stand in my way.

CAEL and I race toward Wate. Byrne told us to leave tomorrow and give ourselves more time to plan, but I won't let my brother live in that hell for another second. And Elana... no. She doesn't deserve to take up space in my head. I can't—won't think about her.

Cael's eyes are dark as we get to the beach, his face stern and set. There is no time for happiness or sorrow tonight. There is no room for emotion. Only violence. Only revenge. We're both armed with enough steel—myself with my father's blades and Cael with several offered up by Hela's Bond—to be considered a military arsenal.

We don't speak as we launch the boat into the waves. We each grab a paddle and row. Only the sound of our heaving breaths fills the air as we cross. Not even the wind dares to blow for fear of what we'll do. Smoke from the burned shack still billows into the air, smothering the starlight. The air tastes foul, like charred bread and dry blood. It's as though the earth knows we're coming and has set the scene for devastation.

When we hit Wate's beach, Cael and I climb out of our boat and stow it in the brush. Our every move is synced. Images of Cass play through my mind with every step: tortured, bruised, bloodied, dead. Falling to the ground, over and over. Screaming. Screeching. I let them take hold. I let the memory drown me until the line between what's real and imagined blurs. Cass is dead. Cass is alive. All I know is that they hurt him. They stole what is ours and Cassien will pay for it in blood.

We follow the plan Byrne laid out, making our way through the city in the darkness. We don't have much time. It doesn't take long to reach the Council building and make our way to the North Halls. Cael crouches when we reach the last door and pulls a set of lock picks out of his pocket. I pull on the feeling at my fingertips and let it rip through me as Cael works. This sensation has always been a comfort and escape from suffering, but as I take two daggers in my hands, all I feel is burning rage. Reprieve is not possible, even as my eyes bleed red. The lock clicks open and the door hinges squeal as Cael enters.

"We're in," he says evenly. My brother's face is wiped clear of emotion, but his knuckles are white around the blades. He craves retribution as much as I do.

I step inside first and come face to face with a bulky man wearing a soldier's uniform. The sleeves of his shirt are rolled up to his elbows and his hands are submerged in a water basin. His eyes go wide as he prepares to scream, but my dagger is pressed tight to his throat before his lungs can constrict. He gasps as I start to run it across—

"Leo."

I look up and lock eyes with my brother. Something shifts in Cael's expression. It's not fear, but it's something close. I clench my jaw as I force my hand to still. The taste of iron stains my mouth as I watch him.

"Reel it in," he whispers. "This is too much. More than we need."

I swallow the growing lump in my throat as I crack my neck. Taking a breath, I try to push away the bloodlust, but it fights back. I'm so angry, and the need for vengeance feeds off my rage. Angry people are easily manipulated. Easily controlled. I won't be controlled. For a moment, I forget I'm holding a man by his throat. I focus back on the present and our current mission, thinking only of freeing Cass. My breathing evens out and my heartbeat slows, allowing my thoughts to clear. I swing my arm and hit the man over the head with the butt of my blade. He slumps into a disorderly pile. Cael watches me intently, as if deciding if I'm all right to continue.

"I'm good. I've got it under control," I tell him.

Though he nods once, his eyes remain tight as he glances at

the man on the floor. "After all the terror they were put through as kids, some of them still have no instincts."

Pity pushes through me as I scan the walls and find the list hanging above a basin just as Byrne said. "Maybe that's just it," I say as I pull the sheet of paper off the wall. "They think they don't need to be afraid anymore. That the worst is over, so they become complacent. I don't know if they're lucky or cursed."

I flip through the pages and my heart stutters as I read the words *high risk prisoner*. That's him.

"Room two-four-eight," I tell Cael.

He nods once, his jaw set. "Let's go."

The hall is sparsely lit and completely silent when we enter. One-five-two. One-five-three. One-five-four. Stairwell. *His room must be on the second floor.* The walls morph from gray painted wood to stone lined with metal bars. Every second, my mind shifts from one brother to another. Altair to Cass. Cass to Altair. Who did I leave alone this time? Who am I searching for today? What state will I find him in?

"Leo?"

"What?" I spit.

Cael blinks as I turn on him. It takes me a second to gather the pieces of my shield that had begun to fall apart.

"We all thought he was dead, Leo. It's not your fault," Cael says softly, glancing behind me.

I nod, even as his words fly over my head. "She didn't. She knew."

"We can deal with later. All we can do now is get Cass out," he explains as a muscle in his jaw feathers.

I force myself to breathe and focus my mind. We quickly ascend the stairs and reach the second floor. I push my ear up against the door leading into the hall. Silence. We push through, and the sense of foreboding tenses my muscles. It's too quiet. This is too easy.

Cael and I reach the door and stare at the numbers. Two-four-eight. Cass is behind this door. Alive. I could smile. Cael eagerly takes the handle and twists. The door swings open. Cael and I share a tense glance as I head toward the cot. He's here. The blanket is pulled tight over his head.

"Cass?" I whisper.

He doesn't move. I repeat his name as I take hold of the sheet and peel it back. A man surges up from the cot toward me, screaming. I startle, stumbling backward into Cael and pushing us both to the floor. The man doesn't stop screeching as he pulls against the thick chain locked around his neck. His eyes are wild when I stand and put the knife to his throat.

"Pretty prince of blood," he whispers as his eyes lock on mine. "No blood left for you. Nobody left to bleed. Pretty prince of bl—" He jerks his head to the side, slicing open his own throat on my blade.

The blood splatters over my face before I can step back. My breath quickens as Cael grips my arm and pulls me away. The man gurgles a laugh as blood fills his lungs. When the door shuts, my eyes stay fixed ahead.

I turn my head as a loud thump rings in my ears. Cael's on the floor. I try to lunge away, but a boot collides with my ribs, sending me plummeting down. I wheeze as I try to lift myself. A knee digs into my back as my hands are tied together. I can't move, but I don't care. I don't care that I'm here in Wate. I don't care that Cass is alive or that Elana lied to me. Not as Cassien stares down at me with a smirk.

I want him dead. I want him hung from a post and left for the birds to tear apart. For what he's done. For what he took from me. Time, family, trust. My mind reels until a fist crashes against my head and all the darkness welcomes me home.

CAEL

My head pounds like I was pummeled with a load of bricks. Slowly, my jaw begins to ache, and sounds buzz in my ears. I try to turn away as light pries through my eyelids. I'm going to throw up.

"Cael!"

A watery voice breaks through what seems to be leagues of space. I swim toward it, fighting against the pounding pain that grows stronger the sharper the sound becomes.

"Cael, open your eyes."

I do. Leo is sitting beside me, his eye swollen shut and his lip split open. Leo's shoulders drop as I try to move. I'm trapped. My hands are chained above my head in a mirror image of my brother. All our weapons are gone, even Leo's sheaths. My breathing picks up as I scan the small, dark room. The *cell*.

Before I can fall into a full panic, the door swings open. My heart stops as Cassien—dressed without a thread out of place

—stalks in and crouches to look us in the eyes. There are stark bruises painting his skin. Elana must have fought back before she left. Leo's eyes light up as he notices.

"You know, I thought my daughter would be smarter when it came to trying to get the boy out, but I'm beginning to believe she did not have a part in this. I'm sure she warned you to stay away, but you just couldn't help yourself, could you?" He steps closer to Leo and tilts his head as if he were trying to understand Leo's mind.

I still when I catch sight of Leo's anger—a *rage* on his face like nothing I've ever seen. He's always had control, but he's losing the reins. Cassien is playing a dangerous game.

Cassien watches Leo for a long time. "You should never have trusted her, but I believe you already know this. Now, the only remaining issue is the hole she's carved in your heart. How are you going to fill it, Blood Prince? How will you live without the girl you so dearly—"

Leo lunges at him, pulling against his restraints until his skin rips. He swings his leg out and catches Cassien's ankle. The man spins away easily, but I see the spark of surprise in his eyes. So does my brother.

Leo slowly smiles. His teeth are stained the same crimson as his eyes. "I'm going to relish the moment she kills you."

My gaze flicks to Leo as his jaw sets tight.

"I don't fear Lady Death," Cassien says as he turns toward the door.

"No, the Lady will be nowhere to offer you mercy when you fall. I'm talking about Elana."

Cassien freezes at the door. His hands slowly ball into fists as Leo continues.

"I want *nothing* more than to rip your heart from your chest," Leo says as though he's recounting a dream. "But I just realized that your life isn't mine to take. It's your daughter's."

"She's too weak."

"You believe, after all these years, you truly failed so greatly?" Leo asks, knowing full well where his weaknesses lie. I don't know where this comes from or where his head is, but somehow Leo is rattling Cassien.

"Her failure is not my own," Cassien spits as he forces open the door and steps out.

Cassien doesn't shut it, instead standing before us. He reaches to the side and pulls Cass forward. A sob grasps my lungs. Cass is pale but looks healthy. Leo's breath catches as he sees our brother. Cassien's smile grows as he takes Cass by the back of the neck and spins a knife in the other hand. Leo and I lurch forward, but our chained arms hold us back. I bite my lip from the pain of the cuffs and force myself to focus on Cass.

"Let him go," Leo seethes.

Cassien grins wildly as he pulls the knife away and runs it along Cass's cheek. I don't know when we start screaming, but Leo and I fill the air with our desperate voices. Cass squeezes his eyes shut. He shakes as we struggle, twisting and pulling fruitlessly at our chains. I'm breathless when Cassien pulls the blade along Cass's skin, leaving a long gash on my little brother's face.

"You know, I once believed in Lady Death. I breathed the air she bestowed and drank the water she purified. I walked the steps she laid before me, trusting she would lead me to greatness. But I grew up and discovered, like all other fairy tales, she is nothing but an old wives' tale. A story. Made up. She does not come to take us before our worst moments, because I knew a woman who had none." He takes a deep breath and looks down as Cass. "I tell you this because I want you to know that there will be no one there to comfort you when I peel the skin from your bones. I want you to know that when I kill you, your brother will hold the memories and suffer for eternity, just as I do."

Cassien's voice reminds me of a soft ripple in a still lake. Calm and welcoming, but a wake must be created by something lurking beneath the waves.

He looks at Leo and his eyes are cold. "I hope she holds the same... feelings you do for her. That way I can sever her last thread of sanity when I take your life."

Cassien pushes Cass into the cell and shuts the door. I can still see his eyes in my mind after he clicks the lock shut. I swallow the lump growing in my throat and focus my attention on Cass. *Cass.*

My chin quakes as I smile at my brother. "Hi, Cass."

He stares at me for a moment, searching my face with wide eyes. *He's terrified.* He takes a step forward and something clicks. His arms wrap around me as he shakes, tears and blood staining my shirt. I push myself to my knees to try to move my arms more freely and hug him as best as I can. I murmur every comforting thought that comes to my mind. A string of *I'm so sorry* and *we're going to be all right* floats through the small room, met only with the silence I've grown to know so well. *He lost his words.*

Tears push at the backs of my eyes. We waited for his voice for so long and now it's lost again. He doesn't pull away for a long time, staying pressed to my chest.

When there's nothing more I can say to console him, the silence of the room becomes deafening. I can still hear Cass sniffling, but not even the sound of a breath can be heard from Leo. Carefully, I turn my head toward him. He hasn't moved. His chest rises in jarring movements as he stares at the spot where Cassien stood, stuck in time. The crimson sheen over his depthless eyes has become so dark, they look almost black.

"Leo?" I mean for my voice to come out strong, but instead

it sounds weak and hesitant, as if I'm trying not to scare a wild animal.

He doesn't react. His eyes are glazed and foggy, and his knuckles are bone white. *He sank.*

Panic bites at my mind as Cass pulls away to look at Leo. I catch Cass's attention before he can look too closely.

"We need to get these cuffs off," I tell Cass, looking up at the iron links as I slowly spin my ring.

Cass's brows furrow as he reaches behind him and pulls a small dagger from his waistband. My mouth drops open as he hands it to me. His eyes are hard and sure when I meet them.

"She gave it to you, didn't she? To keep yourself safe when she wasn't there?"

He dips his chin with confidence and pushes his shoulders back to stand taller. I take the blade and stare at it. *She really was with him all this time.* Guilt floods through my mind as I set to picking the locks. It takes me longer than usual, but eventually they pop open. Rubbing my wrists, I kneel in front of Cass and take his face in my hands to inspect the gash across his cheek.

"Does it hurt?" I ask as I tear a piece of my shirt and fold it up. He shakes his head but winces when I press the fabric against the wound. "Hold that on there tight."

He does as I say before I turn to face Leo. He's still stuck in that trance. That very, very dangerous trance.

"Stay behind me and turn around," I tell Cass softly.

Only when he does do I take a step toward Leo. I won't uncuff him yet. Only the Lady knows what's going on in his head or how volatile he'll be when he comes out of it.

"Leo? Can you hear me, brother?" Even though I'm right in front of him, his eyes look through me. *He doesn't see me.* I bring my fingers up next to his ear and snap. He doesn't flinch. "Leo, you have to come back. You have to wake up."

Nothing. Not even a twitch. I hang my head and take a deep breath.

"Lady, forgive me," I mumble before pulling my hand back and slugging him across the face.

He sways from the force of the hit, but his eyes are still dull. I swear under my breath. I usually catch him before he sinks this deep, but it was so quick this time. Too quick. I watch him for a moment as the realization of what set him off dawns on me. *Cassien found the key to Leo's insanity and unlocked every one of his defenses to unveil his greatest fears and shatter his thoughts with only a few words.*

"Let's see if it can keep a hold over you when you aren't breathing," I say as I slide Cass's dagger behind me and pull my sleeve over my hand.

Ever so carefully, I block Leo's airways, placing one hand over his mouth while the other covers his nose. Still, he doesn't move.

"Come on," I pray over and over. "Fight me."

His hand jerks. I sigh in relief before a foot collides with my gut, sending me plummeting backward. My eyes water as I gasp for air. Leo abruptly backs up into the wall as his wild eyes look across the room. Struggling like a caged animal, he blinks and focuses on me as the sound of his erratic breathing fills the room.

"It's all right," I scrape out as pull myself off the floor. "You're all right."

Leo's eyes track my every step as I move closer and reach for his cuffs. He stays frozen as I break them open, one by one. I slide each cuff off and let them fall to the floor before resting back on my heels.

"What's my name?" I ask softly, keeping my hands in front of me.

"Cael." His voice sounds like scraping stones.

I nod once as a small smile pulls at my face. "And yours?"

He takes a moment to search my face before he answers. "Leo."

I nod again. "Do you know where we are?"

"Wate."

"That's it," I tell him encouragingly as the color returns to his cheeks. "What are we doing in Wate?"

His face sobers as he runs his hand through his hair. "Getting Cass."

Cass steps out from behind me, watching our brother carefully.

Leo's face breaks as his lip quivers. "Hi, Cass."

They collide in an embrace as tears run down Leo's splotchy cheeks. He pulls away and holds Cass's face to get a better look at the gash.

"You're not hurt besides the cut?" he questions.

Cass smiles softly and shakes his head.

"Good. That's good. I'm glad. So, so glad." Leo pulls him close again.

I can see the remnants of whatever had taken over Leo's mind leaving him as he slowly pulls himself back to the surface. He hasn't been that bad in years. Not since around when Dad died.

When Leo levels out enough for us to talk about how we're going to escape, we assess our options. As it turns out, we have very few.

"We could break down the door and make a run for it," he says glumly.

I almost laugh at the thought. Leo still looks as if he's recently died and been resurrected, and the only weapon we have is Cass's dagger, which is no bigger than my hand. Not to mention this time we're gambling with Cass's life as much as our own.

"No. We'd make too much noise getting the door open, and besides, Cassien will have planned for that. There are probably a dozen guards waiting outside," I tell Leo, though I have a feeling he's already aware.

His lips thin as he glances at me before his eyes flicker away.

"What?" I ask.

He shakes his head as he winces. "I know how to get out, but you're going to hate it."

CHAPTER

TWENTY

ELANA

I gasp as my eyes shoot open. By the Goddess, it hurts. *Everything* hurts. Byrne is beside me the minute I manage to pull the golden filter over my vision.

"Where is he?" I grind out, my throat dry as a winter's wind.

Byrne shakes her head as tears gather in her eyes. "How are you feeling, Elana?"

She grasps my hand so tightly I want to recoil. I hold her stare and try desperately to convey the seriousness in my question.

"I'm fine," I tell her curtly when she doesn't answer me. "Where is he?"

I move to sit up, but all at once, seven bodies move to push me back down. When I flinch, they stop in their tracks. I swallow the growing lump in my throat as I scan the room. My surroundings finally register in my mind as my muscles tense. I glance at Byrne as she smiles shyly.

"I'm going to ask you one more time," I tell her, keeping my voice low and severe. I'm panting from the strength it's taking me to stay sitting up. "Where is he?"

Byrne takes a deep breath as she closes her eyes.

"You really should lie down," a thick woman with pin-straight black hair and round glasses says. She has a soft face sculpted around smile lines, though there is no kindness in her face now. Another woman with dark tattooed skin steps in front of her, protecting her. "You've been through a lot—"

"You have no idea what I've been through," I snap.

All six strangers are silent, glaring at me. Byrne flashes them an apologetic look. *Why does she have to do that? She doesn't need to speak for me.* I dig my nails into my palms to fight the overwhelming desire to close my heavy eyes. *I need to know he didn't go.*

"Byrne," I plead one last time, "where is he?" The air punches from my lungs as her gaze shifts to the floor.

"He went to get Cass. They both did."

My heart beats like a drum as I grab her upper arm with all the strength I have. "What did you tell them to do?"

She bites her lip as her eyes rove nervously over the room. "To go through the laundry in the North Halls—"

"Then find his room on the register and get out through the skylight?" I finish for her as a hysterical laugh bubbles up from inside me.

They stare at me like I'm mad. Leo and Cael are headed right into a trap. They're practically giving themselves over to him. I swing my legs over the table as my head spins.

Byrne grabs my arms, stopping me from getting up. "Elana—"

"No. They need help. They're doing exactly what he's been waiting for them to do," I tell her as desperation creeps into my voice.

"What do you mean?" a tall woman with a wine-colored birthmark on her face asks.

I close my eyes as I rub my face. "Cass was never in the North Halls. They kept him by Cassien's office because he knew you would know where the cells are. By the Lady, Byrne, why do you think I waited so long to tell them? Cass was nothing more than bait. We'll be lucky if they aren't already on the post." I shake my head as Byrne covers her mouth with her hand.

"They can fight and they're smart. They'll find a way out," she mutters.

I laugh again and shake my head. "Don't you see? This is a repeat of history. It won't be a fight. It will be a blood bath."

TWENTY-ONE

LEO

"Do you think they'll come?" Cael asks in the darkness, his voice unsteady. He's running his hand up and down Cass's back as he sleeps between us with his head on Cael's lap.

I exhale as I lean back against the wall. "Why would they?" I turn his way and can just make out the stress lines carved into his face. "We'll be fine Cael. We always are."

He stays silent for a long time as he watches Cass sleep. "I don't feel good about this. Maybe we should have waited for Elana."

"We don't need anything from her," I seethe.

Cael sighs heavily before spinning his ring. "I know you're upset with her—"

"She let us believe Cass was dead. She let us *mourn* him."

"Because she knew we would go after him and damn the consequences—"

"Don't take her side, Cael," I tell him coldly.

He takes a deep breath to relieve the tension growing between us. "I'm not. I'm just worried is all. This... everything about this... feels wrong. Like we can't get ourselves out."

"We will," I tell him because what else can I say to that? What could anyone? "We will."

THE LIGHT BLINDS me when the door is pushed open. Cass startles awake as the guards pounce on us. Cass scrambles for the knife, but I kick it over to Cael before he can get a hand on it. Cass looks at me with a quivering lip and I wink. He knows exactly what we're going to do, and I can see the fear in his eyes as I try to smile reassuringly. The reason we're here is to get him out, and by the Lady, I swear we will. They tackle Cael and me within seconds, restraining us brutally as they demand to know how we got the cuffs off.

Cael smirks at one of the guards and quips, "Didn't your parents teach you it's not polite to yell at guests?"

He's punched in the jaw so hard I'm surprised he manages to stay awake.

"I'm sure that's not the best you can do!" I nag the guards, who turn on me.

Cael and I decided to provoke them, because angry guards will easily lose focus of their priorities, like a little blond boy.

"You want one too?" the guard yells.

I hold his glare and paste on the grin of a cocky-faced arena victor. "I bet I won't feel it."

He pushes aside the woman who had been cuffing me and grabs my collar, smashing his fist into my face.

I flush my eyes, drowning the throbbing pain of the punch. I smile with bloody teeth and tilt my head. "You gold-eyes need to train harder if you want to compete with the blood-eyes across the Vallan."

A punch to the ribs.

"You wouldn't stand a chance against them..."

Another to the liver.

By the end of my rant, I'm gasping for air. I catch Cael's steady eyes and I know it's time to stop. His lips press into a thin line. Blood trickles down his chin from a split in his lip. I can almost hear his words in my head: *That's enough, Leo. Reel it in.* I'll take it down a notch.

"You want another?" the guard growls with his fist already raised.

I slouch against his grip and wipe the grin from my face. "No."

An ugly smile paints his face as he leans down so close, I gag at the smell of his breath.

"That's what I thought. You blood-eyes have big mouths, but your words are nothing but sound," he says, cackling.

The rest of their band joins in as they drag us out through the hall. Cass stays ahead of us, but his guard only keeps one hand on his back to guide him. When Cass looks our way, I give him an encouraging smile. *We'll be okay,* I tell Cass silently. *Be brave.* He nods and turns his eyes forward, keeping his head held high. My chest fills with pride. *At least he turned out all right, despite it all.*

The blood leaches from Cael's face with every step we take toward the post. It's only mid-morning, but for the first time in hours, it occurs to me that the royal assembly in Arkezo might be looking for me. They won't find us in time though, even if they bother to come. Cael breathes heavily as they chain us on our knees with our hands behind our backs. I'm pretty sure the guard broke my rib during my earlier outburst, but the discomfort isn't bothering me. I've dealt with worse.

A crowd grows around us, throwing insults into the air. Cass stands at the bottom of the platform along with the three guards who dragged us here. They pay him no heed as they watch us with wide smiles. Their hands twitch toward the blades strapped across their bodies, begging for a chance to make us bleed. I lean my head back and close my eyes.

"This doesn't feel right," Cael tells me from the other side of the post. Cheers erupt as the boards of the platform creak. "Something is different."

My brows crease at the flippancy in his voice. I'm not sure exactly what he means, but strangely, it doesn't sound bad. Maybe Lady Death will bless us with mercy one more time. I've proven to have her fortune on my side.

"This situation isn't exactly something that should feel right," I mutter as I tug on the chains keeping my hands above my head. "But I have faith in chaos."

I open my eyes as Cael's weak laugh reaches my ears. "Chaos is endless, Leo. There is no faith in it, only prayers that it will turn out in our favor."

I shake my head as I grin. My brother, always the wise man. I keep my eyes on the ground as a pair of well-polished boots stand before me. The freezing flat edge of a blade tips my chin up so that I meet Emila's eyes.

"Welcome back, Blood Prince," she coos. I watch her through my brows as she walks around us. "How special that we now have a full set of Heal brothers." She stops in front of me and crouches to look me in the eyes. "A true-blooded, gold-eyed Heal. A getic who wears the Heal ring. And the Crown Prince of Illena who claims the Heal name as if it were a badge of honor." She leans in so close I can see the different shades of silver in her eyes. "So much blood to spill. Pity you aren't actually brothers, or I would have been able to say I wiped out most of a generation."

I want to cut the grin off her face, but I hold back. *Only a few more seconds.*

"It's really a shame that the post hasn't been able to taste any of your blood," I whisper.

Emila's eyes fly to mine. I hear a small click from behind me and smirk.

"Perhaps we should remedy that." I lunge at Emila with free hands as Cael gets to work on his own cuffs.

I catch her off guard and snag two daggers from the sheaths on her leg. I glance to where Cass had been standing and find him disappearing into the crowd, exactly as we told him to do. I spin on a guard as he jumps onto the stage with an axe in hand. He's disarmed with two quick movements, allowing me to replace my dagger with the deadly axe. Emila barks out orders as she scrapes herself off the ground. Two guards come flying at me. I crack my neck before taking my first swing, the axe slicing through air and flesh as I cut them down. Screams fill the air as they fall off the stage. I toss Cael a dagger as he stands to take on another man who jumped up on the steps. Cael backs toward me as he fights off soldier after soldier. Blood roars in my ears as I dance through the movements, cutting down anyone who dares stand too close.

My heart stutters when Cael screams and drops to the ground. The Lady is really testing me today. Panic rages through my bones as a shrill whistle rings through the air. For a moment, the distraction disorients me as I see Emila stand up before me and raise her hand to swing. I move to dodge the blow, but an arrow splits through her shoulder before she can land the hit. She stumbles backward with wide eyes as the soldier who was fighting Cael is hit with an identical arrow. My brother's eyes trace its path and a smile blooms on his blood-splattered face.

"They really do want your favor," he says to me as a

flaming arrow lands in the middle of the crowd. Cael's face drops as he pulls me off the back of the stage.

Flames roar to life, eating at the oxygen all around us. My head throbs before I register the cloaked figure standing over me.

"Hi, Byrne," Cael scrapes out as he pulls himself up.

Relief bleeds through me as she turns and throws a blade at a soldier coming toward us. She drops a bag at my feet and smirks.

"I thought you could use your weapons," she says as I pick up the bag.

I tear it open to find every piece that Cassien's guards took off me. I grin and thank her. "I don't think I've ever been happier to see anyone."

She huffs a laugh and shakes her head. "Come on, we don't have much time before they get the flames under control." She ushers us away from the post and past the Council building. "We've already got Cass. He should be in the boat by now."

Cael nods and I'm overwhelmed with gratitude.

As we run, soldiers see us, but they're taken out by arrows before they get a chance to call out. I push myself to move as faster through the woods, only slowing when we reach the cabin. Or what remains of it. This entire part of the woods has been burned into a perfect circle of ash. Sorrow pangs in my chest as the image of Elana appears in my mind. The bruises and broken look on her face. I swallow the dread and banish away the thought of her.

Byrne stares at the ashes blankly. I see the tears in her eyes, but not one falls. Cael steps to her side and gently touches her arm. She flinches out of her trance and looks at us, but her focus suddenly moves behind us. I spin around at the same time as my brother and bring the axe up in front of his face.

Soren, Kiro, Deca, and Cass appear from the brush, each holding a bow and almost empty quiver of arrows.

"You owe us now," Kiro says with a grin.

I huff a laugh and nod as Cass runs toward us. He stays stuck to my side, carefully eyeing the three members of Hela's Bond.

"That's all right with us," I tell them gratefully as the strain on my body becomes more and more apparent. *At least Cassien didn't bring out the Ruby Tar,* I think with a shiver.

We head to the boat waiting on the shore and launch it into the waves. We climb in as Cael keeps his eyes trained on Wate, and Kiro and Soren row us back.

"Why aren't they following us?" Cael asks quietly, as if to himself.

Deca grins dangerously, but it's Kiro who answers. "This isn't our first rescue mission, Blood Prince. We know how to keep people off our backs."

A deafening boom sounds from Wate. I grab Cass as Cael and I duck down. Kiro laughs deeply as he watches us, shaking his head.

"What was that?" I ask, watching as birds fly from the trees around Wate and smoke billows into the air.

"An explosion," Deca says calmly.

Cael and I share a confused glance as I let my grip loosen on Cass.

"Emmani is a chemist," Soren states with a proud smile.

Deca straightens and looks out at the water. "She creates weapons using chemicals and powders, like the explosion that just went off. She finds different reactions between the substances and amplifies them so that they create fire that burns longer or a blast so large it can destroy buildings. That's what we just heard, and it will keep them occupied long enough for us to get back."

I nod slowly and take in the trio before me. Somehow, I think we stumbled upon the best allies possible.

"Who taught you to fight?" Kiro asks. "You two look terrible, but by all hells, you took on more than two dozen of them by yourselves. I was so impressed I almost didn't fire any arrows."

Soren smacks the back of his head.

"What did I say?" Kiro exclaims.

"You honestly don't hear what's wrong with what you just said?" Soren deadpans.

"I didn't say anything—"

Kiro's cut off as Deca hits him over the head as well. I smile at the ease in their dynamic. She shakes her head as Soren looks at Cass.

"So, this is the brother you risked it all to save," he says softly. "My name is Soren. This is Kiro, and that's Deca." He points at them each in turn.

When Cass stays quiet, Soren's eyes jump to mine.

"He doesn't speak much," Cael tells Soren as he places a hand on Cass's back.

Soren nods as understanding flashes in his eyes. I turn to face Byrne as I hear fabric ripping from behind me. She smiles and hands Cael and I several long strips of the material.

"You're both bleeding," she says tightly.

My gaze pins on Cael as his eyes scan me. By the Lady, I hadn't even noticed the injuries we'd sustained.

"Thank you," I tell her as she looks back toward the approaching shore.

Cass leans into me as the waves rock us, and in this moment, I don't care about anything else. Nothing matters more than the small boy beside me and that we got him back. He's safe and I can finally breathe.

TWENTY-TWO

ELANA

"Stay still," Emmani mutters as she pats a damp cloth over a cut on my forehead.

I wince but stay put, training my eyes on the floor. I woke up about half an hour ago with only a young boy in the room. He ran out the minute our eyes met, and a woman with a red birthmark covering half her face stalked in with Emmani and the boy on her heels. The woman introduced herself as Red and the boy as Gray. They assured me I was safe. She's been quiet since then, sitting in the corner and moving her hands to communicate with Gray.

"I don't understand why your father would do such a thing to you?"

I grimace as Emmani moves on to another one of my wounds. "Do you have a father, Emmani?"

She huffs a laugh and shrugs easily like a child who's never seen the world outside of her mother's arms. "No, but I have a mother. Soren and I grew up on a ship in the Corsair Isles until we were too old to *safely* live amongst the getics. I never knew my father. My mother never told him about Soren and stopped seeing him altogether after she became pregnant with me.”

“Emmani, give the girl a moment to think,” Red interjects.

Emmani’s cheeks flame as she smiles sheepishly. “Sorry, I get carried away sometimes.”

I nod emotionlessly as she glances back at Red with thin lips.

“You should be glad you’re away from your parents. They can’t hurt you that way,” I say. My throat is so dry.

Emmani stops tending to the injury on my stomach to meet my gaze. Something deep sets into her eyes as her jovial demeanor drops away. She suddenly looks years older.

“You let your hurt dictate how you view the world, Elana. There are good people who live and love every day. Just because you aren’t used to it or haven’t witnessed it doesn’t mean they don’t exist. I love my mother. She is a good woman, and I believe that my father is a good man. I know you’ve been unlucky in the hand the Gods dealt you and I’m sorry you have lived a life that’s led you here, but seeing the world as a reflection of your misfortune will only weigh you down.”

I don’t know what to say. Without skipping a beat, Emmani continues with her work. The braided halo on her forehead casts a strange shadow on her face, making her seem almost inhuman. I blink and shake away the chills running up my back.

“They went to get him, didn’t they?” I ask, finally putting words to the fear that has been floating around in my mind.

Emmani nods stoically. “Deca, Kiro, your sister, and my brother have been gone almost a day now. They left shortly after you passed out again after finding out Leo and Cael had gone back to Wate.”

My heart stutters. It was a trap. I knew it would be. That’s why I never told them about Cass in the first place. I was waiting for the right moment when Cassien let up his guard. I should have fought harder. I should have gone back and stayed with Cass.

The door flies open, and multiple cloaked figures walk through. Within seconds, Byrne is crushing me in a hug.

"How are you feeling?" she asks, scanning me with frantic eyes.

I plaster on the best smile I can muster. "I'm all right. You're not hurt?"

I take my turn looking over her features. She shakes her head as she pulls me into another hug. My blood goes cold at the touch of her skin against mine. I force my hands to wrap around her until she finally pulls away and my breath comes easier. Disgust clouds my brain at the relief that floods through me. She's my sister. I shouldn't feel like I want to pull away. I shouldn't be scared of her touch. She's not Cassien. She would never hurt me. But still, I can't help but relax without her arms trapping me in her embrace.

They lower their hoods, and the two men and the woman I haven't met head toward Red at the back of the room. They speak in hushed voices, but I can barely concentrate on their words as my eyes find Leo's. I bite my tongue to stop the tears as I notice the wounds marring his skin. But more than that, it's the distance in his eyes that splits my soul. For a moment, I catch what seems like worry on his face, but it's gone before I can grasp it. The boy who made me laugh, who listened to me and cared for me, is nowhere to be found. *He's put on his murderer's mask so I won't see him.* I feel nauseous at the thought.

Something shifts by his waist and my mind goes clear as Cass looks at me from behind Leo's legs.

"Hi, Cass," I say, my voice no more than a whisper.

He moves to step toward me, but Leo put his hand on his brother's shoulder, keeping him in place. Cael's gaze flies to Leo as he mutters something only they can hear. Still, Leo doesn't release Cass until Cael grabs his arm and pulls it away. With Cael's encouragement, Cass walks over to me timidly. The gash on his cheek is stark against his pale skin. He takes my outstretched hand and smiles softly.

"Are you all right?" I ask.

He nods before pointing at me.

"Don't worry about me. I'll be just fine. I'm just glad you're okay."

His lip quivers as I place a hand on the side of his face. He glances at Leo before turning back to me with wide, questioning eyes.

I force my lips to turn up. "He's upset with me because I didn't tell him you were alive."

Cass frowns as his head tilts.

"I knew Cassien would be waiting and didn't want you to get hurt. That's all. I swear all I wanted to do was keep you all safe," I plead, looking at Leo.

Leo's indifference feels like a stab to the gut, but Cass nods as if he understands. He covers my hand with his and I can feel his acceptance in the gesture. He's so young, and yet somehow, he's forgiven me.

"Thank you," I whisper.

He squeezes my hand and steps back toward Leo and Cael. I look at the brothers and take in the amount of blood splattered across them.

"How bad did he hurt you?" I ask.

The color instantly leaches from Leo's face. Cael glances Leo's way before placing a steadying hand on his shoulder.

"It was nothing we couldn't handle," Leo says drily, but I hear the edge in his voice.

Kiro shifts closer to us and leans against the wall. "But what did they do to you?"

"Kiro, that's not something—" Emmani starts, but Kiro pushes on.

"No, I want to know. If we're going to make them a part of Hela's Bond, I want to know what they've had to endure. I've heard you've done terrible things and I want to know how much you've *suffered*." He's trying to prove a point, rubbing it in that they saved them. Kiro has no idea what he's asking. He steps closer to Leo and my throat tightens. "We've been neglected. Beaten. Tortured. Scarred and abandoned. What have you been through, Blood Prince? What makes you so special that you can survive being captured, chained, and attacked with your head still intact on your shoulders? What would you do without allies to watch your back? What did you live through to learn how to fight like you did in Wate?"

"That's enough, Kiro," Red intervenes, her voice cold.

Cael shrinks into himself, but beside him, Leo's lost every ounce of humanity. His eyes are dark and he stands deathly still, ready to pounce. Kiro recoils under Leo's stare, suddenly losing his confidence.

"You want to know what we've been through?" Leo asks coldly.

Kiro dips his chin as the room stays silent.

"Where do you want me to start?"

Kiro blinks. "What—what do you mean?"

Leo's lip pulls up in a mechanical movement. "Do you want to know that my mother gave birth to me shackled to a post and was killed minutes after I took my first breath? Or do you want to know that they chained my father up when he came to save her and left me lying in the dirt just out of his reach before slowly bleeding him to death?"

Kiro swallows as the tension in the room rises.

"Do you want to know that I watched my sister hang for flashing her gold eyes in Tominay? Or how the man who took me in as his son was struck through the chest with a blade while I ran away? Or how his wife all but gave up after he was murdered and died while I held her newborn baby in my arms? Perhaps you want to know that I fought in the arenas to earn enough money to feed my family and became so skilled in taking lives that a boss took me under his wing and forced me to become a mercenary by threatening my family's lives? Or maybe that I was shot with eight arrows before being dragged into Wate and used as a test subject for drugs that stripped my ability to bleed my eyes?" Leo's head tilts as his eyes narrow on Kiro. "You may have lived through terror, and I'm sorry you've suffered, but I don't take kindly to people who question my right to live for lack of suffering. If you choose to trust us, then so be it, but we can't be allies if it's only because you think we've endured sufficient hardship."

Everyone stays quiet as Kiro's gaze flies around the room. Red shakes her head, as if to tell him she won't help. This is his mess, and he has to deal with the consequences. Leo leans back, and in the blink of an eye, the color returns to his features and the shadows that had gathered over his face fade away.

"I'm sorry. I didn't mean it that way," Kiro sputters as he averts his eyes.

Leo sighs and nods, clearly exhausted by the conversation. Cael spins his ring as he glances at Leo, something strange flashing in his eyes. It almost looks like... fear.

"It's fine. We're all on edge. Thank you for helping us," Cael says with a genuine smile.

Leo nods softly as he places a protective hand over Cass's shoulder. "You have no idea how much it means to us."

TWENTY-THREE

CAEL

Even though it has been two weeks since Cass was rescued, my body still aches. I wince as I lean back on the couch, shifting beside Antares as he sleeps fitfully against me. He's been as exhausted as the rest of us. We spend nights with Hela's Bond, sneaking out as darkness takes the sky, to visit Cass and Elana. Leo was more than skeptical about leaving Cass there without us, but there's no way to explain to the royals why we were in Wate, never mind why we now have another gold-eyed brother.

We barely got away with making an excuse for why we had all but disappeared for a day. At least Antares had the mind to make up something about us visiting the city. The queen herself had come to scold us about leaving the palace alone. Leo and I burst out laughing the moment she left the room, but the whole thing left a sour taste in my mouth.

Leo walks out from the bedroom with Saiph in his arms,

gently bouncing her up and down as she sleeps on his shoulder.

"Did she finally fall asleep?" I whisper.

He nods, the dark crescents under his eyes accentuated by the orange light of dusk filtering through the window.

"You should sleep again, Leo."

His eyes narrow on me as he tenses. "I slept this morning."

"Five hours isn't enough," I dispute.

He turns his eyes away. He knows I'm right. He was like a ghost when he came out of the terror, as if the nightmare had taken hold of his mind and shaken him awake.

"I'll be fine," he says shakily. "My body isn't tired. That's all that matters."

My eyes narrow on him. Before I can tell him his body is clearly as exhausted as his mind, a knock sounds at the door. Leo's shoulders straighten as he glances toward the hall. Byrne steps out of her room and comes to stand behind the couch as I shift Antares's head off my side. He stirs but doesn't wake, so I pull the blanket over his shoulders. We stand together as I grab hold of the handle and open the door to reveal the queen in a deep yellow gown that almost shines gold. Ceto and Ares, wearing similar colors, are positioned close by her side.

The queen lifts her chin, and we step back to let her in. The door stays open as the trio enters, providing a clear view for the guards. I'm still not used to their presence, but it's easier to accept them when they stay in the hall.

"If you don't mind, I would ask that we keep this conversation quiet," Leo says, still holding Saiph.

The queen nods as her jaw tightens. She clears her throat and looks between the three of us.

"Of course. Children need their sleep." She inhales deeply and straightens her shoulders. "We've received word from our Anateyan delegates that their queen has requested a meeting.

She has specifically asked that we send you as our representative."

"We have discussed what to do about your position here, and since you've made it clear you do not want to take your birthright, Her Majesty thought it would be suitable to make you an ambassador. It would allow you to be in close contact with your Bloodline while also having the solidarity and peace you desire," Ceto continues with a tight-lipped smile. "It is the perfect compromise."

Leo blinks as he stares at them. "You want us to travel to Anateya?"

The queen nods. "You would become the head of our Anateyan Embassy. This position would give you status within the Bloodlines as well as give us a reason to keep you all here. You will also be able to learn the ways of the court and our politics. You will sit in on the court's reports and meetings while in Anateya. We will also have the prior ambassador present to ensure a smooth transition and demonstrate your duties. This first trip will be relatively short, an introduction to the position. Your main objective will be to meet with the queen and to charm her. I hope this is within your abilities."

Leo doesn't have a choice but to accept and we all know it. I doubt he'll be offered another chance if he doesn't agree to this. He fidgets, though I know it's not out of fear of the queen but because we will be leaving Cass again.

"Of course. We would be honored," he says.

She smiles and clasps her hands together. "Good. You will leave tomorrow morning. Ares will join you of course, along with a few Bloodlines who have offered themselves as security for your travels."

"Who?" I ask, not catching myself fast enough to stop the word from spewing from my mouth.

Leo glares at me, but the queen doesn't notice the slip.

"Emrys Ceruleen, Demia Alinsky, Enoha Kalu, and Kaja Damaris will be joining you as your... personal entourage. Each has previously traveled to Anateya at least once. They will be there for your protection as well as anything else you may need."

And to keep you in line, is what she doesn't say. My heart skips a beat and I feel Leo's eyes on me as I try to nod casually.

"And I assume we'll all be going?" Leo says, dragging the trio's attention away from me.

The queen's eyes wander to Saiph sleeping on his shoulder. "Of course. I had doubted your cooperation if we had suggested sending you alone."

Leo looks pasts her with a mock-smile and nods. "We'll be ready by tomorrow."

"... then I ran into their father and that's how our family ended up together," I tell Hela's Bond and the Cassien sisters as we sit scattered around the living room of their quarters.

Cass, Gray, and Antares sit in the corner, engrossed in their own conversation, somehow communicating though they all speak different languages. We've been here for just over an hour now. It was hard to break the news of our leaving to Elana and Cass, but as the shock and fear faded, stories of all sorts flowed through the room, easing the tension. Cass is the most averse to the idea of us leaving without him, and though I don't feel great about the idea either, I know he'll be safe with Elana. She cares for him deeply and would give her life for him. It's the only thing allowing my conscience to consider going to Anateya at all.

"Well, that's one hell of a sob story," Kiro says from across the room as he leans against the wall. He grins at us and pulls back his shoulders. "But let me get this straight, your first name is Cael and the one random family you ran into had the last name Hael? So you coincidentally got the name Cael Hael?"

Leo tries to hold in his laugh beside me, failing miserably. I shove him with enough strength that his chair rocks sideways. He barely manages to catch himself before he tumbles to the floor. I take great satisfaction from his glare.

"It just proves it was meant to be," Leo says as he rights himself with a grin.

Saiph saves him from being tossed aside again as she wanders over and sits at his feet with her doll. Now he knows he's immune and it only makes his smile grow wider.

"Anyways, even though that's one hell of a story, I bet I can beat it," Kiro challenges.

Leo leans forward in his seat and rests his elbows on his knees. "Oh yeah? Try us."

"My mother was an addict, strung out my entire childhood. I lived in a few boxes tied together with rope until I was ten. I was fighting off deadbeats and Bloodlines while my ma was passed out in some alley or another. I had to keep her fed before I was even old enough to know what the stuff she was injecting into her veins was called."

"How'd you get out?" I ask, my head tilted.

Kiro smirks before leaning back on the wall. "Red. She and Gray had just gotten out of their own hell and bought this place. I was the first of our group she picked up and took in." Kiro looks at her gratefully.

Red stands in the doorway, pride shining in her eyes as she watches him. She built their family, and by the Lady, she did a good job.

"What happened to your mother?" Elana asks.

Leo's gaze flickers to her briefly, the pain clear on his face.

Kiro huffs a laugh before glancing at where Deca sits braiding Emmani's hair.

"When I never came back, some motherly instinct finally kicked in. She got off the drugs and got a job. She rented a room a few streets over and came to find me. It took us a while to reconnect, but we're good now. She knew I was happy here and never pushed me to live with her again, but I see her a few times a week. She'll most likely barge in while you're all here at some point."

"Gods, I love your mother. She's such a sweet woman," Emmani gushes as she meets Deca's eyes. The corner of Deca's lip kicks up as Emmani looks at us.

"She loves you two more than she loves me." Kiro pouts. "She always gives you all the good food."

We all laugh at his childish tone as Soren waves his arm through the air from where he sits on the couch.

"Poor you, with a mother that brings over homemade meals and coddles you like a child," Soren mocks.

"Like your mother doesn't drop off a chest of coins for each of you every time her ship docks," Kiro says defensively, though a laugh runs through his words.

When everyone settles, Byrne turns to Red. "What's your story?"

Everyone stills as if the air was stolen from the room. We've all gone through our life stories and Red is the only one left, but from the way she carries herself, I thought her story was one we'd have to fill in with our imaginations. Apparently, Byrne hadn't interpreted it that way.

For a moment, nothing happens. No one speaks. No one moves. Not even a breath can be heard as Red's face grows stoic. Just as I start to think of ways to break the silence, Red's gravelly voice cuts through the air.

"I was born a Bloodline. Second in line to my family's

throne. I had five siblings, including Gray, which meant fighting with everything I had to get to the top. No matter if those you're cutting down are your own siblings. I was born with this," she says confidently, gesturing to the wine-colored mark covering a large portion of her face, "and it made me a target. I was the runt, the mutant, the disappointment. Once my siblings tied me up and tried to cut the mark out of my skin. They were caught before they could skin me, but they never faced more than a harsh word from my father."

Leo's face pales as his fingers drift to the numbers on his wrist and the scars surrounding them.

"When Gray was born, they barely cared. They tossed him to me without a thought. Until he proved he could be something amazing, they wouldn't look at him twice." Gray's watching her from the corner, but Red doesn't lift a hand to sign. "He was the quietest child I'd ever seen. When the doctors examined him, they told my parents that he had profound hearing loss and may be completely deaf." She huffs a short laugh as something manic passes through her eyes. "They told me to bring him to the Riv and dump him for the rats."

The entire room holds their breath, visibly reeling from her anger.

"That night, I took him and stole the most valuable pieces from my parents' prized jewel collections. Then I went to my eldest sister's room, tied her up, and repaid the debt I owed her. I walked out of the house with Gray and we haven't been back since."

I swallow, remembering the brutal scar I saw on one of the women at the royal dinner. *She did that.* As I look at Leo, there's something calming about his expression. His complete attention is on Red, captivated by the story. *He understands her because he would have done the exact same thing.* I swallow the dread clogging my throat and look at Saiph. *Maybe he already has.*

ELANA'S EYES track Leo as he disappears to help Soren and Kiro get more food from the pantry after the boys started whining about being hungry. Even Gray joined in, teaming up to make an unbeatable force. I lift Saiph off my lap and hand her to Byrne, then I move toward Elana. She watches me skeptically as I drop down to the floor beside her. No one pays us any heed, deep in their own conversations.

"You care for him, don't you?" I ask Elana, keeping my voice low so only she can hear.

"I don't know what you're talking about," she says, her voice breaking.

I smile at my hands as I take in a deep breath. "I can see it in your eyes, in the way you look at him. It might not be obvious to everyone else, but I can tell."

Her eyes meet mine cautiously and I swear I see her lip quiver.

"And if I did? What would you do?"

I take a moment to think about it. I hadn't really considered what I would say to her before I came over here. She's been stealing glances at my brother all night, sorrow painted on her face. I was so mad she kept Cass's survival a secret, but I can't find that anger anymore.

"I would tell you that I'd never say anything about this conversation to him. And that I'm here to listen if you want to talk," I reassure her.

She relaxes slightly and meets my eyes. There's a storm brewing behind hers. "He won't look at me. I know what I did wasn't right. I know that. But I've tried to apologize. I've tried to stay away. But he barely looks at me."

I nod and spin my ring around my finger. "I understand why you did it. I may have been upset earlier, just like Leo, but I know why you didn't tell us. We almost got ourselves into a situation with no solution because we didn't listen to you. In that way, you were right to keep it from us."

She swallows and closes her eyes as she hangs her head and pulls her knees up to her chest.

"But what you need to understand is that Leo trusted you more than he realized. You broke through every one of his defenses and he trusted you so completely that when you kept Cass from him, when you stayed in Wate, you stabbed him where he was most vulnerable." I take a breath as she raises her glistening eyes to mine. "He let himself trust you and that terrifies him. He's been hurt more times than you can imagine, in every way a man can be tortured. His trust is the only thing he has left."

"So what do I do to get him to trust me again? How can I fix it?" she pleads.

"Just give him time to work through it. He needs to heal. I can't guarantee that when he does, he'll trust you again, so all you can do is be there for him."

She smiles softly and dips her chin. "Thank you, Cael. For all of it."

I can see everything she means in her expression—for coming over... for forgiving her... for being willing to trust her again. I never thought I would meet someone who would understand Leo the way I do, but here Elana sits. For some reason, I feel as though she knows him better than anyone. For a moment, I see him reflected in her eyes and I can't decide if I should be happy or terrified.

TWENTY-FOUR

LEO

The horse makes my back ache with every minute that passes. None of my siblings have ever ridden on horseback before, but when they were presented to us the morning we left, we had no choice but to jump on and hope for the best. It was difficult at first, but with some instruction and a few days of practice, we got the hang of it. I have Antares with me while Cael is holding Saiph. Altair rides alone beside us. As it turns out, Byrne already knew how to ride. She explained it was a mandatory skill taught at the Academy. Cael and I couldn't help but scowl at her words.

We've been traveling through the mountains to get to Enzly for four days now. Though it's not the capital, Enzly is one of Anateya's oldest cities and home to one of the queen's palaces. I'm not bothered in the slightest about not being able to see Terechnova, Anateya's grand capital city, since I can't bring myself to be away from Cass for more than a few days. We're traveling through miles of wide, winding tunnels that were carved through the mountains centuries ago. Emrys explained that these tunnels date back to a time before the Death Dancers and no one really knows how deep they go.

Being that we're riding in the dark, we also learned about Emrys's... interesting Bloodline and their ability. While the Matteuses can heal extremely fast, the Ceruleen line can... glow. When we entered the caverns, Emrys pulled up his sleeves and lifted his hands, casting bright greenish-blue light throughout the cavern. Emrys explained that his Bloodline has DNA that allows their cells to become bioluminescent whenever they call upon it. He explained that we all emit light on some level, but his family's is magnified to a strength that allows the human eye to detect it.

Since then, he has guided our way, allowing us all to see— and more importantly, keeping Cael from losing his mind. Even though we stay close to Emrys, I can tell Cael is uneasy. He only sleeps intermittently when we stop to feed and water the horses in the narrow streams that follow our path and flow toward Illena. Whoever built these caves planned them out with incredible ingenuity.

"There's light ahead, we're almost out," the scarred Alinsky girl announces.

My stomach twists when I hear her voice, knowing what she did to Red. I've never seen a lick of empathy or emotion in her expression. My attention shifts to the previous ambassador, who is openly glaring at me, something he's been doing a lot. He doesn't seem so happy that I took his position, though I can't figure out why. Instead of Anateya, he'll be working on relations with the Corsair Isles, an equal trade with far less travel, so there must be something I'm missing.

We finally exit the tunnels and I feel as if I haven't taken a breath of fresh air in years. I close my eyes and inhale, noticing the crisp smell of autumn and the sound of rushing wind and chirping birds.

"This is incredible," Cael says as he pulls his horse up beside mine.

When I open my eyes and look over the horizon, I observe the details completely unlike Illena and Tominay. The trees are all evergreens with navy needles hanging from long branches, and in the distance stands several stone pillars towering over them all.

"Let's keep moving," one of the guides calls from ahead of us.

We follow, taking a narrow path through the woods. My lips curl into the beginning of a smile as I take a deep breath and let myself sink into the sound of the hooves hitting the soft earth.

"You look happy," Cael says from my right.

I look over at him while keeping my arms tight around Antares as he sleeps against me.

"It's been a while since you've smiled like that."

I hang my head and sigh, knowing he's right. I've been in a mood for days. "Sorry. My mind's been... occupied."

He straightens as his brows raise. "With Elana?"

My head snaps toward him as he grins. "I don't want to talk about her."

"But maybe you should..."

I grind my teeth together as anger rises in my gut. "We're not doing this right now," I snap, my words like a sword swinging the final blow.

"Yes, we are," he pushes.

"Cael—"

"No," he catches me off guard with the harshness in his voice. "We're going to do this now because if I let you put this off any longer, you'll never face it." His face is hard as he stares, daring me to contradict him.

"Fine. But what do you want me to say? She betrayed us, Cael. After everything we did for her, she *lied* to me for *months.*" I try desperately to control my anger. "I don't know what you want me to say. I can't forgive her if I can't look at her, and right now, every time her face crosses my mind, I want to light something on fire." My hands are shaking as I grip the reins.

"You're angry because you're scared," he says matter-of-factly.

I still as I consider his words. "No."

Cael shakes his head and looks forward. "You like her, Leo. And you trust her."

I don't respond as his words reverberate in my mind.

"I think you still trust her even after she lied, but you don't understand why."

The air rips from my lungs.

Cael takes a deep breath. "Whether you believe it or not, the reason Elana let us think Cass was dead makes sense. She was trying to protect you. To protect us. She knew it was a trap and that we would run in blindly if we knew he was alive. And we did exactly that."

My heart beats too hard as the world around me blurs.

"Something in me will always feel betrayed by what she did," he admits, "but I understand why she did it." I meet his eyes as his face softens. "I can forgive her for that much."

I can't pinpoint what it means, but I want to recoil into my own skin. I close my eyes and Elana's face appears in my mind. She's smiling like she did when we ate sugar tarts in the cabin and her eyes sparkle as they did every time I met her on the shore. It seems like so long ago now. As the last remnants of my anger fizzles out, all I feel is loss. A gaping pit inside me. Fear forces my eyes open, and I swallow as I look back at Cael.

"I'll try. I need time, but I'll try," I tell him.

He tilts his head and smiles softly. "Good."

I speak the thought that pops into my mind before I have a chance to think better of it. "Why do you care so much if I forgive her?"

Cael huffs a laugh as he wraps his arms tighter around Saiph. She's been staring at the trees since we came out of the caves, reaching her arms up as if she could grab a fistful of the pine needles.

"You know, for a long time before we met Elana, I hadn't seen you smile. A real smile. But you looked at her and one day you seemed... peaceful." He grabs a blue pinecone off a low-hanging branch and hands it to Saiph. "I think you did the same for her too. Made her smile like she hadn't in years."

Elana's smile reappears in my thoughts, and this time, that sadness wears away.

Cael looks at me with nothing but honesty in his face. "I don't care what you are to each other or even if you decide not to forgive her. I don't care if you're friends or something else, but I think you need to find closure. The two of you understand each other, and I want you to be able to spend time with a person who reflects you like that."

For a moment, his words are the only thing that matter. I know he's right, but I'm still skeptical. I wasn't lying when I told him I would try to rebuild the unstable bridge Elana and I started to cross. I'll try to make things right with her. I look at the trees as we near the city and realize that for some unthinkable reason, that thought doesn't terrify me.

TWENTY-FIVE

LEO

The gates around Enzly shine a deep blue that matches the thick pine trees from which we've just emerged. I shake Antares awake and he barely has the chance to complain before the words are stolen by the sight before him. Archers stand at attention at the top of the wall, bows slung over their shoulders. I feel their eyes on me as the dark metal gates slide open, allowing us through. Soldiers with stoic faces and clad in blue wear bronze helmets so low their eyes are almost completely concealed. They hold their positions unflinchingly as we move into the city.

There's too much around to take in all at once. Blue and silver banners hang from houses and businesses, every building unique in its frame and material. Pine trees of all sizes decorate the streets. Each one is covered in silver strings glistening in the sunlight.

As we head deeper into the city, people amass in the streets. Children stop to stare as the adults set down their tasks, each wiping away the flour, and dirt, and clay, and paint from their hands. They smile at us as they touch the fingers of their right hands to their foreheads. During our travels, Ceto taught us about the sign of respect the Anateyans use as a greeting. Seeing so many people greet you in such a way instead of treating you as a threat with fear in their eyes is surreal.

There are no walls around the palace. Tall gray-blue stone pillars are scattered around the grounds and stretch up high enough to bite the clouds. We stop before the garden leading up to the front steps and dismount our horses. A stable hand arrives to grab the reins, allowing me to clumsily slide off my horse. I hold out my arms and help Antares down. He stands on the ground for barely a second before his legs give out and he's lying on his back.

"Leave me," he says dramatically as he throws his arm over his face. "I'm done for."

I huff a laugh as I pull him up and set my brother back on his feet. "How will you meet the queen if you're lying on the ground?" I take Saiph from Cael's arms, allowing him to dismount as Altair joins us.

"I don't think I'll be able to walk up the steps to meet her," Cael says with a wince as he rubs his back.

"I doubt they'll let us in smelling like horse," Byrne adds with a grin.

Cael and I laugh as we pull our belongings out of the saddlebags.

"What are you doing?" Ares demands as he rounds the horse.

My brows scrunch together as my hands hold the bag. "What do you mean?"

"Why are you opening the saddlebag?"

Cael and I exchange confused glances as I shift my arms to hold Saiph against my hip.

"To get our belongings," Cael replies, stating the obvious. "Why else would we open the bags?"

Ares scoffs as if it's a joke, looking at us for a reaction. When he realizes we're serious, he says, "The embassy will gather our belongings. We are Bloodlines, cousin. We have more important things to do than to carry our own bags."

I want to laugh, but the seriousness on his face stops me. I catch the other Bloodlines sneering as if we'd been about to commit a crime. "We're all going to the same place—"

Ares interrupts me. "You're the Crown Prince of Illena, Leo. With your position comes tradition and expectations. I'm only trying to help you when I say leave the bags to the others." He glances at the Bloodlines behind him.

I take them in, noting the sharp eyes tracking my every movement as they wait to see what I do next. *This trip is a test to see how you hold up against them,* Ceto had said in the tunnels. *You have to play along to earn their respect. You must calculate your every move or they'll rip you apart.* I nod to Ares and step away.

"Of course. I'm still getting used to my bloodright," I tell him, the words tasting foul.

Ares smiles reassuringly and walks toward the palace. "Then shall we head inside?"

We follow close behind him with the rest of the Bloodlines on our heels. I feel the stares of the rest of the embassy burning into my back as we walk away, leaving them to deal with the horses and our luggage. Workers sporting navy bear crests swarm in to help.

The garden itself is like nothing I've seen before. Only manicured in a way to keep it tidy, it's as if it was left to grow by its own means. There's a wild feel to the place. Something you only get when you're walking so deep in the woods, humanity seems to fade away. The air smells like fresh spring.

The wide doors are pulled open by soldiers. Ceto steps up to the front of the group as I stop, frozen by the sight of the woman standing before us. Queen Aerya of Anateya. The queen of snow and spies. She smiles as she steps away from her entourage. Ceto touches his fingers to his forehead before taking the queen's hand.

"How happy I am to see you again, Your Majesty. It's been far too long," he greets her with reverence.

She squeezes his hands and dips her chin. "Indeed. I should have called upon you long ago, my friend. You are well?"

"Still busy as ever." He smiles fondly as he steps back and gestures for me to step forward.

I glance at Cael before doing so. I feel Ares's eyes burning the back of my head as I stand before the queen. Something in her expression flickers as she looks me up and down.

"So, this is the famed Blood Prince," she says, leaning closer to Ceto as if she were sharing a secret.

"It is. May I introduce you to His Royal Highness Leo Matteus, Dirix's son and the Crown Prince of Illena." My skin prickles at the title, but no one else reacts as Ceto continues without skipping a beat. "Those behind him are his siblings."

The queen's eyes narrow as she scans us. "They are not related."

"Not by blood, no," I explain.

Her head tilts as the group goes quiet. Slowly, a smile blooms over her face.

"You know, Ceto, it has been quite a while since I spoke to someone who was not trained in the customs of court— outside of when I take concerns from the people of course, but they tend to be either nervous or reverent." I hold my breath as her eyes bore into mine. "It's refreshing, in a way, to meet someone so undeterred by power. Both mine and his own."

Instantly I understand why Ceto is fond of the queen. She seems... human. Though the lines in her face hint at a harsher side, the fact that she allows herself to smile is a nice change for me as well.

***

"So, what are your thoughts on Anateya so far?" Ares asks as he straightens the collar of his coat.

We had the grand tour about an hour ago, seeing everything from the wide halls of the palace to the city surrounding it. Though the queen didn't join us for the tour, her guide explained that the eastern side of Anateya was left practically untouched by the Great War because of the towering mountains that safeguarded it. Though there were tunnels, the Anateyans were easily able to block them, stopping the Death Dancers from infiltrating.

The ancient Gods still worshipped today can be found carved into walls and weaved into tapestries throughout the city. Candles burn on windowsills for the Goddess of the Air, doors are painted blue for the God of the Water, and stars are carved above doorways for the God of Night and Day. It's remarkable that these people have managed to maintain their old traditions. Even the greeting they use dates back to a time before the war. It is meant to show the person's true respect for who they show it to.

Sadness tangles inside me as I think of Tominay and the cities whose histories were lost or erased. Tominay had once been prosperous, but the Death Dancers not only burnt the buildings, but the people and their ancient culture along with them.

"It's a wonder," I tell Ares.

I pull Antares forward and set to fixing the buttons of his shirt, which he has somehow managed to fit into all the wrong holes. He groans as I fiddle with the hem and straighten his sleeves. My younger brother rolls his eyes when I tell him to stay still.

"When did you become so picky?" I ask Antares as I smooth the fabric.

"When we forced him to leave his old comfortable shirt in Arkezo," Cael says as he sits beside me on the velvet upholstered divan, still holding Saiph. He sets her down and she grabs at Antares, begging him to play.

"We'll be back soon enough," Ares says with a smile as he takes a seat across from us.

He cracks his knuckles as Byrne comes over with Emrys and Kaja. The rest of the congregation has taken up the space on the other side of the room, speaking in hushed tones as they periodically glance our way. Our rooms are all connected to this parlor, each branching off from three different halls. One is designated for Cael, Byrne, Saiph, the boys, and me, another for the Bloodlines, and the last for the rest of the embassy.

"So, you've all been here before?" Cael asks Ares as Kaja, Byrne, and Emrys find their seats.

Cael's eyes follow Kaja as she steps up beside him and sits while the others give her a wide berth. There's something of a challenge in her eyes as they stare at each other, but Cael only smiles.

"Yes, though I've only been once. Kaja and Emrys, on the other hand, have visited several times," Ares explains as he leans back and crosses his arms.

"You have?" Cael asks, turning to Kaja.

Her chin dips in a nod. "For security purposes. And perhaps

to show our nation's... superiority. The power we wield should Anateya ever decide to end their treaty with us."

Emrys holds his breath as Kaja stares at Ares. He tilts his head as the corner of his lips kicks up at the accusation. Ares is a Matteus and the brother of the queen. He would be the one to have knowledge of such things. Maybe he even suggested it.

"Perhaps," is all he says.

A loud knock rings through the room and all heads turn toward the door. One of the members of the embassy rises and opens it without hesitation. A tall steward clad in a navy uniform stands with his hands tucked behind his back, waiting to deliver a message.

"Your Highness, Her Majesty would like to see you in her drawing room," he announces.

His lilting accent reminds me of someone, but I can't quite place who. Their face floats at the back of my mind as I spot the silver bracelets around his wrist. Ares fixes his coat and starts toward him. The steward's eyes thin.

"Her Majesty would like to see the Crown Prince," he amends with a raised brow. "Without the entourage."

For the first time, I catch Ares stutter in his movements. His hands still as he blinks. "Of course. I only wish to accompany His Highness to provide guidance."

His attempt to cover his misstep is believable, but I see the muscle feather by his jaw. The steward looks at me expectantly.

"Can my family join me?" I ask.

His lip pulls into the beginning of a smile. Ares's eyes bore into me at the question. We all know I wasn't asking about him.

"As you wish," the steward responds. "The queen did mention she thought you may make such a request."

I nod in thanks and stand with Cael. I pick up Saiph as Altair pads into the room.

"I want to stay," Altair announces.

Cael and I turn to him. I glance at the embassy members as they hungrily watch our exchange. Altair walks toward us and takes the seat I vacated. Ares watches him carefully as he sits, tracking his every move.

"Are you sure?" Cael asks him worriedly.

For a moment, Altair stays quiet as if he's made the decision without really thinking about it.

"You can if you want to, we won't force you to do anything," Cael adds.

Altair glances at the other end of the room, then at the steward still waiting at the door.

"I want to stay," he repeats, though without as much certainty.

"I'll stay as well," Byrne announces.

I smile gratefully at her as Altair lets himself sink deeper into the couch.

"What about you Antares?" I ask.

He glues himself to my side as he fidgets with his shirt. "I'm coming."

I smile and place a comforting hand on his shoulder. "Then let's go see the queen."

GUARDS LINE the hall as we enter the drawing room. The queen's eyes raise to us.

"Please, sit," she says as the doors shut behind us.

Saiph squirms in my arms as Antares, Cael, and I sit across from her. The room is ornately decorated in blue and gold detailing, paintings and tapestries hung on every wall. On the periphery are shelves filled with books that look older than the walls around them and display tables holding swords and crowns.

My gaze snags on one particular item at the far end of the room, and the world around me goes fuzzy. It's a black blade with runes pressed into its flat. My ears ring as I stare at it. The darkness of the metal seems to consume the light around it.

"Leo."

The blade fades out of my gaze and the room around me comes crashing back. Cael's face is in front of mine, his brows furrowed with worry. Saiph whines in my arms as I blink.

"You all right?" Cael whispers.

I nod and shake away the confusion. "Yeah. Yes, sorry."

The queen walks toward us. "You find that blade interesting, Blood Prince?" She stops beside me and stares at the weapon. "That is the Ash Sword."

My mouth goes dry as I bounce slightly, instinctively trying to calm Saiph.

"Like the Ash Sword from the stories?" Antares asks, standing behind us.

The queen smiles down at him and nods. "Exactly that, my boy. It is said that Lady Death forged this blade on the beach of Arkezo from the ashes of the fallen and quenched it in a vat of blood. Blood from which your kind was created. The process turned not only the blade the darkest shade of night, but the sands surrounding it as well."

"I've seen the beach," Antares says with wonder in his eyes.

"It's quite amazing, isn't it? Legend has it her Bloodline is called to the blade. And that the one who wields it is bound to be a great ruler... or the ultimate destroyer." Her eyes land on me.

Cael pulls her attention away. "How did it come to be in your possession if it has so many historical ties to Illena?"

The queen motions for us to follow her lead and return to our seats. "After the war, the other three countries wanted to destroy Illena. They feared what the people could do if they became dissatisfied, and rightfully so. But the Illeneans had led the turning tide in the war. They'd liberated themselves and then western Anateya. They rallied forces in the south, and after a long and hard push, crushed the Death Dancers. The other countries refused to hear them out even after everything your ancestors had sacrificed and suffered to free them. My aunt of many generations ago knew of this injustice and convinced the other nations to give Illena a chance to live in peace. Though there were stipulations in place, all your people wanted was to live free of cages and my aunt gave them that gift. In a show of good faith and to assure future relations, the first Illenean Queen gave my aunt the Ash Sword for safekeeping, and it has been here ever since."

I look at the blade and my mind stumbles. A shiver slips down my spine as I pull my eyes away. All I want to do is take it in my hand, but something in my mind screams for me to stay away. I force myself to focus on the queen.

"Why did you call us here?" I ask, my breath slightly wheezing.

Emotion washes over her face. "I wanted to learn what type of person you had become and see if they had ever told you about us."

I blink.

"Who do you mean?" Cael asks.

"Your parents."

The breath is ripped from my lungs. "My parents died shortly after I was born."

"No, not those parents. I had been informed they died soon after your birth, and I am sorry for your loss. I told you that a long time ago, but you were far too young to understand or remember," she says tenderly, her hands folding together on the front of her gown.

My heart is pounding.

"What are you implying?" Cael asks, voicing the question bouncing around in my mind.

The queen's lips tilt up, as if reliving a happy memory. Her light crystal eyes meet mine, and for a moment, I feel the pain I see in her face reflected in my soul.

"I knew your birth father, long ago. The prince grew up here. The former king, your grandfather, had worked so very hard to secure and strengthen foreign ties with Anateya and the Corsair Isles, so he wanted Dirix to be well-versed in foreign politics. He spent six months of every school year in our palace, learning alongside my children. I cared for him like one of my own." She takes a moment to breathe as a frown pulls at her face. "It was barely three months after the last time I saw him when I received the letter carried by a haggard messenger. He said the Prince had ordered him to deliver it straight to my hands without ever touching another soul's skin."

I hold Saiph tighter as the queen pulls out a yellowed piece of paper and hands it to me. The creases are as smooth as the paper itself, as if it had been opened and refolded many times. I stare at the folded letter, unable to read it.

"He wrote to tell me that something had happened, and he was afraid a dear friend was in danger. He asked me to offer her refuge in Anateya if he was unable to solve his issues in Illena."

Cael slides closer to my side, but I can't stop staring at the letter. My father wrote this. How is it possible that I had four parents, and now all I have left is a pile of papers? Ink-stained pages that somehow hold the power to rip through me with every word.

"I sent out a runner with a reply immediately," she continues, her voice barely over a whisper. "But that letter was returned to me. When I asked my people in Arkezo where he was, I was told Dirix had not been seen in days. I could only assume the worst, so I dispatched every soldier I had to search for him. It was months later, when the parents who raised you appeared at our gates, that I found out what happened to them."

Silence hangs thick in the air as we realize our parents had been here... with me.

"I... I've been here before?" I ask, the question feeling foreign in my mouth.

"You spent a year here, in fact. Your mother was pregnant with your sister when they arrived with you. They had been hiding in the woods, but your father knew how dangerous it might be to deliver a child by themselves with no medical supplies or clean water. And you... you were so frail. I don't think I'd ever seen a baby so small. That was the reason they came to Anateya. Your parents knew they would receive no help if they went to Tominay," she explains sadly.

I shake my head as my thoughts race. "But I've never been sick. I can go days without food, water, or sleep and barely feel the repercussions."

The queen breathes a laugh and leans back. "Maybe now, but when they showed up at the gates, I thought you had been born days before, never mind six months earlier. When I found out who you were, we provided every treatment we could, but you refused to eat. And you were always so... quiet. We thought that it could be caused by the grief of losing your parents. We did everything we could, but nothing worked. Your adoptive mother knew how grave the situation was and spent as much time with you as she could, walking from room to room around the palace. When you passed by this room, you wailed like a baby with strong, healthy lungs." Her gaze flickers over to where the sword stands before returning to me. "When we tried to take you back outside, you went silent once more, so here you stayed for months. In this room is where you finally grew. You took your first steps and said your first word here, you know."

"What was it?" I ask as my throat tightens.

She smiles softly. "Mine."

"Mine?" Cael repeats as his brows knit together.

She nods. "You looked up at the Ash Sword and said it. It was as if you were connected to it, though as some stories go, the Bloodlines were created from the Child whose blood it was quenched with, so we always pinned it to that. I guess you never outgrew the connection."

"What child?" Antares asks, nearly entirely hidden behind Cael.

"You do not know of the Child?"

We shake our heads in unison as a familiarity sparks in my mind, though I have no idea why. The queen blows out a long breath before pinching the bridge of her nose.

"I guess it makes sense that they would erase that specific part of your history." She sits straight again, resuming the picture of regal posture. My mind stutters at the blip in her countenance. "Long ago, when the Death Dancers dug the tunnels through the mountains, they discovered a cavern laden with ancient drawings and symbols. At the very center, they came upon a large pile of black bones, ancient artifacts from the precipice of the world itself. The mountains roared when the Death Dancers stole the bones, and many of the tunnels collapsed on the thieves. There was only one survivor who fled, managing to salvage a single bone. She was later found floating in Arkezo's bay, her flesh waterlogged and eyes eaten by the fish.

"The bone still found its way to a laboratory, and from that sliver of a creature that existed so long ago, they decoded the DNA and created a child. Though the Child looked human, its body grew twenty times slower and its mind was already thousands of years old. It had a body that could heal, and it wouldn't sleep or eat for days while remaining in perfect health. It held all the powers of the Bloodlines combined: bioluminescence, holding its breath under the waves for hours, seeing and hearing like no other, and most interestingly, connecting neurologically to any living thing it touched. When it breathed, it was said that the land breathed with it.

"They kept it in a lab for over a century before the war, dissecting the poor thing to shreds while it sat strapped to a table, day after day. When the war came around, the Death Dancers pulled apart its genetic code and implanted it into the prisoners whose genetics they'd already been changing, creating weapons of war. Each Bloodline received a trait from the Child, like your ability to heal yourself and that of your blood to heal others."

"What happened to the Child?" The air feels thick in my lungs as my thoughts latch onto every smooth-spoken word uttered by the queen.

"When the first of your people were escaping the laboratory where they were held, they found the Child. It was nothing like anything they'd ever encountered. It had the presence of something that should not exist in our world. When they decided to leave it behind, the Child looked at the first Matteus and asked her to put an end to its misery."

"So they set it on fire and watched as its flesh melted to ash." My voice startles me out of the trance the story had put me in.

The queen swallows and nods, her eyes thinning as she watches me. "Exactly."

I feel Cael's eyes piercing the side of my head, but my gaze wanders back to the sword behind the queen. I need to get out of this room. I need to get away from that sword.

"I think we should go," I say as I run a hand through my hair, but the queen makes no move to stand.

She tilts her head before her eyes slide to Cael. "I think your brother still has questions."

I look at Cael and see what she means. His face is blank as he nods skeptically.

"You said his blood could heal?" he asks. "We knew it could heal him, but it can help others as well?"

"Ah yes. Matteus blood not only heals you but can protect others from infection and speed up recovery should they be wounded. Some say it's even powerful enough to bring souls back to life if they are teetering on the edge of death. It works best if it's delivered directly into another's circulatory system, but if your blood is potent enough, it could even have healing effects if you cut your hand and placed it on an open wound."

"So, you're saying my blood is... magical?" I say, dumbfounded.

The queen laughs and shakes her head. "Perhaps in a sense. But there is a more concrete explanation in your genetics and the healing cells found in your blood. Though, I'm sorry to say, I don't know enough detail to explain anything of that level."

I nod absentmindedly, ready to cut the conversation and ponder over everything she's said, but a thought suddenly takes over my mind. "Why did my parents leave? If you housed them and healed me, why would they take us to a country where we were hunted and killed for our lineage?"

The queen sighs as her jaw works. It's as if she's trying to fit together the right words and that look alone makes my stomach flip.

"When your parents first arrived, they asked me to swear

to keep their stay a secret. They knew if the Illeneans found you, they would have killed you and declared a civil war on the gold-eyed people. It would have been a slaughter, so they tried to keep you hidden. After your sister was born, the king and queen of Illena sent people to come looking for Dirix, thinking he may have come here. They ravaged the palace in their search even after I assured them I had not seen Dirix in some while. It was enough of a pretense to start a war, but what bothered me more was that your parents were gone when I came to survey the damage. They'd left a note declaring their gratitude and apologies for having created such strife within the city. The only reason we did not retaliate was for fear of what a war would do to our people. Anateyans are a peaceful population, and I would not disrupt this to give you safe haven."

There's clear sorrow in her eyes as she looks at me, then scans Cael and Antares. "I am sorry about the loss of your sister as well. Even though I could not allow you back here, I sent many a spy to watch over your family. They tried to save her that day but couldn't get to her in time."

Confusion and sorrow scream in my chest as my breathing goes shallow. I hear the door open behind us and swivel my head. The air whisks from my lungs as two old, weathered faces appear. Tears well in my eyes as I take them in.

"Ah, yes. These two are the best of my spies, and they've been keeping an eye on you for quite some time. I think you know them well."

"I... I don't understand," I stutter as my head spins.

Right in front of me stands Mrs. Ortaga. She hasn't changed since I last saw her, dressed in a deep blue dress with silver bracelets that clink on her wrists. Doc stands beside her with a gentle smile. He told me people would soon rely on me, and I could never have imagined all the ways he was right.

"Have all my teachings really gone so quickly from your head, boy?" Mrs. Ortaga says with that too-familiar accent.

All at once, the pieces fit together. Her lilt is the same as the queen's, though I never put it together because her years in Tominay must have influenced her speech.

"Of course not," I say, feeling winded. A smile pulls at my face as I stand.

She comes toward me and takes my hand.

"You gave me too much homework to forget," I tell her.

She laughs wholeheartedly as she always has. Her hair is more silver than I remember, but she's still the same woman who helped me every time I felt lost. She saved my family from starving more than once. She gave me hope when I was so sure there was nothing left for us, and now she's in Anateya, her home country.

"Does that mean you both knew I was a prince this whole time?" I ask as Cael and Antares stand by my side.

Doc nods, and Mrs. Ortaga flashes a daring grin.

"Do you think the people called you the Blood Prince at random?" She winks as my mouth falls open.

My title was mine for years before I knew about Illena, and I never considered the reason. I always thought it was a coincidence. "You spread that title?"

She nods proudly, as if I were asking her about a grand accomplishment. I can't help but laugh as I look at Cael.

"Everything connects, doesn't it?" Cael says to me as the corner of his lips kicks up.

I smile as I look at the people who've been watching over me since infancy. "That it does."

TWENTY-SIX

ELANA

"Would you two stop bickering?" Soren says as he rubs his temple.

Emmani and Kiro have been arguing about Goddess knows what for over an hour. Cass left with Gray as soon as they came in the door, escaping to the roof. They've become close in the past few weeks since we arrived. They seem to understand each other's silence in a way no one else can. Cass has even taken up signing, and though I've learned a few signs from watching them all speak and translate, I still get lost in the quick, agile movements of their hands.

"Only if Kiro admits he's wrong," Emmani presses.

Kiro puffs up his chest as he stares at her on the rafters. "I'm not wrong. I would survive *any* explosion you concocted. I'm simply that fantas—"

His sentence ends in a shriek as a blade hits the wall

behind his head. Kiro lifts his hand to his ear and his fingers come away smudged in red. My eyes retrace the path of the dagger and land on a smirking Deca. Kiro stares at her aghast.

"You nicked my ear!" he shrieks.

Kiro pulls the dagger out of the wall and launches it back at Deca. It misses her head by a sliver, but the woman doesn't even blink. Her eyes thin. She is made even more threatening by the artwork tattooed to her skin.

"If you can't dodge a knife, how will you escape an explosion?" Deca coos as she continues sharpening one of her axes.

Kiro starts to speak but quickly shuts his mouth. Emmani screeches in delight as she leaps off the beam and trots over to Deca. She sits on the arm of her chair and kisses Deca's cheek before turning back to Kiro.

"Are you speechless, Kiro? Can't argue with Deca's beautiful brain now, can you?" she gloats.

Color brightens Deca's face as her eyes land on everything but Emmani. *Now, that's interesting.* I laugh as Emmani falls without grace over Deca's lap, snickering all the while. Deca stares at her as a rare smile graces her lips.

Red stalks into the room with Gray and Cass on her heels. Gray takes a seat beside me with a grin. I want to return the expression, but something about Red's face stops me short.

"What is it?" Soren asks as Emmani straightens herself on Deca's chair.

Even Kiro stops sulking to pay attention.

"The Bloodlines are out hunting again."

Curses ring through the heavy air. Soren goes deathly quiet in the corner as his eyes close in an expression of pain.

"Have they gone back to Ridge Palace yet?" Kiro asks, translating with his hands for Gray.

Red's lip curls up gruesomely as she scans us. "No, not yet. They're making their way deeper into the Riv as we speak.

They'll most likely go right through, then make their way up to the cliffs."

"Do we know how many people they already got to?" Emmani asks, her hands moving as she stands and heads toward the cupboard of medical supplies.

"Three. Two veterans and a fresh one," Red says.

They all move furiously around the room, gathering weapons and supplies.

"Do we know them?" Kiro asks as deep grooves cut into his face.

Red sneers as she shoves a dagger into a sheath on her leg. "The Lendiger brothers again, and the Sings' daughter."

Everyone stops in their tracks.

"She can't be more than ten," Emmani whispers, glancing at Soren.

"She's not," Red agrees.

They move faster than before, grabbing and packing bags. Within minutes, they're ready to leave. Red hands me a few blades, and without saying a word, I understand I'm going with them. This must really be bad if they need us all to help. While the room buzzes with activity, Soren stays still against the wall. Emmani whispers something to which he only nods. I don't miss the concern in her eyes as she walks away.

"Cass, if you feel up for it, you can go with Gray and Emmani to help the wounded. Elana, you're with Deca, Kiro, and me," Red says.

Cass and I nod. I look at him and he smiles. He enjoys being helpful, but I can't help but worry even though he won't be fighting whatever I'm walking into.

"You'll be careful?" I ask Cass.

He nods and gives me a look as if to say *of course I will.* I smile and follow the rest of the group out of the door. Soren is the only one who doesn't follow, still standing at the back of the room when Red locks the door.

We speak in hushed whispers as we head deeper into the Riv. Any souls lounging in the streets move away as we pass, their eyes filled with awe. They know exactly who this group is and revere them. One old man bows his head in respect, leaning heavily on his warped wooden cane.

Emmani walks to my left and I can't help but notice the tension in her face.

"What exactly are we stopping?" I ask her. There are a million unasked questions in those words, questions I know she catches as she glances my way.

"The Bloodlines have a certain... tradition. For a child to be considered an adult in the eyes of their families, they come into the Riv and hunt our people. The rules are clear. They cannot get caught by patrols or be seen by any commoner as they lure and trap their prey. Most people in the Riv have lived here long enough to recognize a trap, but the children... they don't know better, so they are usually the victims. I would bet that the Lendiger brothers walked into it on purpose so that a child wouldn't. It's torture to be caught, but it's better when you know what to expect. Most people in the Riv can take a beating, so we all try to shield the children. When we fail to hide them from the terror this place brings, they turn into us, continuing the cycles of pain and misery. That poor girl will never be able to get out of the Riv now."

"What do they do?" I ask as disgust builds in my throat.

Emmani sneers and it catches me off guard. I've never seen her unhappy before.

"When they trap us, they tie us up and brand us with the crude seal of whatever Bloodline captures us. The branding irons are made with spikes that clasp onto your skin to make them hurt more." She looks forward and takes a deep breath before pulling up the edge of her shirt, revealing a gruesome scar of a triangle with a small flame captured within. "I got caught when I was fourteen. They were smart. Most of them were Keres kids, but it was a Kalu who branded me. He was around my age at the time, but he was no child. There was nothing but satisfaction in his eyes when I screamed." Her eyes go dark as she fidgets with her shirt. "We've all been caught at one point or another. Even Red has a brand, and Kiro's been caught three times."

My every breath is short as I clench my teeth. My own branded hip burns as if to remind me of its presence.

"And Soren?" I ask softly, my curiosity speaking before my mind thinks better of it.

Emmani's hands fist as she stares straight ahead. I'm about to tell her that she doesn't have to explain when she speaks. "It was the first time our mother left us here alone instead of taking us with her on the ship. She'd received enough backlash and fear from her crew that she had no choice but to leave us. She thought it would be best for us to learn how to survive on our own. I still don't know if she was right to think that way.

"She rented a room for us to stay in for the duration of her travels. Soren and I took turns going out to get food and any supplies we needed because we were scared the owners would throw us out if we left together. One day when it was my turn, I decided to explore. I didn't realize how much time had passed, and when I returned, Soren was gone. He'd left to look for me. I waited for days, but he never came back. About a week later, Red found me in that room. I hadn't eaten in ages because I wanted to be there when Soren came back. Red told me she'd found him, but he was in bad shape."

Emmani swallows and takes a moment to breathe. "When Red brought me to see Soren, he was asleep. We hadn't grown up in the Riv, so we didn't know the rules. Unbeknownst to him, Soren had walked right into a Bloodline's trap. They'd kept him for an entire day and had their fun, each taking their turn to brand and beat him before dumping him in an alley. That's why he doesn't come out on these jobs. And none of us will ever make him."

I nod and straighten my back. I don't know how to respond to that, especially not as pieces of my own past come dredging back from the depths of my mind.

"I'm sorry," is all I can muster.

"Don't be. It's not your fault." She glances at my side. She must have seen the brand Cassien left after Leo brought me here. They all must have. I feel sick at the thought. "We lead unfair lives. All we can do is keep living and hope what we do reduces the suffering of others."

RED, Deca, Kiro, and I never went into the house where the two men and the girl were being helped, but we all heard the screams and the rush of frantic feet from outside. Cass had a terrified look in his eyes before he entered with Emmani and Gray, but I could see resolve there as well. I had asked him again if he was sure he wanted to help and he nodded without hesitation. I can't imagine the types of injuries he's witnessed and the things he's had to stomach with Leo as a brother.

My heart beats twice as fast as we head farther east. I run my hand along the walls of the scattered buildings, most of which are nothing more than ruin and rubble. I pull my hand back in surprise when the surface of the wall becomes smooth, interrupted only by deep grooves carved into the stone. I stare at it in the low light, trying to decipher the markings.

"We call this the Wall of the Soul Scribe," Kiro whispers, having shifted his gait to keep pace beside me. "Chances are that if you live in the Riv, you don't have enough money to burn or bury your loved ones when their bodies are found, which in and of itself is a rare occurrence. The Bloodlines don't want us to live long lives or be remembered when the time they allot us is over, so they offer us no way to celebrate our dead. They drag the bodies to burn houses every few days and use the ashes as fertilizer for the fields." He smiles softly as he looks over the wall. "But a slumblood loves nothing more than to spite a Bloodline, so this is how we remember. Since our people have lived in the Riv, we've been writing the names of the dead on this wall. When we run out of space, we make it longer, taller. When we find bodies that can't be identified, we put a notch on the bottom. That way there's something left behind in their honor."

I look down at the hundreds, if not thousands of notches carved one after the other.

"How far does the wall go?" I ask him quietly as my heart beats in my throat.

"Three blocks so far. There are gaps between for people to pass through, so in truth there are three walls, but we consider them to all be connected."

Sadness drenches me as I think about how far the wall reaches and the names wrapped around every side. As I stare, I can't help but feel a kind of peace. This wall has been a way of rebelling for generations. It holds not just the names of the dead, but the hope and dreams of a community stuck in a cycle of violence. It's incredible to see so many people abide by such a tradition for so long, but I guess it may be the only thing that bonds them. Here they are born, here they will live, and here they will die. Never escaping the fate they're given at birth.

After another few minutes of traveling through winding streets and crossing lopsided bridges, I hear a scream. It's high in pitch, though not high enough to be a child. We move faster as Red directs us where to go. I take two long daggers into my hands and head toward the opening of an alley. Deca stays silent beside me while Kiro and Red move around the other side.

Five Bloodlines stand around a girl who may be just a year or two younger than me. A small fire throws light onto their faces, morphing their features into ones of monsters. The girl lies on the ground, her face bloodied to match the color of her eyes as her chest moves with panting breaths. There's fear in her expression, but rage blazes in her eyes as she watches the group turn the branding irons in the flames. They've already burned her twice, but when one of the Bloodlines approaches emptyhanded with a grin, she fights back. The Bloodline swears when she hits him in the stomach, but the sound morphs into a laugh as he stands over her like a predator playing with its prey.

"When Red gives the signal, we get the girl. If the Bloodlines don't fight back, don't engage. If they run, don't follow. The last thing we want is to provoke them further. If they do fight, don't hit to kill. They can't pin us for giving them bruises because they would have to explain what they were doing here, but if we murder one, they'll cut through the Riv and burn every soul to ash. Understand?" Deca asks.

I nod, though her tone leaves a chill under my skin.

I take a breath and steady myself, remembering the years of torture at the Academy. Even though it almost killed me, at least it taught me to fight. I don't know what the signal is supposed to be, but when a flash of light and a bang that makes my ears ring bursts from the alley, I run forward without another thought. Kiro and Red are already locked in combat by the time I get to the girl. Deca follows close on my heels as she stares down a man, her axes held tightly in her fists.

I kneel and touch the girl's face. She startles backward, her eyes are wide and confused as I help her stand and lead her out of the alley. Before I get two steps away, a burly woman rams into my side. I crumble into the wall, the breath crushed from my lungs. No person is that strong. I straighten my thoughts as a name pops into my mind. Cadmus, *the Bloodline whose strength is unmatched.* How wonderful.

I pull myself to my feet and step in front of the wounded girl as the woman's eyes bleed red.

"What are you doing here, gold-eyes?" the Cadmus woman prods in a way that feels like an insult.

I crack my neck and lift my hands. "Getting rid of you."

She launches herself at me as her fist flies toward my head, narrowly missing me as I sidestep out of her path. I fly around in constant movement, trying to evade her perfectly timed attacks. I expect her to have the agility of a stone, but here she is, keeping up with my every move.

Take away her weapon. I hear Cassien's barked commands echoing in my thoughts. Without allowing myself time to consider, I follow every one.

I dodge, spin, slice. She lands a hit to my face that splits my lips and will surely swell my eye shut, but I take a page from Leo's book and read the recoil of her arm. Moving with it, I run my blade from her elbow to her wrist. The growl that escapes her is feral as she strikes again and again, slowly leaving more and more holes in her guard that I can take advantage of. I hit her arms again and again, slowing her movements as she tires. Finally, I see the gap I was looking for and strike her shoulder, hitting the nerve with my knuckles. The Cadmus's eyes go wide as her arm dangles limply by her side. I spit the blood from my mouth and lift my hands in front of my face, daring her to attack again.

"Dirty *slumblood,*" she barks with wild eyes. She backs away slowly and is almost knocked over by a man stumbling out of the alley holding his face. She follows with two others on her back, screaming and cursing us to the Lady.

Breathing heavily, I turn to see Deca and Red as they recover, stretching limbs and wiping away blood. Relief floods through me as I scan them. They don't seem to be badly hurt. I tear my gaze away to look for the girl, but she's gone.

"You slumbloods looking for something?"

We pivot toward the scratchy voice and still when we see a boy no older than Altair holding the girl by the throat. She fidgets as she fights against his grasp, but her face is frozen, unable to move. When he steps forward, so does she. It's as if they're connected to each other.

"Damaris," Red seethes with a venomous tone.

The child smiles, showing his crooked teeth. "In the flesh. And *you* are a bunch of slumbloods playing hero. Now drop your weapons or I'll shut off her airway."

I glance at Red, but her eyes stay pinned on the boy's hand. Her jaw grinds as she grips her blade tightly. Seeing it, the Damaris boy laughs in time with the girl's gasp. Red drops her weapons. Her hands twitch as the girl gasps a breath, tears flowing freely down her face.

"That's right, you are nothing compared to m—" He screams like a wounded dog as a blade embeds itself in his thigh.

Kiro steps out from behind him, a look of satisfaction on his face. The Damaris boy's hand falls away from the girl's neck, allowing her a moment to pull away. I expect her to run behind us, but instead she makes for the small fire still burning between us. No, not the fire. The brands. She pulls one of the glowing spikes from the fire and turns back on the boy. We don't have time to react before she's pressing it against his hand.

Red appears by her side and drags the girl away, but not before she's had a chance to do significant damage. She fights to get to Damaris as he stumbles away with fresh fear in his eyes. Tears run down the girl's face as she screams, begging Red to let go. Finally, she slumps to the ground. Red leans down to look her in the eyes.

"What's your name?" Red's usual cold tone has completely disappeared.

The girl sniffles and meets her eyes. "Kirya De Cal."

Kiro runs a hand over his face as Deca turns away.

"Did your mother pull through her sickness?"

Kirya's lip quivers as she shakes her head.

Red takes a deep breath and meets the girl's eyes. "Do you have a home?"

Another shake of the head.

Red pulls the girl to her feet and takes a small canteen from her belt. She opens it and hands it to her. "Then here's what's going to happen. I have some friends who can give you a clean place to stay and take care of your wounds until you are better. Then, if you choose, I know of a couple who have grown old and need help with their business. You can work and live in their spare room if you wish. I can ask them to take you in, if you trust me?"

The girl's eyes go wide as she stares at Red. Her brows knit together with confusion as she tries to decipher the truth. If she could truly have a home. Kirya lifts her chin and stands as tall as she can. "I trust you."

TWENTY-SEVEN

CAEL

I jolt awake at the sound of the door opening. I blink as my eyes take their time adjusting to the darkness of our room. Altair is sound asleep in the bed on the far side of the room while Antares takes up three-quarters of the space in the one we share. Saiph stirs between us as I sit up and look at the doorway. *Leo's not here.* I stand and pull a sweater over my head as dread knots my stomach. I shake Altair and he jumps awake. He stares at me for a moment before laying his head back down on his pillow.

"What is it?" he mumbles drowsily.

"I'm going out for a few minutes."

His eyes thin on me. "Why?"

I spin the ring on my finger as I glance at the door. "Leo went out. I'm going to go find out why."

Altair rolls his eyes and turns over with a yawn. "He's probably just tired of sitting in the dark by himself."

I watch him for a moment, staring at the boy showing barely a slip of worry for the brother who raised him. "Even so. Watch Saiph if I'm not back when she wakes up."

He turns back over and scans my face as if he were trying to read my thoughts. "Of course I will." For a moment, his face takes on that childish joy he grew up with, and it fills my chest with light. "You don't have to worry."

I return a grin and nod as I step away. "Thank you."

I move toward the door and put on my boots. I stop short as I go to tie them. Leo's boots are still here. He left without them.

The main room is completely silent when I step through the door. There's a single candle lit on a table in the middle, allowing me to see around the looming space. My head swivels toward the main door as I hear something shift outside. *Why would he have gone out?* I move toward the main door but freeze a step away from it.

"What are you doing?"

I slowly turn to see Kaja standing in thick woolen pajamas. Her hair is down, lying straight over her shoulders. I blink as she crosses her arms.

"Leo's gone," I say.

Her face pinches. As she comes toward me, I feel the storm of panic and confusion stirring inside her. "What do you mean *gone?*"

"I heard him leave the room, and he's not here," I tell her, trying to stay calm.

"That's not possible. There are guards at the door, and they don't let us out to wander at night."

Panic surges through me. Something's been unsettling about Leo since we went into the queen's drawing room a few days ago, but he's gone on as if nothing was amiss.

"Nothing is impossible when it comes to my brother." I turn and pull open the door.

Four armed guards immediately put their hands on their weapons.

"You do not have permission to leave. Please return to your rooms until sunrise," one of the guards says with a thick accent.

My stomach drops as my heart rate quickens. "No one has come out of this room in the past few minutes?"

They look at each other with confusion before their eyes land back on me. "This door has not been opened in hours."

I swear as I run through the last few days in my head. *Where could he have gone?* A thought jumps to the front of my mind and steals the air from my lungs. I swallow the fear that rises in my throat.

"I know where he is," I say as I move to sidestep the guard.

They immediately form a wall in front of me, blocking me in.

I sigh as I try my best to keep my fear under wraps. "My brother is in your palace somewhere. Escort me if you want, but I need to find him before something happens."

The guards shift their weight as their eyes fly from me to Kaja.

"That is impossible, no one—"

Steps pound down the hall toward us. A slim guard in the same uniform stops breathlessly before them. He speaks to them sharply in the Anateyan's mother tongue. Their eyes go wide with panic.

"You said your brother disappeared?" one of them asks.

I don't reply before I set off running through the halls. I hear feet pounding behind me as I sprint, turning the corners I recognize until I stand before the queen's drawing room. Kaja stops beside me as I stare at the door.

"You should go back," I tell her as I reach for the handle.

She places her hand on mine, stopping me. "What's in there?"

I don't respond as I push open the door and step inside. I hear the guards stop at the doorway as I slowly enter the room. The light coming through the window sets Leo's back in shadow, painting him as a dark figure against the moonlight. I swallow and move toward him, feeling Kaja behind me. Something is *very* wrong.

Leo doesn't move. It doesn't even look like he's breathing. I say his name, but he remains silent. I stop when I understand what he's doing. He's standing in front of the Ash Sword. My hands shake as I curl them into fists. Memories from another time fill my mind as I see the moment reflected in him.

"Look at me," I say.

Leo's head twitches to the side. "I don't think you'll like what you see, getic."

The voice isn't Leo's, but it comes from his body. The tone is old and cracked, as if from ages of being left unused. It has been years since I heard that voice.

"I can smell your fear, you know. It's the same as it was all that time ago." I freeze as he glances over his shoulder. The sound of steel being drawn rings from behind me, but all I can focus on is his eyes. His entirely black eyes. His head tilts as he smirks.

"Let him out," I say, my words shaky.

His terrifying smile grows even wider. "Now why would I do that, when I just got hold again."

I hear Kaja breathing shallowly at my side, but I don't dare look away from Leo.

"I've been building my strength for years to be able to come out, waiting for the perfect moment. I simply couldn't resist seeing my blade again." He turns back toward the sword and runs his hand along the glass encasing it. "I will return for you soon," he whispers to the blade before shifting toward us with calculated, feline movements.

"And as for you," he says to me, "I don't have much time today, but I will be back. This time, you won't be able to be rid of me." He steps toward me, and I instinctively step back. "He doesn't have many threads of sanity left. When the last one snaps, I'll be waiting."

The door across the room slams open and the queen charges in. "What by the Gods is the meaning of this?"

When I glance back at Leo, he's kneeling on the floor. I let out a tight breath and sprint to him before going down on my knees beside him. "Leo?"

He looks up with clear silver eyes. He blinks at me, then around the room. His eyes lock with the queen's and he scrambles to stand. I pull him up as he sways on his feet.

"I won't ask again," the queen demands.

Leo shakes his head as if he's trying to set his thoughts straight. "You'll have to forgive me, Your Majesty, but I... I don't know."

The queen stares at Leo.

"I was asleep and now I'm here," he says, his voice raw.

The queen nods as her eyes land on me.

"My brother has been known to sleepwalk, Your Majesty. It comes with the terrors."

Leo stiffens beside me, knowing I'm telling a blatant lie. The queen doesn't look as if she believes it either, but she doesn't push the point.

"This will not happen again," she says to me. Something in her eyes tells me she knows exactly what happened, or at least, has a very good idea. "Go back to your rooms. The guards will accompany you."

Leo and I nod as I turn him toward the door. Kaja moves to

my side as we pass by the wide-eyed guards. I don't know how much they could have seen or heard from outside the drawing room, but they know something was amiss. They keep multiple paces back as we head toward our room.

"What happened?" Leo asks breathlessly.

I glance at him, and I know he can see the fear lingering in my expression. "I don't know."

I hope he won't dig further. He stares at me as if he's going to say something, but in the end he only nods, keeping quiet until we get back to our room.

We enter the main sitting room and head toward our bedroom. Kaja stays by my side as I open the door and Leo walks in. I meet her eyes and see the questions in them as she takes a seat on one of the couches. I step into the bedroom with Leo, leaving the door open behind me. Kaja is going to want some kind of explanation.

"Do you really not know what happened, or are you just not going to tell me?" Leo whispers as his gaze falls to the floor.

I take a deep breath and shake my head. "I don't know."

Leo runs a hand through his hair as he sits on the bed, his head hanging in defeat. "Don't lie to me, Cael. I trust there's a reason you won't tell me, but don't lie and tell me you don't know how I ended up in that room." I'm at a loss for words as he moves to sit against the headboard, so I don't say anything. Finally, he raises his tired eyes to mine. "Go see her. I trust you enough to be all right without an explanation, but I doubt she'll be content without some semblance of an answer. False or truthful."

I nod and turn to leave the room but freeze before I step out. "I just... I don't know—"

Leo stops me with a smile. "There are things about me that are better left unknown for my own sanity."

That word sends a bolt through me, but I bury the fear before it can surface. I nod and return a shaky smile. "Don't do anything stupid until I come back."

He grins and crosses his hands behind his head. "I wouldn't dream of it."

I step out of the door and Kaja's eyes meet mine. I remind myself to breathe as I sit on the chair next to hers. We stay silent for a long time, staring at each other and everything else.

"Why were his eyes black?" she asks quietly, breaking the thick silence I had hoped would last forever.

I spin the ring on my hand as I look at the floor. "I don't know. It's happened only once before, a long time ago. When our father was killed, Leo felt so guilty he didn't speak for days. He didn't eat, didn't sleep, didn't move. After Leo dragged my father's body home, all he did was stare at the wall. We were all grieving in our own way, so we decided to leave him alone. One night, I woke up and heard him leave. I don't know how he got out, because at that time we had a padlock on the door, and I had the key. Our sister and I went out to look for him, but we never found out where he went. After two weeks, we needed food, so I went into Somereil and I saw him coming out of an arena. I'll never forget the moment I saw his face. His eyes were black as tar, and he was covered in blood. He looked at me and smiled, but it wasn't his smile. I was looking at Leo's face, but the thing that walked out of that arena wasn't my brother. I threw up when he walked away.

"Our mother was very sick at the time, but when I approached her about it, she flinched. I'd never seen her so terrified. She told me that Leo was special and what made him strong was not only his own soul, but the soul of another. She said that she had been warned that his mind could become confused as to which soul should connect to his body. Now that I think of it, she probably learned about it when she was here with the queen." I shake my head, remembering Mum squeezing my hand so hard I thought it would break. "I didn't understand what she was telling me at the time. I thought it might just be babble because she was so sick, but she made me swear never to tell him about it. So I stayed quiet. Even after Pleiades and I caught him and dragged him home, even after we tied him up in a room and waited for Leo to come back, I never told him. Neither of us did."

Kaja stays silent for a long time, staring at me with wide eyes as she absorbs the information. "You're telling me that another soul lives in the prince's body? That was who I heard speak earlier?"

I nod as I force my hands to stop shaking. "I have no idea how it works, but I haven't found another explanation. When we spoke with the queen, she did say something about the Bloodlines having part of the Child in their DNA. Maybe that's whose mind is tangled with his..." I shake my head as a million thoughts spin through my brain. "All I know for sure is that I'll never forget the sound of that voice. The things it said the first time Leo sank too deep. Mum told us that to get him back we would have to weaken his body, to in turn weaken its bond with the soul. So we tied him up and locked him in a room with no food or water for three weeks. He spoke to us the whole time in that voice. Then one day it stopped, and he was back."

I lift my head and Kaja meets my eyes. She smiles as she raises her hand and hesitates. Slowly, she places it over my mine and closes her grip around the back of my hand. I stop fidgeting at her warm touch. She blinks as she watches me, as if she expects me to pull away. I don't.

"I won't say I understand what happened," she says softly. "But at least he's back now."

I nod and turn my hand to intertwine my fingers with hers. My skin prickles where it touches hers as I mirror her smile. "At least there's that."

TWENTY-EIGHT

LEO

My mind is still swimming by the time we leave for Arkezo. Cael's avoiding my questions about what happened last night, always spitting the same excuse like a rehearsed thief. *You must have fallen into a memory and wandered the halls. The queen said you spent time in the drawing room as a child. You knew that place, so that's where you went.* I don't believe a word of it. He's too cautious. His words sound almost fearful. He hasn't left my side since Ceto told us we were cutting our visit short. He said that there was no need for us to stay longer, so we were to take our leave. He left out the part where he went to see the queen before most of the others had awoken.

When Cael, Byrne, the boys, and I went to say our good-byes, the queen asked Cael to stay behind. She spoke with him for only a moment, but what I saw in his expression as she spoke quietly terrified me. He looked haunted, but not the way he does when he wakes up from a nightmare. My brother seemed like he was scared to move. Scared to breathe. I caught the queen glance my way as she spoke to Cael. I couldn't hold her eyes. Something happened last night, and I can't figure out what.

That night plagues my mind for days as we journey through the caves. Cael speaks more with Kaja than me for the entirety of our trek, only managing to send me further into my own head. I know he doesn't mean to, but his diverted attention hurts. Maybe I'm just not used to seeing Cael spend so much time with someone else when I depend on him so deeply.

When we breach the cave back into Illena, the air doesn't seem as clear as when we left. I scan the tree line before our descent. The color looks as if it's been leached away from the leaves. The air is thick and silent as the hooves of the horses stick in the mud. Something seems wrong, like the wind itself is holding its breath, waiting.

"We're returning just in time for The Blaze," Ares says by my side.

I blink and turn to face him, careful not to wake Antares as he sleeps against me.

"Is that some kind of celebration?" Cael asks as he catches up to us. He had been speaking with Kaja when we came out of the tunnel.

I don't miss the upward turn of Cael's lips when he nears her or the way his shoulders relax. I have yet to decide if his comfort is something we should be wary of, but Kaja has done nothing to make us think badly of her. Even though I'm skeptical, I trust Cael's judgment. It's how we've survived all these years.

"The Blaze is only the biggest celebration in Illena. All the villages and cities come together to watch the stars fall across the sky. Most people only use it as an excuse to get rip-roaring drunk though," Ares laughs as he smirks.

I glance at Cael as he shifts on his horse.

"What does it entail me doing? As heir..." I wonder aloud.

Ares's grin grows as he cracks his knuckles. "Your entire family will be obliged to attend the party our Bloodline hosts at the Ridge Palace and, most importantly, will be expected to socialize. It's quite a special occasion, so you'll be dressed in the finest silks." My face twists and Ares must catch it because he continues. "Don't worry. This is an informal affair. Very little scheming goes on during The Blaze. It's truly the only night the Bloodlines are inclined to take off. When we were young, it was the one day my mother and father would allow us to play without having to keep up the façade of perfection."

I nod as I imagine the stars falling across the sky. Mum told us about them as children. She painted beautiful images of dark skies splattered with hues of greens and blues so bright they lit the streets. I've always wanted to see them, but they never appear in Tominay. Now I finally will.

***

"What are you going to say to Elana?"

I spin on my heels, almost ripping the button off my coat. Ares was right when he spoke of the silks. I didn't think the clothes could get more expensive than the ones we'd already been wearing, but these are... something entirely different. The black fabric is softer than fur but thin, and it mimics the coloring of ink, shifting from indigo to black to blue with the light. The hems are embroidered with a deep blue thread that blends and shines with the material. The Matteus seal is strategically positioned over my heart, expertly stitched in with the same thread. I inspect myself in the mirror. My father's weapons are well concealed beneath the fabric. I can barely make out where they sit under my coat. I had been staring at my outfit so intently, I hadn't realized Cael had come back into the room.

"What?" I ask, startled by the question.

Cael rolls his eyes and sits on the bed with the ribbon meant for Saiph's hair in his hands. He wears a suit similar to mine, though the fabric isn't quite as dark and the stitching is a vibrant purple.

"Elana? She's been out the last two nights we went into the Riv to see Cass. You haven't seen her since we got back from Enzly," he says as he pulls Saiph over to him.

She squeals as she pulls away, trying to keep the ribbon from being tied in her hair. When she discovers her struggling is useless, she melts to the floor as if her bones had turned to sand.

"Why do I have to say anything to her?" I ask as I turn back toward the mirror.

Cael rolls his eyes as he wrestles to braid Saiph's hair. I've been considering how I should go about trying to forgive Elana since Cael and I spoke, and the longer I go without seeing her, the more my mind conjures her image. I see her face every-where. When I look at the bakeries in the streets or catch a flash of a gold ring. Even when I smell the fresh water off the bay or feel the wind sweeping through the trees. By the Lady, I think of her when I looked at a damned roof.

"I never said you have to say something to her," he says defensively as Saiph slips through his hands halfway through the braid.

I catch her before she can run out the door and throw her in the air playfully. She giggles as I deposit her back in front of my brother. He nods his thanks as I sit beside them, letting her trace the swirls of embroidery on my jacket as Cael finishes weaving the ribbon into her hair.

"You made it pretty clear it would be in my best interest to do so," I tell him.

He glances at me with a grin. "We both know you want nothing more than to speak with her."

I look away, heat rising to my face.

"We're going to the Riv after the Bloodline celebration. You should speak to her then. Ares did say this is a time to spend with the people you care for."

My head whips up. "I never... I never said—"

Cael finishes with Saiph and sets her on the floor before crossing his arms and staring me dead in the eye. "Come on, Leo. Don't try to tell me she means so little after everything. By the Goddess, I wouldn't be surprised if she took up most of the room in your fogged brain."

I run a hand down my face as I laugh mirthlessly. I need to get out of this room.

"You know, every time someone says her name, you snap to attention. Byrne mentioned her sister when she was speaking with Emrys, and you immediately stopped talking to me."

"Liar," I mumble, knowing full well that indeed did happen.

Cael rolls his eyes and stands. As I'm about to retort, Antares and Altair barge into the room with their matching suits. I smile as Antares frowns, looking down at his clothes. Somehow, it looks as though he's put his jacket on inside-out, backward, and twisted.

"I tried to help him, but I have no idea how to undo this," Altair says as he jumps onto the couch he's turned into a bed.

Cael helps Antares out of the discombobulated piece of clothing and starts on the puzzle of straightening the fabric.

"It's a wonder you don't have your shoes on the wrong feet," I tell Antares with a raised brow.

Cael stops and looks down before bursting out in laughter. "Honestly, Antares, would it pain you that much to pay attention to what you're doing?"

Antares pouts as he flops onto the floor and pulls off his shoes. "These took me forever to tie."

"I tied them for you," Altair points out.

Byrne knocks on the door and pushes it open. Her hair is done up in a crown on top of her head the way I saw Elana's a long time ago. She smiles as she takes us in. "Emrys is here to take us down. Are you all ready?"

I nod and stand. I have to run to grab Saiph before she can escape past Byrne. "Monster," I tell her as she cackles, going limp in my arms.

By the time Emrys leads us down the hall, Antares has his jacket back on and his shoes tied up. I can hear the people well before we get to the doors of the ballroom. Floating aromas of food fill the air, changing from sweet to spicy to savory with every step.

I don't know what I was expecting when I walked into the ballroom, but this was not it. A soft orange light filters over the space as hundreds of nobles, Bloodlines, and anyone who must mean anything in Illena gather, deep in conversations. Servants carrying platters of food and liquor move smoothly through the guests like dancers avoiding their partners' fumbling feet. We're barely two steps in before Ares finds us, wearing a wide smile. When I look for Byrne and Emrys, they've already peeled away, heading toward a secluded corner of the room. The neck of Ares's shirt is crooked, and his cheeks are flushed as he greets us. I catch Cael's concerned gaze before turning my eyes back to my cousin.

"Welcome to The Blaze!" Ares announces, his words

slurred in a controlled way. He throws his arm over my shoulder and pulls us into the crowd.

People turn to look our way, whispering and glancing without a care of being caught. So much for having fun. At least we won't be here long.

"It's really wonderful, isn't it?"

"It is," I tell Ares with forced sincerity.

Ares grabs a drink off a passing platter and takes a sip.

"Ares, I hope you aren't stressing our cousin and his brothers on their first Blaze?"

Ares tenses as he turns toward his sister and quickly melts back into the picture of ease. "Now why would I do that, My Queen?"

She smiles at him as he pulls away from my side.

"I should be going. Lots of people to see." Ares looks at me and winks. "And drinks to down."

The queen shakes her head as she watches him saunter off through the crush of people.

"Honestly, I thought he would be over drinking his own weight by now," the king says as he comes to the queen's side. She rolls her eyes before taking his hand.

"My brother never skips an occasion to enjoy himself." She turns to us and laughs. "Ares is the most serious man you will meet when it comes to getting what he wants, but when the opportunity presents itself, he never fails to run off during a party."

Cael and I smile, remembering times we had our own type of fun. Fond memories are few and far between from over the years, but the joy never dampens in my mind.

"So, do we truly get to see the stars fall?" I ask as the royals lead us to the balcony. The air is warm, enveloping me in a blanket of comfort.

When I put Saiph down to run around with Antares, the

two of them immediately wind through the few people who have come outside. Cael tries to warn them about running into the other patrons, but the queen waves him off.

"Let them run. They're children," she says. For a moment, sadness flashes across her face. The king steps closer to her when she clears her throat. "And yes, in fact, any minute now we should be able to see them. But that's not the only thing that makes this night special in Arkezo."

I frown and open my mouth to speak, but Cael beats me to the question.

"What else happens?" my brother asks.

The queen smiles and exchanges a glance with her husband. "You'll see."

We speak for a while of Anateya and the things we learned while we were in the country. Cael's head swivels toward the wide doors as Kaja comes through in a shining purple dress. There must be thousands of crystals sewn into the fabric, each moving as one as she nears. She bows to each royal, including myself.

"It's a beautiful night for The Blaze, Your Majesties," she says with a practiced grace.

The queen dips her chin. "It is. How have you been, Kaja? I have not seen your Bloodline in quite a few days."

Kaja lowers her eyes and crosses her hands over the front of her dress. "I'm sorry to say there has been some unrest within the populus as of late. We have heard reports of strange noises and people moving through the woods."

The queen frowns and looks at her husband. "Why was this not brought to our attention?"

"We only learned about it today, Your Majesty. We believe a virus is moving through the livestock. Some of the animals have escaped their pens and been running rampant through the woods. The people in the smaller villages are prone to believing in folk tales and myths and consider it to be some type of a sign. The livestock have been taken care of and my cousins are currently exploring the specimens to find out what we can about this new ailment."

The queen nods and settles back into her relaxed demeanor. "Very good. I'm sure you'll inform us should anything arise."

"Of course, Your Majesty. We are at your service," she says, bowing deeply. Kaja turns to leave but stutters a step as she catches Cael's lingering gaze.

He looks at me as she leaves and I huff a laugh, seeing the question in his eyes. He smiles and turns toward the royals.

"If you'll excuse me as well, I have some friends I'd like to speak to," Cael says.

The queen tilts her head as she watches him closely. "I'm glad to hear you are making acquaintances. Enjoy the party."

He dips his chin and turns away, following Kaja's trail.

"You should perhaps warn your brother about the Damaris Bloodline," the king says with furrowed brows.

I grin as I shake my head. "I trust Cael knows what he's doing. He has a sense for these things."

Though they seem unsure, the royals move on. We find an easy balance in speaking of all the new things Illena has taught me until a spark flashes across the newly darkened sky. Our heads swing toward it as all eyes turn to the stars. People funnel outside in droves. Another blue flash goes by so fast I barely catch it. Antares and Saiph come barreling back toward us. Within seconds, the entire sky is covered in blue-green streaks of light, illuminating the air. It's like nothing I've ever seen. Altair, Saiph, Antares, and I stare open-mouthed at the sky, trying to catch the movement of every star.

"So this is why everyone celebrates," I say with wonder. I tear my eyes away from the stars as the queen laughs.

"That part is beautiful, but I told you there would be more to The Blaze than just the sky."

As if on cue, the water of the bay starts to glow. At first, I think it's reflecting the moving lights from above, but it grows brighter. Soon the bay and every stream that runs from it is glowing a blue brighter than the stars. I don't know where to look. Up or down. Down or up. The queen grins again as I turn to look at them with awe.

"How is this possible?" I ask.

"Once a year, tiny bioluminescent phytoplankton flow from the Glass Sea through the Vallan and end up in the waters of the bay. It just so happens to be the same day the stars fall across the sky," she explains with bright eyes.

Music rings through the air as I take in the beauty of the colors. The royals say their goodbyes, but I can't tear my eyes away. They laugh airily as I hear their steps recede. People all around sing and dance, but all we can do is stare at the blazing lights flowing up and falling down to meet in the middle in shining arcs.

Antares pulls on my sleeve, tearing my attention away from the show. "Can we go see Cass?"

I smile and nod, wondering what my youngest brother must be thinking right now. I move my gaze toward the Riv and notice for the first time that not only does the blue water shine from the canals that lead from the bay, but bright orange bonfires burn brightly in the streets. Even though I knew we would go down to the Riv tonight, my mind is still uneasy about seeing Elana. I haven't decided to forgive her yet. I'm just... confused. Every time I think of her, my heart flutters in sync with the alarm bells in my head. I don't know what to think or how to feel, but I know for certain that Cael is right. I need to see her. At least once, I need to speak with her.

"Yeah, let's go."

We carve a path through the crowd, stopping to say a few words as various nobles and Bloodlines move to catch our attention. I make polite excuses to get away, mostly to do with Antares not feeling well and bringing him upstairs. Being dramatic, Antares plays the part and sways with every step, tripping over his feet as he clutches my arm.

When we finally clear the room, Antares lets go and jumps ahead of us through the hall. He turns with a smile lighting his face and walks backward. "Can I go swimming with Cass and Gray when we get there? I wonder if the water is hot because it's glowing... but the light kinda looks cold so I don't really know how it's gonna feel. All I want to know is how fast I can swim and maybe I'll go faster because the blue—"

Cael grabs Antares's arm as we round a corner right before he walks into the wall. Antares looks up at Cael in a daze.

"You weren't watching where you were going," Cael scolds him with a smile.

Antares grins sheepishly as he spins away and lifts Saiph into his arms. I stop beside Cael as Antares talks Saiph's ears off. She responds while simultaneously deciding to comment on every blue thing we pass, invested in a conversation I'm not sure she can understand. Kaja comes around the corner, keeping a few steps away. Color stains her cheeks as a smile lingers on her face.

I turn my gaze to Cael, and I'm caught off guard by the ease of his expression. That same genuine smile is evident on his face, as if it were built into his features.

"I'll meet up with you later," he says as he spins his ring around his finger.

I nod as I try to conceal the smirk pulling at my lip. "Don't do anything stupid."

When I walk past Kaja, she nods in greeting but doesn't say a word.

"I wouldn't dream of it," I hear from behind me.

By the Lady, I hope he knows what he's doing.

THE SOUND of instruments and singing rides the wind as we get closer to the Riv. The streets near the bay are packed with eager citizens and tourists alike, battling for a glance at the glowing waters. We bypass them and head straight toward the Riv. Small crowds grouped around towering fires become more frequent the deeper we go. Instruments I can't name play symphonies I've never heard, sounding like songs from times of old played with a new reverence. I feel alive, the air itself holding a charge as we head toward Hela's Bond.

"Leo!"

I skip to a stop and turn toward the sound. A giant bonfire blazes near a canal as kids jump and splash in the water, sending droplets of light flying everywhere. Emmani waves us over with a bright smile from where they've assembled around the fire.

"So, is Blaze night all you expected?" Emmani says as we join Hela's Bond.

Cael and I nod as Cass sprints over from where he had been sitting with Gray. I lift him into the air and flip him upside down, holding him by his feet. My heart stutters as I hear him laugh, the sound coming from deep in his diaphragm. I set him back on the ground and put an arm around him.

"By the Lady, I missed you," I tell him. Cass smiles from ear to ear as he pulls away. "You've been good?"

He nods vigorously before Antares tackles him. They wrestle, each trying to get the upper hand as Saiph stands over them, giggling. The rest of Hela's Bond comes over as Saiph decides to jump on her brothers. They calm and let her pin them to the ground, feigning defeat.

"How was the Bloodlines' half-hearted Blaze Fest?" Kiro asks as he sits on a rickety stool.

I shrug and take my own seat. "Proper."

Cass has Antares pinned when Gray moves his hands in a quick motion. Cass stands and looks at the canal then back at me.

"Is it safe for them to swim in it?" I ask Red.

She nods as the corner of her lips kick up. "It's as safe as it is any other day."

The boys run toward the canal without another word. Cass and Gray rip off their shoes and launch themselves under the metal bar bracketing the waterway to jump into the canal. Their hair glows a muted blue when they resurface. Antares hesitates for a moment before slipping in, staying close to the side. Saiph tries to go in after them, but I jump to my feet and scoop her up.

"Maybe we'll swim later," I tell her as she huffs.

I turn to head back toward the bonfire but stop dead in my tracks. Elana's eyes lock with mine and the air empties from my lungs all at once. I don't know what to do with myself as we stare at each other. She looks devastated, her eyes sad and lips thin. *Talk to her*, my mind screams. *Forgive her*. I blink and force my feet to move. Her eyes track my every move as I head toward where the group sits. I take a deep breath and turn to Altair.

"Are you going to go in with them or stay here?" I ask him.

"I'm not swimming in there," he says with a grimace.

I force myself to keep my eyes on him as I feel Elana approach. "Do you mind watching Saiph then?"

His gaze focuses behind my shoulder for a moment, then

moves back to me. He nods and holds out his hands to take her.

"Thank you," I tell him. "And will you—"

"Just go talk to her already!" Emmani blurts. Deca touches her arm, and Emmani clears her throat. "I only meant we'll watch the boys. They'll be fine."

I smile tensely and turn toward Elana. Neither of us says anything as we walk over the bridge. There are no bonfires here, the bulk of people seeming to have taken up celebrating on the other side of the canal. We stand shoulder to shoulder, leaning against the railing above the glowing canal. I stare at the moving water, watching the vibrant colors swirl and sway. A piece of the railing is missing a few paces away, leaving a gaping opening to the water below.

"Leo..." Elana says, and my eyes dart to her. "I'm sorry. For everything. I've said it before and I'll say it a million times if I need to. I never... I didn't mean for things to happen the way they did. There's no excuse for any of it. I don't need you to understand it or accept it, but I need you to know that I'm sorry."

My eyes don't waver from her face when she finally meets my eyes. I swallow the dread rising in my throat and take a deep breath.

"I understand." Her face relaxes and my soul hurts knowing what I'm going to say next. "But I don't know if I can forgive you."

Her eyes flutter shut as she nods.

"He's my youngest brother, Elana, and you let me mourn him. I thought he was gone. I thought I'd watched him die." My voice breaks. "You let me believe he was dead. You sat with me while I reminisced and blamed myself."

"Leo—" she says, but I cut her off. I need to say this before its buried back inside me.

"No. I trusted you. More than I wanted to, I trusted you. I leaned on you. Confided in you. Told you my fears. And you betrayed me."

Her head hangs as she chews on her lip.

"But you also saved me."

Her head snaps up so fast it's a wonder she doesn't get whiplash. "What..."

She meets my eyes and I smile softly, ripping away the mask and letting her see the emotion underneath. I never thought I would be able to let that facade drop, but here I am, not caring if my feelings are written on my face. If I'm hurt because of this, because of her, I don't think I'd regret it. Elana's eyes glaze as her head tilts.

"No matter how many times I tell myself what you did was wrong, I can't forget what I did when I found out he was there. You knew I would run into Wate. You were trying to save me from myself." I take a breath and shift closer to her. "I should have listened to you. After everything, you were right. I ran into Wate and got caught. I would still be there if you hadn't told Hela's Bond how to get to me out. So, I'm sorry." She shakes her head slowly, as if about to deny it, but I don't give her the chance. "I'm sorry I yelled. I'm sorry I pushed you away when you tried to explain. I should have trusted you. I shouldn't have been scared to trust you."

We stand there, side by side, staring at each other for what could be seconds or hours. The rail creaks as I lean against it, needing the support. The world falls away as her face glows in the light, and for the first time, I see how truly beautiful she is. How her eyes shine like raging rivers of silver and her gilded skin glows. I notice the little things I've neglected to see: the small scars that have faded with time, the shadows under her eyes, the line on the left side of her lip that only appears when she's holding back a smile. She blinks and I'm mesmerized.

"You threw my entire life upside down. But for some reason, I can't help but trust you, Leo. And worry about you—"

"And think about you," I finish for her.

Color rises to her cheeks as she looks away. Hesitating, I raise my hand and bring her face back to look at mine.

"No matter how hard I try not to, I can't stop it," I whisper, moving closer until we're only a breath apart. "Always in my mind. In every sound. In everything I see. You're consuming my thoughts, Elana, and I don't know what to do about it."

She swallows and searches my face before locking her gaze with mine. "I think I know what to do about it, but it might make things worse."

She smiles as her gaze jumps to my lips. I grin and take her face in my hands, gently running my thumb over her cheek.

"I don't think I can find it in me to care about the consequences," I tell her before pressing my lips to hers.

We melt into one another, stealing each other's breath without meaning to. I'm breathing hard when I pull away, but I can't stop the smile that appears my face. Cheers go up from the other side of the canal and I turn us away as my cheeks flame, shielding Elana and myself from the prying eyes of Hela's Bond.

"I never would have taken them for gossips," she laughs as she meets my eyes.

I smirk, unable to worry about anyone but the girl standing in my arms staring up at me.

The rail whines against my back and gives way too fast for me to catch my balance. I plummet backward with Elana still in my arms, landing hard in the glowing water. I come up to the surface with a gasp, spinning around as I search for her. Elana emerges with wide eyes. I choke out a laugh as Elana folds her arms over her chest.

"Look what you did." She pouts.

I pull her into me and wipe away a drop of water from her cheek. "You're glowing."

She scoffs as color rises in her cheeks. "We're in a river of glowing water, what do you expect?"

I grin as I watch her, that earth-shattering smile lighting her face. Staring at her, I realize something I never thought possible—I would die for my family, but this girl in front of me, who burst into my life unexpectedly, makes me want to live.

CHAPTER

TWENTY-NINE

CAEL

Kaja was waiting for me when I left the thick crowd in the ballroom. I walk to her side and follow as she leads me through the halls. After a few minutes of silence, I ask where we're going.

"I don't like big crowds," she states.

I don't push for details, feeling that wherever she's leading me will be better if I'm patient. We head deep into the palace and climb up flight after flight of stairs in complete darkness. I run my hand against the wall, feeling markings worn into the damp stone. I don't know what they mean, but Kaja seems to be following them with sure steps. When we reach the top, she pushes open a wooden hatch and stands back as moonlight floods inside. I squint against it before I look at her.

"Go on then," she says, tilting her head as if it were a challenge.

Do I trust her enough to go through first? I look up at the sky and nod as every possible scenario runs through my mind.

If she wanted to kill me, she could have done it long ago. I pull myself up onto a small platform. I'm taken aback by the view of the city from so high up. It's beautiful, the moonlight reflecting off the bay. Fires rage in the Riv and I can almost make out the crowds of people celebrating around them. I'm careful not to step on the blanket and flask set on the roof as Kaja pulls herself up.

Without thinking, I extend my hand to help her. She hesitates and meets my eyes. I wonder how many people in her life have offered her a hand. After a moment, she grabs hold and pulls herself up with enough grace for me to see that she would have done fine without me. Once she's on the platform, I realize how close we are to one another. I can't make myself move as my eyes follow her. She crouches to close the hatch then sits, pulling the blanket around herself.

I'm teetering on my feet when a flash catches my eye. I turn around and I can't help but smile as the bay glows, thousands of stars lighting the earth and the heavens. I don't know if I'm breathing as I take in the sight.

"You can't see them in Tominay, can you?" she asks.

I turn and look down at Kaja. She nods toward the small space beside her, inviting me to sit. I do. I forget about the light show as I meet her eyes.

"No. There's nothing like this in Tominay," I tell her.

"What's it like?" she asks, opening the flask and taking a swig.

She offers it to me, and I take it without hesitation. The smell alone burns my eyes as I bring it up to my nose. I cough as Kaja breathes out a laugh.

"What is this?"

"In simple terms, it's very strong alcohol." I stare at her, but she only shrugs. "These are perilous nights. People generally fear me, and any other day, I'm used to the way they gawk and whisper, but the Blaze is different. It's the only informal night of the year and the Bloodlines get so drunk they forget to fear me. This soothes my nerves." Something flickers in her eyes as she looks at the bay. "But it's also good to fight against the cold."

Just then, a gust of wind picks up, sending chills down my spine. I take a swig from the flask and immediately want to spit it out. I force myself to swallow, feeling as if liquid fire is burning down my throat. Kaja laughs as I set into a coughing fit and shove the flask back into her hand.

Even with the drink, I can't help but shiver. Kaja opens the blanket and offers me the end. I smile and shift closer to pull the blanket tightly around us both.

"Tominay is very gray."

Her head swivels toward me, her face riddled with confusion as her brows knit together.

"You asked me what it was like. Tominay."

"Right. I did," she says, smiling. "Is it really as bad as the stories you've told the Matteuses?"

I think about how to answer that question. Tominay was my home until a little less than a year ago. It was all I had ever known, and even through the bad, there were so many good times. But the terrible moments... they never failed to rip your soul to shreds and then leave you cold and hungry to sew the pieces back together.

"Most people were dejected, and those who weren't were either high on drugs or power."

"It sounds like the Bloodlines," Kaja whispers as she curls into herself. "We're a very lonely people. Even within our own lines, it's everyone for themselves. Survival of the fittest. If you forget for a moment to watch your back, you're dead. And you'll never know if the final blow will be by the knife of a rival or your own mother."

I nod, knowing the feeling well. "Why do they fear you so much?" I ask before I can think better of it. "The Bloodlines are clearly rivals, but they treat you differently. Are you truly that dangerous?"

She swallows and hangs her head. "Have you ever killed someone?"

I blink and take a moment to register the question. "Yes." I don't elaborate, letting that loaded word hang in the silence.

"Why did you do it?"

I take a deep breath as her eyes meet mine. Something like desperation passes over her face.

"He was going to murder my brother," I tell her.

She nods and turns away. "On Blaze night when I was seven, my uncle grabbed me. He said he wanted to show me something special. I hated him and knew the things he had done with other women. Girls. I screamed when his fingers touched my skin. I made his heart beat so quickly it stopped. He died before he could say where he wanted to take me. For others of my Bloodline, it can take at least fifteen years to learn how to gain enough control of a body to kill it. I did it when I was a child. They locked me up for two years until I proved I could control my power. From the day I was released, I was given assignments, ordered to destroy people my parents said had committed wrongs, but I knew the queen just wanted them to disappear. Painfully."

She takes a deep breath, as if reliving the moments. "I still did it though. Entered their bodies and minds to learn how they worked. How to heal and destroy. That's why they fear me. Because by the time I was ten, I could control twenty people with a simple touch. I can tunnel into minds and break memories, imprint ideas, flip ideologies. I can make a person go mad with a single thought."

For a moment I want to laugh, and she must see it on my

face because she moves to shift away, but I fold my arm around her and pull her tighter to my side.

"I'm sorry that happened," I tell her.

"Why do you look like you're going to laugh then?"

I smile softly, holding her gaze to make sure she sees my sincerity. "Because no matter what I do, I always end up with the most dangerous people. Leo, my brothers, the Cassien sisters, you." I shake my head and sigh. "But the good thing about that is I'm not scared of you. There are two things I'm fearful of in this world and that story you just told me doesn't faze me in the slightest."

She watches me carefully and I feel her start to relax. "I guess having a crown prince blood-eyed mercenary as your brother would desensitize you to most things."

I huff a laugh and roll my eyes. "Oh, you have no idea."

We watch the stars, and I don't think I've been this content in years. No worries plague my mind, no blood stains my hands, and no screams fill the air to torture my ears. I almost don't know what to do with myself. For a moment, my mind wanders and I wonder if Leo worked up the courage to talk to Elana. He needs her as much as she needs him. I hope they find a way to forgive each other or at least find some type of peace.

"What was that thing you spoke to the queen about earlier? About the animals running rampant?" I ask, abruptly cutting through the silence.

Kaja's face pinches as she looks up at me. "What do you mean?"

"You said people were uneasy because they'd seen livestock running through the woods."

Kaja nods, but her face remains strained. She takes a moment to think before responding. "We don't really know what's happening. People in many of our villages have said they've seen soldiers, but none of our reserves have been deployed anywhere near those areas. We have no good explanation for what's going on."

Something in my stomach drops at the thought of soldiers walking through Illena's woods. A familiar memory floats at the back of my mind, just out of reach.

"But there is a disease?" I ask her skeptically.

She shakes her head. "No, but when people have time to come up with their own conclusions, they do so, and it creates chaos."

"You lied to the queen then?"

"Not exactly. It is possible there are virus-stricken animals out there. It has happened before and there are some signs in the woods that point to this. We just don't have proof yet. The Bloodlines don't like to show weakness. If something is happening we don't know about, some military movement or band of civilians causing havoc, it makes us look like we are not in control. We can't have that."

I shake my head as a pit of dread sits heavily in my stomach. "No, we can't."

CHAPTER

THIRTY

LEO

I can't stop smiling as we all walk back toward the Ridge Palace. I keep replaying every second of the night in my mind, and for once, I don't want to stop seeing the memories.

"If you keep smiling like that, your face will freeze in a grin."

I look up at Cael and feel my cheeks flush as I secure Antares on my back. Cael was already holding Saiph, a bag of leftover sweets, and the boy's wet clothes, so I had to carry Antares, who refused to stand after falling asleep against my stool.

"I could say the same to you," I tell him.

He's been sporting that overjoyed expression since he joined us a few hours ago, just before the sun started to rise. He huffs a laugh as he looks at the sky. "That's the best night I've had in a while."

I gasp. "You mean to say that you had fun without me? Impossible."

He rolls his eyes, but I know he can see my own thoughts reflecting his. I don't think I've ever felt this... normal and happy. This is the life I've dreamed of, and we finally have it. We finally made it to where we wanted to be.

Someone running by crashes into me from behind, almost making me drop Antares. I steady myself and turn on the man, but he's already sprinting away.

"That was strange," Cael says, following the man with his eyes.

I nod as I put Antares down, my brother having woken from the jolting movement. As we continue, an unsettled feeling forms in my stomach. An all-too-familiar feeling.

Cael turns and looks down one of the roads leading to the cliffs. I stop in my tracks as I see Ares walking our way with a smile. He strolls down the middle of the street with his hands tucked behind his back, seemingly unfazed by anything around him. His clothes are muddied and out of place. One of his sleeves is ripped and hanging on by a thread. I call his name and his head jerks our way as he stumbles over his feet. In a fraction of a second, his expression is relaxed and his hands sway by his sides.

"Heading back so soon?" he asks.

I glance at Cael as Altair and Antares stay a step behind us. When Ares comes closer, I realize his lip is cut and face is newly bruised, the swelling not having given over to the coloring just yet.

"I'm more than ready for bed," Cael says, pulling a smile to Ares's lips as he laughs. "It seems like you had a good night?"

Ares looks down at himself, scanning his clothes. "I may have gotten a little out of hand." He rubs the back of his neck. "To be honest, I don't remember much of the past few hours. I think I passed out somewhere. I take it you all enjoyed your first Blaze?"

"It was definitely magical," I say, waving a hand through the air for dramatic effect.

"Good. And now that you're here, you can live dozens more. They get better every year." I smile as he looks past us at the palace. "I'd better get back. We can never get too comfortable with this peace."

"Of course," I tell him as he walks away. I shake my head. "He seemed drunk last night, but not that drunk."

Cael glances back in the direction Ares left. "He could easily have had more after you last saw him. I don't think it would be too hard."

I nod, but I'm not convinced. Who knows? Maybe Ares took the one night he didn't have to deal with the Bloodlines to blow off some steam. I'm sure I would do the same.

A scream rings from a few streets away. Our heads swivel toward the sound, barely managing to step out of the way of another two people hurrying in the direction of the water. Without a word, we follow their paths to the bay. The crowd thickens almost immediately, making it nearly impossible to break through. I clench Antares's hand as we push forward. With every few paces, more people pack together.

Something is wrong. My stomach lurches when I see the first person in tears. Then another. And another. Bystanders hold each other while others stand with their hands over their mouths, frantic eyes roaming the crowd. When the people realize who's pushing through, they step back to allow us to pass.

I don't know what I expected to see, but this isn't it. Two bodies are being lifted off a small fisherman's boat, their faces barely covered by a blanket. My heart stops as I watch them carry the bodies onto a dock, then onto the black sand. Soldiers flood in to push the crowd back.

They don't touch me as I drop Antares's hand and step forward. They track my steps, two guards falling in line behind me as I stand over the bodies. They aren't my usual guards. They're royal sentinels meant to protect the monarchs of Illena. The world goes completely silent, as if every person has stopped breathing. I crouch beside the bodies as my heart beats like a drum in my ears. I reach out and peel away the blanket. The ground tilts and sways.

"Your Majesty, you have to come with us."

I don't look at the soldier speaking to me. I don't move. I can't.

"The council must speak to you about the arrangements. We must prepare you for what comes next."

I blink. I run the words through my mind. Over and over. Again, and again.

I know Cael is standing behind me. He must have told the boys to stay back, but I know they can see the bodies. Everyone can see them. There's no mistaking the faces of the Queen and King of Illena.

CHAPTER

THIRTY-ONE

CAEL

People scream and cry as we're marched back to the palace. I had to pull Leo off the ground to get him to move. He doesn't say a word as we're pushed through the streets, surrounded by the king's guard. I keep close to his side, his face a ghastly shade of white. I catch sight of Red and her eyes lock with mine. Her expression is pained, but not with sadness like the rest of the mourners. She's scared, fear written across her face. I swallow as I turn back toward the path, holding Saiph tightly. This is not good.

THE KING'S guard ushers us into our rooms without a word. A click rings through the hollow space behind us. *They locked us in.* Leo starts pacing as he clenches and relaxes his fists, staring everywhere but at us.

"Antares, take Saiph. Go into the bedroom and don't come

out until I come get you," I tell him. He takes our sister but hesitates to follow Altair into the room.

"What's going to happen now?" Antares whispers, as if speaking too loudly might set something dangerous in motion.

I shake my head as I fail to muster any type of comfort. "I don't know."

"Is Leo going to be king?"

"No," Leo interjects, his voice sharp as he stops moving. "Ares will be king. Ares is next in line."

"Then why do you look like that?" Antares presses.

"The queen and king are dead. I don't know if this changes our ability to stay here," Leo whispers, as if to himself.

Antares looks back at me with wide eyes as Leo stares past him out the windows.

"I'm sure they have a plan to deal with this. We'll figure it out," I assure him.

Antares takes his cue and turns away. As he shuts the door behind him, Emrys and Byrne step out of her room but stop short before approaching.

"What happened?" Byrne asks softly.

"The king and queen are dead," I tell them.

Emrys blinks, his face blank as he barely registers the words. "What do you mean?"

"A fisherman just pulled their bodies out of the bay."

Emrys stands frozen with horror. Byrne moves closer and wraps her arm around him.

"That's impossible," Emrys whispers as his eyes search my expression. After a moment, he swears and runs his hands down his face. "This can't be happening..."

"Emrys, we need to know how this is going to go," I say carefully. A change in monarch can mean so many things. So many possibilities that uproot the peace we've just started to accept.

His glazed eyes land on Leo as something dawns on him. "They had no heirs." He takes a deep breath as he shakes his head. "They never designated a successor."

"What does that mean?" I push as my mind goes blank.

"She didn't dictate that Ares would get the crown if they died, which is the only way to divert the line of succession from its natural course. Making your brother next in line. Leo is the king of Illena. The title passed to him the moment the queen and king died."

The room seems suffocating as Leo freezes.

Emrys pushes a hand through his sleep-messed hair. "I need to go. The Bloodlines will be salivating at an empty throne." He whispers something to Byrne before grabbing the jacket he'd had on last night and slipping out through the window.

Seconds later, a knock sounds at the door.

"I'm going to stay with the children," Byrne says.

I nod and turn toward Leo, hearing the bedroom door shut behind me. He hasn't moved a muscle. I step closer and wave my hand in front of his face. His eyes snap to mine as panic grips his expression.

"Don't let them in," he pleads. His hands are shaking furiously as whoever is behind the door pounds against the wood again. "Please, Cael."

I shake my head and gently lead him onto one of the couches. I feel his gaze tracking my steps as I head toward the door. I take a deep breath and pull it open. The king's guard steps out of the way, leaving six council members in matching black finery standing before me. Ceto steps forward from the group, cutting off a bitter-looking man before he has the chance to start.

"I'm sorry to do this, but we have to speak to him."

"You can't talk to him right now," I tell them. I start to push the door shut, but Ceto holds it open.

"We don't have a choice, Cael. This isn't something that can wait," Ceto presses.

I search his face and sigh in frustration when I see the question lingering in his eyes. "He didn't do it." A woman scoffs from the back of the group.

"We have more to speak about than just that," Ceto says.

"Leo doesn't want any of this. He never has. You won't change his mind. We were told he wouldn't have to take the throne."

Ceto smiles sadly, as if he understands the impact of his presence. "I know, but circumstances have changed, and we must do this formally. There are things concerning the crown that you both are not aware of, and he can't make the decision to reject it without being completely informed. But we have important matters we need to discuss before we get to that."

I glance back at Leo. He's staring at the floor, his chest moving with shallow breaths.

"The guards won't come in," Ceto reassures.

I shake my head. Leo can't do this. He needs time to think, time to process. We all do.

I'm about to tell Ceto to leave again when he interrupts. "We can't go until we speak to him, Cael. I don't want to make this difficult."

I glance back at the guards as their hands shift to their weapons. I close my eyes and swallow the helplessness rising in my throat. *Let the Goddess forgive me for this.* I step aside and let them in.

I sit beside Leo and watch the councilors carefully as they take the seats across from us. Leo doesn't look up. He doesn't acknowledge their presence in any way.

"Your Majesty, where were you last night after you left the party?"

"You can't honestly think we could have done this?" I say. Ceto's eyes flicker back and forth between Leo and me.

"I need an answer from him. He has the most to gain from having committed such a crime. We need to make sure there was no foul play before we move on with succession."

"I didn't do it," Leo says, his voice weak. "We went to the Riv to see the bonfires after leaving the party. The boys swam in the canals. Their wet clothes are in a bag on the table. They were handing out different sweets every hour in the Riv. We have pieces leftover. We saw Ares when we were walking back this morning. We were in the Riv all night. We never saw the royals. We never saw them after we left. We never saw them."

Ceto exchanges a look with a council member who moves from behind the couch towards the table where we set everything from last night. He takes out the sweets and the wet clothes before nodding back to Ceto who seems to deflate before our eyes, satisfied with the evidence.

"Now that that's settled, you know what we must speak about, Your Majesty," Ceto says. When Leo makes no move to answer, he continues with a soft voice. "Both the queen and king reigned for many years, but it was not expected for them to die so suddenly, together, without a clear heir. Though you had a verbal agreement with them, they never named another line of succession. This makes you the rightful heir. Do you understand?"

The room stays silent.

"I won't be your king," Leo whispers. He raises his eyes, burning with flames.

Ceto's lips tighten with grief. "I need to explain every fact before your decision can be final. And before you make your declaration, I need you to comprehend and acknowledge what

I'm saying. Do you understand you are currently the rightful heir to Illena?"

Leo stares him down with a crippling gaze. Ceto only lifts his chin, as if he's been through this many times before.

"Yes."

"Good," Ceto says, relaxing ever so slightly at the cooperation. "What you may not know is that your father never officially abdicated, and his right to the throne was not terminated because he died. When the late king had to choose his heir, instead of naming his eldest, Ares, he chose his second born, Kalani. He never divulged why, but he made us swear to never allow Ares to take the throne. This is why we are here. We swore an oath, and we will do everything in our power to keep it."

"That's why you're damning this country? Because of an oath you made to a dead king?" Leo argues heatedly. "I *don't know how* to rule. Don't you understand that?"

Ceto nods slowly. "We do. We know that Illena has only briefly been your home and that court is not where you wish to spend your days, but there are more reasons for us to be here than just an oath. Whether you have seen it or not, the people respect you. You saved strangers from a fire without a second thought. You walk the streets without fear. You have a family with which you have strong relations, as many of our people do. All these things have led them to trust you. If you refuse to take the throne, the council will be forced to rule as an intermediary. The people will not be satisfied with this, but worse, the Bloodlines or others seeking power will see it as opportunity. They will fight for the throne and throw this country into a civil war. They will murder you and your family to keep you from stepping back in. They will cause chaos on an extreme scale."

I stare at him, aghast. "How could you possibly know all of that?"

"There are already whispers of plans in progress. This is why we need you to decide now. The faster we announce your succession, the safer you will all be."

"You don't know they will kill us," Leo seethes.

Ceto looks at him with pity. "You are a threat. If you don't maintain the order, they will destroy you. You could try to run, but you will be no better off than before you arrived. And even if by chance you manage to escape, Anateya will no longer be able to protect you as you may have once planned. You are already familiar with the laws dictating the survival of our kind in the other three countries. Only this time, the Bloodlines will be hunting you down as well." He sighs as he leans forward. "If I could help you, I would. If not for your family's sake, then for your father, but there is no place you will be safe if you do not take the throne."

Leo swallows hard. After a moment, he runs a hand through his hair and leans back. "My family could die if I don't do this?"

"Hundreds will die, including your family. This is in the best interest of everyone, Leo. We will teach you how to rule. There will be missteps, but you'll figure it out. You will learn."

Leo turns his head to look at me. I see the desperation in his eyes, but I have no answer for him. We can't afford to lose this place as a home. As much as I hate it, Ceto's logic makes sense. There would be nowhere for us to hide if someone uncontrollable took the throne and decided to tie up loose ends. For the first time in our lives, this is a decision Leo has to make completely on his own. He must see it in my eyes because the little strength he has left crumbles away.

"I'll do it."

PART TWO
FALSE KING

CHAPTER
THIRTY-TWO

LEO

I can't breathe. My lungs are too tight. My words play over in my head again and again. *I'll do it.* How could I agree? How can I lead *thousands* of people when I can barely keep my own family alive? *I'll do it.* I hear the door close somewhere behind me, but I can't make myself move. My lungs heave as my heart pounds in my ears. *I'll do it.*

"Leo, you need to breathe."

I can't tear my eyes away from the floor as my body refuses to move, to think, to see, to breathe. I gasp for air, but my lungs refuse to constrict.

"Leo, you need to breathe!"

I'm suffocating, drowning, choking on my own throat. Panicking. I can't breathe. *I'll do it.*

My arms are folded against my chest as a hand wraps around my chin, forcing my eyes up.

"Try to breathe with me."

I do as Cael says, watching my brother's chest inflate and

deflate, finally feeling my own begin to do the same. I blink as my mind quiets. Cael exhales gratefully as he pastes on a thin smile.

"Better?" Cael asks as he moves to sit beside me, leaning his head back to look at the ceiling. "You scared me there."

"I'm scared," I reply as I squeeze my eyes shut, trying to imagine myself in a different place, without a roof or walls or a future in chains.

"Me too." Cael shifts as if he's thinking about what to say next. "You should go see her."

My eyes shoot open. "What?"

My brother smiles softly. "You need to get out of here. Go see Elana. Work through your thoughts. Then when you come back, we'll figure out how we're going to handle this."

For the millionth time, I'm amazed by how well Cael knows me.

"Are you going to be all right with them?" I ask, nodding toward the bedroom.

Cael scoffs. "When have I not been able to handle them?"

I roll my eyes and manage a weak smile. "Thank you." I should probably tell him that more often than I do. "For under-standing."

Cael smiles sadly. "What else is a brother for?"

I stand and head toward the window as Cael calls, "Don't do anything stupid until you get back."

I huff a laugh and watch through the window as guards clamber by. When I get my opening, I swing myself out. "I wouldn't dream of it."

I DON'T LOOK toward the bay as I head for the Riv. I hear the people crying and screaming. Singing and praying. The streets

I walk down are filled with guards and soldiers searching for anything suspicious. Every other soul has gone to the black sand to pay their respects. Looking around, there's evidence of last night's festivities everywhere. Charred wood and broken shards of glass litter the streets. I wonder if they'll ever get cleaned up.

When I get to the lopsided building that Hela's Bond calls home, I don't go to the door. Instead, I scale the wall and slip in through the open window as I did long ago. When she was strong enough, Elana took the room we'd first entered. I haven't climbed the wall again since, but each time we come, I find the window propped open.

My feet land on the floor and I close my eyes instantly as I feel cold steel bite at my throat. I push away panic, forcing myself to calm my racing heart.

"You know, a simple hello would suffice," I say, trying to sound aloof but failing miserably as my tone falls flat.

The steel drops away, but I keep my eyes shut. I don't move for fear of shattering. A gentle hand lands shakily on my cheek. I open my eyes and Elana is staring at me, her lips pressed into a thin line. She stands barely a foot away. I lean into her touch and wrap my arms around her.

"What is it?" she whispers.

I clench my jaw to keep my lip from quivering. I feel my eyes glaze as my breath gets caught in my chest. She steps closer as I sway, and she lowers her hand to hold me steady.

"I'm going to be king."

Her face stays blank as I feel mine falling apart. She seems to be working out what's happened in her mind as she takes in my words. I try to muster a smile, but all that breaches the surface is a sob. Tears fall as I am consumed by the pressure, pushing away every rational thought. I bury my face in her shoulder as her hand runs up and down my back, trying to comfort me. It only makes the pressure worse. All at once my mind is cracking, breaking into pieces. I don't know when I collapse, but one minute I'm standing and the next I'm on the floor.

Elana doesn't leave my side. She waits until my panic abates and turns my face so I can look her in the eyes. "You'll make a great king."

I shake my head, words bubbling up without time for my mind to think them through. "I can barely keep myself alive. I've lost so much, so many people. How can I keep a whole country safe? How can they expect me to do this?"

She sits silently for a moment, trying to put the best words together. "But in the face of everything you've been through, you got your family here. You got Byrne and me here. You may have suffered, but that makes you better suited for this. You know what's at stake. It takes suffering to know how to fix a problem. You can do this. You can adapt. You'll find a way to lead, and we'll never leave your side."

"And what if I can't? What if I fail?"

She huffs a laugh and wipes a stray tear with her thumb. "Then you start again. If you make a mistake, you fix it and make the country better than it was before. A villain will never be written as a villain if they rebuild a better home than the one they burnt."

I take a breath and feel my fear abate. Maybe I can do this. Never have we found a place to live peacefully. If they wish to force my hand, maybe this is my chance to make one.

THIRTY-THREE

LEO

Two weeks after the death of the queen and king and there's barely an hour left before I take their place. Ceto's been carting me around from sunrise until well past sunset every day for political meetings and official gatherings with the Bloodlines. Every day has been planned down to the second, cramming my brain with strategy and teaching me every detail about the last five centuries of Illena. By the time I get to see Elana and Cass every night, I'm exhausted.

The funeral took place three days after the royals passed. I've never seen so many people in mourning, but I've never known a country to respect its leaders so genuinely. We've toured as many cities and towns as possible over the three days, and for the first time, I really understand how large Illena is, and I've only seen a small portion of the land I'm going to rule.

"How are you feeling?" Cael asks as the tailor finally leaves our rooms.

I've been practically sewn into my outfit. It's made of a deep burgundy fabric embroidered with a huge black double-dog that wraps all the way around my torso. The old queen was against my wearing my father's weapons at the coronation, but I'd refused to attend without them. It had been my only stipulation, so she'd folded easily enough. The only change I've made is to hang my slayers at my hip instead of on my back. Even though it feels unfamiliar, I must admit it does look more... regal. I turn to my brother as the solid black cape attached over my right shoulder sways over the floor.

"Like I'm going to vomit," I tell Cael as my stomach churns.

He smiles weakly. "It will be over before you know it. Plus, Ceto promised no surprises, remember? We both know exactly how this is going to go."

I nod, remembering the lecture. *You'll walk in slowly, each step just under a second. The music will start, and people will stand. You'll keep your eyes straight on the podium and your chin high. Do not stop. Do not look around. When you get there, I will say the opening line of the coronation in Keyonic, and you will kneel. Do not be concerned about what we will be saying. These are the words of the Death Dancers and are meant as a blessing. Then you will stand, turn to face the people, and repeat the phrase I taught you while I set the crown on your head...*

No matter how many times Ceto ran through the proceedings and assured me every coronation has gone smoothly, I can't shake the dread clouding my mind. Ares came by this morning to wish me luck, and I could sense that he was off. I've been told some of the other Bloodlines aren't happy I'm taking the throne and my cousin has been trying to keep the peace. Thank the Goddess for him.

"None of it makes me feel any better," I tell Cael weakly.

He sighs as he straightens my jacket. "I like this just about as much as you do, but you *were* born to be king. No matter what you or I want to believe. You'll figure it out like you have everything else."

"What if I get people killed? What if I burn Illena to the ground?" My heart is beating like the hooves of stampeding horses.

Cael smiles reassuringly, stepping toward the exit. "Then you rebuild it from the ashes." He opens the door to four waiting guards. Each one nods in respect. "And become the king you want to be."

———

CAEL WENT to take his position on the dais behind the council, and I'm left standing in a crimson room with half a dozen guards. They don't speak, but I feel their eyes. More accurately, I feel their curiosity. My head is seconds away from exploding under the tension of their stares when the door to the throne room opens.

I walk in slowly, noticing everything is bright: the tapestries hanging from ceiling to floor, the light shining through the stained-glass windows, the hundreds of eyes watching my every move. I count the seconds in time with my steps and look anywhere but at the pedestal. That iron crown, taunting me, pulls me ahead. My eyes lock with Cael's and he nods reassuringly.

Byrne, Altair, Antares, and Saiph are to my left, standing in the front row of pews. Altair keeps his eyes forward, while Antares does the opposite, looking everywhere around the room. He can't sit still, fidgeting with the lapel of his coat. I want nothing more than to do the same.

I glance back at Cael and follow his eyes upwards toward

the rafters. I stifle a laugh as I catch sight of Hela's Bond, Elana and Cass watching over us from high above the room. My heart stutters at Elana's smile and the confidence in her gaze.

I straighten my shoulders and return my attention to what's before me, finally allowing myself to see the crown. It's old, made without jewels or adornment, with a peak that stretches up at the center, like a mountain bursting from a plain. For being such a high society, their crown appropriately reflects the exact opposite. The hardship and struggle. The iron backbone of Illena. The crown is carved with sweeping engravings... Words. Ancient words. Similar to those I read in the tunnel under the royal grounds. My blood goes cold.

When I step up to the dais, the music dies with the muttering of the crowd. Ceto speaks in a language I don't understand, harsh tones mixed with guttural letters, yet somehow, the sounds are familiar. I watch as he moves, and I recite what he has taught me. My heart beats slowly, easily. Ceto watches me with flitting eyes as the words flow from my mouth like a song. I know their meaning without thinking. *The land is mine, and my soul the land's. The sky my breath, the sea my blood. The air my thoughts, the fire my heart. I own all and the great will own me, forever more, for death is only a doorway to a life of greater power.*

Ceto raises the crown above my head and switches to his mother tongue as he addresses the crowd. My blood buzzes at its proximity. "For generations, Illenians have hidden in fear and fought for our lives. For years, we have survived, and for centuries onward, we will thrive!"

Cheers roar through the room as Ceto lowers the crown. This is it. This is the moment I've dreaded. And yet for all that worry, in this moment, I can't feel anything thing but ecstasy. I realize this is who I was meant to be. This is my fate.

"With the blessings of Illena in my hands and generations

of Illenean rulers in my mind, I crown Leo Matteus, son of Dirix Matteus, the rightful ruler of the people and land, King of Ile—"

I hear the whizzing sound a fraction of a second before it passes through the space where my head had just been. No one dares to breathe as the crown clinks against the wall, ripped from Ceto's hands by an arrow, now firmly wedged in the mortar between two stones of the wall. Slow clapping rises from the back of the room. The echo of weapons being drawn rings out in time with the appearance of a cloaked figure standing from his seat. I keep my hands pinned to my sides as I look at Cael. He takes the cue and moves toward the boys. I steal a glance at the ceiling but don't see Elana or Hela's Bond. I push the thought aside as I face the figure.

"You know, I fought with myself over whether I should let you be crowned. You *are* the true heir, firstborn son of the King Who Never Was."

I hear Cael stumble as the voice of the man registers in my mind. He moves toward the aisle I walked up only moments ago. People try to intercept him, but the guards, *my guards,* carve him a path. People cling to each other as he approaches, calm and sure-footed.

"So many great stories you so conveniently stepped into. Embodied even. Meanwhile, I've been working for *years* and bided my time. Waiting. So, I think this is an appropriate moment to intervene. Because that crown isn't yours..." He pulls down the hood. Gasps ring out through the room as I clench my jaw. "It's mine." A vile smirk curdles Ares's face.

"You agreed to let me take the throne," I tell him, keeping my chin raised as Cael moves closer to Byrne and the boys. I don't know where this is going, but with the number of soldiers in the room who are turning toward me, I know I need to stall.

"I don't recall ever saying such things." He steps closer and pulls the cloak from his shoulders, revealing the exact same regalia as the one the tailors sewed for me. This isn't a spur of the moment decision.

Heads swivel as a scream booms from outside the doors I'd just entered. The Bloodlines are huddling close together, gazes flying as they try to figure out what's happening.

"When you showed me the numbers on your wrist, I was convinced you were the rightful heir, but I'm not so sure now," Ares continues.

"I don't know what you're talking about," I tell him as Cael reaches the boys.

The Bloodlines have armed themselves—all but the Damaris line, who have sunk into the back of the room. I don't see Kaja as I glance their way.

"Did you really think you could get away with coming to Illena and stealing the crown? It cannot be a coincidence you arrived claiming not to want the crown, then my sister and her husband mysteriously drown on a night you and your entire family disappeared from court."

My brows crease as I shake my head.

"I trusted you. Opened my arms to you and your usurper family as if you were my own blood, but all you were after was power, wasn't it? So, you committed regicide."

The gasps that rise in the room are barely louder than my pounding heart.

"I haven't killed anyone here," I announce loudly.

He looks devastated, but I see the malice in his eyes brewing like a storm. "But you are a mercenary, no? Accomplished and renowned for the *hundreds* of lives you brutally stole in Tominay?"

I stay quiet, caught off guard.

"And you very conveniently went to your room early the

night my sister was murdered. But no guards let you into your room. No guards saw you on the floor at all."

"I was in the Riv," I say, doing everything to keep my voice from wavering as Ares stops in the middle of the wide hall.

"The *Riv?* You expect us to believe you left the most lavish party in the country to spend the night with *slumbloods?* And what's more is that even though you claim to be a Matteus, you don't take the name, do you? You go by Leo *Heal*. What true heir would renounce the name of their crown?"

People mutter as they turn their angry gazes on me. Ares is getting to them.

I open my mouth to retort, but he's two steps ahead of me. "Even if you don't believe me, you should believe him."

The door swings open and the air punches out from my chest. I hear Byrne muffle a scream as Cassien steps into the hall. His face is flat as he looks around the room, stopping only momentarily on Byrne.

"I present the High Lord of the gold-eyed people, Solius Cassien. This man has come to me with disturbing information," Ares announces.

"Leo Heal was taken in by a generous family from my city of Wate. They gave him shelter to keep him safe but ended up dead."

Blood roars in my ears as I grip my slayer so hard the skin of my hand feels like it's tearing.

"When he came to us, we welcomed him. We gave his *brothers* a true family and education, but he wanted control."

I shake my head as memories flash in my head.

Cassien continues, "He burnt down buildings and terrorized families. When we tried to stop him, he took my daughters as captives, swearing one day he would erase me from this earth."

"That's not true," Byrne says as anger rages through her.

Emrys has made his way behind her, keeping only steps away. "We left of our own free will to escape you. You were the one who kept us captive."

"You see?" Cassien says, wearing a mask of dismay. "He's made you think he saved you. But how could stealing a daughter from her father be a blessing?"

Byrne's face is pale as she shakes her head.

"You need to leave," I tell him. "Both of you need to leave."

Ares steps in front of Cassien and tilts his head with a smirk. "How, in good conscience, could I leave someone like you to take a throne that is not rightfully yours?"

A blast goes off somewhere in the distance outside. I pull my blades as I stare Ares down. Screams fill the room as more guards throw open the doors. Ceto steps in front of me.

"This is no way to take the throne," he tells Ares. "Your father warned me about what you might do. He made me swear to never place the crown on your head because he saw no righteousness in you."

Ares's face shifts to pure rage as he grinds his teeth. He straightens his jacket as the Bloodlines watch, confused by the exchange.

"Well. It's a good thing my father isn't here then," Ares says as he raises his hand toward me. "Bring me his heart."

THIRTY-FOUR

LEO

My mind whirls as arrows rain from the sky. The Bloodlines move in practiced units as they escape through the pack of guards now marching toward me. They're following Ares's commands. I'm jerked back abruptly as the guards still loyal to me create a wall, weapons drawn and knees bent as they wait for the oncoming crush. Before I can blink, I'm being shoved through a door at the back of the room. I turn and lock eyes with Ceto as he pushes an object into my chest. The crown.

"Go to the Killarian market and find the chemist. Your Riv friends will know where to find him. Wait for me there." I open my mouth to speak, but he stops me abruptly. "Go!"

With crazed eyes, Ceto pulls a dagger from his belt and slams the door closed. I grip the crown and turn to where Cael stands, holding Saiph tightly.

"We need to go," Cael says.

I swallow my panic and nod. Emrys has Byrne's hand as he

looks back at us from farther up the hall. He's deathly pale as he urges us forward. Screams rip through the walls as we turn a corner and enter an abandoned kitchen.

"They closed this part of the servants' wing when they built the addition above it, years before I was born. They never bothered to repurpose it, so it sits empty," Emrys says. He heads toward a cupboard and throws open the doors, sending a thick layer of dust flying into the air. Coughing, he grabs a few coats and a blanket before throwing them our way. "My cousins used to spend time here and use this passage to smuggle in their drink from the city," he explains, answering my questioning glance as he pulls on a dark jacket.

I shove the crown inside my coat before buttoning it and pulling the hood over my face. I grab Antares's hand as Cael wraps the threadbare blanket over himself and Saiph. "Hold on to my jacket and do not let go. Do you understand?"

Antares nods shakily.

I take a deep breath and kneel to look him in the eyes. "We're going to be all right. But I need you to stay by my side no matter what. Promise me you won't let go?"

"I promise," he whispers, sniffling.

I nod and stand to face Emrys. "We need to get to the Killarian market."

His eyes go wide as he shakes his head. "Absolutely not. We need to get to the underground tunnels you and Cael found and hide until the fighting settles. We have no idea what's happening out there. We're not running into the most popu-lated place in Arkezo."

"Ceto told me to find the chemist, so that's where we're going."

"Your own *cousin* just tried to kill you and is in the process of stealing an entire kingdom from under your feet. Why do you think Ceto would help?" Emrys's hands are glowing slightly as he grinds his teeth. He's terrified.

A giant blast goes off from somewhere nearby, shaking the walls and sending us stumbling.

"Ceto had his chance to kill me, but instead he pushed me in here and told me to go to Killarian. I don't care what you want to do, we're going to the market. You can come or hide by yourself." I look at Cael and he nods with me.

Emrys runs a frustrated hand over his face and grumbles as he starts toward a door to our left. We follow quickly, turning corners and sprinting down halls. A guard spots us as we exit the servants' quarters. He doesn't have time to scream before his eyes roll back in his head. Emrys stares at me as if he's seeing me for the first time—with crimson eyes and a bloodied blade in my hand. His lips thin as he turns away and continues forward, holding Byrne's hand in a death grip.

When we reach the outside of the palace, rain beats down in sheets. People run through the streets screaming as fires blaze from every intersection. Soldiers wearing gold armbands march in unison toward the Riv, cutting people down along the way. Some are being detained and thrown into black carriages while others are left bleeding and crying alone on the stone pathways. My heart pounds as I realize what they've done.

"Ares is using Cassien's legions to take over." I look at Byrne with wide eyes. "The crates of weapons. The training. He's been planning for this."

"And they're burning the houses," Cael says, his eyes looking to the south where most of the smoke can be seen. I step toward it, but Cael grabs my arm, his eyes crazed. "We can't help them now. We need to get out."

"Cass and Elana might still be there," I say.

He shakes his head furiously. "The Bond are smarter than

that. Even they can't fight an army by themselves. Not like this."

"How will they find us?"

"Red signed to me before they disappeared. They're going to find us outside the gates."

I shake my head as my thoughts swim. "Then let's go."

I push forward as I pull my slayers into my hands. I let my eyes bleed red and feel a blanket of calm pull over me. A dark voice whispers at the back of my mind, filling my head with noise. I have to push the voice away. I won't sink now.

We run through the chaos of scampering and screaming people. Thunder rattles the sky as I step in front of Altair, stopping the heart of a lone soldier who had his eyes set on my brother. Another soldier with a gold armband runs at us with raised fists, but Emrys intercepts him, pushing him to his knees before placing a blazing hand over his eyes to blind him. That voice in my head laughs at the sight.

We stay in a tight circle when we leave the royal grounds and fold ourselves into an alley between two shops. The downpour of rain continues as crimson streams flow through the stone roads toward the bay. Legions of soldiers with bright red armbands join the fight from the north, marching in tight formations. They move through the gold soldiers, beating their own people to the ground as they advance toward the Riv.

I realize something as I spin behind Cael and pull a gold soldier to the ground before stomping on his spine and kicking my heel into his jaw. Cassien's gold soldiers weren't dispatched for any purpose but to create chaos, a cover for the blood-eyed legions to march on the Riv and tear it to shreds.

"Leo!"

I turn so quickly my feet almost get caught beneath me. Elana's running toward us with Cass by her side and Hela's Bond at her back. I sheathe my blades and kneel to look at

Cass. He's a bit shaken but doing all right. I stand and scan Elana. She wipes a smear of blood from my face with shaking fingers. Her eyes are hollow as they meet mine, her wet hair is stark against her pallor.

"It's not mine," I tell her softly as I raise my hand to hold hers.

I open my mouth to ask if she's hurt, but Red shifts between us. There's a gash on her shoulder, but she's moving as if she can't feel it.

"We need to get you out of here," Red says hurriedly. Her hand grips Gray's sleeve so hard she's ripping through the fabric.

"They're going to destroy the Riv," I blurt.

Red's eyes go wide as her head swivels toward the legions marching south. I watch the anguish on her face as the pieces click together in her mind. The silence becomes too heavy to bear. Red closes her eyes and turns to Kiro. Soren grabs him as he understands what's happening.

"My mother. I can't leave her! Let me go!" Kiro says, thrashing.

Red steps in front of him as Soren begins to lose his grip.

"We can't go back," she tells Kiro.

"What are you talking about?" Kiro pleads breathlessly. He hasn't stopped struggling against Soren's hold.

"We need to get Leo out. We can't risk Ares finding him."

Kiro's eyes flit to me then back to Red. "You don't need me. I can get to her!"

"We had a plan for this. Trust that she'll follow it and get out. By now the alarms will have gone off and she'll be deep in the woods with hundreds of other people. If you go, you chance revealing their location and getting yourself killed. So you won't go. I won't allow it."

Kiro shakes his head furiously but doesn't say another

word. *They knew something like this could happen. They prepared for it.* The thought echoes through my head as Red turns back toward me with a question on her face.

"We need to get to the chemist in the Killarian market," Cael says on my behalf.

Red nods as her brows furrow. "I know the way."

THE FARTHER NORTH WE GO, the more deserted the streets become. People have either fled or taken refuge in their homes, barring doors and windows to protect themselves against the onslaught of soldiers that will march through. The air is too still as Red leads us through alleys and backstreets toward the Killarian Market. When we turn into New Corsair, the streets are completely abandoned. Belongings are strewn on the ground and doors are boarded up. They must have been prepared to evacuate to have done it so quickly. I can hear the racket of the ships sailing out in the distance as we head deeper into the city.

"They haven't been here yet," Cael remarks as he scans the streets, looking around for any evidence of blood stains or broken bodies.

I nod as a chill runs down my spine.

"Knowing Ares, he'll send his forces here soon. If he wants to ravage the city's undesirable corners, he'll run through the first floor of the market. It's just a matter of time," Emrys says quietly.

Deca looks at Emrys with a rage that could melt the flesh from his bones, but at the touch of Emmani's hand, her gaze sobers. Soren stays close behind Kiro who periodically glances back toward the Riv, murmuring things under his breath I choose to ignore.

We reach the market, and all the aromatic signs of flourishing life that had filled the streets have disappeared. Most of the brightly colored mats and flags have been taken in, presumably to avoid ruination. Only one tattered red cloth remains, whipping in the wind against a stone pillar. I breathe and let go of my instincts. Crimson tears fall down my face as I swallow my dread and head through a back door blocked by crates.

When we enter the building, my eyes water. The air is thick with the smell of chemicals and unwashed bodies. I keep Cass and Antares tight to my side, and I shift closer to Elana as she coughs. The point of the crown digs into my chest as we walk close together through the winding maze of stalls. People sit on ripped carpets with their goods gathered in satchels lined up in front of them. Some yell to us as we pass, while others stare through us. Red moves swiftly toward a woman who has a ramshackle booth set up near the wall. I grip my dagger as I inspect her wares—bones of all sorts, hanging haphazardly off the dilapidated posts and heaped together in piles.

Red takes out a pouch and hands it gently to the woman. Her fingers twitch as she opens it and brings it up to her milky eyes. The woman smiles toothlessly, giggling as she jumps with excitement. She curls her finger for Red to come near and whispers in her ear. Red motions for us to follow as she pulls away from the haggard woman.

Red nods to a few vendors as we weave through the stalls but doesn't say a word. Each peels away quietly and disappears into the darkness. Red finally stops near the back and pulls open a curtain. Emmani teeters from foot to foot as we file in. I glance back before the curtain swings shut and catch some of the vendors frantically folding away their possessions.

The air here is thick with yellow smoke. I lift my hand and

swirl my fingers. The air does loops around them, flowing like a river's current around a stone.

"I would have preferred if Emmani came alone like usual, Red."

I turn abruptly and my eyes land on a boy, maybe a year younger than Antares. His clothes are tattered, and his face is smeared with soot.

Emmani wraps her arms around him. "I missed you too, you little cockroach."

He pushes her away, but I see the comfort in his eyes. She pulls back and the boy runs his hand through his greasy hair.

"So, what is it today? Obsidian powder? Carbon shards? I've been working on synthesizing some new concentrates that might make that cold fire of yours burn longer," he says, nodding toward a table of jars behind him.

"You know it's coronation day?" Red interjects, moving her hands swiftly to translate for Gray.

The boy's face goes blank. His eyes shift to me and go wide with understanding. There's no fear in his open expression and it makes me wonder what it must be like to live his life. "Why is the king in my workshop?"

"Ares led a coup. His army marched on the Riv and I wouldn't be surprised if they're making their way here as we speak." As I say it, a blast goes off from somewhere in the distance.

The boy grinds his teeth as he looks to Emmani for confirmation. He grumbles when she nods, but it seems more out of annoyance than concern.

"We're supposed to meet the head of the royal council here," Cael says as the boy moves around his shop, pulling out and packing up jars of powders.

He yanks the curtain aside and yells at someone to prep more chemicals, the names of which I couldn't pronounce if I tried. He leaves us staring in silence for a few minutes before moving a cart stacked with coils of wire that run up the walls and disappear into the murky darkness.

"Ceto sent you?" he asks.

I nod.

The boy laughs as he grabs three packages and tosses them to Emmani. "The regular and some extra toys. I added some notes in with the last pack," he says to her before turning back to me. "That old Bloodline loves to poke his head in places he doesn't belong. He's a Goddess-damned good chemist though. And smart for sending you here. No ruler in their right mind would destroy the biggest market in the country and upset the international vendors who sell here. So instead, Ares delays his attack to give the merchants time to evacuate while isolating the people who have nowhere else to go."

Right as he says it, a hooded figure yanks the curtain aside and enters the room. Ceto pulls his jacket off and takes us in, hesitating when he sees Red and Gray before blinking in recognition. Hela's Bond draws their weapons slowly. Ceto straightens his back to stand taller against the show of strength.

"Ares's blood-eyed forces are marching here as we speak. We have only a few minutes if we're lucky," Ceto announces.

I find Elana's hand beside me and intertwine our fingers. The touch grounds me enough to clear my thoughts. "Then we have to go. I'm hoping you have a place in mind?"

Ceto nods with certainty. He glances at the boy, taking a moment to consider his words. He shakes his head before meeting my eyes. "There is a royal safe house carved into the mountains. It can fit hundreds of people and has enough resources to last a long enough to figure out our next move. It was meant as a shelter in case of an outside invasion, but I believe this qualifies."

"We can bring people with us?" Kiro pushes as desperation shines in his eyes.

"It has the facilities to house a small army and a passageway to Anateya. The Death Dancers carved it out centuries ago and we have kept it stocked in case of disaster. Only a handful of people who knew of its existence: myself, a team of ten soldiers I watched Ares cut down at the coronation, and the late Queen and King."

I ponder his response, feeling as though this option is too good to be true.

"We're sure Ares doesn't know about this place?" Cael asks skeptically as Saiph clutches his shirt.

Ceto shakes his head. "We were sworn to secrecy, a breach punishable by death, and no records were ever kept. This fortress is secure."

"But can we get to the mountains without being caught?"

Lines crease Ceto's face as he watches us. "The fortress is meant for an army, not as an evacuation center. Not only that, but the chances of being followed should you allow citizens inside would increase tenfold. If Ares marches on that base before you have forces in place or a way to hide, there will be nowhere else to go."

"You would let your people be vulnerable? Left without resources or shelter?" Soren presses incredulously, keeping one hand on Kiro's shirt as Kiro's fists shake.

"I would take the only chance this country has at dethroning a man who just slaughtered hundreds his own people," Ceto counters. "Regardless, we don't have time to discuss the others. We need to leave now."

I glance at Cael with a storm of thoughts in my mind, then turn to Ceto. "If the people meet us in the forest, could we lead them to the mountains?"

The old man watches me for a moment, taking me in. He

nods as a smile appears on his face. My heart stutters when I catch the pride in his expression. I shake the feeling away and turn to Red.

"Can you get them there?" I ask her.

She nods without hesitation. Red and Deca move the curtain and step out without another word.

"I'll show you out," the boy says, having put on a thick vest.

We walk through a narrow hall, and I check over my shoulder every few paces, counting heads again and again. Elana takes my hand and holds Cass's shoulder with the other. My heart is light as I watch her check on my brother.

"Why don't you come with us?" Emmani asks the boy as we turn a sharp corner.

"We're the rats of the Killarian, Emmani. We live and die within these walls. No one can take us away from the shadows." I hear the smile in his voice as he speaks.

Emmani slings an arm over his shoulders. "Just be safe. Promise me that."

"I'll survive. I always do," he says with a smirk.

We reach a wooden door at the end of the hall and Emmani kicks it open. The rain seems to have settled. We pull our hoods back over our heads and step outside. Red and Deca reappear behind us, sweat shining on their faces.

"We need to move. They're trying to breach the building," Red announces.

The boy, who I realize never told us his name, gives us a grin that smothers his face in excitement. "Good luck, Your Majesty. Remember we did you a favor, will you?"

With a wink, he shuts the door and locks it from the inside. I turn toward the mountains towering over us from the north. They must be a few hours' walk away. I swallow my apprehension and pull my shoulders back. We'll make it. There is no other choice.

CHAPTER

THIRTY-FIVE

ELANA

I keep my eyes on Byrne and my hand on Cass as we run. Leo's only a step behind as we follow Hela's Bond through the streets. I don't let myself think past my next step. *Cassien's here.* I shake the thought away as my heart pounds. We cut through a residential district and it's deathly silent. The rain has let up, but thunder still rumbles in the distance.

Ceto yells the directions to the compound as we run. "Go toward the middle peak. There is a line of boulders with ancient markings carved by the Death Dancers that will show you the way. Follow the symbols up the mountain to a wall with a final marking, different from the rest. Find the stone that's loose and pull it out. A lever behind it will open the door, and another inside will shut it again. Once it's locked from the inside, no one will be able to get in from the outside."

Cael freezes as we turn a corner. Leo stops right behind him and pulls out his slayer, his eyes bleeding red in an instant.

Hela's Bond look back at them as I pull the two daggers Deca gave me from their sheaths.

"We have to keep moving," Ceto urges. He's on edge.

Cael shakes his head slowly, glancing in every direction. He mumbles under his breath and Leo tenses, pulling Antares and Altair close.

"What did you say?" Kiro asks.

"They're everywhere," Cael breathes.

All at once, soldiers appear from the alleys and streets, surrounding us. Their numbers multiply with every second that ticks by. Emrys and I step in front of Byrne as a symphony of steel sings through the air.

The soldiers are all different ages and most wear red armbands while others are flaunting gold, sending shivers of hate down my spine. I grew up with these people. They were raised to loathe blood-eyes, yet here they fight alongside them. I wonder if they even care or if it only matters that they get a taste of the action. Hela's Bond spreads out, making a protective circle around the children.

A figure steps out of the crowd. I stop breathing.

"Hello, Elana." Cassien smiles as he tilts his head. "We've missed you."

Leo steps closer to me in time with Byrne.

"You're sick," I tell him as my face pales. I know he can see the fear in my eyes.

Cassien laughs mirthlessly as he folds his hands behind his back. "I thought I taught you to be fearless, my daughter." He sighs. "I guess I'll just have to bring you back to Wate and restart your *education*."

I barely catch Leo's movement before a knife flies through the air. It grazes Cassien's cheek before he can move away, landing in the eye of a soldier standing behind him. Leo is breathing hard as he stares at Cassien.

"You won't touch her," Leo seethes, his hands eerily still.

Cassien wipes away the drop of blood dripping down his face. "I'm going to have fun playing with you."

Cassien smirks as his eyes narrow on Leo, before raising his hand. The troops launch into an attack. I don't think as my eyes shift gold. We stay in a tight formation as we fight to cut through the onslaught of soldiers. A man comes bolting at me with a double-edged axe. I feint left and stoop low, missing the blade by an inch as it swings through the air. As he recoils to control his momentum, I pop up and split his left leg from his knee to his hip. He screams and fumbles, giving me enough time to stab through his stomach and send him plummeting backward.

Another assailant comes flying forward. I blink as I recognize her face. Emila's gold band shines against her gilded eyes. I push away from where Hela's Bond fights, stabbing and dodging as Emila and I lock into a spinning battle. Another soldier comes barreling toward us, but Emmani embeds an arrow in her shoulder before I'm outnumbered.

I focus on Emila as we exchange blow for blow. She snarls as my fist collides with her jaw. She sweeps her feet behind my knees, sending me falling backward. Leo catches me just before my head hits the ground and pulls me up. He barely gets the chance to look my way as he moves on to his next opponent. Red is yelling orders I don't take the time to understand as Emila closes the space between us. I swipe at her shoulder and roll against her as she evades the blow. Her blade slices through my side as I kick her down. I'm on her back in seconds with my arm tightening around her neck.

"You... traitor," Emila wheezes as her eyes flutter.

I squeeze harder as my lip curls. She goes limp and I push myself to my feet. My skin pulls numbly at my side while my lungs heave. Emmani yells something I don't process as I scan the scene in a daze. She throws a powder into the air, and it sets off a series of small blasts. Thick smoke floats down from the sky and I can barely see a few feet in front of me.

"Leo!" I yell, breathing hard. "Byrne!"

Screams go up all around me, blending with the sound of clashing steel. I walk blindly toward where the children had been and plummet forward as a body rams into my back, forcing the air from my lungs. I blink heavily, stunned as I lie on the ground, unable to take a breath.

Kiro's foot collides with my side as he wrestles with a man wearing with a ripped gold band. I turn onto my stomach, trying to get my bearings. I gasp as Leo spins into view, locked in combat. He starts to gain the upper hand, but another opponent appears out of the smog, stealing his attention. Leo pushes the first assailant to the ground. The first man slowly pulls himself up as Leo turns his back to face the second soldier. The bloodied man takes a step toward Leo, then another. Leo never turns.

Get up, I tell myself. My muscles scream as time slows. *He doesn't know there are two.*

Leo manages to overcome the second man and lifts his arm to finish him off, but the first man is only a step behind with a dagger aimed for the kill.

My mind blanks as my muscles take over. I'm moving. My blade is in my hand.

Leo finishes the man on the ground, ignorant to the assailant taking aim behind him. I push harder and grit my teeth as I lunge, forcing my blade into the groove between the man's jugular and collarbone. *Just like I taught you,* Cassien's voice whispers in my mind. Leo turns with wide eyes as the man crumbles to the ground. He closes the space between us without a thought.

"I'm all right," I tell him, but the words come out weak.

Leo pulls me to him, and for a fraction of a second, I'm safe and I want to cry. I want to crumble right here. He places a swift kiss on my forehead and pulls away to meet my eyes.

"We need to go," he says, worry playing across his face.

I nod, exhausted. He notices the blood soaking my shirt from my side and places his hand tightly against it as his jaw tics.

Somehow, he finds Cass, Antares, Gray, and Altair holding Saiph through the smoke. Red and Kiro soon appear as well.

"We need to go," Red urges. "We have to disappear by the time the smoke fades, and Emmani said it won't last much longer."

"We can't leave Cael and the others," Leo interjects, pulling Antares toward him as he scans his brothers.

"They'll find their way," Red assures.

Leo looks around frantically as we move. I can see Leo's thoughts spinning in his mind. We clear the smoke, and two soldiers stand waiting. But they only manage a few steps before Kiro has one on the ground and Red has the other's throat in her hands.

Leo turns to look back. "Cael, are you in there? I have the boys!"

Red's eyes go wide at the volume of Leo's voice, but no one steps closer to stop him.

"I'm out, Leo. Go!" Cael's voice bounces out of the fog.

Leo swallows hard and moves, helping me forward. I look up at the mountain ahead and, with a deep breath, push myself to run.

THIRTY-SIX

CAEL

"Cael, are you in there? I have the boys!" Leo's voice resounds as I finally find my way out of the smoke.

Relief hits me like a stone as I breathe fresh air. I turn in circles, trying to pinpoint where he is.

"I'm out, Leo. Go!" I call back, praying he'll get to the mountain.

I heave a sigh as I look at the gash on my leg. It's deep. I hadn't seen the soldier coming when she barreled through the fog. Thankfully, without the element of surprise on her side, she was easy to beat. I clench my teeth as I wrap a piece of my shirt around the wound. Standing up straight, I spin the daggers in my hands and tell myself to walk despite the blinding pain. *I need to find a way to the mountains.*

"Cael!" someone calls.

My head swivels toward a building to my left. Soren, Deca,

Byrne, and Emrys are huddled together in an alley. I limp over as they argue.

"We're not pulling it out!" Deca says, motioning to the dagger sticking out of Soren's shoulder.

"I'm not leaving a knife in my shoulder!" Soren says as he reaches for the grip.

"No!" I yell as I get close.

Byrne sighs in relief when she sees I'm mostly unharmed.

"Let me look at it," I tell them.

Soren reluctantly agrees and turns away. My brows furrow as I watch him grind his teeth.

"You can feel pain even though you've bled your eyes?" I ask him, mostly as a distraction as I tear his shirt to get a better look.

He winces and nods. "My mother is a getic and my father was a blood-eye. Emmani and I can still bleed our eyes and have the heightened senses, but we feel some pain, though it's dull compared to what a pure-blooded getic would experience."

"That, and he's a child," Deca notes absentmindedly as she looks into the fog that seems to be getting thinner with every passing minute.

I turn to Emrys. "When you light up your hands, do they heat up?"

He considers for a moment before nodding. "Normally, no. But I think I can focus the energy to make them heat up enough to burn."

I look back at Soren and his eyes go wide as he realizes why I asked. "Actually, I'm feeling much better, we can leave it in—"

I shake my head and tell Emrys to hold onto the portion of the blade sticking out of his shoulder. Soren squeezes his eyes shut as the blade heats up, cauterizing the wound. When the smell of burning skin reaches me, I grab Emrys's hand and pull, bringing the blade with it. Soren screams and I place my hand over the wound, forcing it closed.

"By the Gods," Soren swears as he blinks away tears.

I give him a pitiful smile and replace my hand with his as his head sways, looking as if he might pass out.

"Try to keep yourself—" I don't get to finish my phrase before a scream rips through the air.

Deca's already running toward the fog when I realize who it must be. Emmani. I stand and look at Emrys and Byrne.

"Keep him awake," I tell them before pushing away to follow Deca. I run blindly into the fray, trusting myself to find her.

"Emmani!" Deca screams.

I block out my senses and let my feet guide me. Deca is spinning in circles with wild eyes when I find her. She almost takes my head off as I grab her arm and pull her with me. A shape appears on the ground and Deca steps in front of me, kneeling beside Emmani. Her cheeks are tear-stained and there's blood everywhere.

"Where are you hurt?" Deca demands, her voice tender as she holds Emmani's face.

"My ribs. He broke my ribs," Emmani wheezes. "We need to get out. We need to go!" Deca meets her gaze and tells her to breathe, but Emmani's face twists with panic. "The Bloodlines are here. It was a Cadmus who rammed into me."

I look around wildly as my stomach flips. If the Bloodlines are here... we have no choice. We need to run.

"How did you get away?" I ask.

She shakes her head as we pull her up. "I don't know. One minute he was on top of me with his fist raised, the next he was frozen and convulsing. I crawled away before I saw what happened."

I shake my head as confusion lashes through me. No one can control a person like that. My mind quiets as the smoke shifts. I stop walking and drop Emmani's arm.

"Someone's here," I whisper.

I pull my daggers as three figures appear through the mist. Three soldiers approach with crimson eyes and weapons at ready. Deca grips her axes.

"Hela's Bond and the false king's getic," one of the soldiers snarls. "How we will be praised by the true king for bringing back your heads."

I steady my breathing and shift my weight to my good leg. "I'm afraid your tyrant is in for a disappointment."

They lunge at us, one swinging toward me while the other two attack Deca and Emmani. I dodge the first hit and grind my teeth as I duck and pop up behind my assailant. She moves quickly, forcing me onto the defensive. I feign one way, but she reads the move, targeting my injured leg. I only manage to nick her arm as she sends me plummeting backward. I stumble as I pull myself back up, but before I get to my feet, she kicks me in the chest, forcing the breath from my lungs. I cough as my eyes water. The soldier pins me against the ground and places the tip her blade against my side.

"How pathetic," she seethes as she pushes the blade deeper. I wince and shift my grip on my dagger. Taking a deep breath, I swing my weight and kick her leg. She falls onto my dagger with a scream before pulling herself up. She touches the wound and her lip curls back as her fingers come away painted in red. "You're going to regret that—"

I wait for the next strike, but it never comes. She's frozen in place as I watch her heaving for breath. Crimson tears fall down her face before her lungs stop filling. A figure steps out from around her.

"How pathetic indeed," the figure says.

My eyes go wide as she comes into full view. Kaja. The soldier's eyes roll back as blood spews from her nose. Kaja's head moves ever so slightly, and the woman drops into a lifeless heap. She turns, and I can't help but smile as relief floods through me. Kaja's face softens as she steps forward.

She opens her mouth to speak but stops short as her eyes lock on something behind me. Her hand reaches for me as I realize there weren't three soldiers, there were four. I move to turn, but I'm sluggish. Slow. Too slow. I hear Kaja scream as a blinding pain splits my skull. There's no fading moment to look at her as I fall or a second to wonder what I could have done differently. There's only all-consuming darkness as I crumble to the dirt.

CHAPTER

THIRTY-SEVEN

LEO

Saiph sleeps deeply in my arms as we hike up the mountain. The symbols Ceto instructed us to follow are the same as those inscribed in the tunnel under the palace grounds. My stomach flips every time my eyes find a marking, unable to shake this looming feeling of dread. When we find another symbol carved into the stone, we stop and gather around it. We're too cold and exhausted to be encouraged by the thought of finding the entrance, so we all just stare in silence. I finally step closer as I shake the worry from my bones and start feeling around the stone for a loose piece.

"Look at this," Antares says. He crouches, staring at a circular stone that seems to have been carved out from the mountain side and placed back in the same spot.

Antares wedges his foot against the ground and leans his weight back to pull against the stone. It finally dislodges, sending him stumbling. I wince as Saiph stirs at the ruckus. I kneel to take a closer look. An iron lever sticks out from the hole in the wall.

Kiro steps up and pushes on it. After a few tries, the mechanism finally gives way. The giant stone beside us pushes backward and slides to the side, revealing a long hallway. We step forward skeptically, squinting to get our bearings. The air is stagnant and dry, but I hear the faint sound of running water coming from far inside the tunnel.

Red steps in and traces her hand along the ledge of the wall. She grasps something and pulls. A loud whirring rumbles through the tunnel before a line of stone lights up. I stare at the light in amazement.

"It's lumina stone. They used to mine these mountains for it before it became scarce. When you run a current through it, the stone creates light," Red explains as she places her hand on the wall. "There must be a turbine built into the mountain that feeds power into this place."

"Emmani is going to pass out when she sees this," Kiro whispers.

We move in slowly after placing the stone back over the lever outside. As we walk deeper in the mountain, Red discovers a crude, faded map painted on the wall. I drag my fingers over the paint and read the symbols.

"This is the common room," I say. "And the infirmary... the sleeping quarters and the kitchen." A line traces from the top of the map and splits into different rooms. I look at the markings and the corner of my lips curl up. "That's the water source. It must flow from a reserve through the compound. And look, up there is the turbine."

The silence behind me is deafening. I turn slowly and I'm met with half a dozen stares.

"How do you know that?" Gray asks, the words stringing

together gruffly as he shifts his gaze from where he had been watching Red's hands sign.

I blink and glance back at the map. "It's not obvious?"

Gray shakes his head. Even Antares looks spooked. I shrug as I push away the unease rising from my gut.

"I can read the symbols," I say as they continue to stare open-mouthed. I swallow and proceed to walk through the hall. "We should get a count of supplies before more people arrive."

They snap out of their trances and nod. We split into groups, Elana and I going to see the sleeping quarters while Gray and Kiro head toward the kitchen. The rest move to the infirmary to start patching up their wounds. The sleeping quarters aren't big, but there's more space than the cellar Cael and I shared in Wate. There must be over two hundred rooms with two to three cots in each. What's better is that every room has lumina stone lighting that can be controlled with its own switch.

"This must have taken years to dig out," Elana wonders quietly as she runs her hand along the smooth walls.

I nod as I glance inside another room, noticing that some even have furniture to store personal items. I stay close to Elana's side as we walk slowly through the hall. I go back and forth with myself, wondering if I should take the moment to speak to her about Cassien. I almost don't realize when she stops.

"Don't tiptoe around me," Elana says as she lifts her chin.

I take a breath and smile softly, hoping to seem supportive. "I just wanted to thank you for saving me."

Elana breathes a laugh and winces. I shift near to her and move to put a hand around her waist but hesitate as I meet her eyes with the question on my face. Color rises to Elana's cheeks as she nods, leaning into me. She sighs in relief as I take some of her weight.

"Let's keep going so we can patch you up properly," I tell her, looking at the makeshift bandage tied around her side.

It only takes a few more minutes to scour the rest of the compound. Beside the sleeping quarters is a large room with tubs dug into the ground. Each can be filled by a stream of water flowing out of the wall. Before heading back, we stop by a storage room and find crates packed with clothes, weapons, and most importantly, food.

"There's enough in here to feed a village for weeks," Elana remarks, staring at the dozens of boxes piled against the wall. "It's incredible they keep all this here just in case of emergency."

"I'm thankful either way," I tell her.

We head back to rejoin the group, but along the way, a dark hallway catches my eye. We walk toward it slowly, the temperature dropping as we approach the doorway. There are stairs that lead down, but something about it makes me uneasy. *It feels like death,* I realize suddenly. There's a symbol on the wall by the first step and I run my hand over it, knowing immediately what lies below.

"It's a prison. Cells."

Elana looks at me with a pinched face. "Let's leave this until tomorrow."

Her face is pale as I nod. We turn back to the infirmary, keeping each other close the whole way. I can't bear the idea of being away from her. Not when Cael's not here. Not when so many people are lost.

Red and Kiro are in the infirmary when we arrive. We fill each other in on what we found as I gather some supplies to patch up Elana. I already checked over Antares, Altair, and Cass, and thank the Goddess, they were unharmed. Antares did roll his ankle as we ran, but it doesn't seem too serious. Red is sewing up her own wounds as she speaks to Kiro, who translates for Gray.

After spreading out the supplies, I finally get the courage to speak the question that's been floating in my head.

"How are you doing? With seeing Cassien, I mean," I whisper. I keep my hands busy and eyes down as I unwrap the bandage around Elana's side. Wiping away the blood, relief floods through me as although it was bleeding quite a bit, the wound isn't as deep as I thought.

She leans back, her face void of emotion. "I don't know."

When she stays silent, I meet her eyes, urging her to continue. I can see the words on the tip of her tongue, begging to be put to sound. Finally, she relents.

"It terrifies me," she admits. "And the fact that Byrne is still out there makes me crazy. I know Cael and Emrys and the rest of the Bond are with her, but if anything happens to her... I don't think I'd be able to live."

Gently, I put my hand on her chin and guide her welling eyes to mine. "You have to believe that they're all right. That they'll walk in any minute with only a few scratches and bruises."

She nods even though her face mirrors the concern gnawing at my mind. "How do you deal with it? The killing and the fear of always losing them," she whispers.

I think about it for a minute, unable to find a proper answer. "I don't have a choice. We have to live, so I swallow the worry and keep going." I take a breath and look at the door, always hoping Antares will sprint in to tell me Cael is alive. "You get used to it all, after a while. The killing and the running. The only way to be safe is to improve the way we live, and the world won't change unless the people in control lose their authority. You never know if dethroning them will be worse or better, so I deal with the consequences of my actions as they're thrown my way. As long as I'm trying to protect those I love, every sacrifice is worth it."

I never break her stare. Her hand runs over the scar of the tripoint on her hip as she tries to form a smile. "It's all worth it if they're safe."

I place my hand over hers and nod, not knowing what else to say but grateful that she understands or at least is willing to listen. I take a bandage from the pile and look at her wound when a memory from Anateya resurfaces. *Matteus blood not only heals you but can protect others from infection and speed up recovery. Some say it's powerful enough to bring souls back to life if they are teetering on the edge of death.*

I grab my dagger and run it across my palm. Elana's eyes go wide as I place the bandage over my wound.

"Why did you do that?" she asks in disbelief.

"My blood heals," I tell her with a shrug.

After a moment, I take the bandage away from my hand and wrap it around her newly sewn gash. Her brows crease as she watches me. When I finish, her mouth opens to speak, but the sound of pounding footsteps cuts her off.

I'm on my feet in seconds. Byrne and Soren come in first, supporting Emmani between them. Emmani looks terrible. Her face is bruised, and every breath is barely more than a wheeze. Elana jumps up and runs toward her sister. I look at Soren as Red, Kiro, and Gray approach.

"Where's Cael?" I demand.

Soren's face crumbles when he looks at me. I clench my jaw and move around him toward the door, refusing to believe... no. I won't think it. It's not true. Cael is going to walk in and tell me not to worry. He's going to be fine. He has to be fine.

Deca and Emrys carry in a stretcher, sweat covering their

exhausted faces. Kaja has her hand on Cael's barely moving chest. Her expression is drawn and set with concentration.

"What are you doing? What happened?" I push, panic coursing through my veins as I look helplessly at Cael. His head and leg are wrapped in blood-stained bandages, and he's covered in bruises.

"Do you have medical supplies?" Kaja asks without looking at me.

"Tell me what happ—"

She turns to me suddenly, her eyes firm and tired. "Right now, I'm the only thing keeping blood pumping through your brother's heart, of which he has very, *very* little. I need you to get me medical supplies before his body gives out and I'm sending electrical pulses through a corpse!"

My breath hitches as she tries to stay calm, keeping her chin held high. I nod and point her towards the first empty bed. Elana already prepared a box of medical instruments and supplies, half of which I've never seen before. They set Cael and Kaja gets to work rummaging through them with one hand.

"Do you see that box of needles and that tubing?" she asks me. I lay both in front of her. "How good is the healing quality in your blood?"

I raise the hand I just cut. "I did this ten minutes ago."

She takes a moment to look at the closed wound. Kaja directs Elana to connect the needles to the small tube and hold my arm still. Kaja finds a vein before inserting the needle tip, then does the same to Cael. The speed and precision with which she works is mesmerizing. She blinks as we sit in silence, her brows creased.

"No wonder they call you immortal. The cells in your blood are incredible," Kaja says.

I glance at Elana before noticing the boys have gathered

around us. I try to say something to comfort them, but nothing comes to mind. All I can think is that I left him. I left him and now… now. I shake away the thought. Cael will be fine. He has to be all right.

"What are you doing to him?" Red asks Kaja, though it seems as though she already knows. There's a dagger in her hands and mistrust in her eyes.

Kaja raises her eyes without hesitation. "He got hit in the head so hard it cracked his skull. Not only that, he barely has any blood left in his system. So I connected to his nervous system and diverted the passageways from his brain to allow him to rest while also synching his heartbeat and breathing to mine to keep them steady. Leo's blood has qualities that allow the cells to split rapidly and clot easily, so I'm stimulating the blood cells to multiply and stop the bleeding in his brain while being careful not to give him a stroke and making sure to control his hormone levels to stop his body from creating swelling that would press on his brain. Now, I would appreciate if you didn't question me further so I can concentrate on keeping him alive."

We sit in silence and stare. There's still unease in Red's eyes.

Kaja sighs in frustration. "I'm a Damaris, and a skilled one at that. You know what I'm capable of, but I swear I don't associate with the Bloodlines. I've been wronged by them too many times. All I want to do is help, and whether you like it or not, I'm the only reason your king's brother is still breathing. Even if you tried to get rid of me, he won't let you," she says, nodding to me.

I don't need to agree for Red to know that she's right. Red finally relents and steps back. Kaja doesn't bother thanking her as she closes her eyes and continues to work.

We sit for several minutes, taking in the events of the day.

After everything we've been through, everything I've fought for, we're in a worse position than when we started. How is that even possible? How could I have screwed this up so badly?

Elana takes my hand, pulling me out of my thoughts. I smile weakly.

My head swivels toward the shut door as it slides open. Kiro went out a few minutes ago to look for survivors who might have gathered in the woods. The cacophony of voices, cries, and screams make my head ache as a wave of people enter. The Bond, Emrys, Elana, Byrne, and I exchange panicked looks. Exhaustion and stress pull at our faces, but each of them walks over and start triaging. Kaja puts her free hand on my arm and pulls the needle free, then does the same to Cael.

"What are you doing?" I ask. I look at Cael as his chest moves with shallow breaths.

"You've given enough," is all Kaja says.

I shake my head. "Does he need more?"

She stays quiet.

"Then take more. I've survived with less."

Her eyes narrow as she meets my eyes. "You need what you have, Leo. I've already let you give more than I should have. Cael has enough for now. You need to allow your body to replenish what you've lost."

"No, I don't."

Kaja shakes her head, and for a moment, sadness takes over as she looks at my brother. It's a feeling so deep and painful that I recognize it well. "Yes, Leo. You do. There are other people who need help. You can't aid them if you're in a coma. I won't in good conscience let you give more."

There's no arguing with her. I grind my teeth and stand, my legs feeling weak. I know she notices me swaying, but she doesn't comment.

Antares and Cass watch me move away from the bed. I go

over to where they're sitting with Saiph and crouch to look them in the eyes.

"Where did Altair go?" I ask.

They shrug.

"He said he was going to help," Antares says.

I nod slowly and scan the room for my brother. He's nowhere to be found. *Altair's old enough to take care of himself. If he wants space, I need to leave him be.*

"How are you two doing?" I ask them as I turn back.

They stay silent.

I smile softly and gather them in my arms. "It's going to be all right."

"Is Cael going to die?" Antares asks as I pull away.

I look at them both, about to say no, but the seriousness in their eyes stops me. They aren't children anymore. They haven't been for a while. "I don't know."

A bolt of pain splits through me, but they deserve the truth. It's the least I can do. Antares and Cass nod stoically, taking my words in stride.

"We want to help," Antares tells me as Cass nods. "Tell us what to do."

I don't think I've ever been prouder. I take a breath and do my best to smile. "Why don't you go around and find out if there are kids without parents. You can bring them all into the first room there." I point at one of the rooms in the sleeping quarters. "Tell Red what you're doing and bring some food and supplies in there for them, that way we know all the kids are accounted for and being taken care of. Can you do that?"

They agree and stand tall. I pull them in one last time before I send them off. I give myself a moment to watch them go, savoring the simplicity of knowing I must have done something right.

When they disappear, I'm left by myself, and I don't know

what to do. There are so many people in pain. Everyone is running around trying to help, gathering children, sewing up wounds, moving the dead. My mind is spiraling at the chaos.

So I do the only thing I can. I step up to the first bed where a man and child are huddled together. They gawk at me as I take a bandage and split open my hand as I did with Elana. I soak the bandage in blood and, after doing my best to sew the man's arm back together, wrap the bandage around it.

"You're the king," he says as I get ready to move to the next bed.

I blink. "No."

"You and your brother saved a family in the Riv. We watched you do it." I don't know what to say as they look at me with reverence. "The Bloodlines watched it burn and you jumped into the flames."

I stay silent.

"Are you going to fight him? Fight Ares?"

I raise my eyes and feel the crown in my jacket burn against my skin. I forgot it was there. "I don't know."

They don't seem satisfied with that answer, but they nod none the less.

"You're giving us refuge. You're bandaging up your own people. Even if you don't stand against him, you've already done more than any other before you. We won't forget that."

I force a smile and move away. *I need to get this crown off me.* I step into the first empty room of the sleeping quarters and rip off my jacket, breathing hard. The space is bare, equipped only with two cots and a chest. I take the crown in my hand. There's blood on the point. It must have sliced through my skin. I open the chest, wrap my jacket around the crown, and toss it in. *I can't do this.*

I leave the room as my mind swims. My feet move toward the next bed. A woman lies with a gash across her head. She doesn't say a word as I work to patch her up, slice my hand, and wrap the wound. Over and over, I force myself to breathe. Get up. Find a bed. Clean the wound, patch the wound. Slice my hand. Wrap the wound. Stand up. Move. Find a bed. Breathe. Slice my hand. Bleed. Stand. Breathe. Move. Slice. Get up. Bleed.

"Stop."

I blink. My neck creaks as I look at the old woman sitting on the bed beside me. Her arm is bandaged. Maybe she needs something. I open my mouth to ask, but the words don't leave my throat. I blink again.

She stands slowly, using the frame of the cot to push herself to her feet. "Sit, Your Majesty."

I think I'm shaking my head. "I have to move to the next person." The words echo too loudly in my ears.

She looks at my hand as I feel a drop of warmth roll down my finger and fall to the floor. The woman turns to a young girl and waves her over. "Go find someone to help the king."

My brows crease as I straighten. The world tilts as I stare at her. "I'm no king."

She smiles softly and takes my arm. I'm not sure if it's for her balance or mine, but I lean against the wall as my vision crosses. Sounds swim in my mind as colors shift before me. The floor is rising as hands touch my skin, but I can't tell who they belong to. I close my eyes slowly as the world shifts and my legs give way before my mind finally goes dark.

CHAPTER
THIRTY-EIGHT

"How much time do we have?" I ask Hela's Bond.

Kiro is the only one of them missing. His mother showed up and he's refused to leave her side even after we told him about the meeting. I was helping with the wounded when Emmani pulled me into the common room. She said it would be a quick conversation, but I've been listening to them go back and forth for half an hour.

"I don't know, but we need to get in touch with our contacts as soon as possible," Red says. "The faster we evacuate people from the cities, the faster we can plan a counterattack."

"So, this is war then? There's no trying to find a way around it?" I ask.

"The Bloodlines are bred to seek power, Elana. Ares won't stop until Leo is dead. He's the only one preventing Illena from falling completely into Ares's hands. As long as Leo breathes, Ares's reign will be threatened," Red explains. She crosses her tensed arms.

I nod slowly, wondering for a moment where Leo is. He should be here by now.

"We can't fit thousands of people in here," Soren remarks. "How can we possibly evacuate that many?"

"When we can't sustain the numbers, we move people into the woods just north of Desai. That town has been fostering a blistering hate for the Bloodlines since its foundation. They won't turn us in."

We stare in silence as the reality of what the future hold hangs heavily in the air.

"After we have escape plans in place, then we can start hitting Ares. I have resources available that will help, but not enough to dethrone a king, so we have to figure out our next steps," Red says.

I nod absentmindedly and glance at the door. Emmani said she'd told Leo to join us when he was done helping.

"Did Leo respond to you when you told him we were meeting here?" I ask Emmani, stopping the conversation.

Emmani's face pinches in thought. "He nodded."

"But did he look at you?" I press.

She shakes her head. Dread sinks like a stone in my stomach as I excuse myself and head toward the infirmary. A young girl comes running down the hall and barely manages to stop herself from crashing into me. I catch her arm, stopping her in her tracks.

"Are you all right?" I ask her.

She nods somewhat frantically before trying to pull away.

"You shouldn't be running. There are injured people all over this place. Never mind that you could hurt yourself."

She shakes her head and holds my gaze. "Miss Hein told me to find help."

My forehead creases as I bend down to her eye level. "Who needs help?" I ask her softly, feeling my heart speed up.

"Miss Hein said to find someone to help the king because he's bleeding."

I don't have the time to think before I'm sprinting toward the infirmary. The smell of blood and waste makes my head spin as I step around people rushing from bed to bed. I catch Byrne sewing an elderly man's leg up at the back of the room and Kaja, still with one hand on Cael's arm, setting a man's broken leg. Her concentration barely manages to mask her exhaustion as she orders someone to get her a splint. Finally, I see him. Leo's leaning against the wall, his forearm and hand dripping blood.

"Please sit. I know what excessive blood loss looks like and you shouldn't be on your feet," an old woman holding his arm coaxes.

Leo gently pushes her away, refusing her help. His eyes snap to mine when I stop in front of him. He looks like death. His red eyes are glazed, and his face is pale and gaunt. His breathing is labored as I take his arm and slip it over my shoulder. His eyes don't move from my face as I lead him to the back of the room where there are two open beds. Leo shakes his head and plants his feet.

"I don't need to sit," he says, air wheezing from his lungs.

I step away from him and he sways, barely able to keep himself upright. When he finds his balance, he meets my gaze.

"Bleed your eyes," I tell him as I cross my arms.

His eyes widen with panic as he swallows. "What?"

"You heard me. Bleed your eyes. If you're fine, you'll be able to stay standing without pulling on your instinct. So do it and I'll let you go back."

He stares blankly for a long moment as despair fills his face. His jaw clenches as he averts his gaze. "I can't."

My heart cracks as I muster a thin smile. I move beside him and pull his arm back over my shoulder. He sighs gratefully as I support part of his weight.

"Then you need to let me help you. You need to stop bleeding yourself dry to patch people's wounds."

He nods weakly and leans his head against mine. "Anything for you, Elana."

I roll my eyes. He lets me lead him to the bed and sits down. Leo rests his back against the wall as I grab some medical supplies and take his severed hand. It's ripped to shreds. His gaze never wavers from me as I clean the wound and wrap his hand. He doesn't make a sound as I clean the rest of his wounds and then step away to get him some food. I walk down to the kitchen to find that a few of those who were unharmed have been busy preparing the food found in the crates. I bring Leo back a steaming bowl of stew, but he doesn't even glance down as I set it on his lap.

"I'm not leaving until you eat," I tell him.

He smiles softly, his lips pale. "You sound like Cael."

I know he means it as a joke, but the pain in his words rips open a cavern in my chest. I take a deep breath and hold his good hand. He still has his sheaths strapped on.

I move to undo them, but he stops me. "Not yet."

I nod in understanding. He takes the bowl off his lap and shifts to make room beside him. He looks at me, then at the space.

"I'm not going to reheat that if you let it get cold," I tell him pointedly, ignoring the look he gave me.

He rolls his eyes and takes a few bites before setting the bowl on the floor. I smile and stand awkwardly. I don't know what I'm doing. Color rises to my cheeks as he watches me.

"Come on, Elana." He sighs and rubs a hand over his face. "Are you really going to make me ask?"

I stare at him blankly.

He huffs a laugh and scoots over until he's sitting on the edge of the small cot. "Would you just come sit with me? Please?"

My stomach knots as he reaches for one of my belt loops, hooks his finger in it, and pulls me toward him. I shake my head as I relent and sit. The cot is small enough that there's no space for either of us to move for fear of rolling off. He sighs softly as he rests his head on my shoulder and shuts his eyes. Panic bolts through me at the thought of him falling asleep.

"If you need to sleep, we can go—"

He grumbles and opens his eyes. "I'm just resting, Elana. I won't fall asleep."

I smile hesitantly. He drapes his arm across my torso and lets his eyes shut. After the events of the day and despite the chaos around me, my eyelids droop. I hadn't realized how exhausted I am, and the warmth radiating from Leo isn't helping me stay awake. Maybe it's the fatigue. Or maybe, just maybe, it's the blood-eyed mercenary, ousted king sitting beside me who makes me feel safe.

THIRTY-NINE

LEO

I sit with Elana until my hands go numb around her. Still, I don't move. Her presence eases the stress and exhaustion pounding in my skull. I know I have things to do, people to think about, and decisions to make, but for these few hours, I only have the will to do this one simple thing. Sit with her. Let her rest without worry. Let her heal.

Red came looking for us about an hour ago. She didn't even blink when she saw Elana asleep, curled up against me. She went through everything they had spoken about together: the amount of people and resources we currently have available, what we're going to do when too many people show up, and how we need to contact her network soon.

People are trickling in from all different cities across the country. We have citizens from Arkezo to as far as Delos near the southern border. Apparently Ares and Cassien sent their troops to every city and town with a population of more than a few hundred people. The whole thing makes me anxious. I feel responsible somehow. I can't figure out what I could have done to stop it, but I know I should have done more.

Over the next two weeks, we spend our time counting heads and resources, arguing over what steps to take next, and sending letters with runners asking for information and aid. Though Red says we should avoid involving outside nations, I point out that Cassien has been using Tominay's resources for longer than we know. So no one opposes when I write to the Queen of Anateya. I'm not sure how to make an official plea for assistance, so instead I write the words that come to my mind. I tell her of the coronation and the dead. The destroyed. I tell her about Cael. I entrust the letter to Emrys, who promises to deliver it swiftly. He's the only one I trust who also knows how to navigate the caves. I know Kaja would go had I asked, but I... we need her here.

We decided last night that we would split into groups to try to contact Red's network and spread the word about the compound for those still left without housing. Hopefully, by the week's end, Emrys will return with news from Anateya. We're running out of space faster than I expected.

Sitting by Cael's bedside with that needle in my arm, I let hope spark in my mind. I've been giving him small amounts of blood under Kaja and Elana's supervision for the last few weeks. Kaja says he's finally stable enough to survive without her constant intervention. His heart has been strong enough to beat without help and he has been breathing on his own for the last few days. But despite every good sign, Cael still hasn't opened his eyes. Kaja spends most of her days at his side, working to restore the parts of his brain that were damaged.

I shake myself out of the thought and focus on Cael's chest rising and falling in even motions. Elana watches me as she leans against the doorframe. We've barely left each other's sides since the coronation. Thanks to Kaja initially having to keep her connection with Cael, she's taken to sleeping in this room. Elana and I took the one where I ditched the crown, and the boys took the room next to ours, though most nights they sneak in with us to sleep in our second bed.

I sigh as I glance at the door. Hela's Bond has been standing in the hall since I entered, waiting to set off.

"That's enough," Kaja says under her breath.

I let her take out the needle to tend to my brother. She sits up and takes a shaky breath, her eyes never leaving Cael's face.

I don't stand for a long time. I know Hela's Bond is waiting for me, but the notion of leaving Cael makes me want to throw up. Not only do we need to contact Red's network, but there are others to find. Kaja assured us that there are Bloodlines opposed to Ares's rule and we need to get to them before they change their minds. We also discussed the Issue of Ceto. He's one of our biggest liabilities, and we have no idea if he's even alive. The question arose as to who would take up the task of approaching these Bloodlines and finding Ceto's location, and the only reasonable answer was to ask Kaja to make the journey to Arkezo. But that means leaving Cael. Kaja and I fought against it, but there was no use arguing against reason. We need support from the Bloodlines, and Kaja knows them inside and out.

Cael will be all right, I tell myself as Elana steps to my side and puts a hand on my shoulder.

"Don't do anything stupid until I get back," I whisper into the silence.

I stand and take a step. I feel myself slip deeper into darkness with every inch I move away from Cael. Even though Kaja assured me Cael is stable enough not to need her, I can't bring myself to feel any type of comfort.

I don't let myself contemplate anymore as I head to the

entrance and take Cass and Antares in my arms. I hold them tightly until I can't delay any longer.

"Are you both sure you'll be all right here with Saiph? The offer is still open if you want to join us," I tell them as I pull back. I don't know if it's better that my two youngest brothers are here without me, out of harm's way, or with me in the field.

Unlike them, Altair jumped on the chance to come with me. Everyone has a designated pair for their travels: Elana with Byrne, Deca with Emmani, and Red with Kiro. Soren and Gray are staying behind to hold down the fort.

"We'll be all right. We're needed here," Antares says confidently.

Saiph runs toward me from where she's been standing with Altair. I pick her up and spin around, filling the room with the sound of her laughter.

"By the Lady, at this rate you're going to be as big as me by the time we get back," I tell her before placing a kiss on the top of her head. I pull Cass and Antares in close one last time. "Be good. We'll be back before you know it."

They nod, and I'm overwhelmed by how much they've grown up. Gone are the young kids Cael and I carried out of Wate and through the woods. I couldn't be prouder.

I put down Saiph and grab my pack. I wave one last goodbye to the boys and walk out with Altair, Byrne, and Elana. The rest of the group—Deca, Emmani, Red, and Kiro—decided they would leave shortly after us. Partly because we didn't want to attract too much attention and partly because Kiro refused to get out of bed.

We don't speak as we descend the mountain and enter the woods. When we reach the point where we're meant to split paths, I turn to Elana. I stutter on what to say as she meets my eyes.

"We'll give you a minute," Byrne says with a smile as she hooks her arm over Altair's shoulder and leads him away.

His brows furrow in confusion as he looks at her arm, but nonetheless, he allows Byrne to take him away. I breathe a laugh as I watch him.

"He's still different, isn't he?" Elana says softly.

I nod sadly. "It's better. Than it was, I mean. I don't know what they did to him in Wate, but I see a bit more of the real him every day." I run a hand through my hair as I look to where Altair and Byrne walked off. "Maybe he'll never be the same. I don't know if that's a bad thing though. A person doesn't stay the same forever, right?"

I look to Elana for an answer. She steps in close and loops her arms around my neck. I place my arms around her waist and pull her in.

"No, they don't. I'm sure he'll figure himself out."

I nod and lean my forehead against hers. "You're sure you're going to be all right?"

She raises her brow dramatically. "Leo Hael, are you doubting my ability to survive?"

I wince with mock hurt. "How dare you think that? Especially since I've taught you *so much* about fighting. Shall we go over how to make a fist again, Your Highness?"

She scoffs and starts to pull away, but I hold her tightly. Elana laughs as I kiss her, melting into my touch. When I finally move away, reality swoops back in to knock my head straight.

"Promise me you'll be safe," I whisper.

Her gaze never leaves mine as her chin dips in a nod. "I'll be safe."

I place a kiss on her forehead.

"And you'll be smart? You won't run into the flames of a burning home with an army shooting arrows at your heels?"

I hook my arm over her shoulders and paste on a look of confusion. "Whose army are we talking about here?"

She punches me in the side hard enough to make me double over.

"I won't run into any burning buildings while being chased by an army of archers," I swear with a gasping breath.

"Good. Because I won't be there to save you," she sings.

I laugh as we walk and something terrifying occurs to me as we head in different directions. *I have no idea how I'm going to spend a week without her.*

FORTY

ELANA

It's been three days since we left the mountain, and so far, we've done well. We met with the first contact in Amana, and though the woman seemed skeptical, she told us there were families who'd been looking for a way out and would take advantage of the information we'd given them. They'd also been nice enough to house us, though not without taking the necessary precautions.

Amana is an important city for Illena's economy, so we were happy to hear of its people's willingness to help. Ares's troops had already ravaged the streets before we arrived, leaving devastation in their wake. Those who'd tried to fight back were either killed or beaten half to death. The soldiers stationed in Amana decided that the killing hadn't been enough and hung a body at every corner as a reminder of what happens when the people step out of line.

The second town we reached was much less receptive. It made sense, seeing as they were higher in social class. Those people were on councils directing agriculture and overseeing the mines. They had workers to clean their homes and were able to lock their gates before the soldiers ran through. It was clear there had been disturbances in the streets, but there were no destroyed homes or bodies hanging from poles. The man we met with didn't even own a home. He worked as a servant for one of the richer households and lived in designated quarters on their property.

The man told us the soldiers had been there but didn't do anything worse than sack some businesses catering to the workers and burn a few shelters used by the homeless. They didn't touch the homes and businesses belonging to the wealthy, so in turn, the rich did not hate them. In fact, the man said the upper class admired Ares for ridding the city of their poverty-stricken population.

It was the perfect combination for compliance. Ares instilled fear by enforcing his strength over people who could not protect themselves, while making the rich feel valued and powerful.

"So, how's the whole Leo thing going?" Byrne asks as we eat our lunch.

I shake away my thoughts and look at my sister as my stomach churns. "What Leo thing?"

Byrne rolls her eyes. "Come on, Elana. How come you can question me about Emrys, but I can't ask about Leo?"

I raise my brow. "I never questioned you about Emrys."

She stops packing up the last of her food and stares me down. "Then what did we talk about all last night and the day before? We've barely spoken about anything other than Emrys and me. And when we don't speak about my relationship, we still never talk about *you*. I'm your sister. Sisters share juicy details about each other's love lives. So spill."

I blink. What am I supposed to tell her? I pack up my food, no longer hungry.

"What do you want to know?" I ask as my cheeks flush.

"Anything? Everything. Come on, Elana. This might be our last time alone for a while. Share something with me. Do you love him?"

I stop breathing, choking on the thought. "What?"

She throws her head back and laughs. When she finally gets a handle on herself, she takes a breath and, to my disappointment, focuses back on me. "Fine, we'll ease into it. What do you like about him? Is he sweet? Does he—"

"If we're going to have this conversation, you're going to need to be a lot more patient," I deadpan.

She stays quiet, waiting for my answer.

I sigh and shake my head, not seeing why this is so important. "He makes me feel... safe. And I trust him."

She grumbles something I choose not to hear but presses when I don't continue. "But what do you *like* about him? Those things are the bare *minimum*, Elana. There must be more."

I think about it for a moment, going back and forth in my mind. "I like that he would do anything for his family. And that through everything, he tried to keep them from seeing the terrors he lived through. I like that he took the time to understand why I never told him about Cass even though it hurt him. I like that he doesn't come at me too fast or touch me without checking that I'm all right with it. I like that he notices the small things and can make me smile. He understands my morals and the things that drive me to live because he shares them, and I like that I see pieces of the person I want to be in him"

I stop as Byrne gapes at me. Her eyes are piercing.

"Stop looking at me like that," I mumble.

Her face softens with a smile. "I'm sorry. I've just never heard you speak like that before."

"Like what?"

"Happily. And I don't mean I've never seen you happy, but this is an unrestricted type of happiness. One that won't slip through your fingers if you look the wrong way."

I don't know what to say. Am I that kind of happy when I'm with Leo? I've been with other people before and it's never felt this easy, but I've never believed this kind of relationship really exists.

"He looks at you the same way, you know. Like he'd burn down the world to keep you safe." Byrne's speaking so softly she sounds like our mother when she used to tell us stories before bed. The memory makes me want to cry.

"Do you think Mama would like him?" I dare ask. My voice is barely above a whisper.

She takes my hand and squeezes it with a smile. "I think she would have loved him." Her smile grows more devilish. "Especially because he's a king who has rights to the most powerful nation of the continent, maybe even the world, but you know that's just one of his qualities. He's also not bad on the eyes."

I laugh and wave her off. "I won't disagree with that."

She giggles. "You know, I think he's in love with you."

My head spins toward her so fast I wince.

"I did say I would ease into the love conversation," she says defensively.

I sigh and look down at my hands, butterflies taking over my stomach. "You can't know that."

She snorts rather loudly and crosses her arms. "I've seen the way he acts with you. He's fallen head over heels."

"Is this really an appropriate discussion when there's a war going on around us?" I make a point of saying, trying to deflect.

Byrne has none of it. "Yes, for that exact reason. We need people to keep us sane, and I'm just pointing out that the boy who is clearly smitten with you would make a perfect partner. So, we've covered that he's crazy for you, but how do you feel? Love wise?"

I huff a laugh and shake my head. *This is ridiculous.* But I have to admit, being able to gossip like this is nice. It feels like the most normal thing I've ever done. "I think I maybe, perhaps am... falling for him."

"Falling in love?" she prods with a wide smile.

I roll my eyes as my face lights on fire. "I'm falling in love with Leo," I admit, and it feels good.

Byrne shrieks. I can't help but smile as she throws her arms in the air. "My big sister is finally in love! You're a real person now, Elana!"

I shush her, but Byrne isn't one to back down. I walk away, but she pushes back to my side, batting her lashes. Somehow, I spill all my heart's secrets as she manages to pry every detail from me. Byrne can't wipe the prideful look from her face, smiling from ear to ear.

A few hours later, we get to our next destination, a city named Keria. It's eerily silent. The sun is beating down as we walk along the streets. This town is twice the size of the last, yet there's not a person in sight. A strong stench of rotting flesh fills the air, intensifying as we creep deeper into the heart of the city. I pull my shirt over my face as the source of the smell reveals itself. Bodies. Hundreds of them lie stacked in piles in the city's center, teaming with flies and scavengers looking for their next meal.

"We need to get out of here as fast as possible," I tell Byrne.

She nods without hesitation, the ease that had found us on the way here has completely dissolved. We still have two people to meet, if they're alive.

We stay close to the shadows and make our way around the dead bodies to get to our destination. A moan sounds, and I draw my weapons. Byrne arms herself as we spin, looking for the source of the cry. I hear it again and turn toward the nearest pile of bodies. Someone is still alive. Byrne's face is void of color as she comes to the same realization.

"Stay here," I tell her.

She nods and sinks further against the wall.

I creep forward and find a woman buried underneath the dead bodies. Her face is covered in flies and caked in blood. A crackling sound escapes her failing lungs with every breath. Her breathing deepens as I touch her arm.

"I'm going to get you out," I tell her. "Just hang on."

I set to pulling at her arm, trying to release her from beneath the crush. Slowly, she takes my hand. I freeze as her red eyes meet mine. I lower my ear as her lips move, trying to pick up on her words.

"Run."

I blink as I straighten. Her lips continue moving in the same pattern. *Run. Run. Run. Run. Run. Run.*

I look back at Byrne as panic makes my heart beat out of my chest. She's gone. I look back at the woman. She's stopped moving, stopped breathing. Her arm is stretched out, her finger pointing in the direction Byrne and I came in.

They were following us. I jump up as fear wraps around my chest and squeezes. I don't remember to say a prayer for the woman as I sprint.

"Byrne!" I push my legs forward, gripping the hilts of my daggers so hard my fingers turn white. "Byrne please!"

I slow as I come to another courtyard surrounded on all sides by tall buildings. I don't think as I run again. I refuse to look at the archers following me with the points of their arrows from the windows high above. I can't. Not when there's a post—stained like the one in Wate—directly in front of me. Chains hang from the top, holding my sister, my Byrne, from her wrists. Blood drips from her mouth.

"*Bryne!*"

Her eyes meet mine and her terror rips me in half. She shakes her head, and I push myself faster. My feet are taken out from under me. I blink as my eyes flash gold. I barely manage to throw out my hands and break my fall before there's rope around my feet. I pull on it and try to get my blade to the cord, but a boot steps on my back with a crushing force.

"Well, how beautiful is this?"

I know that voice. I move to spin out from under my attacker, but a hand grabs my neck while the foot pushes down. My ribs are on the verge of cracking under the pressure as Byrne screams.

"Get her up."

Suddenly, I'm standing and gasping for breath. Two soldiers hold me up as a pair of irons are strapped onto my hands and feet. The daggers I'm carrying are stripped from my grasp, along with all the weapons hidden within the layers of my clothing.

Ares steps into my line of sight with his hands neatly folded behind his red tailored jacket. Flames lick at the outskirts of my mind as he smirks.

"No words for your King, Elana?"

I'm breathing hard. "Usurper."

My ears are ringing before I comprehend what's happened. Ares recoils and rubs his fist. He *hit* me. I pull on the chains and grind my teeth with rage. The metallic taste of blood fills my mouth.

"When will people get the truth straight?" Ares says. He steps closer, his face a breath from mine as I struggle against the chains. "The throne belongs to *me*. Not my soft-minded, half-breed of a cousin. I didn't wait all these years for the poison to deteriorate my father's insides, then push my weak sister up a cliff for some getic-minded *slumblood* to swoop in with convenient digits on his wrist."

My eyes go wide as he holds my gaze. "You killed them. The king and queen."

He laughs loudly, throwing his arms in the air. "Oh, don't be so naïve. Of course I killed them. How else is one supposed to mold the world's strongest country other than by spilling blood?"

Trust. You build it through trust and loyalty. Leo would have built it on trust.

"And really, it was simply too perfect of an opportunity to waste. I had been planning to take over using your father's troops for quite some time. Most would never have supported me if my sister were still alive, and with my cousin's appearance, I was faced with a slew of new challenges. I followed Leo into the Riv that night planning to rid myself of the nuisance, but it just so happened my sister and her husband decided to take a walk under to moonlight up the peaks to watch the stars. When I weighed my options, leaving your naive love as my sole opponent seemed to be the smarter choice."

Ares takes out a dagger and balances the edge on his finger. "In any case, you know as well as I do, Elana, that the best way to gain power is through fear." He's whispering as he slowly places the tip of the dagger against my throat. His eyes bore through my skin.

I force myself to keep breathing, to stay still as my body shakes with revulsion.

"And with fear comes order," he continues. "How long did Cassien beat you before you decided to leave?" My blood freezes, and his smile widens as he searches my face. "It still holds power over you, doesn't it? The fear?" Ares sighs happily.

I'm going to rip his head from his shoulders and make it *hurt*. "You were the best student because of that fear. You were honed into the perfect weapon. Your mind is a copy of your father's ideals, and you would have done anything to further his reign. That's what this world needs." He turns and heads toward Byrne.

I'm going to kill him.

"Right now, people murder each other for sport. We starve each other, work the poor until they break their spines, then leave them to be eaten by the rats. These people are so desperate to escape this world that they poison themselves with chemicals and drink for a moment of reprieve." Ares shakes his head as he flips the dagger in his hand and watches as the blade cuts through the air. He nicks himself as he catches it, his eyes following the blood as it drips to the ground. "It needs to change."

"So you'd destroy entire populations? To save the lives of those who have yet to exist?" I pant.

Ares bursts into laughter, the sound booming in the quiet space. "What I'm doing is bigger than saving people, most of whom are too far gone to accept what needs to be done. No, I'm preparing the world for a new generation. This will be the beginning of a better world where people do not suffer. There will be no more greed. No more fighting. Starting anew with a clean slate." He sighs and turns to Byrne. He runs a hand over her cheek as she struggles against her bindings. "So pretty."

"Don't touch her!" I scream.

Ares turns back to me and drops his hand with a smirk. "I'm sorry. I was distracted," he says, each word calculated.

My wrists are becoming bloody as I pull against the chains.

"Where was I? Ah yes, fear. Once those who will not change are gone, that leaves room for a better generation. The people remaining will be too afraid to go back to their old ways, allowing me to mold a new, *improved* world."

"That's a world without freedom. People won't accept being caged," I seethe as my mind struggles to find a way out.

"They won't have a choice!" Ares screams. He takes a breath and composes himself. "They will obey, or they will not live. This world is broken, and I am the only one who is willing to do what it takes to fix it. No one will stand in my way." He places the tip of the dagger under Byrne's left ribs.

Her breathing quickens as she looks at me.

"Everyone can change if the right price is wagered," he taunts.

Ares pushes the blade in slowly. Byrne's pleading sears my ears as I scream.

"Every will can be broken."

Tears fall down Byrne's face as Ares buries the blade beneath her skin. She stops speaking. Byrne is looking at me. There's blood on my sister's shirt. Too much blood. I pull at the chains.

One of the men holding my arms steps closer, allowing me to move my feet under him. He stumbles and plummets to the ground. I spin and hit him over the head with my iron-bound hands before wrapping the chain around his neck. The other soldier doesn't attack as the man sputters and faints. I don't let go as my heart pumps.

"By the Lady, are you done?" Ares demands from the post.

He's let go of the dagger, the blade still stuck in my sister's chest. He waves to another set of guards. They set to untangling me from my victim and drag him away. They tighten the cuffs and chains while one of the guards keeps a giant hand wrapped around the back of my neck. The force of his grip is so crushing my eyes water. Ares waves the soldier forward and the man drags me with him. He sets me a foot away from

Byrne. I can smell the blood staining her shirt. I try to fight, but the man's fist collides with my jaw and my head goes numb. It takes me a second to recover my senses as Ares watches.

"I should have warned you not to fight back," he says cheekily. "This man with his hand around your neck is a Cadmus. And a strong one at that. You won't break his grip no matter how hard you try." Ares sighs as I ignore his warning. "You'll only hurt yourself, but do as you like. You'll comply with me soon enough."

Blood roars in my ears.

"Now that you're closer, would you like to say anything to your dear sister before I pull the blade from her chest?"

I struggle against my restraints, begging and pleading for her life. This isn't happening. This can't be happening.

"Elana," Byrne whispers weakly, "it's all right."

I shake my head furiously. "No, don't do that."

"Don't blame yourself. You did everything right. You let me live."

Ares places his hand on the hilt of the dagger. His smile grows wider as the color drains from Byrne's face.

"Please, I'll do anything," I plead, tears rolling down my face.

Ares shakes his head. "This is for the greater good. You lose so that the future doesn't have to. It's a sacrifice we all must make."

"I love you, Elana. I should have told you more often. I love you," Byrne whispers, faster now.

I'm screaming. Time slows as Ares pulls the dagger from Byrne's chest. Blood spews from the wound. Something snaps inside me as I watch her eyes flutter closed, the life draining slowly from her face. I drop to my knees as I hear her lungs stop filling. The hand holding my neck drops away. I can't breathe, and my chest ceases to move in time with my heart.

"Well, now that that's done, let's move on. We're behind schedule. We need to move back to Arkezo and set up a meeting with my dear cousin," Ares says.

His words blur as one thought becomes clear in my mind. The Cadmus holding me has a blade in his belt. I move faster than light, the dagger in my hand before the guards can blink. I jump up and spin, launching it toward Ares. He catches the hilt before it cuts too deep, but he's hit. He tosses the dagger away, red staining the blade. Blood spews from under the hand he places over his cheek. A broken laugh sounds my chest as the smirk finally fades from his face.

"I'll make it deeper next time," I wheeze as hysteria takes hold. "Fear works both ways. Now you will remember to be afraid."

His jaw tics as soldiers rush to his aid, but Ares pushes them away. I'm still laughing when a fist collides with my jaw and my mind goes black, sending me plummeting into darkness.

FORTY-ONE

LEO

I think it was good for me to spend time alone with Altair. At first, we didn't speak much, but after a few days, he opened up. We spoke about Tominay and Wate, the way it was before and what comes next. We talked of our parents, my parents, his grandparents. He never mentioned what they did in the lab though—almost as if the time had been erased from his memory. Either way, I finally feel as though I've got my little brother back.

Every town and city we visited was receptive. We almost got into some trouble when a soldier spotted us outside during a lockdown, but thankfully, the woman we were meeting saw us and was able to buy him off. Most of those we met were willing to help in some capacity, but a few weren't willing to go against Ares. They're still afraid. I think they wanted to meet me to know that someone is looking out for them, even if they can't bring themselves to fight. I don't blame them. Ares is using fear as a scythe to silence the people, and he's done it effectively.

When the week is up and we return to the mountain, reality comes crashing back down. I knew what I would be walking into, but I still hoped Cael would be awake. Kaja arrived shortly before we did and is sitting in Cael's room as I step in.

"How is he?" I whisper. She starts at my voice. "I'm sorry, I didn't mean to startle you."

Kaja smiles tightly as she looks at her hand lying on my brother's arm. "It's all right. I was just trying to read his vitals and lost track of time."

I stare at her blankly. She sighs and nods for me to sit on the chair next to the bed.

"Is it better? His... brain function?"

She takes a second to breathe and shakes her head. "I can't tell for sure. His body is doing everything it's supposed to and has been able to sustain its state. The wound is healing well, thanks to your blood, which is good as well. What worries me is I can't feel any of his thoughts, something I would normally be able to do."

My brows crease as I look at Cael's face. I can almost pretend he's sleeping. "You can feel thoughts?"

Her chin dips. "When I connect to someone, I am essentially making myself a part of them. My nervous system becomes one with theirs. When I was young, I could only hear thoughts when I connected with people, but as I trained, I learned to be able to pinpoint electrical signals in a person's body and manipulate them. That's how I was able to keep Cael alive when his brain was damaged. But in essence, yes. I can feel and see people's thoughts when I am connected. I can go so far as to unlock long-forgotten memories or even implant my own."

I know I'm gaping, but I can't stop myself. "That's why they fear you."

Kaja nods. "Most of my Bloodline can perform most of the same skills, but none with the agility I've honed. I once tore through my cousin's mind and was able to recite the names of every person he'd ever met. I reconstructed his entire personality to make him laugh at things that would make others cry. Until I set him right, he thought his parents were going to eat him." She looks at me. "Does that scare you? Knowing I could take anything from your mind or stop your heart with a touch?"

I think about it for a moment and shake my head. "No. Not really."

She breathes a laugh. "You know, I've never met anyone like you and your brother."

"What do you mean?" I ask, leaning back.

She smiles and looks at Cael. "You both have a habit of walking toward things that want to kill you. Even after being beaten again and again, you continue to attract danger and laugh in its face as if it hadn't almost torn you apart the moment before."

I smile. She's not wrong. "When you're afraid for long enough, the feeling becomes less potent. Cael and I went through a lot as children. Maybe our brains rewired themselves along the way because fear was all we knew. It became our default, like returning to your childhood home after spending years away. We're attracted to fear instead of craving happiness. Even so, my mind wouldn't be pleasant to rifle through. It might even be nice to have a little rearranging."

"That... makes sense," she says with a soft laugh. She gets lost in her thoughts for a moment before turning back to me. "Through it all though, I think it's made you both stronger. You would never have survived had you not lived through what you had, as terrible as it is to admit."

I nod, not knowing what to say.

We sit in silence for a long while. I shake myself out of my trance when the boys come in with Saiph. It's only been half an hour since I left them to come here, but it feels good to have them around again. I pick up Saiph and set her on my knee.

"How is he?" Antares asks Kaja.

Her face softens when she meets his eyes. "Just about the same."

Antares nods and pastes on a smile of his own, though I can tell it's difficult.

"As long as he's not worse," I say as I pull him into me.

Antares shifts away and stands in front of Cass. My youngest brother moves his hands in two quick movements. At first, I struggle to decipher the signs and ask him to repeat them.

"Where's Elana?" I ask, speaking the words he signed.

He and Antares have been spending a lot of time with Gray and Cass has learned more signs than I can understand. I've been getting better though. Cass smiles and nods.

My brows knit together. "I don't know. She's not back yet?"

Cass shakes his head.

"Weren't she and Byrne supposed to get back first?" Kaja wonders.

"Yeah. They were." I get to my feet, keeping Saiph in my arms.

Bryne and Elana had one less town to visit, so they should have been back this morning. They may have been delayed for a few hours, but it's dusk now. They should be here.

Antares and Cass are on my heels as I trek through the compound, searching for Red. I find her with Gray, Kiro, and Soren in the storage room we've been using as a meeting area.

"Leo," she says in greeting. Her brows crease as she catches my expression. "What is it?"

"Elana's not back yet."

She leans back in her chair as she signs my words for Gray. "Delays happen some—"

"She was supposed to get back this morning," I interrupt.

She pinches the bridge of her nose and closes her eyes for a moment.

"Were you never late coming back when you worked as a mercenary?" Kiro says curtly.

"Only when I was *hurt*," I snap. "We need to go out and look for them."

"Do you not think her capable?" Kiro presses.

My jaw locks as Cass takes hold of the back of my shirt, keeping me planted. I force myself to breathe as I look back at Red.

"She's more *capable* than I'll ever be," I say, "but that doesn't mean she couldn't run into trouble or get caught."

Red takes a breath and nods, gesturing for Kiro to back off.

"I know our resources are stretched thin, but I won't leave them out there," I add.

"If Byrne and Elana aren't back by sunrise, Soren and Deca will go with you to look for them."

I nod and thank her before turning away. A gnawing dread eats at my stomach with every passing minute. I busy myself with helping those who've taken refuge, setting up plans with the Bond, and spending time with the children, but I can't help worrying.

A few hours later, I'm sitting outside with Saiph asleep against me. The air is cold, burning my lungs in a way that's almost soothing. I can see Arkezo in the distance as its lights burn into the sky. The only thing stopping me from running down the mountain is my sister. It surprises me sometimes that she can still sleep so peacefully. Maybe through all this, I did something right. Maybe if she gets a chance to grow up, she'll be proof I wasn't always a monster.

The door opens behind me as the sky begins to brighten. It will be a beautiful morning.

"Are you ready to go?" Soren asks.

I laugh sullenly and stare at the horizon. "Always."

Antares, Cass, and Altair are behind Soren and Deca. I stand carefully and pass Saiph off to Antares as Altair picks up his pack.

"You decided to come?" I ask him. He was unsure when I told him I was leaving again, but I can't say a part of me isn't glad he'll be with me. I smile when he nods.

I turn toward Antares and Cass to tell them to be safe, but Antares beats me to it, repeating the words I tell them every time I leave them alone. I laugh and pull them into a tight hug before forcing myself to walk away. For some reason, it's harder to go this time as I follow Soren down the mountain.

We push hard through the towns, finding those where Elana stopped and quickly moving on. The first day, we walk through half the night before Soren and Deca refuse to go any farther. I kicked myself for having to push them so hard, but I can't stop thinking of all the places Elana could be.

The next night, I stop with ample time for them to rest. But by the beginning of the third day, my mind is in shambles. I don't speak as we walk. We're ahead of schedule, but we still aren't going fast enough.

"Are you listening, Leo?"

I turn toward Soren. "No." I don't have it in me to apologize.

"You should eat," he says, handing me a package of dried meat, fruit, and crackers.

"I'm all right," I tell him, but he pushes the food at my chest.

"We haven't seen you eat since we left."

I start to deny it but realize he's right. I've given Altair all the food I've opened over the past three days.

When I stay quiet, Soren sighs. "At least take it for later. I don't know how I would explain to Red that you died of starvation when we had four packs full of provisions."

I scoff and take it reluctantly. "I can go weeks without eating, you know."

I open the package and eat. I didn't notice how hungry I am until I take the first bite.

"Let's test that another day, shall we?" Soren suggests.

We continue on our path, finally reaching the next city. Wind whistles past the buildings as we stalk through the streets. The only living things here are the rats feasting on bodies. Altair takes in the sight with wide eyes, turning green. I take a cloth from my pack and tie it around his face to help with the smell.

"Breathe through your mouth. If you're going to throw up, make sure to lift the mask," I tell him as he nods shakily.

"What did Ares do?" Deca whispers. She holds an axe in each hand and walks as if an attacker might just appear in front of her.

I shake my head. "I don't know. This is Keria, right? Wasn't this known as the muck city? One of the Bloodlines owns it and almost everyone here worked on the labor lines?"

Soren nods stoically. "These people created some of the most beautiful goods imaginable but were the poorest of Illena. The Alinsky Bloodline owns every building and person here. Their homes and the grounds around them are a wonder to behold, but the rest of the city has been left to rot for generations. Ares must have had a bone to pick."

I hear a shutter close in a building ahead. Someone is watching us.

We creep forward slowly, passing piles of undisturbed bodies. We finally get to the place where Elana and Byrne were supposed to meet a woman who ran a large part of the underground market that fed into the Killarian. I rap my knuckles against the door. Nothing.

"There's no one left," Soren murmurs in the eerie silence. "We need to move on."

I nod and start to turn away, but a creak in the house stops me short. I grab the knob. It's locked.

"Leo, what are you doing?"

I step back and kick in the door. Soren and Deca let out a string of curses as I step inside and swing open every door, looking through every room. Another creak bounces through the air as I leave the kitchen. I crouch and run my hand along the wilted floorboards, finding a trap door. I grip the planks and pull. It folds open easily. Before I have the chance to look inside, a knife flies by my face. My eyes bleed red as I jump out of the way.

"I'm a friend. I swear I'm not here to hurt you," I plead. I lean over the hole as another blade comes at me. I swear and signal for Altair, Deca, and Soren to stay put as they barge into the room.

"Who are you?" a shaky voice demands from below the floor.

"My name is Leo Heal. I'm looking for two friends who came through here a few days ago."

Aggressive murmurs fill the air before a man with shining silver hair clambers out of the ground.

"You're the king?" he asks carefully.

I sheathe my dagger and drain my eyes. "I was never officially crowned, but yes."

The words taste foreign, but for the first time, I don't mind saying them. Not when the man's eyes light up with relief. Fourteen people, including an elderly couple and five kids, climb out from the space below. Each is bloodied and dirty. Some are bandaged with linens that look as if they've been dragged through the mud. We unpack our supplies and set to helping them as best as we can.

"What happened here?" I ask after we've dealt with the worst of the injuries and given them any food we can spare.

"We were finishing our shifts when Ares's troops marched in. We'd heard the rumors about what had happened in Arkezo, but we thought we'd be safe because of our association with the Alinsky Bloodline. Little did we know the soldiers had been camped outside the city for days, holding off their attack until the evening, so we'd be too drained to fight back. The legions had no mission but to slaughter. We've only been able to survive because we were hidden. Our own people burned our buildings and killed every soul they could find before sending in their gold-eyed minions to finish anyone teetering on the edge of life. Only they never came back to burn the bodies, so here we are."

I don't know what to say. We stay quiet for a long time.

A woman, who evidently very recently lost an eye, steps forward carrying an infant. "Do you have somewhere for us to go? Please, we cannot stay here."

I smile and nod, taking the time to explain how to get to the mountain. We're going to have to start setting up the alternate space in the woods soon if we continue to send more people north. Two people leave a few minutes later to inform some others in hiding. When everything's settled, I finally ask the silver-haired man the question that's been scraping at my thoughts.

"Do you know of the woman who was in charge of the black market here?" I ask.

When the man's face takes on a frightened look, I assure him I have no malicious intent in searching for her. I explain that I'm working with Hela's Bond to forge a rebellion. He seems appeased and opens up.

"I knew her well. In fact, Marge and I grew up together. She saved many of us when the slaughter began, but in the end, they got her too."

"I'm sorry," I tell him, but he waves me off.

"If we apologized for every life we've seen taken too soon, there would be no time for living."

I smile sadly, knowing he's right. "Two gold-eyed sisters were supposed to have come through here about a week ago. Have you by chance seen or spoken to them? Or do you know anyone who might have?"

The man's face falls. He moves to turn away, but I grab his arm. I know my grip is crushing, but I don't care.

"What do you know?" I demand.

The man's face is pale as he meets my eyes, and I feel the others get closer. Soren and Deca call me away, but I don't move. The man's face morphs with terror.

"One of them was special, wasn't she?" he squeaks.

I grip his arm harder and push him against the wall. "Where are they? Tell me or I swear on the Lady, I'll rip out your throat!"

The man swallows and puts up his hands. "Fine, fine. Please just let go."

I pry myself away and step back as my heart races.

"We saw them come through, but we had no idea who they were. I swear we didn't know he was waiting. But she was on the post and—"

"Where? Where is the post?" I demand.

He winces and shrinks back. "The next street over, in the courtyard."

I don't think before I'm sprinting out of the house. My lungs heave as I push myself faster. *Please, by the Lady, let them be alive. Let them be all right. I'll do anything.*

No matter how much I pray and hope, the body on the post still appears as I turn the corner. Something in me breaks as I stare at the black hair flowing in the wind. "No."

I sprint up, begging it not to be Elana. No matter how terrible it is, no matter what hell I'll go to for thinking it, I hope it's not Elana. I grab her face, and a twisted pain rips through me. It's not Elana. I close my eyes and force myself to breathe through the agony.

"I'm sorry," I whisper as tears gather in my eyes. "I'm so, so sorry."

I grab a dagger and break open the cuffs that keep her standing. My muscles shake as Byrne's dead weight falls into me. I take her off the platform and set her body gently on the ground. I don't know what to do, so I stare and whisper a word to the Lady. I know Deca and Soren are watching.

Something fluttering in the wind on the post draws my attention away from Byrne. A note is pinned to the wood with a knife. I step up and pull out the blade. It's the dagger Elana left with. My hands shake as I force myself to read the note written in a perfect, practiced script.

My dear cousin,

I want to remind you that you are the one who decided to play games, not me. I only reacted to your trying to steal my crown and start a rebellion. You should have listened to yourself and continued to refuse the throne. Had you done so, poor Byrne's heart would still be beating. I know you must be worried about your beloved. She's in perfect hands, do not fret. I will take very good care of her. Just make certain that you come to the Ridge, unarmed and alone. If you do, Elana will be set free. But if you reject my conditions, I will skin her alive. Slowly. It's in your hands, Blood Prince. These are the decisions a king must make for his people. To save thousands, or one.

FORTY-TWO

LEO

My mind is blank as I cover Byrne with a blanket. A crowd gathers around as I find pieces of discarded wood and build a stretcher. I don't care where Altair is right now, and I don't give Deca and Soren another thought. My heart pounds rhythmically. I count each beat, each breath. I gather anything flammable and place it at the base of the post before throwing sparks into the air. Within seconds, the fire eats at the wood, sending plumes of smoke into the sky.

I don't stay to watch it burn. There's nothing left inside me to take satisfaction from the flames. I want to cut down every person in my path. I shove away the feeling, building walls in my mind and locking my conscience in a cage. I stay numb, trapped inside a box. A small, colorless box. I don't know what I'll do if I have to face the rage roiling in my mind.

No one stops me as I walk through the night. A crowd of several dozen follow close behind us. The people thank me for saving them. For fighting for their freedom and safety. But every time those words are muttered, a new wound rips open in my chest. I am no King. I haven't saved them. And when it comes down to it, I won't choose them.

I force the walls in my mind to press closer, suffocating my thoughts until I can breathe again. The only thing stopping me from sprinting back toward the mountain is Byrne's body lying in the stretcher in my hands. Soren holds the other end, purposefully slowing his steps to keep me close to the group. Altair stays close to my side but doesn't speak or look at me, his face pinched. I don't ask where he was when we found Byrne.

When my feet drag, I bleed my eyes and continue forward. Soren and Deca try to make me drink, eat, sleep. Do the human things that people need to do to survive. But I don't want to survive. I want to fade.

We get back to the mountain in the dead of night. I don't stop to greet the boys. I can't let them see me as my mind is ravaged by my imagination.

I don't know what Soren and Deca tell Red, but none of the Bond question my actions. They watch as we lay Byrne down in a secluded room. Emmani and her brother shed a tear and say a prayer in words I don't understand, touching the braided circlet on their brows.

The people we brought with us are in dire need of attention, so I bandage their wounds and bring them something to eat. I keep myself busy. Busy is good.

Emrys isn't back yet. He should be back soon. I don't know what happens then. What he'll feel. How he'll react. If he really loves her. I hope a bolt of lightning strikes him on his way back so he never has to know and I never have to tell him.

I gather Hela's Bond together a few hours later. My head is

clear enough to get at least one thought straight through the chaos. "Ares has Elana."

Their heads swivel in my direction.

"How do you know?" Red asks.

I unfold the note I've kept tucked in my pocket. I couldn't tell Deca and Soren about it when we found Byrne. I guess they assumed Elana was killed along with her sister. Red reads it and grinds her teeth before passing it to the rest of the Bond. They try their best not to seem eager but jump on the paper as soon as it leaves Red's hand.

"I'm going to get her," I announce.

Their gazes shoot up to me, clearly alarmed. I smooth my face into a mask of calm.

"No, you won't."

I cross my arms and stare Red down. She holds strong for longer than I expect, but soon she folds.

Still, Red says, "You are a king, Leo. No matter who you love, your duty is to your people. To your country. Without you, there is no hope of getting Ares off the throne."

"He'll kill Elana if I don't give myself in. But me?" I shake my head, imagining the terror I'd live. "I'm a prize to him. He won't kill me. He'll bruise me up and parade me through the streets. You'll have more time to get me out."

Red shakes her head incredulously.

"And if you're wrong? What if he does kill you?" Kiro interjects.

"Then make me into a martyr and use my name as a symbol."

They stare at me blankly, searching my face for a crack in my resolution. They won't find it.

"We don't want to leave Elana with him," Red says softly, as if I were a wild animal she's trying to tame, "but we don't have the network to get her out and you giving yourself up will only increase our vulnerability. I'm sorry, Leo, but saving her isn't worth the risk."

I laugh in frustration, hearing the words jostle in my skull. *Not worth the risk.* "So you'll let her die?"

I need to hear her say it. Red sighs and rubs a hand over her face.

"And you would abandon your siblings?" Kiro interjects.

I'm seconds away from pushing a dagger through his eye when Red pulls him back.

"Don't pay him any heed. We'll gather a force as we planned and make getting her out a priority, but these things take time. She'll just have to survive," Red amends.

Not one of the Bond dares to meet my eyes as I look around.

"Cowards," I breathe before turning and leaving the room. "Every one of you is a coward."

There is always a way. When Altair and I were out in the cities, I spoke to a woman whose husband was a king's guard. She said that he would be willing to help if he and his family could get out of Arkezo safely. There must be more like him. All I need to do is ask.

I sit in my room alone, running through plans in my head. Every time I think of something that might work, my thoughts spiral apart. I run my hands over my face and lean back. A quiet knock sounds at the door. Two raps, a pause, then another. The safe knock.

I open my eyes to see Cass, Antares, and Saiph in the doorway.

"Are you all right?" Antares asks.

They sit beside me on my cot as I pick up Saiph.

"No. Not really," I admit.

Cass leans into me as I hook my arms around them both.

"Can we help?"

"No," I breathe weakly.

Antares nods and looks at Cass as he moves his hands.

"It's Elana?" Antares translates.

I nod, tears gathering in my eyes. For a moment, I'm afraid if I speak, the walls will crumble and the flood unleashed will tear me apart. Even in the silence, I can't stop the tears from falling. I feel too helpless to fight against it. Byrne is dead. Cael's on the brink, and Elana will be next.

"You should go get her," Antares whispers.

I blink and look at my little brother. He's so much bigger than he used to be.

"I can't leave you here," I tell them.

Antares considers my words and shakes his head. "If you went, would you promise to come back?"

"No," I reply. I could lie, but what would be the point? I'm too exhausted and terrified to try to put on a strong face.

"Do you love her?"

My head swivels to Cass. I blink. His whispered words send me toppling over the edge. Tears stream down my face as I pull him in and hold him tightly. When I finally get a handle on the sobs ripping at me, Cass looks up at me expectantly.

"I think so," I say, my words breaking.

Cass smiles softly and moves his hands in a sign I understand. *Me too. I don't want her to die.*

"I don't know what I should do," I tell them.

"If Ares had taken one of us, would you stay or go?" Antares asks.

"I would go," I answer without hesitation.

They both nod.

"Then you should go."

My mind blanks. "Even when there's a chance neither Cael nor I will come back?" I have to make sure they understand what they're saying.

"Would you be able to live if she died and you knew that you could have saved her?"

I don't know what to say. My mind imagines Elana living through hell, just as I have hundreds of times before. It's almost too much to bear.

"No," I breathe.

Antares nods solemnly. "We'll be all right. We've survived until now. We can last a while longer."

I nod and pull in my three siblings. We don't speak anymore, but I don't dare move. I don't tell them goodbye when they nod off. I keep my mind focused on the things I'll do to make sure I come back. Because there is no other option than to return. I'll tear the world apart before I let this be the last time I see them.

I stay longer than I should, listening to their breathing level out. I carefully lift them off me and tuck them in. I glance back one last time before shutting the door behind me.

My gaze gravitates toward the chest at the end of the bed where the crown has remained untouched since we arrived. Only Elana and the Bond know it's there. Maybe one day I'll have the courage to put it on, but today is not that day. Today, I get Elana back.

CHAPTER

FORTY-THREE

ELANA

It's quiet. I focus on every breath. In. Out. I need to keep my thoughts collected and my wits straight. I have no time for tears or reminiscing, there's only now—sitting on a horse with a bag over my head and my limbs chained to the saddle. I tried to slip out of the cuffs, but a hand caught my neck before I could move an inch. I can feel the heat radiating off the Cadmus riding beside me.

In this position, fighting is futile, so I bide my time and prepare for my chance. I note the changes in the air and the sound of hooves against the ground. It takes hours before I pick up the scent of bodies cutting through the dampness of the woods. Only one place can smell so horrid—a city, and a large one at that. *We must be getting close to Arkezo.*

I stay still as the horses transition from dirt paths to stone roads. I expect to hear the flutter of people milling in the streets, but instead my ears are battered with the sound of marching boots. Somewhere in the distance, a scream is cut off in the middle of a breath.

Breathe, I tell myself. *Listen to what's around you. Find a way out.*

I grind my teeth as Cassien's voice mingles with my own in my thoughts. He was the one who muttered those words when he would blindfold me and send me into a ring with a fighter twice my age and ability. I never won those fights, but he would always smile when I came out bruised and beaten. *You will be better next time. Learn from what you did wrong and fix it. Then you will become great.* Every time I lost, he repeated the same words. He never told me I was great, but the hope that festered inside my core drove me to keep entering that ring, to keep taking the punches. All for the smirk that would cross his face.

The horse stops after climbing a small hill. *We must be at the palace.* The Cadmus grabs me by the waist, yanks me down, and tosses me on the ground. My body is frozen as I force my lungs to inflate. My entire left side smarts as I roll onto my stomach.

"Oh, don't be so rough with our guest," Ares says from somewhere above me. "We don't want to damage the prize. My poor cousin might not want you anymore if we're careless. Though maybe that wouldn't be a bad thing."

A hand touches my arm and I jolt away.

Ares cackles as he retreats. "Bring her to her room, Cadmus. There's no reason to leave the lady in the dirt."

I'm picked up like a doll and set roughly on my feet. I try every maneuver I've been taught, but with the chains so tight and the hand gripping my neck, I'm stuck. Trapped. Panic rings in my mind when my feet hit smooth tile and the warm feeling of the sun on my body disappears. My foot hits a ledge and I plummet forward. I blink in the darkness of the bag as I'm yanked back up.

"Stairs," a gruff voice grumbles from my left.

My fists curl as I blindly search for the next step. I wonder if the soldiers find this funny or if they even care about what Ares has done. Maybe they're truly so blind they don't see the monster he is.

I count the turns as I'm jerked one way and the next. I'm sure at one point we walk down a hall only to go back the same way, throwing off my sense of direction. After several minutes of trying to keep my feet under me, we stop. A ring of keys clinks together from somewhere to my right before a click and the sound of old hinges squeaking open reaches my ears.

I'm shoved forward so hard I trip onto something soft. A hand lands between my shoulders, holding me down against what seems like a bed. The chains around my hands are undone and relocked at my front. Sweat builds on my forehead as I try to break away, but there are hands all over me, touching me, touching my skin.

My lungs heave as they hold me down. My vision tunnels as my muscles tighten and freeze. I'm trembling when they finally let me go. I slide onto the floor and curl into myself as footsteps recede and the door creaks shut. Even after the lock is set, I can't get myself to move. My thoughts spiral, but my body doesn't react, stuck in a state of terror.

My eyes fall shut in the silence interrupted only by my own shallow breathing. The darkness is calming, inviting. I let myself stay there for a moment and imagine nothing has happened. That I'm home with my mother and Byrne... I bring myself back to my room and imagine hiding under the covers of my bed. I let the darkness swallow me whole. Nothing can reach me here. No one knows where I am.

For a moment, that make-believe notion gives me reprieve,

but nothing is strong enough to keep away the wave of reality. One moment I'm stilled by exhaustion, and the next, the darkness I'd found so comforting closes in, suffocating me. I grab the bag and yank it off. The material scrapes roughly against my face as light beaming through the high window blinds me.

My eyes adjust slowly as I force myself to breathe. I expected to be in some type of cell, but this room is beautiful. There's a bookcase built into the wall by a large window and an upholstered bench. The bed I'm propped against is fitted with satin sheets. I run my hand over the material in wonder. An armoire is placed on the other side of the room beside a standing mirror taller than the door. The only aspect of the room that remotely resembles a prison is the chain pegged into the wall beside the bed. There's even a bathing room.

I stand and drag myself over to it. The chains around my limbs clink with every movement. I run my fingers over the hinges hanging on the empty frame. They must have taken off the door.

I walk over to the armoire as my curiosity gets the better of me. I gape as I throw open the door and take in the army of gowns hanging inside. Each is made of expensive fabrics and layered to be ridiculously thick. I scowl as I take in the weight of each dress. They must be at least sixty pounds each, all embellished with fine stones and delicate embroidery. More than anything, I take in the blood-hued crimson. I feel like Ares is mocking me, filling the room with clothes in the same color he wore to the coronation, which also happens to match the shade of the blood-eyes. Albeit slightly lighter than Leo's, but every blood-eye shares the hue. I slam the door shut as my breathing picks up. I need to get out of here.

My gaze jumps across the room as I force myself to stay calm. I need to find a weapon. Wrapping the chain around my hand, I step up to the mirror and throw my first into the glass, shattering it with ease. I tip it over and shake the pieces onto the floor. After kicking the shards around, I find a piece large enough to use as a knife. I throw open the armoire and rip at the thin fabric. I tie the strips around the glass to stop the edge from slicing my hand.

When I'm satisfied, I rip a few dresses off their hooks and slice the ribbing. The corsets are made with bone and wire, perfect for picking locks. It doesn't take long before I get the shackles undone. I take a moment to rub my wrists and sigh at the small dose of freedom. *I'm going to get out of this.*

I spend hours ripping things apart and knocking on walls, trying to find anything useful. I push at the window, trying to break it open, but the glass is so thick it stays intact even when I smash it with the chains. There's no food, but the bathing room has running water. It takes me ages to figure out how it works, but I remember Leo telling me about the taps in their old room and I'm finally able to turn it on. I stare at the water, mesmerized for a moment before drinking to my stomach's content. It occurs to me that they might have poisoned the water, but I can't bring myself to care.

A full day passes and the door remains closed. I sleep in bouts with the glass dagger held tightly in my hands. My stomach twists with hunger, but the feeling is a welcome familiarity. I find my mind wandering back to everything that's happened. Ares's words replay in my mind in harmony with Byrne's eyes. I can't stop seeing her, hearing her scream. It becomes too much. Isolating me is more torture than skinning me alive. Of all the mistreatments and terrors, my mind has somehow become the worst kind of prison.

I open the books in search of a distraction, but the letters aren't characters I recognize. I throw open every tome, and each is illegible. Frustration grates at my mind as I do the only thing I can muster to keep me from insanity—I rip out every page, one by one. When that becomes too mundane, I decide to make traps. I rip apart the threads in the dresses and tie together shards of glass. I string them up all around the door. When it opens, they should pull tight and get wrapped around the limbs of whoever enters.

I continue to set traps and take them down again for four more days, sleeping every few hours under the bed. It's the only place I feel safe enough to close my eyes. I'm in the midst of cutting into the wall to see what lies behind it when the door creaks open. I grab my weapons and step behind the bed. The door snags on the chains, and balls of glass fall, swinging out into the opening. Two screams ring out from the hall as someone swears and calls for a medic. I can't help but laugh as I bask in the chaos of my own making. The traps were never going to get me out of here, but the satisfaction of knowing that I did not go down without leaving a mark is well worth the slices still stinging my hands.

After a few moments, two guards clear the glass and bone shards I laid out for them. Each carries a crossbow aimed at my chest, pinning me to where I sit on the floor. Ares steps in and takes a look around.

"It seems we don't share a taste for finery," he murmurs. He picks up a piece of a shredded dress, caressing the fabric with his fingers. "You know, the people who made these for you spent days slaving over the material. Two of them are dead now."

My stomach flips as I stare at the luscious fabric in his hands. I force myself to keep still as he lets it fall to the floor.

"We were going to have this room redone anyway. We'll save some manpower now at least," Ares says to one of the guards as he looks at where I've been cutting through the walls.

"What do you want?" I imagine running the glass dagger

through his heart again and again. The thought keeps me grounded.

"Aren't you hungry?" he says with a smirk.

I watch as he ushers in a small maid. Hunched over, she brings in a platter with a tower of food. She steps through the glass without shoes, whimpering with every step. I move to help her, but the guards put their fingers over the triggers of their crossbows. I sink back onto the floor and watch as the maid helplessly crosses the river of shards between us before placing down the food. She raises her eyes to mine and my lungs cease moving. They sewed her mouth shut. I'm frozen in place as she averts her eyes and limps out of the room. My gaze lands on Ares and I'm starting to think it will be worth dying if I can take him with me.

"Don't look at me like that," Ares says, waving me off as he leans against the door. "Her screaming was scaring the children."

My limbs hang heavily as the weight of his words settles on my shoulders.

Ares sighs and crosses his arms. "I'm going to be frank with you, Elana. You have about sixteen days before I start to disassemble you and send the pieces up the mountain for my cousin if he doesn't give himself up. If he does show, I still haven't decided if I'll truly let you live, so you may not have long either way."

"Why would you tell me that?" I whisper, meaning the words to sound stronger.

"Because I want you to cherish your last days if you decide to continue supporting him. I will send in some maids to clean this mess and wash you. Over the next few days, I want you to consider your life and think about how it could improve if you chose to join me."

A laugh bubbles from my lungs. I can't stop myself from

doubling over from the idiocy of the statement. "I'd rather be dead."

Ares shrugs. "Suit yourself. I will be visiting more often from now on." He turns to leave but throws one last remark over his shoulder before his guards shut the door. "Make yourself nicer than this. You look like a slumblood."

I'm stung for reasons I can't identify. I don't know how long I stand in the same place, replaying his words in my mind.

As the sky turns pink outside the window, the door swings open slowly. I raise my hands, expecting Ares to step back inside. Instead, three women file in. Their khaki dresses hang dully on their bones. The last maid is the one I saw before. The stitches in her mouth look mostly healed. They must have been done weeks ago. The other two women mill around, sweeping up glass and resetting books in a mechanical routine. It takes me a moment to realize the other two maids have been maimed as well. One lady, standing taller than her counterparts, is missing three fingers on each hand while the other has partially healed burns all over her face.

"Why did they do this to you?" I ask shakily.

The women stop and glance toward each other. Not a sound comes from their mouths as they return to their work. I watch them closely as they move around, glass crunching under their shoes. I blink. The woman with the sewn mouth hadn't been wearing shoes before. Now her feet are covered.

"Did they take your shoes? When you came in before?" I ask her.

That stops her. She swallows and looks at me with broken eyes. Her skin is pale, and under her eyes lie two dark crescents. She nods shallowly.

"Why?" I press.

"To make her bleed," the taller one says. "They find pleasure in seeing us suffer." She raises a hand to place a book back on the shelf and reveals the band and number on her arm.

I almost break down as I see it. "You're gold-eyed?"

Three pairs of eyes land on me.

The tallest woman turns slowly as her hands fall to her side. "You really are his daughter, aren't you?"

She doesn't need to say his name for the memories to push at my mind. "Yes."

"But you fight with the Blood Prince."

It's not a question, but I nod nonetheless. "I didn't know... I thought the gold-eyes were safe."

I glance at the other woman's wrists. The woman with the burns is also gold-eyed, while the third is blood-eyed.

The tallest laughs. "No. No one was safe when Ares marched. The gold soldiers were all sent to blood cities to ravage, and it gave the blood soldiers a perfect opportunity to take us away. They stole every puppet from the academies, along with anyone who was weak and poor. They ordered each family, no matter their rank, to give up one of their members as a show of fealty as well. The ones who refused were slaughtered, and those who gave themselves in exchange for their family's survival were brought here. We were separated into two groups: individuals they could use for labor, and those they did not need. If we were found *useful,* they took us to the prison under the palace and started to experiment. Testing our reactions to pain mostly, but some were injected with things that killed them almost instantly. The rest were killed on the spot."

Silence hangs heavily between us as they watch me.

"Were you going to try to stop him?" the blood-eyed girl whispers.

I don't know how to respond because of course we planned to stop him, but maybe we were already too late. Even if we dethrone him now, how can Leo fix the damage left in Ares's wake? How could anyone?

"They're still trying," I tell them.

The girl marred with burns smiles. "Then maybe there's a chance."

The tallest nods, but something in her eyes tells me she's already lost hope. "Maybe."

I join them as they continue cleaning, listening to more stories about the terrors they've endured. Somehow, they still believe Cassien had nothing to do with the attacks and that he'd been double-crossed. I don't have it in me to argue. If believing Cassien is good gives them hope, then let them be hopeful. I won't be the person to steal that from them.

When they leave, the emptiness I'd managed to momentarily forget about burns a gaping hole in my chest. I stare at the clean room. There's still a platter of food sitting on the floor. My knees shake as I take in the room. My mind spins and I'm on the floor, heaving for breath. Tears gather in my eyes, but I refuse to let them fall.

I crawl under the bed and curl up. I close my eyes and imagine arms around me, holding me. A voice telling me it will be all right. A warmth enveloping me and transporting me to a place where there is no danger or fear. But no matter how I try, my bones remain cold, and the air stays thin. No matter how hard I try, my thoughts are not reality, and I am alone.

FORTY-FOUR

ELANA

I force myself to eat, swallowing tasteless food as it scrapes down my throat. Ares has not been back. I've been alone. I move through the motions as I have for days: eating, drinking, ripping up pages stained with incomprehensible ink, placing them in piles to make it easier for the maids to clean up if they return, watching water spew from the tap, trying and failing to warm my bones.

Sitting in the corner of the room with my legs crossed has become my greatest pastime. I think of comforts, of Leo and a home. I imagine being safe, having luxury in a small house away from it all. I imagine Byrne living up the road and my mother and father growing old as they'd once dreamed. I imagine Cass, Antares, Altair, and Saiph getting older, and Cael jousting with Leo on a clear day. I dream of everything perfect, of everything I cannot have.

I'm dreaming when the door creaks open. The glass dagger is in my hand, but there is no strength in my arms. The three women step in and shut the door softly. Though we spoke before, they do not open their mouths now. The tallest carries a blood-red gown. My stomach flips as she lays it on the bed. There must be fear on my face because the other two women come to my side and lift me gently from where I sit. They keep hold of me as we step into the bathing room.

I don't have it in me to fight them as they start a bath and strip me bare. The water's warm, but still, my bones shake. I sink under the surface and stay until my lungs shriek for air. Every inch of me is scrubbed clean. They pull a brush through my hair and guide me out of the tub. I shrink away from their touch, but there is nowhere to run. I block them out and let my mind build up the walls that have served me for so many years. I do not feel their hands against my skin as they force me into a dress half my weight, or their fingers as they braid my hair and poke my scalp with pins.

When they've finished, I cannot sit. I cannot breathe with the corset around my chest. I have no mirror to look into, but I know I look regal. Expensive. Dead.

"He wants to see you in the throne room," the tallest whispers.

I nod.

"We have to lock you back in the chains," the burnt one says.

They move swiftly. When they finish, I wiggle my feet, noticing the cuffs hanging so loose I could get out of them. The women smile when I look up.

"You could be killed," I tell them.

The tallest waves me off. "Even if it does not help, we believe you're worth the risk."

I don't know what to say to them, but they smile nonetheless. There are no other words between us as they open the door. The guards take my arms, yet I make myself a promise to try to help them one day. To try. I stand a little taller as I'm pulled through the halls.

When we reach the looming doors of the throne room, I'm roughly tossed inside. At the last moment, I catch myself before I hit the ground as they shut the doors behind me. The walls are lined with soldiers sporting crimson armbands. The gown weighs on me as I raise my eyes to the throne.

"Now, this is what a lady should look like." Ares walks down the steps of the dais.

My hands curl into fists at his smirk.

"The chains though..." His face morphs into something of deep thought before he waves his hand through the air. "Someone take them off. They're clashing with the dress."

I steel myself as a soldier outfitted in a similar shade of red walks toward me. My muscles coil with stored power, preparing as I have millions of times before. My body works separately from my mind as ice courses through my veins, calming me. I will not give up.

The man stoops to undo the bindings on my feet, then releases my hands. As the last click resounds through the air, I act. The dagger from his belt is in my palm in an instant. I move slowly in the dress, but with surprise on my side, I manage to kick the man's knees. He falls with a grunt. I grip his hair with one hand and press the edge of the blade to his throat. The man shakes beneath me as a symphony of weapons being drawn rings through the room. A slow clapping rises above it all.

"Impressive," Ares says bleakly before he crosses his arms.

I pull the dagger tighter against the soldier's throat. He squeaks at the movement, but Ares seems unfazed.

"Truly, I believed we'd be on better terms than this by now." He steps closer and scans the room with furrowed brows.

"You kept me prisoner," I seethe.

"Because you try to kill my men," he explains, looking at me through his brows.

"You murdered my sister," I yell with a broken voice.

"Such a pity. But you were planning on destroying me, were you not? I could not let poor Byrne go for fear of her hurting my beloved people." His words are serious as he stands unflinching, as if this make-believe story he's concocted in his mind is hard truth.

I hold my ground as he watches me. Finally, Ares sighs and shakes his head.

"I've allotted you the best garments and comforts, yet this is how you treat me. I had hoped we could find some sort of… friendship. But if you are so set on destroying my dear, distraught country, we'll have to take a different approach." Ares signals one of his guards and heads back to sit on his throne.

Three soldiers appear, each holding one of the maimed maids. Fear rages through my mind as the women struggle against the iron grip of the guards.

"Now, I have no problem seeing these women killed. They have been annoyances for some time. But seeing as you have spent some time with them, I hope that you have formed an affinity for their lives." I meet his eyes as he smiles and tilts his head. "I have no qualms about you killing my soldier. I hand-picked him to unlock your chains because I knew you would try something like this. He has been funneling people out of the city for days now. I was going to put him in the brig, but I felt this would be a perfect precursor."

More than before, I feel the man shake. The guards holding the women tighten their grips and pull out their daggers. They place the tips under their ribs toward their hearts. My mind spins as I look back at Ares.

"It's your choice, Elana. My soldier, or the maids."

I clench my jaw as the tallest of the maids shakes her head, pleading with desperate eyes. I force myself to breathe and let go, stepping away.

The man I'd been holding feels his neck and turns to me with wide eyes. "No. *No, please!* Kill me! Have mercy, don't let them take me down there..."

Two soldiers march to the middle of the room and grab him under the arms. Another joins them as he fights like a feral animal. They drag him away, and I wince as his screams fade.

"Now that that's been dealt with," Ares says as he picks at his nails, "let's get to the real show."

For the first time, I notice the group of people standing behind his throne.

"I've grown tired of complaints about the gold cities, and I've exhausted their usefulness. I've taken the armies available under my own command and used their families as collateral for their service. Though I do respect the fact that most are simply happy to serve in an army as powerful as Illena's and will do as I command because that is the way they were raised." Ares nods and the small crowd behind the throne parts.

Cassien is staring at me, unmoving. His jaw is tight as Ares folds his hand behind his back. My mouth goes dry.

"How wonderful is this? A family reunion. Too bad your youngest could not attend, Cassien."

I clench the dagger tightly. "If you dare mention her again, I'll give you the matching scar on the other cheek."

Ares smiles and turns to Cassien. Something strange passes through Cassien's eyes.

"Do you know, my dear colleague, why Elana is the only one of your offspring to stand before you?"

My lungs tighten as Cassien's brow furrows. He looks at me

and his face falls. I do a double take as fear passes through his eyes. A man places his hand on Cassien's shoulder and walks him down the steps. Cassien's muscles strain with every step as I realize who stands beside him. *Damaris.*

He's directing Cassien, I realize with a start.

Ares sits on the throne and folds one leg over the other as if this were a show. "I've decided you are now expendable, Cassien. You've proven useful for a time, but I lost respect for you when you asked me to spare your daughters. I cannot have weak men on my council..."

My eyes meet Cassien's as I shut out Ares's voice. He tried to spare us. After everything, he tried to bargain for our lives. Cassien is marched toward me until he is four paces away. He kneels and stays frozen as the man peels his hand away and returns to the dais.

"I've asked one of the strongest Damaris's to freeze him in place for you, Elana. He cannot move until his brain stem is reconnected with his muscular system or he dies."

My eyes shoot to Ares and my stomach plummets. I start to shake my head and step away, but one of the maids still held at knife point gasps as the guard holding her pushes the blade farther into her ribs.

"You can't do this," I tell Ares, desperate for a way out. The longer I look, the more panicked I become.

Ares raises his chin and drops the emotion from his face. "Really? Have you not figured out that I do as I please? I wanted you in a crimson gown and here you stand. I wanted to you to show that you were soft, and you let my soldier go to save the maids. I wanted you to have a dagger in your hand to kill your father and your knuckles are white around the hilt." The ease returns to his face as he leans back. "I wanted a country to command, so I sat on the throne. I take what I want without remorse and your aversion to seeing others die will not stop me. Now, I will tell you this once and only once. I want you to put that blade in the soft spot between your sweet father's shoulder and neck on his left side. With every minute you wait, one of these maids will die. If you take longer than three minutes, I will have a guard kill him, and you will have four deaths on your hands. Make your choice, Elana. Your time is running out."

I look at Cassien kneeling before me. How many times have I imagined this moment? How many years have I wished to stop his heart? Yet now, when he's kneeling helpless before me, I can't bring myself to do it. I glance at the wide-eyed maids and step back as my hands shake.

"Time is ticking, Elana," Ares sings.

I'm heaving for breath.

"Elana."

My gaze shoots to Cassien. He smiles softly. My chest breaks open as I see the man who used to tell me stories and tuck me into bed.

"Don't—" I start, but he cuts me off.

"Elana, please." I freeze at the harshness of his tone. "What did he do to Byrne?"

I shake my head. "You don't get to act like you care. You don't get to do this to me."

My eyes dart to the maids. Ares says something, but I block it out.

"I know I've hurt you—"

"Hurt me? *Hurt me*? You *killed* us, Cassien. You murdered everything good in Byrne and me. You killed Mama's memory. You drank until you couldn't think, then you beat me to near death and paraded me around like a puppet! You don't get to do this. You don't get to redeem yourself."

"Elana—"

"No. You don't get the satisfaction of putting me down one

last time. This is your fault. Do you know why I'm here? Do you?"

He stays silent, grinding his teeth as he watches me.

"Because you decided to give an army to a monster. You decided to help overthrow an entire *kingdom* and hand it to a man with a bloodlust worse even than your own. And while you were here, Byrne and I were hiding, but they found us. And when they did, Ares strung up your daughter and pushed a knife through her ribs." I'm screaming as years of rage and sadness merge to create a tidal wave of emotion.

There are tears in Cassien's eyes as silence surrounds us, and all I can do is laugh. There's no mirth in the sound, but somehow it takes over my entire body, shaking my lungs and limbs.

Still holding the dagger, I can't bring myself to place it against his skin. His eyes bore through me as Ares calls my name. My head shoots up and my heart stutters as his lips curl into a sick grin.

"Your time is up."

"Wait—" I try, but it's too late.

The first guard pushes the blade into the chest of the woman with sewn lips. He pulls it out and it's as though I feel her blood soaking my clothes. The corset suffocates me as the other two maids scream, pleading to whoever will listen. They kick and scream, but it's no use. I'm frozen as I meet Ares's gaze.

"Better be quick. There are only two left."

I steel myself as I step toward Cassien. My heart beats too loudly in my ears. I blink and raise my chin as I place the tip of the blade on the side of Cassien's neck. His eyes never leave my face.

"You made me proud, Elana. No matter what I did, I was always proud."

My entire arm is shaking. I tell myself to push the blade in, but my hands don't move. Ares is counting down in the background as sweat builds on my skin.

"I'm sorry about Byrne. I truly am. I loved her once. I remember that. But everything I did was to make you strong. You will survive as I taught you. You will thrive. And if you must do this, you will."

My jaw twitches as I watch Cassien.

"Stop talking," I force out, gripping the blade so hard the skin over my knuckles threatens to split.

"If you do not, you will prove to me one last time that you are weak. Do not do that to me. I have sacrificed too much to have a pathetic excuse of a daughter."

"You don't get to say that—"

"I get to say what I please, Ella. Because if you do not do this, you will never be good enough to save these people. You will crumble as your mother did, and you will fold. Just. Like. Byrne."

I don't know if I'm screaming or if it's someone miles away. Cassien gargles then chokes. He sways as I pull out the blade. Blood splatters over my face, and no matter how hard I try to keep still, I flinch. I can't tear my eyes away as his eyes go blank and his skin pales.

He's gone. After everything, he's just... gone. I thought it would make everything better, but staring at his limp body makes me want to retch. Nothing has changed.

I raise my eyes as Ares applauds. "I was starting to think you truly wouldn't go through with it." He raises his hand, and the guards who hold the two remaining maids sheath their weapons. Tears roll down their faces as they're dragged away. "But my prior statement stands true. I always get what I want."

Two guards come up from the side and rid me of my

weapon before taking hold of my arms. I'm too stunned to fight back. The blood on my face burns like acid. It's evidence of years of pain all coming to a screeching halt, yet somehow, I don't feel cathartic. I feel hollow. Empty of closure or fear. Just... numb. Broken. *I'm the only one left.*

They drag me toward a door at the back of the room. The mark left when an arrow pinned the crown to the wall is still there, a blemish in a perfectly kept room. A stain in history.

"Elana." The guards stop as Ares speaks, but I don't turn. "It truly was a pleasure to spend time with you. I hope we will meet again."

His words fade as I'm dragged into a small room. I crumble to the floor as the door shuts, leaving me alone. I wonder for a moment if this is the end. If there is an executioner waiting behind the next door. I don't raise my eyes when a pair of boots pound into the room. All I can do is curl into myself and wait for it to be over.

The steps stop in front of me, and the executioner drops to his knees. Shaking hands cup my face gently. I only realize there are tears running down my cheeks when calloused fingers wipe them away. My eyes flutter up at the touch as recognition flies through my mind. A weak sound floats from my lungs as his eyes meet mine, and any resolution I had left, any remnants of defensive walls still barely standing fall away.

"Leo."

CHAPTER

FORTY-FIVE

LEO

"Leo."

"Hi, Elana," I say.

I don't know what to do with myself as she stares at me. Her eyes are broken in a way I didn't know was possible, and it tears open my heart. When I look at the blood splattered across her face, my chest tightens. She breathes my name again as if I were some make-believe being she's scared might disappear.

"I'm here," I tell her. I wrap my arm around her and pull her into me.

She doesn't flinch or tense. She melts in my arms as if she has no strength left. I close my eyes as I keep my thoughts on the present moment and not on the pain I'm about to cause her. Ares said I have ten minutes.

Her lungs heave as she grasps fistfuls of my shirt. I feel the dress drowning her and my brows furrow.

"Get it off," she pleads, kicking desperately at the fabric. She looks at me with tears in her eyes as she yanks at the material. "Get it off. Get it off. Get it off."

I take her hands and make her meet my eyes. She stops as her lip quivers. I sweep the hair behind her ear and kiss her temple.

"Let me help you."

Elana swallows as I tear the material. I undo the corset and take the small blade out of the sole of my boot to rip the stitching connecting it to the skirt before throwing the dress aside, leaving her in only the thin blouse beneath. She shivers as I finish discarding the material and replace the knife in the hidden compartment of my boot. It's the only weapon I allowed myself to bring. I pull off the fleece I'm wearing and slip it over her head before gathering her back into my arms.

When Elana stops shaking, I close my eyes. I don't have much time left.

"Elana, I'm going to tell you something and I need you to promise to listen until I'm done."

She nods haphazardly against my chest. I hold her tighter.

"You have to remember that no matter what's happening, I will always be there. I will fight to be by your side until I take my last breath, and even then, I will find you in whatever comes next. And you..." My voice breaks and she raises her eyes to meet mine. "You are the strongest person I know, Elana. Never forget that. There are people who love you and will do anything for you. So you'll be all right."

She blinks at me for a moment and seems to gain her bearings. "What are you talking about?"

"You're smart. You'll figure out a way to get me out. I'll stay alive until you do."

Her eyes light up as she touches my face. I lean into the warmth as she sits up and looks at me.

"How are you here, Leo? What are you doing?" There's panic in her voice now. I can see it in her expression.

I rest my forehead against hers and kiss her once. Twice. Breathe. "Survive. Promise me that. Promise me you'll survive and know that I'll find my way back to you." She stutters, but I stop her. "Say it to me."

"You'll find your way back to me. Leo—"

"And?" I press, feeling our time slip through my fingers.

"I'll survive. I'll keep going."

"Good. Good," I breathe as relief washes through me.

"Leo, how are you here?" Something seems to occur to her as she glances at the door, then at the pile of discarded fabric. "We need to go." I smile sadly as she gets to her feet and pulls me up with her. "We need to get out. Ares—"

"Ares knows I'm here."

She stops. My hands hang limply at my side as she searches my face.

"What do you mean?"

"It was the only way," I tell her as tears build in my eyes. I didn't imagine leaving her would be so hard. But she'll be okay. If anyone can survive, if anyone can get me out, it's Elana.

"No. No, that's not true. You didn't." She stumbles over her words as a hand flies to her mouth. She pushes me backward, but I stay planted. "No! You're lying. You wouldn't leave me."

I take her hands and kiss her knuckles. "I couldn't bear the thought of you here. Alone."

"So you'd leave me alone out there!" She's breathing hard, her chest moving fast.

"You're not alone out there. You're as much family to the boys as I am. You are a part of Hela's Bond. You and I... if I'm a king, then the only person who could be queen is you. In no world are you alone. And you can't possibly believe I would let you stay here. Not with him." I stuff my hand in my pocket and feel for the rag. "I wouldn't be able to live with myself."

She lets me wrap my arms around her one last time as tears flow down her face. "Don't do this. We can find a way out."

I shake my head. "This is the way out."

I touch her cheek and place the rag over her mouth. Her eyes go wide as she breathes in the gill oil, and within seconds, she's unconscious.

I close my eyes as I hold her against me. "You'll be okay."

The doors through which I entered a few minutes ago open and two soldiers rush in. They have a stretcher between them, and for a moment, I try to think of ways to escape. But the longer I consider, the more I'm sure this will work. Elana will be safe, and I'll be here. Elana will be safe.

"Here are the coordinates to the meeting place. If you get her there safely, your families will both be given shelter. If either of you betrays the location or doesn't get her there safely, both your families will be killed on the spot. Do you understand?"

Both men nod as the tallest takes the folded page I hand him.

"We will get her there, Your Majesty. Thank you."

I lay Elana on the stretcher and tuck the blanket the first soldier had carried over her. I take one last look, memorizing the curve of her cheek and darkness of her hair.

"I love you," I whisper as I place a kiss on her forehead. "Come find me."

She doesn't stir as I pull away.

"Go now. Don't let anyone stop you," I tell the men.

They nod and place a hand over their hearts before picking up Elana and hurrying out the door. I watch as they leave. She'll be all right.

I don't turn as the door behind me opens. Nor do I move as footsteps resound around the room. I take a deep breath as the voice I've been dreading rings in my ears. He stands not ten feet away.

"I'm glad you decided to join me, cousin."

EPILOGUE

ELANA

It's been three days since I woke in the mountain fortress. I've barely been able to stand since then. I awoke screaming. It took both Emmani and Red to bring me down. Even when I came to my senses, I didn't stop yelling. I was enraged. How could they let Leo give himself up for me? He is a king and I'm... I'm replaceable. Unneeded. Apparently, they hadn't known what he was going to do, but I didn't want to believe them. How could they have not known he would give himself up? Leo wouldn't let me suffer. He wouldn't be able to live with himself.

Emrys got back yesterday. He brought flowers for Byrne from Anateya. I was the first he sought out when he couldn't find her. I know I should have cried when he asked me where she was, but I had no tears left in me. I spoke the words without feeling, and his eyes scarred my soul. The sound that came out of his lungs tore me open, but all I could do was blink. I watched as he leaned his weight against the wall and pleaded with me to tell the truth. Only this is the truth. Byrne is dead. I killed Cassien. Leo is gone. I am alone. I haven't seen her body. I couldn't bring myself to go in the room where they'd placed her. Emrys had the courage to see her once more, but his screams, his cries... there was nothing strong about them. It was proof of his soul shattering. Everything in his being broke apart and fell at my sister's feet.

Emrys's face was gaunt and his eyes hollow when he walked into my room last night. He asked where I wanted to bury her, and I told him I didn't care. I told him he should pick somewhere. That he would know where she would like to rest. In truth, I know she wanted to be buried with our mother. We'd both said so when she died so many years ago. But there is no way to get Byrne there now. His voice was but a strained whisper when he told me he'd bury her on the mountain. That there was a small patch of earth along a path outside with a view she would have liked. He buried her there this morning, and I haven't moved since.

My bones feel hollow when I hear someone knock at the door. Antares and Cass don't smile when I look up. Their faces, however, are not as etched with despair as I would have expected. There's a steely calm to their features as they step inside and sit on the opposite bed.

"You're wearing his sweater," Antares says.

I let his words bounce in my empty mind, replaying the sound through my weary thoughts.

"You saw him before he gave himself up?"

I swallow the ball forming in my throat. Their eyes are so young, faces unscarred and naïve. But his words aren't strung together with sorrow or fear. Each letter he pronounces is built of resolve and tied to the next with a weathered confidence gained through years of survival. He knows what Leo did and he's proud. These eleven and fourteen-year-old boys are proud of the brother who raised them and carried them across hell for abandoning them to save me.

"I did," I rasp.

"We'd hoped for that," Antares says.

I blink. "You... you knew?"

Cass smiles and moves to sit beside me. He takes my hand and leans into my side.

"We're the ones who told him to go," Antares admits.

My skin feels too tight over my bones as I look at him.

"Why?" The word isn't more than a breath, but there's something desperate in the sound that slips past my lips.

He sighs and looks at his hands. "Leo once told us that we can't save everyone, but we can save those we love. If the entire world starts to burn and the earth splits open, you save the people who matter most. Ares tore Leo's world apart." Antares meets my eyes, and some deep-rooted pain finally shows, but there's hope too. Dangerous hope. Hope that Leo did everything to keep alive in his brothers. "So, Leo did what he always does. He saved those he loves. He saved you."

The thought makes my stomach flip. Leo told me that before he knocked me out, when I was dazed and so depleted that I barely understood what he was saying. But through all the words he spoke that stuck in my mind in the moment, that simple phrase is clear. He was telling me the rules he'd created, the creed he lived by. He was telling me how to survive.

I stand to leave but stop at the door, turning back toward the boys. They smile softly, as if they understand my thoughts. As if they came in here knowing I would come to this conclusion.

"Go," Cass whispers.

My lungs cease at the sound. Through all the time I spent with him in recovery while his siblings were in Arkezo, he's never uttered a word. But now, maybe when I need it most, he chose to speak. His voice is different than the last time I heard it, but it still carries that same hopeful sound. Somehow, I think this family is the best thing that could have happened to me. I never realized the impact they would have until now, when I have nothing left.

I step out the door and walk slowly through the halls. Conversations stop as I pass. Eyes follow my movements. I keep putting one foot in front of the other. I pull Leo's sweater over my chin and tuck my hands into the sleeves. It smells like him. There's a man at the door standing guard. He doesn't ask my business before pulling on the crank and stepping aside to let me through.

The sun is setting over Illena as I step outside. A cold breeze works its way into my bones even through the layers. I burrow deeper into the sweater and start up the mountain. My muscles strain as I step over loose stones and rubble. Still, I move up the path.

There is nothing left in me when I reach a plateau, but I don't have to give any more. There are flowers everywhere, poking up from the soil like stars in the sky. The sun is sitting right over the horizon, throwing gilded light onto the petals and making them glow a gold that reminds me of Byrne's eyes. I step toward the stone propped against the lone tree that managed to grow between the sea of flowers. There are only two words carved crudely into its face. *Byrne, Beloved.*

I swallow my tears and lie next to the patch of disturbed soil. She would have loved this. I turn my face toward the light and feel the heat seep into my skin.

"I'm sorry," I say to the wind. I pick up a handful of soil and slowly let it fall back to the ground. "I'm sorry I couldn't protect you. From the world. From Cassien. From pain." I look at Illena stretching out far below. "I'll do better now. For you. I'll never make it right, but I'll do my best to fix what's broken."

I take a deep breath and sit up, keeping one hand over her grave.

"You can only save the people you love," I murmur to myself.

I close my eyes and breathe as my mind clears. In this moment, with seemingly nothing left to live for, I find myself knowing exactly what I have to do. And I'm going to do it, no matter if the earth shatters beneath my feet or the wind steals my breath. Not even Lady Death will stop me.

"I'm going to get him back," I tell Byrne, knowing she can hear me. I take a breath and look at the horizon as the sun slips out of view, marking the start of something new. Something dangerous. "And then we're going to take Illena."

The End

Acknowledgments

It took over a year, but somehow, I've written my second book. There are so many things I've wished to do and being two thirds of the way into a trilogy at seventeen is something that seemed so incredibly impossible. I can't begin to describe the joy I feel anytime I think of this series. But through all the months I spent slouched over my computer, I couldn't have done it without the help and support of all the amazing people around me.

To my family, who sat by me every step of the way, thank you. When I doubted myself, you were there to lift me up and hold my hand until I was strong enough to walk again. Mum, you helped me with every piece, from looking over my mess of a manuscript to keeping every receipt and email organized. You are the reason my head didn't explode on multiple occasions, and I'm so grateful. Calum and Dad, you both saw me through each step of this process and were always there to offer an opinion when I couldn't decide on a seemingly unimportant detail that would take over my brain, thank you.

To Anshika, Katelin, and all the rest of the insane people I choose to spend my time with five days a week, thank you for being excited at even the smallest steps. Even when some of you still haven't read the first book because, as you put it, you're just not book people, it means everything that you take the time to ask how my writing is going and listen to every complaint or accomplishment I've chosen to vent about that day. Knowing that I have people like you around makes every struggle and step that much easier, thank you.

Leah, where do I even start? You've been my biggest supporter from before I knew what to call the main characters. Through every test you had to study for or university applications you spent months stressing over (even though I know you have it in the bag), you always made time to check in and see how my book was developing. You celebrated with me at every victory and held my hand through every stress, and I can't begin to describe how much your support means to me. So, a million times thank you, I would never have been able to do this for a second time without my best friend by my side.

Now of course I can't forget to say a huge thank you to the team of people who helped make this book possible. To the editors at Joy Editing, I learned so much from your work and this book wouldn't have been complete if you hadn't been there to help. A huge round of applause goes out to the amazing Hang Le who, once again, created the cover of my dreams. No good book is complete without eye-catching cover art, and you hit the target. To the team at Itsy Bitsy Book Bits and Hidden Hollows Book Tours, thank you for helping me launch The Uncrowned King to the world. Without all of your incredible work, none of this would have been possible.

I also can't forget to thank Laura, who not only jump-started my career, but is still there for me when I have questions or need help with anything. Your guidance has been invaluable, and your support has been priceless. I will never stop being grateful for everything you've done and continue to do for me, so though I can never say it enough, thank you for everything. It means the world.

Last but not least, I want to say a huge thank you to all the people who have taken a chance on The Blood Prince and given me the amazing feedback I needed to be confident in my writing. Because of you, I know this is what I want to do for the rest of my life, and I will forever be grateful for that. I'll see you for the grand finale.

About the Author

Ayla Marie is a Canadian high school student whose love for fantasy started when she was twelve and hasn't dulled since. She will read any book you put in front of her—textbooks do not count—especially when they have action packed storylines and a romantic subplot that makes you want to read as fast as you can, while wishing it would never end. Though writing, reading, and studying take up most of her time—or all her time according to her younger brother—she always manages to find space in her schedule to play some soccer and hang out with friends and family. Her goofy dog and two cats are her biggest fans, and though she could have done without the constantly interrupting barks and meows, she loves their annoying presence very much.

The Blood Prince was her debut novel, but she plans to write many more, deepening her love for writing and literature with every page.

ALSO BY AYLA MARIE

The Blood Prince

The Uncrowned King